# Portrait of Rage
## *The Marcel Experience*

## Cynthia H. Wise

*To Jeannie!*
*Enjoy the Story!*
*Cynthia H Wise*

**outskirtspress**
DENVER, COLORADO

Portrait of Rage
The Marcel Experience
All Rights Reserved.
Copyright © 2014 Cynthia H. Wise
v2.0

Cover Design by Sarah Harden.

Outskirts Press, Inc.
http://www.outskirtspress.com

ISBN: 978-1-4787-2230-4

Outskirts Press and the "OP" logo are trademarks belonging to Outskirts Press, Inc.

PRINTED IN THE UNITED STATES OF AMERICA

*To two very special people: my daughter, Sarah, and my husband, Cliff. Sarah's determination and support helped me break through the barrier of being published. Cliff's belief in me was humbling. His "I loved it" and "I'm proud of you" gave me the confidence to keep writing.*

# PROLOGUE

Dark clouds, pregnant with moisture, loomed in the late afternoon sky. Thunder rumbled in the distance. Slatted shutters had been opened allowing overcast light into the oppressive gloom. The air was rancid with the stench of decay causing bile to rise in the back of Detective Mark Winward's throat. He swallowed hard. His lean, six-foot frame was still as he stood with his fists in the pockets of his brown leather jacket. Besides droning flies, his dark head and eyes were the only things that moved as he scrutinized the nude, male corpse hanging from a rafter in the empty attic. The dead man's silver-white hair appeared stylishly barbered, but in disarray. Milky eyes bulged and seemed to glow red with hemorrhage. Deep gashes marred the neck around the embedded rope. Shredded, mated flesh clung under the dark nails. What remained of the mutilated genitals was a disfigured mass.

He shifted his gaze to the bloody wooden chair overturned beneath the slightly pointed toes and then over to where an antiquated, pearl-handled stiletto knife had been found resting against the baseboard a few feet away. In the dim light of the attic, the slender, blood-smeared blade had appeared eerily menacing.

The clap of wingtips echoed on the bare wood floor. "Mark, George Stelling just arrived."

Ignoring the fat, sluggish flies that buzzed around the corpse and his own head, Winward turned to face his approaching partner. "Good. How's Jenkins doing downstairs with trace?"

"He's wrapping things up." Detective Don Hayes's baritone voice suited his tall, muscular form. His coffee colored skin made the dress shirt beneath his paisley suspenders appear startlingly white. A hip-holster was attached to his belt securing a Glock 9 mm like the one Winward wore snug against his ribs in a custom-made shoulder holster.

Winward nodded and then stretched his arms out to encompass the space around him. "Why is it so clean?" he asked with a puzzled lilt in his voice. "No respectable, unused attic should be this dust free. A few dusty footprints might have at least told us if our pal here had company."

"I have the answer to that," Hayes replied, unconsciously drawing attention to his intimidating biceps as he placed his hands on his narrow hips. "Apparently, the woman who discovered the body owns a cleaning business. A crew was sent in to tidy the place up for a tenant and she came in to inspect their work after being delayed a couple of days. They obviously did a thorough job."

"Why was she delayed?"

"Because she has more than one crew and 'business is crusin'. Her words, not mine."

"Great." Winward's eyes were drawn back to the body. The wounds in the neck and genitals had begun to undulate with hatching larvae. "At least those nasty little guys can give us a time frame." He turned back to Hayes. "Have any reporters arrived yet?" he asked, changing gears in his thought process.

Hayes's expression was grim as he swatted away a persistent fly searching for ripe ground to lay its eggs. "Yeah. Mitchell's in charge of securing the perimeter. So far, everyone's been kept behind the tape, but you know as well as I do that there's always a slippery one in the bunch."

"Damn." Winward turned his dark scowl to the officer who had been guarding the attic stairs. "Pritchett, go down and help Mitchell. Make sure no one gets in or near this house. It might get out of hand if they find out who we've got up here. And tell Jenkins to process that stiletto as soon as possible. Maybe it'll tell us something useful."

"Yes, sir." Pritchett turned and headed down the narrow stairs.

Hayes surveyed the scene and shook his head. "What do you think?" he asked.

"At this point, I'm not sure what to think." Winward thought of the blade of the stiletto as his experienced gaze traveled the length of the corpse. "From the amount of blood on and around the chair, and the indentions pricked into the wood, he sat while the stiletto was used on his genitals. After he was hung, he dangled, clawing at the rope as he was asphyxiated. The question is, did he do it himself or did he have help?" He shook his head. "Hopefully, George will have something for us after he examines the body."

Hayes wore an expression of horror. "I don't know about you, but I don't think I could just sit there while someone came at my pleasure package with a sharp, pointed knife. I'd have to be drugged or bound and gagged."

"I agree," Winward said as he stepped closer to the body. "There don't appear to be any ligature marks."

"If he was incapacitated, he wouldn't be able to try and claw his way out of the noose."

Winward shrugged. "Maybe he woke up. And if he did…."

"That would mean someone put him there. And that's murder."

They heard footsteps on the stairs and turned to watch the medical examiner advance toward them. He was in his late fifties with thinning salt and pepper hair, watery grey eyes, a bulbous nose and thick, moist lips. The khaki pants and white button-up dress shirt covering his thin five-foot seven-inch frame looked like they'd been slept in.

"Hello, George," Winward greeted. "Long night?"

"And getting longer. What have you got?" Stelling asked, meeting the detective's eyes.

"It's not pretty."

"It never is. Any idea who it is?" he asked, waving a limp hand at the fly buzzing around his ear.

"Yeah, we know. It's Theodore Chandler."

Stelling's brow went up. "You're kidding. *The* Theodore Chandler?" He stopped to fully take in the scene. His eyes widened as his thick lips pursed to let out a low whistle. "Not a very dignified way to go. Can he be brought down?"

"Yeah. We've done all we can do."

Morgue attendants lowered the body. Stelling knelt, pulled on a pair of latex gloves, and examined the dark, distorted face.

"Time of death?" Winward asked.

"I'll have a better estimate after a thorough exam. Hell, I'll be able to tell you what he had for breakfast. But I'd say thirty-six to forty-eight hours." He ran his gloved finger around swollen lips and pushed the protruding tongue aside ignoring the infant maggots revealed underneath. "Well, well. Looky what I found."

He retrieved a pair of tweezers from his bag and grasped what appeared to be cellophane. When it was fully extracted, what he found was startling. It was a zip-lock sandwich bag. Inside the bag was a folded piece of paper.

# CHAPTER ONE

The Georgia sun was straight overhead declaring the noon hour. The day promised to be warm with a moderate level of humidity. Cumulus clouds drifted across the cerulean sky, shifting into bunnies and trains—shapes that could be seen if you used your imagination. Automobiles roared by on the one-way, two-lane street, passing through dappling shade created by old oaks, sycamores, and dogwoods lining the streets and gracing manicured lawns. Some of the stately homes were antebellum; others were built as the small town grew. All had seen decades of change and all had stories of past generations to enthrall, sadden, or delight. Most were very well maintained and loved, sporting white trim and stained glass. One or two along the way showed signs of neglect, evidence of economic change, or just a lack of interest and respect.

"For Sale" signs were rare in downtown Marietta, but one stood in the yard of the two-story house at 1122 Church Street, named for the impressive religious structures on either side of the street as you entered the town square. A light breeze stroked the man's raven hair as he stood with his thumbs hooked in his jeans pockets, surveying the house. A surge of excitement raced through his body. A glint in the depths of his ocean blue eyes was the only clue to his emotions, but they were well hidden behind the cover of the shades protecting his calculating gaze from the afternoon sun. A hint of a smile played along the line of his lips. *It needs work,* he thought. The corners of his wide mouth tilted a fraction higher, softening the chiseled, sun-darkened features of his handsome face.

The slamming of a car door drew his attention away from the house. His shuttered expression revealed nothing to the probing eyes of the woman who advanced toward him in a gray dress-suit that matched her straight, bobbed hair. Her hurriedly applied make-up was unsuccessful in hiding a dull, almost pasty, complexion.

"Well, here we are," Mrs. Dempsey stated with a quick, thin-lipped smile. She walked to him with her stork-like gait. "As you have probably noticed, it needs a little work."

"I've noticed." His voice was deep and resonant. His lips twitched with a repressed smile.

"Yes, of course," she said. "Shall we go in, Mr. Shear?"

"Absolutely."

Thomas Shear moved with the sensual grace of a panther as his tall frame fell in step behind the realtor. With each movement, his broad shoulders seemed to caress the thin, white cotton of his shirt, hinting at the sleek, well-defined muscles hidden from view. His faded denim jeans only served to enhance the lean, powerful legs that carried him with a surefooted stride along the cobbled path leading to the house.

"I'm sure you'll realize the wonderful potential the house has once we're inside. They don't build them like this anymore." Mrs. Dempsey led the way up the porch steps to the door. Long, etched-glass sidelight windows flanked both sides of the door frame.

"Our little city is just oozing with Civil War history, you know. There were battles fought all around this area. William Sherman bullied his way through in 1864 on his way to burn Atlanta. The battle of Kennesaw is legendary. Kennesaw Mountain is only a couple of miles from here to the west. It's a national park, you know. You might want to consider a little exploring. The museum is fascinating, and there are wonderful hiking trails through the woods, as well. There are even cannons along the trail up the mountain. And you wouldn't believe the flora." She rolled her hazel eyes up to look at Shear as she placed her hand against her non-existent bosom like she might swoon before inserting the key. "In the spring and summer, everything's so green, and the wild azaleas are beautiful. You really must see it," she said, pushing the door open.

"I'll keep that in mind."

Shear stepped inside. Removing his shades, he revealed long, ebony lashes that framed the deep blue of his eyes. A wavy lock of black hair fell across his forehead. He swept it aside before stepping deeper into the musty interior of the house.

The foyer was broad and spacious with a wide-planked hardwood floor the color of rich honey. The wide staircase flared at the bottom with elegant volutes and curved to the right as it rose to the second floor landing. It split the foyer, allowing for two hallways to lead deeper into the house on either side. A narrow runner of gold carpet covered the steps, revealing the tread of many feet and the passage of time. The banisters were carved oak, thick and sturdy, a work of art in themselves.

As his eyes were drawn upward, Tom saw a crystal chandelier dangling from the fourteen foot high ceiling. Hundreds of tear-drop crystals sloped inward to create a large suspended stalactite that waited to dazzle the eye with shining prisms. From there, his eyes traveled to the crown molding surrounding the room. Plaster rosettes with adorning leaves had been painstakingly carved and set into place by the loving hands of an artisan.

To the left and right of the foyer stood open French doors. The rooms beyond were cavernous and seemed to glow with an abundance of natural light. Tom glimpsed large marble fireplaces in the rooms, each with a carved mantle. More works of art.

As he passed from room to room, the constant jingling of coins stirred by the restless fingers he kept deep within his pockets was the only hint to his mounting excitement. His artist's eyes absorbed the sun-drenched rooms of the first floor while he envisioned the paintings he held in storage, and the ones he had yet to create, hanging on freshly painted walls. Finally, coming to a halt at the front of the house, he stood silent as his mind's eye formed a picture of the gallery he longed for within the walls that surrounded him.

"Besides the obvious, Mrs. Dempsey, why is the asking price so low?" he asked, turning to meet the realtor's gaze.

The directness of the question seemed to fray her cool composure. "The owner has been in dire straits since the death of her husband. She can't afford to maintain the property, so she has lowered her asking price. That's all there is to it."

Mrs. Dempsey's small, pinched face remained polite and attentive, but Shear thought he detected impatience in her voice.

She forced her thin lips into a smile. "Of course, for your own peace of mind, you might consider having it inspected."

"Oh, I intend to."

Shear turned and walked back across the foyer, through the second set of French doors on the right of the staircase, and stood gazing at the enormous, sun-lit room. He lifted is gaze and once again admired the intricately carved crown molding and high ceilings throughout the house. They gave the room the character and depth that was needed to showcase the magic he tried to portray in his life's passion. Shear's heart swelled with the possibilities.

He moved to a long window overlooking the back of the property. The lot was extensive. Additional parking would be easy to arrange.

"What about children?" he asked, seeing a little girl standing motionless in front of an garage-sized metal shed with barn-like double doors. Her piercing gaze seemed to be directed straight at him. The hair rose on his forearms and prickled on the back of his neck. "Are there many around here?"

The realtor came to stand beside him. "Not as many as you'd think. Why do you ask?"

Shear glanced at the woman. When he looked back through the window, the little girl was gone.

"No reason." He turned and walked back into the foyer.

"How soon do you need an answer?"

"Well, considering the current market, a listing like this won't last long."

The corner of Shear's mouth quirked at the ploy. "Don't worry," he said. "I intend to make an offer, contingent upon the outcome of a full inspection, of course."

"Of course."

"Can you have the documents I'll need to sign ready by tomorrow afternoon?"

"Certainly."

"Good. Then I'll meet you at your office at two o'clock."

"That'll be fine." Shear followed the realtor out of the house and across the wide, front porch.

"Well then, until tomorrow," he said, shaking her delicate, bony hand.

"I'll have everything ready."

As Shear turned away and followed the cobbled footpath toward the shining black Jaguar waiting on the wide asphalt driveway, a satisfied grin spread across his face. He pulled the car door open and turned his eyes back toward the house.

"It's perfect," he said under his breath. It was all he could have asked for and more. The roof was high and steep. Perfect for the studio he planned to install in the attic. Of course, he'd have to add skylights for additional lighting, but that would be no problem.

He thought of the rooms throughout the house, spacious and

rich with the exceptional light that streamed in through tall, generous windows. New carpet would have to be laid. That was definite. Fresh paint also, inside and out. These were all minor problems, however, when Shear looked into the future and pictured the finished product. He lifted his hand to the realtor watching from the porch, then slipped into the Jag.

Mrs. Dempsey watched him until he pulled out into the early afternoon traffic. *He's hooked. Next week I'll finally be rid of this place.* "And with good riddance," she mumbled, tightening her grip on the keys she held in her hand.

Mrs. Dempsey turned to lock the gaping front door and was startled by the muffled sound of a child's whimper coming from within the house. She stepped back inside and waited. Breathing soft and shallow, her ears strained for the slightest sound. The silence surrounding her only deepened.

"I know what I heard," she muttered, "and it came from up there." Mrs. Dempsey's eyes followed the wide staircase curving up to the second floor.

"I don't know who you are or how you got in," she shouted, "but I will not tolerate trespassers." She waited, but still heard only silence. "Come out at once." Still nothing. Shaking her head in frustration, Mrs. Dempsey proceeded across the foyer to the foot of the stairs, the heels of her sensible shoes clapping against the hardwood floor.

"If I have to come up and find you, I can assure you your parents will be informed of your ill conduct."

The silence continued. She began the climb up with determined steps and her anger mounted as she passed from room to room, only to find each one empty. With an exasperated sigh, Mrs. Dempsey stepped back into the hallway to await a sound that might give their position away.

A muffled thump sounded above her head. She threw her hands

on her bony hips in agitation. *The attic. I should have known. Well, when I'm through with them, they'll wish they had never started this preposterous game of hide and seek.*

Mrs. Dempsey went over to the narrow passage leading to the attic and looked up. The gloom waiting at the top seemed to deepen and grow into something forbidding. Chilled air enveloped her. Her instinct told her to avoid the attic altogether and leave the house at once, but her legs were suddenly leaden.

"This is absurd." Her voice quavered. She took a deep breath then lifted an unsteady hand to grip the banister before mounting the steep stairs.

Rising through the gloom, Mrs. Dempsey felt the chilly air grow colder and her heartbeat sped up. By the time she reached the shallow landing at the top, her warm breath was misting in the frosty air. Her hand trembled as she grasped the knob and turned. After a gentle push, she shivered as she watched the door swing back on un-oiled hinges.

Standing very still, Mrs. Dempsey gave her eyes time to adjust to the dimness of the attic. She expelled the breath she had been holding and was assaulted by the musty smell. She forced her feet forward.

Swallowing to lessen the tightening of her throat, she stated firmly, "I know you're up here, so you might as well show yourself." With a cautious step, she walked deeper into the cavernous, bare-wooded room.

Bright shafts of light streaming in between the slats of the shuttered widows did little to expel the gloom surrounding her. Shadows clung to the rafters, creating the eerie sensation that she was being watched. She felt exposed and her brittle confidence began to crumble. Her eyes searched the corners and any deep shadow that might hide the small form of a child, but the further she searched the more desperate her plight became. Her thinning confidence vanished altogether with the dawning realization that she was alone.

Then a fleeting whisper passed her ear. Her heart raced as a child's soft moan trickled from the rafters. A tiny whimper filled the stale air, and she spun around, eyes wide, scanning the shadowy corners. Seeing nothing, her fear mounted and a cold, clammy sweat dampened her skin just as the sickening smell of death reeked through the air. Surging vomit filled her throat as she reeled and ran for the door.

"Stop, please! I hurt so bad. I want my mommy! Find my mommy!" The frightened little voice rang in her ears and her quick breath became sobs. Every hair on her body stood on end, tingling against raw, trembling nerves. She was unable to suppress a terrified scream as a seemingly huge presence filled the doorway in front of her.

# CHAPTER TWO

The noise level in Grady's Bar & Grill had risen to a low roar as the lunch rush reached its peak. Thomas Shear tossed his paper napkin on the shellacked wooden table and leaned his elbows against its edge. The excitement shining in his eyes clouded as he watched the man sitting across from him.

Jonathan Fields stood five eleven and was lean muscle thanks to routine visits to the gym and martial arts sparring with Tom. His short, curly hair was blond and his eyes were dark brown. At the moment, his wide generous mouth, usually quick with a smile, was turned down at the corners.

"Okay. Are you going to tell me what's buggin' you?" Tom asked. "You've hardly heard a word I've said."

Jonathan looked at Tom with a rueful smile. "I'm sorry, Tom. I don't mean to put a damper on your good news. It's great, it really is."

"But—"

"But nothing. It has nothing to do with you." Jonathan let out a frustrated sigh and lifted his gin and tonic to his lips.

Tom waited. He crossed his arms over his broad chest covering his black and silver striped tie and watched his friend fidget with the fries that had grown cold on his plate. Muted conversations continued around them. Clinks and scrapes from utensils blended with the voices. Stevie Ray Vaughn, singing about flooding down in

Texas, emanated from ceiling speakers installed throughout the Bar & Grill.

The two men had known each other since their freshman year of college. They were like brothers, but Tom wasn't sure how they had become so close, because they were like night and day. Jonathan was fair and of average height. While handsome, he had a boyish charm that could make the most hardened spinster radiate a blushing smile. Tom was six two and dark. He was more serious, with a sensual charm that made women turn for a closer look. And, what could be more different than an analytical attorney and a creative artist?

"Marsha's talking marriage again," Jonathan admitted suddenly, returning Tom's blunt stare. "Last night she told me to make up my mind which I love more, her or my bachelorhood. She didn't exactly say it, but I could hear the 'or else.' I thought things were going great. I don't understand why she wants to change everything. Our life's perfect the way it is."

"Apparently, she doesn't think so," Tom replied. "Who says things have to change anyway? You're already living together. A legal document somewhere binding you at the hip shouldn't make any difference."

"Oh, yeah? You know as well as I do that after marriage comes kids. It's a huge domestic step. One that I'm not sure I'm ready for."

Tom stifled a smile. "You talk like she's ready to give birth any minute. Marsha's not exactly the barefoot and pregnant type, Jonathan. Besides, I doubt very seriously if she would give up a flourishing career as a criminal psychologist to become the next June Cleaver."

The corner of Jonathan's mouth twitched as he met Tom's eyes. "You're right. June Cleaver she's not."

He let out a slow breath. "I don't know. I guess I'm afraid of turning into a statistic. In my profession, I deal with divorce everyday. It seems marriage always starts out full of love and promises, then something somewhere down the line goes wrong and it turns into a court battle of who gets what and how much."

"How long have the two of you been together? Three years?"

Jonathan shook his head with another sheepish smile. "Four," he said.

Tom's brows shot up. "Four years. No wonder she's making demands." He looked around for their waitress and caught her eye with a quick wave of his hand. "Do you want another drink?"

"Yeah, sure. Why not?"

Tom motioned for two more drinks then sat back in his chair to study his friend. "You may not like what I'm about to say, Jonathan," he said, "but I don't see a problem. I heard what you said about divorce and I understand how dealing with it everyday as an attorney could make you think twice about marriage. But aren't you overlooking something? You and Marsha really love each other. And if you really love someone, you'll try your best to make a marriage work.

"Personally, I can't understand your hesitation," Tom continued, ignoring Jonathan's brooding. "Marsha's a sweet, intelligent, beautiful woman. And she's in love with you. I wish I could be so lucky."

Jonathan remained silent.

"Four years, huh? I must be getting old. I swear it doesn't seem that long."

"You think I'm a total asshole, don't you?"

Tom chuckled. "I didn't say that, you did." He smiled and shook his head. "No. But you're crazy if you let a woman like Marsha slip through your fingers."

He looked up as their waitress approached with their drinks. "Can I get you anything else?" she asked with a soft southern drawl, returning Tom's smile as she cleared the table of plates and empty glasses.

"Not right now, thanks."

As she walked away, there was no mistaking the admiration in his expression for the sway of shapely hips that were hugged by tight, low-riding jeans. As he watched, she gazed back at him and her long, blond ponytail slipped over her shoulder. Tom's lips parted in a handsome grin, seeing the invitation in her whiskey colored eyes, but he made no move to pursue it. Instead, he turned his attention back to Jonathan, catching the knowing gleam in his friend's mocking eyes. "What?" he said, feigning innocence.

"Nothing."

The silence lingered and Tom's disbelieving grin spread. "Don't tell me you're afraid of losing your freedom," he said continuing the conversation.

Jonathan's silence confirmed Tom's suspicion, and a low chuckle rumbled in his chest.

"This may come as a shock to you, buddy, but your freedom flew out the window the minute you laid eyes on the woman."

Tom could see the denial coming before Jonathan started shaking his curly head. He put up his hand to stop the motion.

"Are you going to tell me I'm wrong? You love her enough to give up anything and you know it."

"Of course, I love her. That's not the issue," Jonathan sputtered.

"Then what is?" Tom's amusement shimmered in his dark blue eyes. "Could it be my cold-footed friend is really afraid of the inevitable?"

Jonathan looked stricken. "Me? Afraid? You're nuts. Why don't we change the subject? How'd we get on the blasted thing, anyway? Tell me more about this house you've found. I assume you've had it inspected?"

"Yes. And considering its age, it passed with flying colors. The best things are that the entire electrical system's been rewired, and it has modern plumbing. The house sits on a full acre, and there are big oaks and dogwood trees everywhere. There's a tall hedge that lines the property, so I'll have privacy. Oh, and there's even a huge, barn-like metal shed in the back.

"I'm telling you, Jonathan, it's perfect. The whole street's perfect. The houses have been beautifully maintained. I think mine's the only house on the block showing signs of neglect."

"I've traveled that street a million times on my way to the courthouse. Isn't it still residential?"

"Mostly," Tom replied. "The house is within walking distance of the town square, so there are a few businesses mingled in. I should blend right in after I fix the place up and have a few yards of concrete added in back for parking."

"What about a business license?"

"It's in the works."

Jonathan smiled at Tom's enthusiasm. "You know, with you being a business owner and all, you're going to be asked to contribute to the restoration of The Strand Theater there in the square, along with other historically significant properties in the area."

"I probably will," Tom replied with a grin.

"Have you checked out Eddie's Trick Shop, yet? I picked up a pair of fake ice cubes with bees in them a couple of months ago for a gag. They have everything from clattering teeth to costumes.

"Then there's Shillings. It's right on the square and a great place for dinner. Marsha and I have eaten there several times. The owner gets to know you quickly and then you're an insider, with "the usual" on call."

"I'll keep that in mind." Tom lifted his glass and took a drink. "I plan on doing some exploring."

"Well, while you're at it, you'll want to experience the Theater in the Square. You'll see everything from plays to concerts. Just take a lawn chair and a cooler and you'll be all set.

"Marsha's personal favorites are the antique shops. She loves to browse and could spend many blissful hours skipping from shop to shop." Jonathan's grimace transformed into a mischievous grin. "That's how I learned where all the good pubs are."

Tom's eyes twinkled with amusement as his smile grew. "Geez, man. You're a walking advertisement. But I appreciate the tips."

Jonathan grinned and nodded. "I'm here to serve." He picked up his drink. "Who's handling the closing?"

"Russ Carson. Ever heard of him?"

"Sure I have. I'm just surprised he's handling a real estate deal. His specialty is criminal law, you know. And he's damn good, too," he added. "What time is your closing?"

"Three," Tom stated, glancing at his watch. "As a matter of fact, if I don't get my ass in gear, I'm going to be late."

"Yeah, I need to be going, too. I have a meeting with a new client at four. Let me know if there's anything I can do to help."

"You may regret that offer on moving day," Tom warned, motioning for the check.

"Yeah, I probably will."

<hr>

A petite woman with fiery red hair looked up as Tom entered the reception area of the Carson, Stiles & Bradford Law Firm. The décor was elegant and expensive. Oil paintings of landscapes hung on the walls in ornate frames. Crystal lamps cast a soft glow over the room where cherry-wood tables flanked a leather sofa and chairs. The flaming haired receptionist sat at a desk made of the same fine, dark wood.

"May I help you?" she asked.

"My name's Thomas Shear. I have a three o'clock appointment with Mr. Carson."

She spoke into her telephone, then smiled up at Tom. "Someone will be with you in a moment."

Within seconds, an adjoining door opened and a tall brunette stepped through. Her high-heeled steps were whispers as she crossed the thick carpet. The smile that greeted him was warm and friendly. Her sky-blue eyes seemed to light up and come alive.

"Mr. Shear, hello," she said, offering her diamond-laden hand. "We've been expecting you. I'm Ellen Brighten, Mr. Carson's personal assistant. If you'll just follow me, I'll show you to the conference room."

She led Tom down a hallway decorated in the same color scheme as the reception area. Closed doors along either side piqued Tom's imagination before he was led through the only opened doorway at the hallway's end. The conference room had a long oak table in its center. Honey-brown leather chairs circled the table and more landscape paintings hung on the walls. In the center of the table were crystal bowls filled with an assortment of bite-size candies and mints.

"Am I the first to arrive?" he asked.

"Yes, but Miss Stafford should be along any minute."

"Miss Stafford?" Tom was confused. The name meant nothing to him.

"She's the realtor handling the sale."

"But I thought Mrs. Cutter was doing that."

"She was," Ms. Brighten answered. "But because of personal reasons, she decided to turn the sale over to Miss Stafford. She called only this morning to inform us of the change. I hope this isn't going to cause an inconvenience."

"No, of course not," Tom replied. His mouth quirked. "It's just that I'm beginning to feel like I have the plague. First Mrs. Dempsey, then Mrs. Cutter, and now Miss Stafford."

Ms. Brighten looked startled. "I'm sorry. I was under the impression you had been told about Mrs. Dempsey."

Tom stilled and held the woman's gaze. "Told what," he asked, detecting a heartbeat of hesitation and a slight shift in her direct blue gaze.

"Mrs. Dempsey was killed in an accident."

Tom was stunned. "I had no idea. When I went to the office to confirm the sale, I was given to Mrs. Cutter and things progressed from there. She mentioned an accident, but said nothing about it being fatal."

Ms. Brighten seemed surprised by his reply. "Someone should have informed you of the circumstances," she stated with just the right touch of remorse. "I apologize for the misunderstanding, Mr. Shear."

A buzz from the conference phone halted further inquiry. As she answered, the shocking news of Mrs. Dempsey's death lingered in Tom's mind. He wondered how and when it happened.

"Miss Stafford has arrived," she told him, returning the handset to its cradle. "Will you excuse me?"

"Certainly," he said, and turned to admire a painting of a shimmering lake. Cattails edged the shallows, and a field of yellow wild flowers drew the eye to a snowcapped mountain range in the distance. An adjacent door opened and Tom turned from the painting to see a tall, thin man dressed in a tailored gray suit enter the room.

"Mr. Shear? I'm Russ Carson," he said, flashing Tom a smile before placing a manila folder thick with legal documents at the head of the table.

Tom returned Carson's firm handshake. He guessed the man to be in his mid-forties even though a shock of white hair belied his true age. Returning the piercing gaze he received from dark, calculating eyes, Tom judged his companion to be a beguiling, ruthless man.

"I'm sorry I'm late," a feminine voice replied from the doorway. "I hope I haven't kept you waiting."

Tom turned to the attractive young woman entering the room and was pleasantly surprised by the alluring smile he received. Her lips were full and inviting. Her nose was petite with an impish turn at the end. Her skin was flawless except for the tiny mole that kissed the left side of her mouth. He couldn't help but imagine her bare, slender thighs as they moved beneath the soft fabric of the skirt that exposed shapely knees and calves.

"Ah, Miss Stafford. As a matter of fact, Mr. Shear and I were just introducing ourselves," Carson replied.

Miss Stafford looked directly at Tom and the saliva in his mouth dried up. "I'm sorry to say I haven't had the pleasure," she stated.

Tom took her small hand in his and had to give himself a mental shake to avoid losing himself in the depths of her emerald eyes. "I assure you the pleasure is mine," he managed to say and realized she barely reached his shoulder.

As she turned away and walked around the table, he noticed the way her long, auburn hair hung in soft, gentle waves down her back and felt a sudden, strong urge to reach out and stroke it. Startled by his distraction, Tom stifled the unexpected impulse and found his chair; putting the expanse of the table between them. Still, the soft, musky scent of her perfume lingered in his nostrils like an aphrodisiac.

Carson opened the folder and removed the first set of documents. "Shall we begin?"

# CHAPTER THREE

Chief Bill Swainer sat behind his wood-grained laminate desk with his arms folded over his scrawny chest. His office, like the rest of the building, was painted neutral beige with blue trimmings. A laminate bookcase that matched his generic desk stood against one wall and three tall filing cabinets lined another. Two chairs, made of metal tubing with barely cushioned cloth backs and seats, were as generic and nondescript as the rest of the furnishings. At present, both chairs were occupied.

Swainer gave an inward sigh as he watched Detective Winward shake his head in weary disgust. The detective had worked under him for the past five years, and he had grown to trust the man's uncanny instinct, but there was nothing he could do; his hands were tied.

"The case is closed, Mark," he stated. "You know good and well you sealed the case as soon as you found that confession stuffed in Chandler's mouth. Hell, his fingerprints were all over the place, including the stiletto. What more do you need?"

Swainer glanced over at Hayes, who sat brooding beside Winward. "We should be thankful," he continued. "Six months ago, we had a series of eight missing children on our hands. Thanks to the late Mr. Chandler, that series has been reduced to four random cases."

Mark Winward drew in a sharp breath then expelled it through his long, slender nose. He ran slim fingers through his short-cropped brown hair, and his dark eyes grew almost black beneath thick brows that were creased in frustration.

Winward stood and walked to the window. He gazed between open blinds, seeming to barely notice the sunshine or the few people walking across the parking lot of the Marietta Police Station. His wide shoulders flexed beneath the dark wool of his suit jacket, as if trying to ease the tension that had been building for the past six months.

"That's just it," he said, turning his head to look at Swainer. "After months of dead ends, a neat little package was dropped into our laps. I've tried, chief, but I can't let it go. There are just too many questions without answers."

"Such as?"

Hayes spoke up from his chair across from Swainer's desk. "Why, after all that time, did he suddenly feel the need to confess?"

Hayes was a hulk of a man, but was known for his quiet control. With his bone-crushing strength, coffee colored skin, and black, penetrating eyes, his mere presence was usually enough to intimidate the most hardened criminal. He had been partnered with Winward the year before and, so far, they made an unbeatable team.

"Who knows? He might have guessed we were ready to call in the Feds. Or maybe the man had a plague of conscience," Swainer suggested. "He couldn't live with what he had done, so he confessed."

Winward's lips twisted sourly as he turned from the window to face the room. "I doubt that," he said, crossing his arms over his broad chest. "Chandler was ruthless and self-centered. He was a financial magnate. He lived for the impossible challenge and would never have given in to defeat so easily. So, why did he give us the location of only one body? If he was feeling so guilty, why didn't he tell us where the others could be found?"

Swainer shrugged his shoulders. "Maybe he thought he was making it too easy for us and felt we should work for the rest." He watched Winward shake his head with the expression of someone indulging a child.

"I'm sorry, Bill, but I don't buy it, and neither do you. The body of Kathy Packard was out in the open. If he was that careless with where he dumped the bodies, why haven't we found the others? We've had half the force and hundreds of volunteers combing the city and surrounding areas." Winward planted his hands on his hips and began to pace. "No, there's more to it. Kathy Packard was his last victim. It's almost like she was a plant, the bait to reel us in."

Chief Swainer let out a heavy sigh. He understood Winward's dissatisfaction. The questions Winward raised were questions he had asked himself. Questions that should have had answers, but didn't.

Rising from his chair, Swainer walked around his desk. His dress shirt and pants hung from his bony five-foot, seven-inch frame. For the moment, he chose to ignore his blue and white striped tie that had condiment stains from the burger he'd had for lunch. He could almost feel his dark, graying hair growing lighter by the minute. He knew his pale blue eyes were bloodshot from an ill night's sleep. If his colleagues didn't know him better, they might have suspected him of using drugs.

"It's not up to you to like it, Mark," he said, hiking his skeletal hip onto the front corner of his desk. "It's not up to me anymore, either. The commissioner has the final say here, and he's made himself very clear. As far as he's concerned, the case is closed and has been for the past six months, since you and Hayes found Chandler dead in his attic. Without evidence stating otherwise, there's nothing we can do but continue our search for the bodies of the three other girl's he named in his confession." He patted his shirt pocket in search of the cigarette pack he usually kept there then remembered he'd quit the damned things the week before.

"Look," he said. "If it's any consolation, I'm on your side. I don't like the way things have turned out any more than you, but my hands are tied."

Winward met Swainer's gaze in the silence that followed. The feeling of friendship was strong between them. They respected each other personally and professionally. They admired the instincts and common sense they each possessed. Through the years, their friendship had grown. More importantly, however, the trust they held in each other had strengthened.

"Bill, believe me, I know what you're saying. I understand your position, and I wouldn't jeopardize your command for something I didn't totally believe in. But we're not satisfied with the way this has turned out. We can't be."

Swainer saw the determination in his friend's expression and heard the familiar stubbornness in his voice. He needed a cigarette. Heaving an inward sigh, his resolve cracked. "What are you trying to say, Mark?" he asked.

"If we were to find new evidence, would you back us up in reopening the case?"

Swainer looked over at Hayes and noted his acquiescence.

"You know I can't authorize that. We have a case load a mile high. I can't afford to have you spending the taxpayer's money and the department's time working on a case that's already officially solved."

"We're not talking about doing that and you know it," Winward said. "We have every intention of pulling our weight around here. But this is important. Not only to us, but I think to you, too."

Swainer turned away and walked back to the chair behind his desk. His bushy brows were creased with concentrated indecision. "You'd have to do your investigation on your own time," he stated.

"We understand that," Winward agreed, seeing Hayes's nod.

"You'd have to keep your investigation under wraps. We can't afford to have it leaked to the commissioner that we're working behind his back."

"Definitely."

"And you would have to report to me daily. We'd need enough evidence to blow this case wide open before we went public with it. We'd need enough to ensure the commissioner's full cooperation."

Winward made a vain attempt at hiding a triumphant smile as he shifted his gaze toward Hayes. "Absolutely. We agree with everything you've said." He turned for the door and Hayes stood to follow him out.

"Remember, you two. I want to be kept informed of everything."

"Don't worry. You will be."

Swainer watched his two best detectives stride away and felt the weight on his shoulders grow a little heavier. "I'm getting too old for this," he mumbled, shaking his head.

# CHAPTER FOUR

Jonathan pulled his Mercedes into the driveway and parked behind the rented U-Haul moving van. Even though the yellow and white paint of the structure was dull and chipping, Jonathan and Marsha couldn't help but be impressed. It was like stepping into the mystique of a by-gone era.

"Wow," he said under his breath.

"Yeah, wow," Marsha mimicked in awe.

Its wide, front porch extended around both sides. Large, octagon-shaped gazebos graced each of the front corners. Generous windows faced the street on the first and second floors and were edged on all sides by multi-colored stained glass. Large dormer windows protruded from the roof. Hand-made bricks formed the two fireplace chimneys that stretched skyward on both sides of the house. A colonnade extended from the house on the left side, allowing the driveway to run through it to the back of the house. Even though the wide driveway was now asphalt, one could almost hear the crunch of gravel as coaches and carriages delivered their passengers for afternoon tea or a late night dinner party.

Huge oaks, generations old, dotted the green lawn surrounding the house, with dogwoods scattered here and there. Sycamores ran along one side of the property as if strategically planted by hands that had long since turned to dust. A thick hedge of Red Tip Photinia ran the length of the property line along both sides and back, exposing the front to the street.

Neighboring houses along the shaded street, each different in its own grand style, hinted of past generations while giving promise for new ones to come. The quaintness of a small town existence seemed to enhance the impression of time passing at a slower pace, even though the progress of modern life thrived around them.

Marsha opened the car door and a breeze caught her shoulder-length, molasses-brown hair as she stepped out. She brushed it from her heart-shaped face and tucked it behind one dainty ear as she scanned the house and property. Dressed for labor in a black Lynard Skynard t-shirt and jeans, she stood with her hand shielding her hazel eyes from the bright morning sun and took in the expansive, uncut lawn shaded by the trees. The brilliant red and gold of their leaves were nearing their fall peak. The tweet of a bird's call and the bark of a squirrel mingled with the traffic moving along Church Street toward the square of Marietta.

"Well? What do you think?" Tom called, stepping around the U-Haul and watching their expressions as he held out his arms.

Full lips revealed straight, white teeth as Marsha smiled her approval. "So far, I'm impressed," she said as her eyes were drawn back to the house.

"Wait until you see the inside. The rooms are enormous."

Marsha pulled her gaze from the dormers protruding from the roof in time to see Tom and Jonathan disappear inside. Her brisk stride carried her across the cobbled walkway and up the porch steps. She followed the sound of their voices and found them standing in front of a massive marble fireplace.

"Tom, this is fantastic," Jonathan said, his voice loud and echoing in the large, empty room.

"It is great, isn't it? Come on. I'll show you around before we start unloading the truck."

The first floor was to become his gallery. As he walked them through the four large rooms, he detailed his plans to create a different color scheme for each one. The two front rooms lead off each side of the foyer, while the other two, one down each hallway, were separated by the staircase.

"Each room will have a different atmosphere and mood," he explained, leading the way through double French doors at the end of the left side hallway. "My purpose is to emphasize the variety of themes I manifest in my work.

"As you can see, I've already had the walls and ceiling throughout the house painted. The hardwood floors have been stripped and refinished. New carpet has been laid upstairs as well. The only room that hasn't been carpeted upstairs is the spare bedroom, so it shouldn't stand in the way of moving things in. I don't have any furniture for that room anyway," he said with a grin and shrug.

Jonathan smiled and slapped Tom on the shoulder. "All in good time, my friend."

"I have a question," Marsha said. "Why did you choose the color red for this room?" The textured ceiling was pristine white and the elaborate crown molding was a light crème. The walls, on the other hand, were a dark red, the color of a rich, full-bodied wine that reminded her of blood. She suppressed a shiver.

"I don't understand how your paintings could possibly harmonize with such a dominating color," she continued. "The colors in the other three rooms, the white, ice blue, and soft yellow, I can see. But this deep red is pretty extreme."

Tom shrugged. "I don't know. I have to admit, I was skeptical at first myself. But when the room was finished, I knew it was perfect."

He escorted them from the room and down a narrow hallway that crossed beneath the staircase to a closed door on the other side. "This is the kitchen," he said, pushing through the swinging door. "There's very little that will have to be done in here. New wallpaper, maybe. New tile was installed before I bought the house. The best part is that it's roomy enough for the catering team I'm going to hire to serve the parties and special showings I intend to have."

Inside, they saw a large butcher-block island with a deep stainless steel sink in its center. The countertops were blue tile and the cabinets, many with glass doors, were the color of fresh honey. A generous bay window looked out onto the back lawn.

Marsha stepped to a recessed door and revealed a hidden staircase. "This will come in handy."

"Sure will. Upstairs, I have a den, a study, two bedrooms, and two full baths. My apartment didn't even compare to what I have now."

Marsha and Jonathan smiled at their friend's excitement as the doorbell echoed through the empty house.

"That's probably the carpet layers. They said they were going to finish up today."

"You go ahead," Jonathan said, taking Marsha's hand. "We'll just nose around until you're ready to start unloading."

He led Marsha up the backstairs to the second floor. When they came upon a narrow stretch of stairs that continued to lead upward, Marsha looked into the darkness and felt dread settle in her chest. Her feet became leaden as Jonathan climbed the first step up.

"Come on," he urged, giving her hand a gentle tug. "Tom told me he had the new skylights installed in the attic last week. I want to see how they turned out since this is going to be his studio."

"No," she said and pulled her hand away.

Jonathan turned in surprise. "What do you mean 'no'? Sweetheart, what's wrong?"

Marsha's cheeks felt cold and pale. When she realized she was staring with wide, frightened eyes at the door above them, she pulled her gaze away and looked at him, forcing a smile. "Nothing," she said with a quick shake of her head.

"Honey, I know you better than that," Jonathan said, stepping back down to face her. "Something's wrong. What is it?"

Her brow furrowed. "Don't you feel it?"

"Feel what?" he asked, then ran his hand through his hair and across the back of his neck like he was smoothing a prickling scalp.

Marsha shook her head again. "Never mind." She cast an apprehensive glance toward the stairs looming behind him and rubbed her arms to ward off a sudden chill. "Besides, there's too much to do to be wasting time. The new carpet needs to be vacuumed before Tom's things can be brought in. The bathrooms need scouring. The windows need to be washed and—"

"Baby, all of those things can wait another five minutes." He gave her a coaxing smile. "Come on. Tom really wants us to see it. He's proud of what he's accomplished, and with good reason."

"I can't," she said, backing away from his reaching hand.

"What? Marsha, you're acting silly. It's only an empty attic."

She gave her head another vigorous shake. "I don't care. I'm not going up there." Her hazel eyes betrayed the sudden panic she felt, and Jonathan surrendered with a soft, bewildered sigh.

"Okay." He took her in his arms and held her tight. "You go on down and find Tom," he said, steering her toward the main staircase. "I'll be down in a minute."

When Marsha stopped and looked back at him with drawn, worried brows, Jonathan gave her a reassuring smile. She stood watching as he began the climb up, then whirled, and hurried down the main stairs, only slowing her steps when she saw Tom in the foyer.

"Where's Jonathan?"

Her smile felt plastic. "He's in your studio looking around. Was that the carpet layers at the door?" she asked, then took a deep breath in and slowly let it out to help settle her nerves.

"Yep. They're outside gathering their tools."

"Great. I'll bring in the cleaning supplies," she said and started to turn away. "Oh, by-the-way, I like the carpet upstairs. Neutral, but very plush." She tried giving him an impish grin.

"Thanks," he said, smiling back. "Need any help?"

"Nope. You just go up and fetch Jonathan."

As Marsha moved from room to room with her vacuum, bucket, and rags, Tom and Jonathan unloaded the moving van. The lowering sun went unnoticed as they strained beneath the heavy weight of furniture and packed boxes. By the time each piece had been brought in and arranged, twilight had crept in around them.

"Well, that's the last of it," Tom announced, setting a bulging box on the floor. "Now comes the fun part. It's going to take me forever to unpack."

"What do you mean, 'the fun part'? I've just had an afternoon so full of fun I can hardly move." Jonathan groaned as he sank into a soft, leather recliner.

Marsha raised a teasing brow. "What's the matter, Jonathan? Getting soft with age?"

Tom chuckled, and Jonathan did an excellent job of looking down his nose to fake an air of superiority. "Go ahead and laugh. When a beautiful woman pokes fun at *your* macho prowess, I'll remember this."

"Maybe next time you'll think twice about offering your services," Tom replied, his grin widening. "On the other hand, I'm sure you'll find humor in the fact that I'll still be up to my eyeballs in boxes, not to mention struggling to hook up the entertainment center, while the two of you are snuggling between your sheets."

Jonathan looked over at the wall-mounted forty-six inch flat-screen TV, CD player, DVD unit, and surround sound stereo system. "You've got a point," he conceded and smirked.

"I wouldn't worry about it, Tom." Marsha stifled a yawn as she stretched her tired muscles before collapsing onto the leather sofa. "Everything will fall into place. You don't have to try and do it all tomorrow, you know."

"Oh, I don't intend to. I've got the next few days free to unpack. I'm just going to take my time and enjoy decorating my new home."

"Don't you have to be back at the university on Monday?"

"I'm taking next week off to get settled."

Jonathan's mouth twitched with amusement. "I'm sure your students will appreciate the reprieve."

"Very funny," Marsha said in Tom's defense. "I happen to know Tom's students think the world of him."

"Humph."

Tom stood with his hands on his narrow hips and his eyes sparkled with mirth as he watched his two friends. "Look, I don't know about the two of you, but I'm starving. Do you want to go out? My treat. We'll go anywhere your little hearts desire."

"No," Marsha said, aghast. "Do I look like I belong in public with decent, sweet-smelling people?"

Tom's lips twisted in a rueful grin. "You're right. I'll call takeout," he said and bent to dig out the telephone directory from a box. "I discovered a great little Chinese restaurant that delivers."

# CHAPTER FIVE

Tom raised his hand in farewell as Jonathan's car pulled away. He stood for a moment gazing at the sky as the evening stars glistened against an empyrean of soft, blue-black velvet. He sighed with contentment. In the deepening night, brittle leaves rustled as they swayed in a subtle breeze. He lifted his face to enjoy its touch then turned and entered the house.

He closed and locked the door, set the new security system, turned out the foyer light, then headed for the stairs. The delicate scent of roses stopped him in his tracks. His heart thumped as it wafted around him then drifted away, leaving him aroused as if by a lover's touch. He stood motionless in the dark, half fearing its return, then let out his breath as his heartbeat eased.

*What the hell was that?* Tom looked around then shook his head as he rubbed the hair that had prickled along his arms. It had happened so quickly, he began to wonder if it had really happened at all. "I'm delirious," he said aloud, attempting to shrug it off.

He climbed the stairs and pulled his t-shirt off as he entered his bedroom. The soft light from the lamp on the bedside table made the window appear black. Imagining someone across the way with binoculars; a lonely housewife, a depraved teenager, or maybe a deranged criminal, Tom pulled bed-sheets from a box and tacked them over the dark glass. Satisfied, he finished undressing, anticipating the luxurious spray of a hot shower.

He stood under the pelting water and let it drench his body. The liquid heat felt like a touch of heaven and Tom could feel the tension of the day slipping away as he rinsed shampoo from his dark hair. He was here. He had made it. His dreams were coming true and he didn't even try to stop his goofy grin or child-like chuckle.

After toweling himself dry, Tom returned naked to the bedroom. The new carpet was soft under his feet as he picked up the remote and turned on the TV sitting on his armoire in the corner. Ignoring the boxes stacked against one wall and the bare tops of his dresser and chest of drawers, Tom turned out the bedside lamp, got into his king-size bed and pulled the sheet to his waist. His muscles sighed in relief. He was lulled by the anchorman's voice and struggled to keep his eyes open. Tom barely noticed as the voice began to fade.

Suddenly, a soft whimper came to him through a rising mist that was surrounding him. It grew in volume until his mind filled with the muffled, heart-wrenching sound of a sobbing child.

Searching blindly through the fog, Tom became disoriented and stopped to recover his bearings. His heart lurched when a little girl, perhaps six years old, emerged from the mist directly in front of him. The expression of suffering on her battered face impaled him.

Her brown eyes were huge with fear. One eye had been blackened. Her small jaw was red and swollen. A dried and crusted trickle of blood from a gash at her temple streaked her face. Her arms and legs were black and blue with bruises, some of them resembling large hand prints. Her long, dark hair was matted and stringy, and the blue and white dress she wore was stained and torn. White lacy socks, now grimy, sagged around delicate ankles. She wore no shoes.

The cruel reality of a child being forced to endure the vicious abuse that her little body displayed made him tremble with rage. He longed to ease the wretched sorrow clouding her dark eyes by enfolding her in the safety of his embrace. But as he moved forward to her tiny, reaching hands, he was cheated of the chance by a grasping arm that snatched her back into the consuming fog.

"Please! I want my mommy. Please!"

The desperate, terrified plea shrilled through the air, forcing him to cup his hands over his ears.

"No!"

Tom jerked awake. His heart pounded and his body quaked beneath a cold sweat within the harsh, gray light radiating from the television. Drawing in deep, jolting breaths, he threw off the tangled sheet, swung his legs over the edge of the bed and reached for the bedside lamp. Unsteady fingers sliced through his damp hair before he grabbed up the remote control to snap off the set.

He sat a moment as his trembling subsided and filled his mind with the things that still needed to be done before his gallery could be shown. Then he pulled on his jeans and left the room. He roamed aimlessly through the quiet house and soon found himself standing in the doorway of the red gallery. He switched on the light and the frightening memory of his dream came back to him in a startling rush.

Tom remembered how he had felt when he saw the child's beaten and battered body. He remembered his frustrating sense of futility when the unseen figure snatched her from his grasp. He remembered the rage and paralyzing helplessness that had consumed him. And when he remembered how her desperate cry for help had ripped through the silent mist, Tom suddenly understood the room's purpose, the reason behind its creation and its crimson walls.

He ran upstairs to his studio and searched the boxes in the attic until he found a fresh canvas, brushes and paint. Then, with the empty canvas propped on the easel in front of him, Tom cleared his mind except for the image of the haunting dream.

His hand guided the brush across the canvas and the image of a child began to take form. As her face emerged, her eyes stared back at him and Tom began to feel the sadness of her presence beside him, watching as he brought her heartbreaking image to life. He could hear the sound of her tiny child voice, crying out in tormented sorrow, filling the empty space around him. It seemed to ricochet from the rafters to the floor, bouncing off the walls to engulf him in its desperation. He had never experienced anything so vividly real in his imagination before, and he let it guide his creative hand across the expanse of the canvas.

When the sun began shining through the skylights, Tom stopped and laid his paint and brush aside. The tiny presence that had been his companion throughout the long, emotion-filled night had vanished with the final stroke of his brush and was now silent in the morning light.

Without bothering to inspect the painting, Tom turned and left the attic. He knew she was only in his imagination, but to him, she represented the thousands of battered and abused children throughout the world. In his mind, she was one of them.

# CHAPTER SIX

The morning sun pierced the windows of Tom's bedroom. Feeling its warmth against his naked shoulders, he was vaguely aware of its glaring brilliance as it drew him up from a sound, dreamless sleep. He opened one eye just enough to peer at the digital numbers of the bedside clock, then groaned in frustration as he buried his head beneath his pillow.

Suddenly, the sound of a compressor rumbling to life beneath his window shattered the silence and Tom's eyes flew open. He withdrew the pillow from his head and rose to one elbow. *The painters.* With a moan, he fell back against the mattress and rubbed the sleep from his stinging eyes. Then he slowly lifted his head. *Bare windows.* He looked over and saw that the sheets he had tacked up the night before were in a puddle on the carpet. He stared for a perplexed moment until he heard a shout from outside.

Pushing the discarded sheets to the back of his mind, Tom crawled out of bed. He located clean clothes and began to dress. As he tied his shoes, his eyes strayed back to the sheets lying rumpled on the floor. With a shake of his head, he left the room and made his way outside to find four men in painter's whites standing in the front yard. He could barely make out the sound of their voices over the vibrating hum of the compressor.

One of the men saw him advancing and broke away from the

group. He was tall and rangy, covering the distance between them with a long stride. Tom took in his bald head glinting in the sunlight, then almost smiled at the small animal-like thing on his face. What the man couldn't grow on his head, he made up for on his upper lip. The thick mustache was salt and pepper in color and hung down at least three inches on either side of his mouth.

He greeted Tom with a wide, toothy smile. "Mr. Shear?" His voice sounded like gravel.

"That's right," Tom said, shaking the man's strong, bony hand.

"My name's Joe Douglas. You surprised me just now. I didn't think anyone was home. We rang the bell, but no one answered. You must have been dead to the world."

"Yeah, I guess I was. How long have you been here?"

"Since eight this morning."

"Really?" Tom couldn't believe he had slept through the noise. "I guess there's no use asking if you've had time to look the place over," he said, his lips creasing with a grin.

Joe chuckled. "Did that first thing."

"How long do you think it will take?"

"Oh, I'd say we could have this place looking brand new in about ten days or so. That is if the weather holds. You should be all set for Thanksgivin'."

Tom's brow lifted. "That soon? I was expecting longer."

"Well," Joe drawled, "I know how anxious you are to have the house finished, so I've added a couple of men to my crew."

"I appreciate it," Tom said. "Joe, you've just made my day."

"Glad to hear it."

"I need to return the U-Haul. I'll be back in a couple of hours."

"No problem," Joe said. "Take your time."

Tom turned toward the moving van. The swish of uncut grass beneath his feet reminded him that he needed to look into buying a mower. Considering the size of his lot, one he could ride was a must.

Suddenly, he was smiling at the prospect of having the house completed the following week. Everything was progressing a lot faster than he had anticipated, and his excitement grew as the reality of his first public showing drew near.

He drove through the square and was caught by each red light. As he waited with the rest of the traffic, he made a mental note to check out the antique shops in town, of which there were several. At the next light, he saw Eddie's Trick Shop and thought of Jonathan and his fake ice cubes with bees. Shillings restaurant was on the corner and he added to his mental list to try its cuisine.

To his left stood the multi-floored municipal buildings which were designed with gold-tinted, reflective widows. On this bright, sunny morning, they seemed to glow. The storefronts lining the sidewalks were sheltered with nameplate awnings, which were in turn, shaded by the steady parade of well-spaced water oaks. People on business errands and people browsing walked past curbside shrubs and raised beds of colorful flowers. The centerpiece of this square roundabout was the garden-like park, with an actual old-fashioned bandstand gazebo. In the center, a fountain and park benches were available for whoever wanted to linger.

The car in front of him began to pull forward and he followed. A half-mile south of the Square, Tom turned left onto Clay Street where the U-Haul rental center was located. He parked the lumbering vehicle with the others and got out. Inside the store, he waited at the counter while the male clerk rang up a woman's purchase of boxes.

Sale signs were taped to the plate glass windows and Tom read the words backward through the thin paper. Flattened boxes, separated by size, were displayed in neat stacks. A variety of dollies waited in a row. Tape, packing peanuts, brown wrapping paper, and bubble wrap lined the shelves.

"Congratulations on your nuptials," the clerk said as he handed her a receipt. "Good luck to you."

"Thanks," the woman replied with a smile. She turned with a glance in Tom's direction then did a double-take and met his gaze. Her smile broadened with a flirtatious twist to her lips. "Hello."

Tom's mouth twitched with a grin. He took in the dark hair clasped to her head off her shoulders, the becoming blush coloring her cheeks, soft brown eyes, full, luscious lips—and teeth that were yellow and overlapped in front. "Hi," he responded, then both men watched as she gave him a quick wink and sauntered out the door, hips swaying.

"Women," the clerk stated with a shake of his head. He chuckled and the belly hanging over his belt jiggled. "Can't live with'em, wish we could live without'em. Tie ye up in knots if ye let'em."

Tom's grin turned sardonic as he handed the man the keys. "I'm returning that truck," he said pointing out the window. The man hitched up his trousers and waddled outside to inspect the vehicle. When he returned, he printed out Tom's receipt.

"You have a good day."

"You, too," Tom replied then made his way to his Jaguar that he'd left the day before parked in the lot.

He stopped for groceries on his way home. After putting them away, he fixed himself a smoked turkey sandwich, then carried his lunch up the attic stairs to escape the commotion of the painters outside.

The faint insistence of the doorbell yanked at Tom's awareness. He shook his head to dislodge the heaviness within it, then looked up through the skylights. The light outside was fading. Hours had slipped by without notice.

He realized his hand held a paint-filled brush. Looking at the painting in front of him, Tom sucked in a startled breath as a shocking array of children's faces, distorted by their pain-filled screams, leaped out at him from the canvas.

Some had eyes wide and staring in different shades of blue and brown. Others had their eyes squeezed shut with tears streaming down their pale faces. Also, they were all little girls. Their stricken expressions were so alive he could almost hear the chilling sound of their voices crying out in chorus with the physical and mental pain they displayed. The canvas was covered with this image from corner to corner, some faces overlapping others, making Tom wonder how such a devastating scene could be held within the confining space of one single canvas.

Even though he heard the faint chime of the doorbell once again, Tom was unable to move away from the painting's haunting image or the intensity of its sudden existence. He had to close his eyes against it before he could turn his body away, and, even then, he felt the tormented faces at his back, seemingly straining to keep him near.

His heart pounded as he descended the narrow attic stairs and practically sprinted down the main staircase. He dared not look back, for the shiver that ran through his body was like a warning that had him shuddering within its grasp. When he reached the bottom, Tom forced himself to stop and take a deep, steadying breath before crossing the foyer.

"I'm sorry to bother you, Mr. Shear," he heard Joe say as he pulled the front door open, "but we've done all we can do today. We'll be back first thing in the morning."

"That'll be fine," Tom replied, forcing a smile.

The painter nodded as he looked curiously at Tom's pale face. "You have a good evening, sir."

"Thank you. You do the same."

Tom closed the door thinking of the horror-filled painting upstairs. How could such a painting exist when he had no memory of creating it? And how could he let the entire afternoon slip by without remembering?

Tom shook his aching head then activated the security system and turned out the foyer light. Ignoring the rumbling of his empty stomach, he ascended the stairs in search of the oblivion of a dreamless sleep.

*Don't cry, little girl. Everything will be alright. Why are you so frightened? I'm right here. I'll help you.*

Tom could hear his words in his mind, but could feel no movement on his lips. *What's wrong with me? And why is the little girl suddenly so quiet?* He strained to detect the slightest sound.

*Footsteps!* Understanding invaded Tom's muddled thoughts and a chilling deluge of fear washed over him. *He's coming!* His mental voice grew frantic. *He's coming up the stairs. We've got to run, but how? We're trapped. There's no escape. No escape...except...death.*

*I can't move. I've got to try and get away. Get all of us away. How many are we? Why can't I see? I know they're here. I can feel them. They are all around me.*

Tom heard the rattling of a key in the lock. At the sound of grating hinges, the urgent need for freedom overwhelmed him. He pulled frantically against the cold metal encircling his wrists and ankles, but felt only searing pain as the unyielding bindings cut into his flesh.

The menacing presence drew closer. Footsteps thumped on the bare planks of the floor. Tom began trembling with fear.

*He's getting closer! NO,* his mind roared. *Please, no more!*

The footsteps stopped close beside him. Tom pried his eyelids open, feeling the crust that covered them crack as his lashes pulled apart, and saw the blurry vision of a figure towering above him. He could see the ominous glint of metal dangling by its side and felt his body cringe with terrified expectancy. He watched its arm rise up, holding tight to the threatening object. He quailed in terror as it came lashing down.

Tom was held defenseless against the onslaught. He writhed in pain as the deadly object made contact again and again with his exposed ribs. The sound of cracking bone rang in his ears and he felt his blood go cold with the sense of detachment that accompanies mortal fear, pain, and death.

His feeling of detachment intensified as numbing darkness seized his mind and Tom felt himself begin to rise. Suddenly released from the excruciating pain, he found himself floating against attic rafters. His naked body lay beneath him, bound and helpless, bleeding on the rough planked floor. His horror-twisted face was caked with blood.

Looking around, he searched frantically for a means of escape. It was then Tom noticed the buckled leather straps hanging from the rafters.

With growing curiosity, he began scanning the depths of the attic. He saw a table scattered haphazardly with a grizzly array of blood-stained tools: hammers, pliers, knives, clamps, long screws and spikes, wire, ropes, razor blades, a butane fire-lighter. They were all there, ready and waiting to be used on the tender flesh of the children.

Tom shifted his gaze and a tiny form, huddling in a dark corner, caught his eye. And then he saw another. And another. Looking more closely, he noticed several sets of manacles bolted to the floor around the frightened little bodies. Along the wall, he noticed a large wooden box with holes in its padlocked lid.

Maniacal laughter brought him back to the central scene below and a bone-chilling horror washed over him at the sight of blood streaming across and between his own body's legs from mutilated genitals. The display of his naked body, lying mangled and bleeding on the cold attic floor, left him with a sense of rage more intense than anything he had ever felt before. His blind fury wanted to lash out against his tormentor, but as the man's arm rose up once more,

Tom felt himself being yanked from the rafters by the lifeline he could now see stretching between himself and his body on the floor. His scream of denial gurgled in his throat as the annihilating weapon came crashing down against his skull.

Tom bolted up in bed, shaking, his head throbbing with the pounding of his heart. His choking breaths became sobs as he fought restraining, sweat-soaked sheets to reach the bedside lamp. In the pool of soft light, Tom sat on the edge of the bed, elbows on his knees and chest heaving, running unsteady hands through his damp hair, before stumbling naked into the bathroom. He splashed cold water over his pale face and let it trickle down his neck and chest as he stood trembling, braced against the sink. His head hung limp between his shoulders as he drew in a deep, shuddering breath. Then, avoiding the revealing truth of the mirror, he fled the room.

In the den, Tom retrieved the lap blanket from the back of his sofa. His mother had knitted it in a deep rich blue. "To match your eyes," he remembered her saying. The memory nearly closed his throat and he felt the prickle of tears behind his eyes. He took a deep breath then slowly expelled it as he picked up a John Saul novel. He sat in the recliner, covered his bare legs to his waist, and tried to concentrate. Before long the book began to sag and his eyelids closed. The scent of roses hung heavy in the air as the light from the lamp beside his chair went out.

"You have to help her, love. You have to help all of them. Don't be afraid. I'm here with you."

Tom heard the whispered words from a woman in his mind; they were like a caress. They soothed him with their softness just like the fingers and lips he imagined stroking his bare chest. The lingering touch swept lower along with the blanket and he felt himself grow firm.

"I'm here with you," he heard again, as he gasped with pleasure when enveloping warmth closed around his erection.

# CHAPTER SEVEN

The weatherman promised that the overcast skies would clear up by late morning. Tom could already see blue sky through breaks in the clouds as a mild November wind pushed them to the east. He sipped coffee from his green insulated travel mug then placed it in the cup holder on the console between the Jag's bucket seats.

As he merged into heavy traffic on I-75 headed southbound toward Atlanta and Georgia State University's city campus, he tried not to think of the nightmares of the past week. It would be hard to decide which haunted him more and seemed more real, the imploring children or the erotic presence. Instead, he turned his mind to the workday ahead, with the inevitable pileup of paperwork and anxious students awaiting him.

The lot adjacent to the Fine Arts building was half full by 7:00 a.m. when Tom parked and took his bag from the car. A woman on the Law faculty gave him a second look with his jeans, white dress shirt and baby-blue tie. He smiled and nodded good morning, got his coffee mug and jacket, activated the car's alarm, and entered the building.

As Tom opened the door to his office, he hoped to get a handle on a week's worth of paperwork before his nine o'clock class. He mentally groaned when he saw his in-box and immediately began whittling at the teetering pile.

By 9:00, he was in his classroom leading a fast-paced review of the Quattrocento's major developments which justified the name "Renaissance". This had been the focus of the multiple-choice test which had been administered in his absence, and everyone was anxious to learn of their results. At the end of class, he promised his students that he would have their papers graded and returned in the next two days, and he poured over the material for the next three hours until his stomach demanded attention with a complaining rumble. Tossing his pen on the test in front of him, Tom pushed away from his desk and went in search of food.

Tom, along with most of the staff, still called the cafeteria the Student Union; the students, however, rejected the idea and just called it the Café. As usual, it was alive with the cacophony of voices, laughter and the clank of trays. Aromas from a variety of foods cooking and being served wafted through the air. The whole atmosphere was comforting in its unique way, and Tom felt himself relaxing for the first time in days.

Forking up his last bite of roast beef and potatoes, he wiped his mouth with a thin, practically useless paper napkin, then crumpled it and tossed it on the tray. He looked up at the sound of a familiar voice.

"So, you finally decided to come back." Marsha pulled out the orange, plastic chair across from him and Tom smiled.

"Yep, I'm back," he said, pushing his tray aside and leaning back in his own plastic chair. He watched her withdraw a wrapped sandwich from her shoulder bag.

Marsha's appearance had changed since the last time he saw her. Her make-up had been applied flawlessly, enhancing her almond shaped hazel eyes and high cheekbones. Instead of jeans and a Lynard Skynard t-shirt, she was wearing a skirted business suit the color of dark chocolate and a cream silk blouse. Her dark, shoulder-length hair was pulled up and clasped behind her head revealing a slender, elegant neck. She was all business while maintaining the soft allure of woman.

"How are things going at the house?" she asked, unwrapping what looked like a ham and cheese. She popped the tab of her Diet Coke and managed to keep her manicured nails intact.

"Couldn't be better," Tom answered. "How are things going with you and Jonathan?"

"Good." She paused and met his gaze. "Why?"

"No reason."

"Uh huh. Has Jonathan been talking to you?" she asked and watched his eyes widen with innocence. "He has, hasn't he?"

Tom's brow creased with indecision as she waited for his reply. Then a mischievous grin curved his lips.

"Okay," he said. "We might've discussed a thing or two. But I have to admit, I'm on your side. I can't understand why he's dragging his feet."

"I'll bet," Marsha retorted and dropped her sandwich on her napkin without taking a bite. She folded her arms beneath her breasts and watched him from across the table.

Tom threw up his hands in self-defense. "I'm dyin' if I'm lyin', sweetie." He leaned forward and held her gaze. "One thing's for sure. If you were mine, I'd do everything within my power to keep you."

Marsha's pixie face melted into a heart-stopping smile. "You don't know how much I needed to hear something like that. Thank you."

"You just keep your chin up. He'll come around."

"I hope you're right. I really do love him a lot, you know?"

Tom smiled at the romantic softening of her expression. "I know you do. It'll happen, don't worry."

"What about you?" she asked, picking up her discarded sandwich.

"What about me?" Tom's heart skipped a beat. The memory of being half awakened in the dark of night by the same invisible lover as before flashed through his mind.

The scent of roses had enveloped him. Her fingers, lips and tongue had trailed over his body leaving him engorged and yearning before her sucking lips and throat engulfed his erection, forcing him to climax in an explosion of almost painful pleasure. When he had awakened, he had been shaken by the vividness of the erotic dream and by the lingering reality of it. It didn't fade into a vague confusion of disjointed fragments the way all dreams did in the light of day. There was also the slightly embarrassing physical evidence of his climax on him and on his bed-sheets.

*Wet Dreams. Nocturnal Emissions.* The terms came back to him from the lessons of adolescence. *Succubus* was another forgotten term that arose unbidden in his thoughts. It just fit in with the other unbelievable and previously discounted superstitious concepts that had begun to force themselves toward credibility since moving into the house. *But would a succubus plead help for someone else?* He didn't think so. *And didn't they use sex to drain energy from their victims to sustain their own lives?* Except for a few sleepless nights, he didn't feel drained, he felt good. In fact, he felt great. *Granted, it had only happened twice. How many times did it take to drain a person?*

He was jerked back to the present by Marsha's persistence. "You know perfectly well what I mean. Have you found anyone you're even remotely interested in yet?" She took a dainty bite of sandwich and smirked as he rolled his eyes.

"I should have known that was coming." Tom made a mental note to add "Succubus" to his list of research subjects as soon a possible.

"Well?" she insisted from the corner of her mouth as she resumed chewing.

"No. I'm not even looking. Besides, who has the time to look anyway?"

Marsha gave him a level look and swallowed. "You may not be looking, but that's not to say someone won't find *you*," she said before biting again.

His expression grew daring. "I guess we'll just have to wait and see, won't we?"

Marsha chuckled. "I guess so."

"Enough said about my lacking romantic endeavors. I want to know about you. Anything interesting brewing in the realm of criminal psychology?"

"Actually, there might be. I've been offered the opportunity to analyze a man arrested for beating his son to death."

Tom's expression grew doubtful. "Sounds like fun," he drawled. "Who made the offer?"

"The DA's office contacted me. Someone over there seems to have taken an interest in the articles I've written discussing the psychological theories of crime causation. The main study focused on the social development of individuals with traumatic childhoods, particularly with the element of abuse."

"Sounds deep."

"It is," Marsha said and laughed. She put down her half eaten sandwich and took a sip of Coke. "But it's extremely interesting. Especially to someone who delves into the depths of a criminal's mind. Actually, this could be a big break for me. It's an opportunity to expand my research, but at the same time, it'll give me the chance to explore, in more depth, a hard core element of my profession that I need more experience with."

"Which is?"

"The United States Court System."

"Are you saying maintaining a healthy private practice while teaching classes twice a week isn't enough for you?" he asked, intrigued.

Marsha shrugged. "Maybe not. I do know a few psychologists who would rather have their eyeteeth pulled than have to deal with the courts. Ask me again in a couple of months."

"I'll do that," Tom said and matched her grin.

"So how does it feel to be back in class?"

"I have to admit, it feels good."

"I'll bet your students are glad to see you," she said, smiling.

"Why do you say that?"

"Well, it's not exactly a secret your substitute didn't know a hill of beans about art."

Tom's black brows shot up. "How do you know?"

"I popped in from time to time. Oh, I guess Mr. Jackson's nice enough," she admitted. "He just seemed to be a little on the absent minded side of the fence."

His own laughter sounded strange to Tom's ears. He suddenly realized it had been days since he'd felt the urge to laugh.

"Are you sure everything's okay?" Marsha asked. Her expression was serious, her lunch forgotten.

"Sure I'm sure," he said. "Why shouldn't it be?"

"I don't know," she said, her thin brow furrowing. "But I have this feeling I should be worried about you."

Tom's shuttered expression tightened. "It's unnerving when you go all witchy on me. I wish you wouldn't do that," he announced, startled by her insight.

"That's what Jonathan says, too. I can't seem to help myself. I've always had feelings. But it's nothing more than a woman's intuition."

"I think the word is clairvoyant," he stated, only half-way joking.

"Ahh. Telepathic intuition, huh?" she said, looking intrigued. "Okay, let's go with that. So, just what am I sensing? What kind of turmoil? I feel like it's something connected with the house."

Tom shrugged. "It's nothing really," he edged, wishing he'd kept his mouth shut. "I've not been sleeping well lately. I guess I'm just anxious about my upcoming opening."

Marsha's steady gaze made him want to squirm.

"You shouldn't worry about it," she said finally, picking up the remembered sandwich. "Didn't you say everything's falling right into place?"

"That's just it; everything's going so smoothly. I keep expecting it all to crumble around my head."

"Have you been painting? That always seems to relax you," Marsha replied and noticed Tom's hesitation.

*Not lately it hasn't.* He pushed the thought aside. "I've been keeping myself busy. I've been hanging paintings for the past two days."

She just looked at him. "That didn't exactly answer my question."

"Sure it did. Like I said, I've been keeping myself busy."

Marsha watched him from across the table until the corners of her lips lifted in a knowing grin. "Oh, I get it. You're not going to discuss your new creations until your showing, is that it? Okay. I can take a hint."

"I think you'll be surprised," he said, glancing at the clock on the wall.

"Pleasantly?"

"Surprised," Tom repeated, pushing his chair back before her curiosity and concern created more questions. "I've got to go. My next class starts in ten minutes." He pulled his jacket from the back of his chair and put it on. "Tell Jonathan I said hello." "I will. Don't you be a stranger, you hear? We'd better not have to come looking for you."

He picked up his tray. "Don't worry," he said, before turning toward the disposal window. "I'll be in touch."

Tom loved the smell of his classroom. The scents of paints, charcoal, chalk, and canvas all mingled to create an unmistakable blend. He was in his element here. He enjoyed teaching the fundamentals and then watching the progress of his students as they began to understand and respect the beauty that can be created from their imagination and talents.

A bookshelf along the left-hand wall was neatly crammed with volumes describing and explaining the Masters. He always enjoyed seeing his students' cautious expressions at the beginning of a semester slowly take on interest, then excitement as they absorbed the lives, personalities, failures and accomplishments of Picasso, Cezanne, Manet, Degas, or Monet. As he lectured, hands would begin to lift with questions or comments, debates would be born, some heated, but always intelligent and stimulating.

At the moment, twenty easels held covered canvases. Tom was eager to see the progress his students had made in the last week, but had to wait until everyone had arrived and taken their place.

As students began to trickle in, Jason Stafford, a third year student, bounded into the classroom. A wide grin spread across his face at the sight of Tom sitting behind his desk.

"Hey, Mr. Shear. Where've you been?"

"I've been moving into my new house," Tom answered, smiling.

"Oh yeah? Well, I'm glad you're back. Your expertise has been sorely missed. Do you think I could talk to you later on? I need some advice about the class exhibit next month."

"I'm free after class," Tom offered.

"I'm not. I've got Finance next and if I'm not there on time Mr. Crowley'll deck me."

"Okay," Tom said, "how about meeting me back here at three fifteen. That'll give me a chance to catch up on some paperwork."

"That's no good, either," Jason replied, flashing an apologetic grin. "My sister's picking me up at three."

Tom's amusement increased. He couldn't help but like the young man.

"I'll tell you what. Why don't you tell me where your sister's picking you up and I'll meet you there."

"Great," Jason agreed with mischief in his eyes. "I'll even introduce you."

The afternoon sunlight was bright, creating a short term illusion of warmth as Tom emerged from the building. He looked up for a moment to enjoy the sight of the cerulean sky, clear except for a few, thin wisps of cloud and two vapor trails from jetliners high in the sky. He wondered at their destinations.

He took a deep breath and felt the chilling air fill his lungs. Trees, swaying lazily in the breeze, were in their last stage of fall colors. Leaves blanketed the ground like a patch-worked quilt. Students headed in all directions to different buildings on campus, some at a saunter, some at a dead run. Others were arm-in-arm with here now, gone tomorrow significant others. And then there was Jason waiting patiently on the steps. Even at a distance, he was a striking young man being tall and athletically built. His auburn hair was short and parted in the middle. Moss-green eyes crinkled at the corners when he smiled or laughed, which was often, flashing straight, white teeth that his parents had probably spent a small fortune on. But, as far as Tom was concerned, one of Jason's best attributes was the way he always seemed to find the bright side or humor in things. He was the type of person people enjoyed having around. As these thoughts ran through Tom's mind, he returned the smile on the young man's face and headed in his direction.

"Hey, Mr. Shear. I appreciate you taking the time to talk to me. I know you must be pretty busy," Jason said, falling in step with Tom's stride toward the parking lot.

"No problem. That's what I'm here for."

Tom watched a smile form on the younger man's lips before he looked away.

"What?" Tom asked.

"It's nothing really." Jason gave his head a slight shake. "No, that's not true. You're different from my other teachers. I feel like I can really talk to you. That means a lot."

"I'm glad to hear you say that, Jason. I'd like to think I'm your friend as well as your teacher. So, what problem are you having?"

"It's about the art department's exhibit next month. I didn't know what I was getting into when I volunteered to be on the student committee representing our class. They informed me Friday that I have to pick the best ten pieces from the class to be shown. How am I supposed to do that without having people hate me for not choosing their work?"

"Jason, I can't tell you what to do." Tom sighed and shook his head. "But you can't go through life worrying about hurting everyone's feelings. I'm not saying you shouldn't consider them. You should. But there comes a time when you have to start using your own good sense and judgment. You're going to be making important decisions for the rest of your life, and even though what you decide may not always be right, that's how we learn in life. But when something *is* right, and you know it, you've got to stick to it. You have to learn to trust your instincts and go with them."

"I know you're right, but—"

Jason's eyes were downcast. The teasing fall breeze ruffled his hair, but he ignored it.

"But it doesn't solve the current problem, correct?"

"No, not really."

Tom stopped. He waited until several people passed before meeting Jason's questioning gaze.

"What I'm about to suggest has got to stay between us," he said. "Agreed?" Jason's auburn head bobbed. "It can't get around that I had my hand in the choosing, however small. Am I making myself clear?" Jason's head bobbed again and a conspiratorial smile split his face. "Okay. Why not let the other students have a say on which pieces are to be shown?"

"How do you mean? The committee said it had to be my decision."

"The final choosing will be. But why not let each student pick, say three of his or her best pieces. Then you decide from those which should be shown. That way the best pieces will already have been sifted out. All you'll have to do is choose the best from the best."

"That's a great idea. I'm going to feel kind of bad taking all the credit, though."

"Yeah, I'm sure you will," Tom remarked, seeing the mischievous grin that contradicted Jason's words.

Jason laughed and pointed to a white Lexus sedan parked at the curb. "That's my sister's car. Come on. I want you to meet her."

Tom followed Jason to where the woman waited. He watched his student lean into the open window and found himself frozen to the asphalt as the petite woman stepped from the car.

She wore form fitting jeans and a v-neck sweater the color of peaches. Her long auburn hair was pulled up on each side and secured by jade combs leaving the rest to hang in silky waves down her back. She removed her sunglasses and flashing green eyes met his gaze.

"Kelly, I want you to meet my art professor, Mr.—" Jason's voice trailed off with the look of recognition on his sister's face.

"Mr. Shear, it's a pleasure to see you again," Kelly Stafford said, offering her hand.

Tom's mouth had gone dry. "Miss Stafford, this is a very pleasant surprise. I had no idea you were Jason's sister. Now I see the resemblance."

"I take it the two of you have met," Jason said.

Kelly's smile was bright. "We sure have. I completed the sale of Mr. Shear's new home."

*This has got to be fate.* Tom couldn't help but admire her sparkling green eyes and flawless skin. He watched her cheeks tinge with a slight blush then took in her straight, pert nose before letting his lingering gaze fall to the sensuous curves of her mouth and the kissable mole at the corner.

"How's the house coming, by the way?" she asked.

"It's shaping up great," he answered, managing to ease his eyes from the teasing fullness of her lips, and the beckoning mole, to meet her gaze. "As a matter of fact, I'm planning an art exhibit in a couple of weeks. A sort of formal grand opening for the gallery I've created."

"That's wonderful," Kelly said, obviously impressed. "Let me know when you'll be open to the public. I'm sure with your schedule here at the university it'll only be open on selective days?"

"That's right. But why wait until then? Why not come to my private showing? I'd love to show you around," Tom suggested, subduing his enthusiasm.

"I'd love to. Should I bring a date?" She held his gaze in a subtle challenge.

Tom's lips twisted in a rakish grin. "Well now, that's entirely up to you," he said, "but I'd be happy to offer my services and pick you up if the need arose. I might even be persuaded to give you a lift home, if necessary."

"Why, Mr. Shear. Are you asking me for a date?"

"Would that be so terrible, Miss Stafford?"

"Oh, not at all."

Her soft southern accent was like music to his ears. "Then, I take it, you accept my invitation?"

"With pleasure, Mr. Shear."

"You'll have to promise me something."

"And what would that be?"

"No more of this Mr. Shear stuff. My name's Tom."

She smiled and her low, lascivious laughter seemed to caress him. He lingered in its effect.

"I'll have to let you know about the details."

"I'll be waiting for your call. Tom."

She slipped back into the car and he closed her door. He looked up to see Jason's ear-to-ear grin, receiving a thumbs-up.

"Here, you might need this." She handed Tom a business card.

"Most definitely."

"My cell's on the front, along with the office, as you can see." She started the engine. "Home's on the back," she stated, smiling at him like they'd just shared a secret. "Oh, and Tom?"

"Yes?"

"No more of this Miss Stafford stuff. My name's Kelly."

He grinned as she pulled away, already beginning to memorize the number written in blue ink across the back of the card's white surface.

# CHAPTER EIGHT

The light outside was draining into night as Tom tossed the remains of his microwave dinner into the trash while thinking of the paintings that still needed to be hung throughout his gallery. Each gallery room contained boxes of battery operated display lights that would have to be mounted above each painting after the paintings were in place. Once these things were done, his gallery would be ready. He grinned ruefully, a mingling of excitement and apprehension warring in the pit of his stomach, as he got to work.

Instead of letting his past eat away at his sanity, Tom had discovered a way of transferring his feelings, passions, and heartaches onto a simple white canvas. His paintings were his release for all of the emotions he kept buried inside. This was his dream, his life. Everything had to be perfect.

Three hours later, he stepped back and looked with a critical eye at the painting he had just hung. Yellows, gold, and lavender bled into one another toward the center where streaking reds and a darker gold led the eye to a woman with outstretched arms twirling, absorbing the magical spontaneity of living, of being alive. Seven others with the similar abstract style adorned the walls. Nodding his approval, he turned to survey the room.

Two bright yellow sofas sat facing each other in the center with a low glass and chrome table in-between. The fireplace represented warmth and light. The windows had been installed with indoor shutters that could be opened at will to let in the splendors of light and life thriving outside. The only other furnishings were the eight paintings he had chosen for the yellow walls. These best portrayed the feelings of free spirit and passion. This was his room of "Life."

The blue room down the hallway on the right of the staircase had no fireplace, unlike the two rooms at the front of the house. It held paintings of cold heartache; paintings that reflected the chill of rejection and loneliness. The stark white of a straight-backed, slatted chair facing an unadorned alabaster pedestal, helped to signify the starched and frozen atmosphere created within, as did the two long windows in the back wall with retractable, ice-blue shades. In one painting, cold colors blended to draw the eye to an un-detailed man crouched in the corner of a room filled with shadow people interacting with one another. The man's face was a white mask melting into a sagging display of a distorted mouth and black eyes. The painting, along with six others, gave the impression of the self-inflicted isolation of a wasted existence. This, he called his room of "Ice."

In the white room on the left of the foyer across from the Life gallery, he had created a haven of virgin emotions. Like in the room of Life, the windows had white shutters to either let in the sunshine and the wonders outside waiting to be explored, or to shut out the darkness of night. The fireplace lent the feeling of warm comfort and contentment. Giant, white velvet throw pillows encircled a low, cut crystal table that had an open coloring book and a box of Crayola crayons in its center. A deck of Go Fish cards and a game of Chutes and Ladders lay on the floor waiting to be played. Huge bean-bag chairs, blending like chameleons against the white of the walls, waited for the young at heart. He had instilled the playful, uninhibited atmosphere of childhood splendor, emotions of the young, still untainted by the cruel lessons of life. In one painting, pastels were splashed upon the canvas, color overlapping color, with tiny hand

and footprints pressed into the paint and walking across the surface. This room, with its naïve beauty and charm, he named "Innocence."

The only room he had avoided completing was the room with the crimson walls. Soon, the deadliest emotion of all would be contained there—an emotion so powerful, it could turn the meekest of people into ravagers of hatred. This emotion was one Tom knew well, one he held deep within – "Rage."

He hesitated in the doorway of the dark room and the image of his bleeding, unconscious mother lying on the kitchen floor pushed forward in his mind. He remembered the twisted smile on his father's face as he stepped toward him, unzipping his pants, and a familiar, paralyzing anxiety swelled within him.

Tom shook off the unwanted memory. He walked into the room with its red walls and switched on the overhead light. As he scanned the bare interior, he was suddenly overwhelmed by the sadness and furious heartache of the cloth-covered paintings still sitting in his studio. He had created eleven altogether, only a few of which he actually remembered painting. With the others, it was almost like someone else had guided his hands to create the intense horror the paintings displayed, the appalling reality of abuse and torture.

*You can't keep putting it off.* They were the best work he'd ever done, and the most important. People had to wake up and become aware of the atrocities going on around them. Maybe this was one way of getting their heads out of the sand and opening their eyes.

Tom left the room of Rage and climbed the stairs to his studio. He uncovered two of the paintings and carried them down. He then retraced his steps until all eleven paintings leaned against the base of the red walls.

He picked up the first painting and found himself staring into the solemn eyes of the little girl whose image he carried within him; the very image that mirrored his own.

"Where shall we hang you, sweetheart? It's got to be somewhere very special. You've got to be the first people see when they enter the room."

Like the gallery of Ice, this room had no fireplace to offer comfort. But unlike the other three rooms, the double French doors of the red room had been curtained with rich, thick red velvet on the outside to enhance isolation. The two windows in the back wall had been concealed by thick, black walnut paneling with doorknobs and slide-bolts to represent the dark, confining space of locked closets. There were no pillows, bean-bag chairs, sofas, tables, or games to instill hope, safety, comfort, or to stimulate imagination. Only fear and despair resided here.

He scanned the walls and decided on the space directly across from the curtained double doors. After installing the hanging hooks and wire, Tom secured the painting, then stood back to check its position.

Suddenly the light flickered and the air grew thick. The temperature dropped and his breath came out as shallow, misty puffs. Tom froze as the hair rose on the back of his neck and arms. His scalp crawled. The nerves beneath his skin began to tingle with the sensation of being watched. He whirled, his muscles tense, and found himself immobilized with mind clenching fear.

His eyes widened and a silent scream lodged in his throat. Then his fear slowly transformed into an overwhelming sense of humbled grief and Tom sank to his knees. He ignored the tears that filled his eyes and drank in the sight of the little girl standing a few feet away. He could see her clearly and knew without having to look at the painting behind him that it was the same little girl who had cried out to him on his first night in the house.

She wore the same stained and torn blue dress. Socks, that had at one time been lacy white, were discolored with grime, sagging around delicate ankles. Her starved little body held the marks of purple-black bruises and vicious cuts crusted with blood and the sight made his heart sink.

She looked up at her portrait hanging on the wall then slowly shifted her haunting gaze back to Tom. He watched her mouth lift into a fleeting smile and thought his heart would burst with the whirlwind of emotions that surged through him.

"Are you real? Have you been real all this time?" he asked, his voice strangled. "How can I help you? Tell me what to do."

She lifted her tiny hand and pointed to the portrait. It was then that Tom understood.

"What's your name, sweetheart? Can you tell me your name?"

Her child voice was a mere whisper, but it was one Tom would have recognized without question. "Emmy. My name's Emmy."

"Emmy. That's a very pretty name," he said, his trembling voice growing stronger. "Everything's going to be alright now, sweetheart. I promise I'll make everything alright."

Tom watched as she took a silent step closer and stretched her arms out toward him. Welcoming the embrace she offered, he reached out his hands and felt the loving warmth of trust envelop him as she stepped into his arms before she disappeared.

He remained kneeling and let his empty arms drop to his sides. Even though she had vanished from sight, he could still feel her presence. He could smell her child's sweetness in his nostrils and feel her soft touch against his soul. He knew she had entered his being and he welcomed her with all of the love he possessed.

Slowly, he stood and faced the portrait. The pain and sorrow she felt would be his to relive. Feelings he had kept at bay for years could now be shared and understood as long as her presence remained.

He turned and left the room, returning minutes later with a brush filled with white paint. With gentle strokes, he wrote the name 'Emmy' in the bottom corner and felt the sorrow around him lessen, the air around him warmed.

A heavy sigh escaped him as he turned and picked up the next painting. With each painting he hung, the vivid memories of the nightmares he had experienced while painting them lashed back with blinding reality. *Were they really only dreams? Or are they all as real as Emmy? Could all I've seen actually have happened?* He shook his head at the thought. *I don't know, but I'll find out.*

Two hours later, Tom stepped back to survey his room of Rage. He was glad to see that Emmy wouldn't be alone, and yet, he was remorseful to see that others had had to suffer as well. For hanging beside her were seven others; seven once happy, beautiful little girls with the same tormented, tear-stained faces.

Turning away, the sorrowful room was veiled in darkness as he turned out the light.

# CHAPTER NINE

The automatic headlights of Jonathan's Mercedes flicked on as the lowering sun sank behind the tress. Traffic on Sandy Plains Road was thick as commuters headed home. After passing through the broad intersection of Sandy Plains and Shallowford Road, he soon came upon his left turn onto Wigley. Nickelback sang about photographs and coming to terms with the past and Jonathan's head bobbed along with the beat of the song. He wondered if any of the other homeward-bound commuters noticed and grinned. He didn't care if they did. He liked the song.

At six o'clock and a mile and a half down Wigley Road, he made a right turn into his subdivision. As night took over dusk, he could see the gas light in front of his house illuminating the driveway and sidewalk. It was a single story, contemporary brick ranch the warm color of apricots. The lot was elegantly landscaped in front with aged gardenia and camellia bushes, azalea hedges and a couple of tall, wide spreading dogwoods.

Jonathan stopped by the mailbox at the curb then pulled into the garage and closed the door behind him with the remote. He got out and stepped through the door into the mud-room. When he entered the kitchen, he found Marsha waiting, her body swaying seductively to the Eagles' "I Can't Tell You Why" emanating from the den. He stood a moment taking in her faded, well worn jeans, baggy yellow sweater and bare feet. Her toes screamed with bright red polish. Her soft, brown hair hung to her shoulders, shining like satin under the overhead lamp. Her smile was warm and her hazel eyes sparkled.

"Hey there."

"Hey yourself." He sat his briefcase down, tossed the mail on the counter out of the way and gathered her in his arms to return the welcoming kiss she offered. "Mm, something smells good," he said, giving her a tight squeeze.

"It's called dinner. Why don't you change out of that suit," she suggested and wiggled out of his arms. "It'll be ready in a few minutes."

"I won't be long," he promised, sneaking a nibble of her ear.

Marsha's grin softened as she watched him saunter from the room, then she turned back to the stove. She loved to cook and her spacious kitchen was her favorite room in their cozy home. Oak cabinets of every size lined the walls. The countertops were black granite and plentiful, giving her unhindered workspace and elbow room to be creative.

After checking the chicken baking in the oven, she filled a pot with water to boil. She lifted the lid to stir a simmering pot and smiled as the aroma of home-made marinara wafted up to fill her nose.

"Is that a look of ecstasy?" Jonathan asked from the arched doorway. He was now dressed in an old UGA bulldog sweatshirt and faded jeans. His grin was appreciative and teasing.

"Absolutely," she replied, replacing the lid.

"I've seen that look before, but it had nothing to do with spaghetti sauce."

"Is that a fact?" she asked, trying to hide a grin. Boston's "More Than a Feeling" encouraged the mood.

"Definitely." He stepped closer. "Shall I remind you?"

She pulled a knife from the butcher block and couldn't contain a giggle when he took on a look of horror and threw his hands up in self-defense. "Jerk," she said, laughing. "Like I'd actually do something to hurt my playground." Grinning, she shook her head and began slicing tomatoes for a salad. "Tell me about your day."

"My day was terrific." He ran his hands beneath her sweater, up her bare ribs, then wrapped his arms around her waist. "I won the Petry case today. And guess who was the presiding judge?" he asked low against her neck.

"Don't tell me Judge Hartwell," she said, laying the knife on the chopping block and turning in his arms to face his smug expression. "You won a case with Heartless Hartwell while you were defending the husband in a custody case?"

"Yep."

"I've got to hear this," she stated, returning to her chopping block and vegetables.

"Actually, it was an open and shut case," Jonathan replied, releasing her from his hold and turning to the refrigerator. He reached in for a bottle of ale. "We had a substantial amount of damaging evidence against Mrs. Petry to prove she's an unfit mother. All Hartwell had to do was look at what was presented. No one in their right mind would have allowed those kids to continue living under the conditions she forced on them."

"Such as?"

"For one thing, she lives in a pig-sty," he said, removing the cap with a bottle opener. He took a drink then leaned his hip against the counter. "The house, if you can call it that, is nothing but a three-room shack. And the yard is a disgrace. Its main purpose seems to be a dump for the empty beer and liquor bottles discarded by her and the many guys she screws around with.

"She has all of these lame excuses for not finding a decent, honest job. Can you believe she actually expected to receive child support?

She makes her living by turning tricks and sponging welfare, for God's sake. The woman's a tramp, not a mother. And we proved it today."

Marsha's emotions were a mixture of sadness and frustrated anger. "This has got to be devastating, not to mention frightening, for two small children. What does their father have to offer? Will they be happy with him?"

"I think so. He has a decent home, in a decent neighborhood. They'll have their own rooms with clean, warm beds and a big back yard to play in. Nice clothes." He took a sip before continuing. "You wouldn't believe how she made them dress for school. They tried to play hooky half the time because they were ashamed of wearing the same dirty clothes day after day. But the most important thing they'll have with their father that they didn't get from her is love, love and understanding. Two things they've needed the most, but lived without."

"So, the case unfolds with a happy ending." Marsha wrapped her arms around Jonathan's neck and hugged him close. "I'm proud of you, sweetheart. What you accomplished today is marvelous."

"I have to admit, it feels good. Just knowing those kids now have a chance at a better life is reward enough."

"Why don't you set the table while I open a bottle of Merlot to celebrate."

"I'm up for a celebration," Jonathan agreed in a low, seductive voice, once again slipping his hands beneath her sweater. He cupped her naked breasts, massaging their rising peaks. He was already hard and pressed against her as his lips found the sensitive skin beneath her ear.

"What about dinner?" Her voice was husky with rising passion.

"Later." He reached for the controls of the stove and turned them off. "Come on. Let's go celebrate."

Content in the circle of Jonathan's arms, Marsha sighed and snuggled closer. "I should get up and finish dinner," she purred and placed a kiss beneath his chin.

"It can wait a few more minutes," he said with his eyes closed, tightening his hold.

"Oh, yeah?" She chuckled low in her throat. "Tell that to your stomach. That's the third time it's growled at me."

Jonathan groaned as she pulled out of his arms and slipped out of their king size bed. He watched with lingering passion as she covered her nakedness with a robe.

"Need any help?

"Yeah. You can open that bottle of wine I mentioned earlier."

"Done."

After dinner, Jonathan carried the remainder of their wine into the den. The room was large and comfortable with two dark blue sofas, matching recliners, and inlaid tables. A large, flat-screen TV took up one corner and a rock fireplace engulfed one wall.

"Did you remember to bring in the mail?" Marsha asked.

"Yeah. It's on the counter in the kitchen," he replied, reaching for the remote control.

Marsha retrieved the stack of mail and sat down in a corner of the sofa, curling her legs beneath her. Sifting through its contents, she came across a small, gold embossed envelope. Curious, she slit the top open and read the word 'Invitation' on the front of the card. A smile came to her lips.

"Hey, Jonathan, guess what I have?"

"What's that?"

"An invitation. To a grand opening."

# CHAPTER TEN

The December evening was chilled by a breeze whispering through what remained of season-aged leaves. A shining full moon hung heavy in the night sky. It cast its glowing radiance creating moon shadows, a haunting beauty that enhanced Tom's feeling of expectation as he pulled the Jaguar into the driveway.

"Wow," Kelly exclaimed. "Tom, the house looks wonderful. You've done so much with it. It's a showplace."

Tom smiled with pride. The refurbished house did look remarkably bathed in the security lights. The house was white. Rails, columns, and trim were light gray and long, slatted shutters flanking each window were black. The oak front door had been stripped and stained red, a sign of welcome. The oval, etched glass in its center was encircled by a colorful pattern of stained glass that matched the flanking sidelight windows. Light from within and the light outside made it sparkle richly. The house itself seemed to stand proud and, like its owner, welcome the praise it received.

Tom pulled through the colonnade to the back of the house and parked. A soft smile played along his lips as he turned to admire the woman sitting beside him. She wore her thick auburn hair gathered in a French twist, revealing the tempting curves of a slender neck. She pulled her white cashmere wrap tighter around her and he lifted his gaze. The eyes he saw staring back at him caused his breath to quicken, but he'd noticed how she had used her wrap almost like a shield. He'd also noticed how quiet she had become as he drove and they drew closer to the house.

"Is there something wrong, Kelly?"

Surprise flashed in her eyes before her expression softened and her smile became more genuine. "No. Of course there isn't." She placed her hand on his forearm. "I'm looking forward to tonight, Tom. I have been all week."

"Shall we go in, then?" he asked.

"Oh, yes."

Kelly watched Tom's sleek form as he rounded the car and opened her door. With a becoming smile, she accepted his hand and stepped out.

As Tom watched, Kelly glanced up at the back of the house to the dark dormer windows protruding from the roof. She shivered and pulled her eyes away to meet his gaze.

"You're cold," he said.

"Only a little."

"Then let's go inside."

With his hand resting lightly on the small of her back, he guided her across the footpath leading to the porch and to the front door. They entered the house and were met by soft instrumental music coming from speakers Tom had installed throughout the first floor. Two long tables laden with food were set up in the spacious foyer. A short, well-rounded woman in her early forties, giving last minute instructions to a young man in a waiter's uniform, greeted them with a wide smile. She advanced toward them.

"Ah, Mr. Shear, you're back. A few more minutes and everything will be ready."

"You have plenty of time. My guests shouldn't start arriving for another thirty minutes or so."

Tom took Kelly's wrap from her shoulders and felt an uncomfortable tightening in his crotch. Her long-sleeved, ankle-length pearl white dress hugged her body, caressing her slender curves. The low dip of the neckline revealed satiny mounds and tantalizing cleavage. He wondered what would happen if she bent over too far, then wrenched his gaze away before he was reduced to an ogling schoolboy. With a huge measure of control, he turned away to hang her concealing wrap on the coat-rack, then turned back to introduce the two women.

"Kelly Stafford, my caterer, Mrs. Reading."

"Pleased to meet you," Kelly replied. She smiled as her gaze swept the preparations. "Everything looks and smells wonderful."

"Thank you. We aim to please." The caterer's hearty chuckle made her plump body shake. Eyes the color of blueberries twinkled.

"Have there been any problems?" Tom asked, grinning as he shrugged out of his dress coat, to reveal the tuxedo he wore.

"None whatsoever," she answered. "The bar is set up down the hall. Would you care for anything while you wait? I can have a server bring whatever you like."

Tom gave Kelly a questioning look.

"Chardonnay."

"Make that two."

He smiled as Mrs. Reading flashed him a grin and waddled off.

"She's a remarkable woman. I was lucky to find her," he said, turning his gaze on Kelly. "Would you like a tour before the others arrive?"

"I'd love one."

With a light touch, he guided her into the room of Life.

"Oh, Tom, they're beautiful," she said as she stepped into the yellow room and looked around wide-eyed at the paintings hanging on the walls. "The color is spectacular. They seem to come alive and dance with the joy they display."

"You seem to know quite a bit about the expression of art," he said, surprised. "This happens to be my room of Life."

"Your room of Life. I can understand why you chose the name. It fits the atmosphere you've created perfectly. My cousin Katie is an artist, pencil and charcoal mostly. When we were kids, I used to sit and watch her draw. I became fascinated by the concept of art's creation. I guess it's my secret passion. I even took a few courses in college. That's where I discovered my true talent in the art world."

"Which is?" he asked, intrigued as he handed her a glass from a waiter's tray.

Kelly flashed a grin. "My talent is definitely observing. When it came to creating, I had two left thumbs. My work was terrible. I'm glad I took the courses, though. It taught me how to appreciate a true artist."

"I have to admit, I'm pleasantly surprised by that admission."

"Why?"

"I was afraid you'd be bored out of your mind tonight. Most people don't know enough about art to appreciate it."

"You don't have to be an expert to see the talent hanging on these walls, Tom." She looked up into his eyes.

Tom suddenly felt himself engulfed in her emerald gaze. Unable to pull his eyes away, he felt himself sinking in an emotional undertow. The chiming doorbell broke the spell and his expression slammed shut, concealing the emotional maelstrom he had just experienced.

"Someone's early," he said. "Will you excuse me?"

"Certainly."

Tom turned toward the foyer and felt Kelly's green-eyed gaze follow him from the room. The smile playing along his lips widened as he opened the front door and found Jonathan and Marsha waiting on the other side.

"Hey, buddy," Jonathan greeted as he followed Marsha inside. "The parking lot out back was a great idea. But I see you have the coveted space in front."

"Of course. It's my gallery," Tom said, closing the door. "I take it you saw the parking sign and followed the arrow?"

"Naturally."

"Come here," Marsha said, wrapping her arms around Tom's neck. "Enough about parking. Only a man could get excited over such a thing."

Tom laughed and hugged back. Jonathan wore a lopsided grin and nodded. "You've got us pegged, babe."

"Marsha, you look sensational," Tom said as he took the black, quilted satin stole from her bare shoulders. Her hair was artistically piled on top of her head leaving wispy bangs. Her dress was long, black and shimmered. It clasped at the back of her neck revealing her back in a daring display.

"Thank you," she cooed. She ran a hand over the soft lapel of his tux. "You look pretty spiffy yourself. The sight of the two of you is enough to make a proper lady swoon."

Jonathan turned from hanging his coat and held out his arms. "Here then, darlin', allow me to catch you."

"Sorry, sweetheart," she said, laying a caressing hand on his chest. "I'm not the swooning type."

Jonathan pulled at his collar. "Mercy. Did the temperature suddenly rise or is it just me?"

Tom's laughter rumbled. "I think it's both of us. And just think. The night's just beginning."

"Yeah well, I know we're early, Tom, but Marsha couldn't wait. It's all she's talked about since we received your invitation." Jonathan directed a sly grin at the woman beside him. "Isn't it dear?'

"Oh, you just hush," she retorted. A soft blush colored her cheeks. "Of course I'm excited. This is Tom's big night."

"Well, I'm glad you're early. There's someone I'd like you to meet."

"Oh, really," Marsha said, her brow rising.

A grin lit Tom's face as he crooked his finger in a gesture for them to follow. At the sound of their footsteps, Kelly turned from the painting she had been studying. It was one rich with color, and if you looked closely, delicate wings could be seen attached to the tiny bodies of fairies dancing in flight.

"Kelly, I'd like you to meet my two closest friends, Marsha Webster and Jonathan Fields. Guys, meet Kelly Stafford."

"It's such a pleasure to meet you, Miss Stafford," Marsha said. Her pleased smile broadened. "I see that Tom's been keeping secrets."

"Am I a secret, Tom?" Mischief glimmered in Kelly's eyes.

His seductive expression brought a blush to her cheeks as he held her gaze. "Not anymore." He motioned to the attending waiter. "Would anyone care for a drink?"

"Capital idea." Jonathan turned to the waiter.

"I've just been admiring Tom's work," Kelly said. "He's wonderful."

"I've been telling him that for years." Marsha tossed Tom a mocking smile. "I'm just glad he's finally able to open his own gallery. He deserves some recognition. Are you in the art field as well, Miss Stafford?"

"No. I'm in real estate. And please, call me Kelly."

"Marsha."

Tom watched the two women exchange smiles only females understood as Jonathan clapped him on the shoulder and asked, "How about a tour before the other guests arrive? I want to see what you've done."

Tom grinned, nodded, held out his arms and said, "This is my room of Life." He then guided his guests through the other two rooms he had opened for the showing. Each room was illuminated by track lights in the ceiling and lamps above each painting. The hardwood floors glowed warmly and tapped out their footsteps as they passed from room to room. When they emerged from the last, the room of Ice, he led them back into the foyer where candlelight danced from sconces hanging on the walls and from centerpieces on the tables. The crystal chandelier high above their heads sparkled brilliantly.

"What you've accomplished here is marvelous," Jonathan said. "And you've managed to put it all together in a remarkably short period of time. I'm impressed."

"I think we all are. But haven't you forgotten something?" Marsha asked, raising an expectant brow.

"I don't think so," Tom replied.

Marsha turned and walked down the left side hall to the closed French doors covered with thick red velvet. She placed her hands on the knobs. "Have you decided what to do with this room yet?"

"Marsha, wait," he called, but was too late.

She threw the doors open and entered. When light flooded the room, they heard her startled gasp. Jonathan hurried into the room and stood frozen as he gazed at the exquisitely poignant horrors displayed.

Kelly looked up and caught a glimpse of Tom's anguish before his expression shut down. "Tom, what's wrong? What's in there?"

"Something I hadn't planned on showing tonight," he replied. "Come on. You can see for yourself." He gathered her hand in his and led her into the room of Rage.

"Tom, how—" Jonathan started, but was unable to find the words to express his thoughts.

"This is my room of Rage," Tom explained. "I hadn't planned on opening this room tonight."

"Why not?" Marsha insisted. "You have to. I admit it's a bit frightening, but it's the best work you've ever done. The paintings are exquisite."

Kelly looked around the room with wide eyes. "They're heart-breaking," she said. "But they're so beautiful and alive. It's almost as if I can hear them calling out to me in their anguish. The vibrations of the room are so vivid, it's uncanny."

Tom looked at her sharply and watched her walk deeper into the room. He hadn't expected to hear her say the very words that matched his own secret thoughts.

"I agree with Marsha, Tom," she said, standing in front of Emmy's portrait. "You've got to show them. Not just for the possibility of making a sale, but for the very statement and impact these paintings make. This room exhibits more real-life heartache than mere words could ever express."

"The ladies are right, Tom," Jonathan conceded. "You really have no choice. These paintings have to be seen. If only for the thousands of children who are being abused as we speak. What you have here is a testimony on their behalf. Mental and physical abuse of children happen everyday. I know, because I've seen its effects too many times in court. But maybe you're right about tonight not being the appropriate time," he finished thoughtfully. "You apparently have your reasons."

"What are you talking about?" Marsha demanded. "Tonight's perfect."

"Perhaps," Jonathan responded.

"It seems I'm outnumbered," Tom said, giving in to their logic.

"Why were you going to hold back?" Marsha asked. "You should be proud of what you've created here."

"I'm not sure. I guess it's because, right now, they're so private. They're a part of me like no other work has ever been."

The chime of the doorbell sounded loudly in the soft silence that fell around them.

Jonathan gave Tom a pat on the back. "Get ready. The troops have arrived."

Before long, the gallery rooms were filled with a vast assortment of people, and the one thing they all had in common was their love for art. With Kelly by his side, Tom passed from guest to guest. They ranged from art dealers to collectors, with a few critics mingled in. Some were gallery owners as well.

People shifted from room to room admiring Tom's work. He received praise from all corners and felt his confidence crest at an all time high. Although offers were made for several of his other pieces, the initial shock came when an offer was made for the entire Rage collection.

"I'm sorry, but the paintings in the room of Rage are not for sale," Tom replied. "I plan to add to the collection in the future and I need to keep it intact."

Craig Raymond smiled politely at the rejection. The smile barely reached his cobalt eyes. He had a straight and narrow Norman nose and a thin lipped mouth. His thinning gray hair was neatly trimmed and his robust, barrel-chested frame filled the tux he was wearing with only a hint of a thickening midriff.

"I fully understand the sentimentality an artist has for his work, Mr. Shear, but I am willing to offer a substantial sum. You're very talented. One day your work will be displayed in fine galleries all over the world. I want to be the first to promote that success."

"That's very flattering," Tom replied, "but I'm afraid I have to decline your offer for this particular collection. Maybe in the future I'll change my mind. But right now, my decision's firm."

"Well, if you should change your mind, and I hope you do, I want you to come to me first. I want that collection."

"If I decide to sell, I promise you'll be the first person I call."

"Even though I'm going to hold you to that promise, it doesn't mean I'm not interested in your other work," Raymond said. "I meant what I said about promoting your talent. Why don't we have dinner next week and discuss featuring some of your work in a few of my galleries? I think it would be beneficial for us both."

Tom's smile was subdued. "I appreciate your interest. And I accept your invitation. Thank you."

"I'll call you early in the week to set a time."

"I'll be waiting."

"In the meantime, my son Michael will be by to pick up the two paintings of Ice I've decided to purchase. Is Wednesday afternoon too soon to have them ready?"

"Not at all. I'll be here anytime after four."

"Excellent."

Craig Raymond's expression changed abruptly. Tom realized why when he detected the subtle, sweet smell of roses hanging in the air. He watched, fascinated, as the man seemed to suppress a shiver like he had been physically touched.

"Are you alright?" he asked.

"What? Oh, yes. Yes, of course."

"You seemed out of sorts for a moment."

"Did I?" Craig Raymond gave Tom a wavering smile. "Not at all. I only caught the scent of roses which reminded me of someone. Isn't it odd how small subtleties can retrieve memories thought long forgotten?"

"Odd, but nonetheless a reality," Tom replied.

Raymond's smile was quizzical. "Well put, Mr. Shear. Until next week then."

Tom shook the man's hand and watched as he disappeared in the mingling crowd. With questions still filling is mind, he turned to see Kelly standing with Marsha at one of the buffet tables. He strolled over to join them.

"How's it going?" Marsha asked as she filled the plate she held in her hand.

"Great. I've already sold five paintings and had an offer for the entire Rage collection."

"You're kidding," the women blurted.

"I saw you talking to that gentleman over there," Kelly stated. "Your conversation seemed pretty intense. Is he the one who made the offer?"

"Yep. His name's Craig Raymond. He's one of the most respected collectors in the United States. I have to admit, he drove a hard bargain. He wasn't going to take "no" for an answer. I had to promise him first dibs if I decide to sell."

"You mean you turned him down?" Marsha asked, astonished. "Why?"

"Because I don't want to sell it right now, that's why."

"I swear, I'll never understand the mind of an artist," she stated, shaking her head in bewilderment. "The criminals I study are easier to figure out than you are."

"In case you didn't know," he said to Kelly, "Marsha's a criminal psychologist."

"I know. We've already been through the preliminaries. I think what she does is fascinating."

"How's it going by the way?" he asked. "Did you take the DA up on his offer?"

"Of course. Was there ever any doubt?"

"Not really. I knew your tiger instincts would come through. Have you begun the interviews?"

"Yeah. Last week."

"And what's your diagnosis, doc? Did he do it?"

"There's never been any question of whether or not the guy did it. The DA only wants to make sure he's capable of standing trial. It's rumored that the defense is looking into an insanity plea because he was abused as a child."

"Can they really get him off with that?" Kelly asked.

"Not entirely. If the defense plays their cards right, it's more probable he'll get a reduced sentence. They'll probably push for extensive psychological treatment. Depending on his progress, it's very possible he could make early parole."

"And what about his son, the victim?" Tom asked. "The one he murdered? Where's the kids justice if his father gets out on good behavior and doesn't serve his time?"

"The victim's dead. He can't be helped now, but the father can." Tom shook his head in disgust.

"Yeah, I know," she said, her tone matching his expression. "Sometimes our judicial system really stinks."

"To put it mildly."

"Hey, aren't we supposed to be enjoying ourselves here? Enough of this depressing conversation. I'm going to find Jonathan."

As Marsha retreated, Kelly found herself the object of Tom's watchful gaze.

"Everything's going very well isn't it?" she asked.

"Tonight's success has gone beyond my wildest dreams. Mr. Raymond and I are going to meet next week to discuss a feature of my work in a couple of his galleries. If it works out, it would mean some heavy duty recognition."

"Tom, that's wonderful."

"I'm glad you're here. Tonight would have been empty without someone to share it with." Tom's heart constricted with the gentle smile he received.

"I'm glad you chose me to stand by you," she replied, searching his eyes.

He raised his hand and traced the delicate line of her jaw. "I hope you realize I plan on spending a lot of time with you in the future, Kelly. Tonight's only the beginning."

"Is that a promise?"

Leaning down, he gave in to temptation and kissed the tiny mole at the corner of her mouth. "Most definitely."

# CHAPTER ELEVEN

Tom released a groan of frustration. He groped the beside-table for the shrilling telephone and fumbled the receiver from its cradle.

"Hello." His voice was half muffled by the pillow pressed against his cheek.

"Tom, it's Marsha. Have you seen the morning paper?"

He cracked one eye open and peered at the digital clock with a gimlet stare. Weak morning light was leaking around the edges of the curtains. "Do you know what time it is?" he asked.

"Of course, I do. It's time for you to get up," she said, a bit too cheerfully.

"Let me get this straight. You called to wake me up at seven o'clock on a Sunday morning just for the hell of it? What are you, my new alarm clock? How do I turn you off?"

"I can't believe you," she said, laughing. "I expected you to be up at the crack of dawn buying out the newsstands."

"I take it you've seen my reviews," he said, feeling a twinge of stirring excitement.

"I most certainly have. And they're raving. You're a success, Tom. A big success. Why don't you and Kelly come over tonight for a drink. We've got to celebrate."

———))(((○)))((———

Barrett Parkway was thick with motorists going to or from Towne Center Mall as Tom drove toward Kelly's apartment. Up-scaled strip malls and restaurants were passed by unnoticed as his mind replayed the events of the night before.

Even Kelly's reaction had not been what he'd expected. Instead of being repulsed, she had been overcome by the intense sadness the paintings evoked and had surprised him by expressing the same feelings and concerns he had felt from the very beginning.

As he made a left at the light onto Barrett Creek Boulevard, he noticed the trees lining the sides of the four lane street. Bradford Pear trees ran in a row along the median. Late falling leaves floated toward the ground, dancing in the gusting wind created by the traffic. He made another left into The Cameron at Barrett Creek Apartments and drove slowly over the speed bump a little distance into the complex. At the gate, he punched in the code Kelly had given him and the gate swung open. The buildings were three floors high, made of stone and lap wood-siding the color of warm cream. The complex was well maintained with designer landscaping.

Tom wound his way through the complex until he came to building E. He parked, took a deep breath, then got out. The steps led up and he took them two at a time. Standing in front of Kelly's door, Tom looked at the flowers he held in his hand, then he looked down at himself. Satisfied, he took another deep breath, pressed the doorbell and heard it chime deep within the second floor apartment. When the door opened, his heart thumped against his ribs.

Kelly's long hair was loose and hung in waves. The soft green of her long sleeved cashmere dress caused her emerald eyes to sparkle beneath the sooty black of her lashes. It clung to her body and accented her sensual curves to perfection. Unlike the dress she wore last night, this one's neckline was modest around her slender neck.

"Oh, Tom, they're beautiful," she said, accepting the bouquet of white lilies.

Her voice sounded low and seductive to his ears. "They're not nearly as beautiful as you."

"Thank you." A light blush colored her cheeks as she smiled. "Come in. Do we have time for a glass of wine?"

"Sure. There's no hurry," he replied. "Jonathan and Marsha aren't expecting us for another hour."

"Great. Then let me take your coat." He slipped out of the garment and she hung it on a coat-tree by the door. "Would you mind doing the honors with the wine while I put these in water? It's chilling in the refrigerator."

"I'd be happy to."

He followed her through a spacious living room made cozy by warm colors, a lush, over-stuffed sofa, a matching chair and ottoman, and rich oak tables. Merlot colored pillows, lamp shades, and candles added the perfect accents. An oak entertainment center lined one wall and was filled with all of the necessary electronic equipment. At the moment, TOTO drifted from the speakers. Family pictures hung on the walls and he caught Jason grinning out at him with seeming approval.

In the open, modern kitchen, Tom retrieved the bottle of wine as Kelly filled a crystal vase with water. He removed the cork with practiced ease and filled two glasses. As they sipped in silence, Tom watched her over the rim of his glass, smiling inwardly when another light blush colored her cheeks.

"Why don't we sit down," she suggested, moving toward the sofa. Her dress was several inches above her knees and when she sat and crossed her legs, he caught a peek of lace on her sheer, thigh-high hose before she smoothed her dress into place.

*She's wearing a garter belt.* The arousal he was already feeling grew more intense and his penis thickened at an alarming rate. He had to stifle the impulse to kneel in front of her and run his hands up her thighs beneath the hem of her dress to find bare skin. Instead, he sat down beside her and searched his mind for something to say.

"I hope you had a good time last night."

"Oh, I had a great time. Which reminds me," she said as she gave him a heart-stopping smile. "I think congratulations are in order."

"Thank you. It did come off rather well."

"I'm talking about the reviews in this morning's paper. Everyone thought your work was superb." She seemed marveled by the glimpse of surprise she caught in his eyes. "Didn't you read them?"

"Yes, I did. I'm just surprised that you did."

"Why? It was the first thing I looked for this morning. I think it deserves a celebration."

Tom smiled at the idea. "As a matter of fact, I've made reservations at Aspen's tonight to do just that. I thought we could have a nice, quiet dinner after our visit with Jonathan and Marsha."

"That sounds wonderful. I'd thought of treating you to a celebration dinner of my own, but since you mentioned Aspen's, I think it can wait."

"Mm. Now that sounds enticing." His eyes began to smolder, giving meaning to his sly grin. "Tell me more. I might just have to cancel our reservation and make you cook for me."

Her soft, throaty laughter warmed his blood. He was mesmerized by her smile and her shimmering green eyes.

"I was thinking of cooking you a gourmet dinner served by candle light," she said, looking back at him. "A superb bottle of wine would, of course, accompany the meal while soft, relaxing music drifted in the background." She paused to let the effect sink in. "How does that sound?"

After an imagining pause, Tom found his voice. "It sounds very romantic, that's how it sounds."

"What's the matter with a little romance?" she asked, the flush on her cheeks deepening. "I understand that we've just started getting to know one another, but we're both adults. Sharing a romantic dinner doesn't mean we have to bare our souls. And besides, a little romance hasn't killed anyone yet, has it?"

Tom threw back his dark head and laughed. He could feel the tension leaving his body. "As a matter of fact, it has. Just look at what happened to Romeo and Juliet. And then there's—"

"Okay, okay," she interrupted, trying to simulate an air of indifference. Her twitching lips gave her away. "So it has pushed a few people to an early demise. If you don't want to take the chance, then I guess there's nothing I can say to change your mind."

Tom stopped smiling. He caressed her chin in a gentle grasp and forced her to meet his gaze. Her cheeks were rosy and her green eyes darkened.

"There's nothing in the world I'd rather do than spend an evening alone with you, Kelly."

He released her from his gaze, stood and pulled his cell phone from his pants pocket. He scrolled, pressed a button, and held the phone to his ear.

"This is Thomas Shear. I have a reservation for two tonight that I need to cancel. Yes, that's right. Thank you."

He hung up and extended his hand. "Shall we go?"

Tom pulled the Jag into Jonathan and Marsha's driveway and turned off the engine.

"Nice place," Kelly said, her realtor's eyes assessing.

"Yeah," Tom replied, grinning. "They're both doing really well."

He escorted her to the front door with its oval of beveled glass and rang the bell. When the door opened, Jonathan's smile was welcoming as he stepped back and pulled the door wide.

"Hey, you two. Come on in." He was dressed casually in jeans, a blue t-shirt with a bright yellow smiley face, and socked feet. His grin widened, uncannily matching the one on his chest, as he gave Tom's shoulder a solid thump. "Congratulations, buddy."

"Thanks."

From the stereo, Steely Dan was telling Jack to do it again as Jonathan led Tom and Kelly into the den and motioned for them to sit down. "Make yourselves comfortable. Would you like a drink? Just name your poison," he said, taking their coats.

Tom looked at Kelly. "Wine?" he asked and at her nod, lifted two fingers.

"Coming right up."

Marsha appeared carrying a plate of hors d'oeuvres, which she set on the coffee table beside a couple of lit vanilla scented pillar candles, then gave Tom a hug. Like Jonathan, she was casually dressed in jeans. Her sweater was turquoise and her feet were bare.

"Congratulations," she said, squeezing hard. "I'm so proud of you I could bust. How does it feel to finally have your dreams come true?"

The battered image of little Emmy standing before him flared in Tom's mind. As his heart began to swell, he suppressed his sadness and forced a smile.

"I think you're exaggerating a bit, but I have to admit that I feel pretty good about the whole thing."

"Can you believe this guy?" Marsha asked, looking at Kelly. "Modest to the end."

"Marsha's right, Tom," Jonathan said, handing them their drinks. "Admit it. You're an overnight success."

"That's yet to be seen," Tom countered. "Before we go overboard with the praise, let's wait and see how business is after I open my doors on Friday."

"Well, if last night's any indication," Marsha surmised, "you'll have more business than you can keep up with."

Jonathan cast Tom a quizzical glance as he sat across from them.

"I still can't believe you turned down that offer for your Rage collection," he said, reaching for a piece of toast with pâté. "From what I heard, it was a substantial sum."

"It was. But I'm not ready to sell. I have a feeling I'm going to be adding to it."

"What do you mean, you have a feeling?" Kelly asked.

Tom shrugged, keeping his expression neutral. "Like I said, it's just a feeling. I'm inspired in that direction and I don't feel I'm finished with the theme."

"You've been having a lot of these feelings lately," Marsha said. "You're beginning to sound like me."

"What do you mean?"

"Wasn't it just a feeling that prompted you to paint the room red in the first place?"

"Basically." Tom took a sip of his wine.

"Leave the poor guy alone, Marsha," Jonathan said as he retrieved another bite of food. "I don't think an artist's mind was meant to be understood when it's in action."

"I think you're right, Jonathan." Kelly leveled her gaze on Tom. "Let him keep his secrets. As long as he keeps producing his wonderful art, who's to question his inspiration?"

Tom smiled his thanks for her allied forces and picked up a shrimp puff hors d'oeuvre. "These look great, Marsha. You shouldn't have gone to so much trouble."

"Tom, for you, I'd do almost anything," she said sweetly. "And now that you've so obviously changed the subject, I have a question. How did you meet the lovely creature sitting beside you and how did you manage to keep her a secret from us?"

"I think that's two questions, darlin'." Jonathan turned his laughing gaze toward Kelly. "Just grit your teeth and bear it, Kelly. You've got to understand that Marsha's been trying to play matchmaker for years. She can't stand the fact that Tom's found someone without her help."

Marsha had the decency to blush, slapping Jonathan playfully on the knee.

Twilight had faded and the temperature had dropped when Tom and Kelly said goodbye to Jonathan and Marsha. After escorting Kelly to the car and securing her in the passenger seat, Tom slid behind the wheel and started the engine.

"I'm sorry I put you through that." He cast Kelly a rueful grin. "Marsha can be a little aggressive sometimes."

"Don't apologize. I had a great time. I really like Marsha and Jonathan."

"I'm relieved to hear that," he said, backing out into the street.

"Why?" she asked and laughed. "Were you afraid I'd bolt from the house, pulling at my hair and screaming to get away?"

Tom imagined the scene and his throaty laughter filled the car. "Not exactly, but I *was* afraid you might push the panic button. You have to admit, Marsha practically had us married back there."

"I can't argue with that, but I am flattered she thinks I'm good enough for you."

Kelly looked over at Tom's shadowed face and saw his grin widen, then snuggled deeper into her seat with a contented smile.

With his eyes on the road and his grin turning mischievous, he asked, "So, what are we going to need for this romantic dinner you've promised me?"

# CHAPTER TWELVE

The unease she had felt since their arrival at the gallery was finally beginning to fade as Kelly busied herself in Tom's kitchen with the preparations for dinner. The inability to understand her unfounded fears unsettled her sense of security and control. There was no doubt Mrs. Dempsey's death had been a horrifying experience, but she refused to think it showed a weakness by letting it rule her emotions every time she stepped inside the house where the tragedy took place.

There had to be another reason for what she was feeling. Although she had always been very sensitive to the vibrations around her, she had never been one to exaggerate her emotions. But then again, nothing had ever unsettled her like the warning fear that had taken her in its cold grasp.

"How's this?" Tom asked and her thoughts scattered. He had arranged a bouquet of flowers in a vase and was awaiting her approval.

"You do have a flare for beauty, don't you?" Kelly looked at him and grinned.

"Let's just say I know it when I see it," he replied, stepping close.

She breathed in his spicy, male scent and her heartbeat sped up as she watched his deep blue gaze darken and fall to her lips. As he lowered his head, she lifted her face and her eyes fluttered shut.

Their lips met with tantalizing languor. Tom pulled her close and Kelly's knees trembled as she pressed her body against him. She slid her hands up his chest and around his neck to draw him closer. The tip of his tongue brushed her lips and she opened wider to let him in, gliding her tongue against his, then again, sucking, loving the taste of him, drinking him in.

Her gasp was breathless as she pulled away. "Damn, this is crazy," she said in a voice barely above a whisper. She could feel her cheeks growing warm as the taste of him lingered in her mouth. She swallowed. "We hardly know one another and I'm acting like a dime store hussy on our second date. I can only imagine what you must think of me."

"What I think is that I'm extremely attracted to you, Kelly," Tom said, his fingers gentle beneath her chin as he forced her to meet his gaze. "It makes me feel good just being with you. And tonight, the kiss we just shared, proves to me you feel the same way."

Kelly searched his eyes. She knew her own longing mirrored his.

"I can't deny what I felt when we kissed or what I feel when I'm with you. That's what scares me," she admitted softly, turning away. She picked up a set of tongs and began tossing the Caesar salad.

Tom stood watching as if trying to digest her words. Then he placed his hand on hers to stop their motion.

"I've never had feelings this intense for anyone either, Kelly," he said. "That's why I'm willing to push my fears aside and explore them. I can't let something that could be the most wonderful thing in my life slip through my fingers just because I'm afraid to let it happen."

Kelly was silent as she searched his face. Then, pushing the turmoil of her emotions aside, she took a deep breath and stepped closer.

"Then let's let it happen."

She stood transfixed as Tom ran one hand beneath her hair to caress her neck and placed his other hand on her hip to draw her close before slowly lowering his head. As he began teasing her lips, they parted beneath his touch. Her pulse quickened as he dipped his tongue into the wet warmth of her mouth then slowly withdrew it. When hers followed suit and the tips of their tongues met, his hold tightened, and she found herself intoxicated by the feel of her own yielding body.

He left her mouth to nibble a path along her jaw to the sensitive lobe of her ear. His warm breath against her skin made goose bumps rise and she shivered with pleasure. His teeth nipped, his lips sucked, and his tongue scorched a trail down her neck to settle on her pounding pulse. Her core throbbed and released enough wetness to soak her panties. Kelly's breath was becoming ragged as his hands caressed and explored her back then worked their way down to the curve of her hips and lower. Tom filled his hands with her, lifting her high on her toes and pressing his hard body against her. A low moan escaped Kelly's parted lips when she felt how big and hard his erection was against her belly.

Kelly gently pushed away, looked into his eyes, and saw her own smoldering passion reflected in his heavy gaze. Even though her body ached and throbbed for his touch, her better judgment pleaded caution.

"You know, this could get out of hand," she said, her voice husky as she slid her hands down his chest to feel hard muscle beneath his sweater. "Maybe I should cool things off a bit and finish dinner."

Tom released her and watched her put on a pair of oven mitts. "I'm sorry if I offended you."

The corners of Kelly's mouth quirked as she retrieved the soufflé from the oven. "In case you didn't notice, I was enjoying every minute of it." Her eyes fell to the floor before rising to meet his curious gaze. "I think that's the problem. I enjoyed it too much. I don't want to let things happen too quickly and ruin everything."

Tom smiled his understanding and stroked her cheek with his fingertips. "Then, I guess I'll have to learn to keep my hands to myself.

It'll be tough, but I'll manage somehow," he said, looking like he was unsure whether or not he could pull it off.

Kelly's laughter was soft. Her eyes were shining as she wrapped her arms around his waist and pressed her body close to his.

"I only suggested we move a little slower," she corrected.

"Oh yeah? Well, in that case—"

Tom enfolded her in his arms. He smothered her startled protest with a kiss and thoroughly savored her mouth before relenting to her feeble attempt of escape.

"Whoa, Tiger." Her laughter was low and enticing.

"You shouldn't tempt a hungry beast, my lady," he said, nuzzling her neck.

"Oh, but I think I should." She backed away from him and her sly grin widened. "I've got to keep you on your toes."

Tom's brow shot up in surprise. "Well then, I think it's time to change the music. Theory of a Deadman is a great band, but a guy singing about how his relationship's not meant to be isn't exactly setting the mood we're talking about. Something to tantalize the senses, perhaps?" A wicked smile played along his lips.

Kelly's breath caught as she watched him. He really was the most gorgeous, sexiest man she'd ever met. "I've heard that over-stimulating the senses can be deadly."

"There's only one way to find out."

Kelly smiled as the kitchen door swung shut behind him. She could still feel the touch of his kiss and hands on her body and she felt a soft blush warm her cheeks. She shook her head in awe of her own unhindered response and turned to the task of preparing the table.

The china sparkled as she lit the candles, watching each wick ignite into a glowing flame. Otis Redding's "Dock of the Bay" drifted to her ears as she dimmed the lights.

"Perfect," she whispered, surveying the scene. She raised her wine glass in a silent salute. A caress from eyes behind her softened her smile as she turned.

"Everything's ready—"

Kelly's smile wilted as the delicate crystal she held in her hand slipped to the floor with a splintering crash. She shook her head in denial at the little girl standing a few feet away and cringed beneath the haunted, forlorn light-blue eyes that pleaded for help. They seemed to bore into the very depths of Kelly's soul, and she shuddered as the little girl lifted her hand, beckoning her to follow.

"Please, help us."

The hollow sound of the childish plea sent chills down Kelly's spine. The door suddenly slammed open and a whimper of fear lodged in her throat as the little girl who had seemed so real only seconds before disappeared.

Tom halted as Kelly stared back at him with eyes wide with terror. A racking sob shook her body and he stepped forward to gather her in his arms.

Kelly wiped the tears from her cheeks and pulled away to face Tom with an expression that made him recoil. The undeniable fear she had felt only moments before had been replaced by startling, snapping anger.

"What's going on here, Tom?" she asked, her voice strained and trembling.

"I think you should sit down," he said as he steered her away from the shattered crystal toward a chair. Ignoring the wine on the counter, he opened a cabinet and took down a bottle of brandy, then handed her a glass filled with a generous portion.

"Here, drink this."

Kelly was startled by his calm demeanor and her sense of dread escalated as she watched him retrieve a broom and dustpan to sweep up the shards of glass. "Why haven't you asked me what happened? You come rushing in to find me hysterical, and you don't seem the least bit surprised," she said. "Should I tell you what happened, or should I let you tell me?"

Tom was silent as he dumped the contents of the dustpan into the garbage.

"I saw a little girl just now," she continued. "She was marred and disfigured by bruises and bleeding cuts. I could actually feel her anguish as she held out her hand to me, begging for help."

Kelly studied Tom's expression as he put the broom away and turned to face her, but saw no sign of the indignation she half-expected to see.

"Why aren't you stunned by this absurd admission? You're looking at me like you've hard this story before."

She sat back in her chair as the stunning reality hit her. Suddenly, the mystery behind Tom's hesitations and awkward discomfort whenever the Rage collection was mentioned became clear. She stared at him with wide eyes.

"Her name's Emmy," he said in a low voice. He pulled a chair around and sat facing her. "She came to me shortly after I moved in. She inspired my paintings in the Rage collection."

"You actually talked to her?" Kelly asked in disbelief.

Tom ran agitated fingers through his hair. "Yes. When she first appeared, I couldn't believe she was real. I was scared stiff. But as we stood there watching each other, my fear faded and I finally saw her for what she was. A frightened little girl who had suffered in a way you and I can't even imagine."

He stood up, got another glass, and poured himself a drink. "I'd assumed she had a purpose for coming to me. At first, I thought she wanted the world to see how she had suffered. How all of the children in the paintings had suffered. And I thought I had done that by opening the exhibit to the public. But now I'm not so sure."

"What do you mean?" she asked, watching a confusing play of emotions cross his face.

Tom hesitated before answering. He seemed immersed in a personal struggle.

"I'm not sure," he said, more to himself than as an answer to her question. "She's obviously not satisfied with what I've done. Why else would she show herself to you and plead for more help?"

Kelly looked at him in bewilderment. She was at a loss for an explanation of what she had just witnessed, and Tom's admission only added more questions to the ones already swirling in her mind. Taking a deep, calming breath, she placed her glass on the table, stood, and walked from the kitchen. She had to find out what part she played in this spectral drama, and to do that, she had to confront her fears head on.

Ignoring the warning voice inside her head telling her to walk out and never return, Kelly proceeded with determined steps through the dimly lit, narrow hallway beneath the staircase until she came face to face with the closed doors of the room of Rage. Tom stood watching her rigid back and saw her shaking hands falter on the cold knobs of the double doors. Pushing her gently aside, he opened the doors wide and turned on the lights.

She stepped inside and stared at Emmy's portrait for several moments. "This isn't the little girl I saw," she said.

"What?"

"The little girl I saw was older and had blond hair."

Tom looked at Emmy's portrait. Her long, dark hair hung in unkept strands across her small shoulders.

"But if it wasn't Emmy, then who?"

Kelly moved to a painting on the far wall and stood in silence as she took in the familiar face. In her peripheral, she saw Tom take a step toward her, then stop abruptly. As she turned, her body grew stiff. The air became frigid and the lights flickered as they both watched a shimmering veil of mist rise from the hardwood floor. As it floated toward Kelly, the dim shape of an adolescent came to life in its veiling center. The little girl's body grew more defined in its advance, until every detail of the portrait at Kelly's back focused and came alive before them.

Her white t-shirt and pink shorts were caked with blood and dirt, the shorts urine stained at the crotch. A grimy ankle sock covered one foot, the other was bare. Straight, blond hair hung in unwashed, matted strands around a bloodless oval face and huge, light-blue eyes were dark with circles that looked like bruises. More bruises were visible on her arms and legs along with bleeding cuts and abrasions. Red, angry patches looked like burns with oozing blisters. She was about ten years old, but her wide eyed, fear engulfed expression made her look much younger.

Kelly was unable to look away. The bone-chilling apprehension she'd felt only moments before faded. She took in the expression of the child and her heart ached with the loneliness and despair that filled the room. She was unable to resist the girl's reaching hand and was shocked by the firm grasp of it. Then a fog settled over her mind and she saw with dim eyes that she was being led from the room. Her last thought was the impression of being consumed before everything went black.

Suddenly, she convulsed after being shaken by a strength born from sheer terror. Her glazed eyes focused and Kelly saw Tom's ashen face in front of her. Her mind made a vague mental note that she was in the upstairs hallway at the foot of the attic stairs before it registered an underlay of emotions that weren't her own. Then his bruising grip released her shoulders, and she was enfolded in his arms.

"I'm here, Kelly," he rasped. "I'm right here, sweetheart."

Her body shook with grief as she collapsed against him. "She's inside me, Tom. I can feel Jenny inside of me."

Tom rocked her gently in his arms. "I know, baby. I know," he said, blinking back his own hot tears.

# CHAPTER THIRTEEN

The morning chill was damp with the promise of rain. Low, gray clouds, casting a gloomy shroud, complimented Winward's brooding mood as he sat in a corner booth of The Morning Express Café on the out-skirts of the square of Marietta. The breakfast rush was in full swing and the sounds around him blended into a blur of noise as he watched through the plate-glass window for the man he'd been expecting for the past thirty minutes.

"More coffee?" His waitress held out the round glass pot. Once again, he felt sorry for the chartreuse and polyester uniform dress she wore because it was filled to full capacity. He could almost hear it cry out in agonized strain as it held its seams together. The apron looked smaller than what the other waitresses wore, but he knew it wasn't. The front of it flapped over a bulging midriff and the ties that went around a non-existent waist were hidden deep between two rolls of fat. Her muddy brown hair was pulled tightly away from her pudgy face and wrapped into a bun on the top of her round head. He bit his tongue to keep from suggesting a wax, or even a razor, for the hair that darkened her upper lip.

He brought his hand down from where he had unconsciously been rubbing the space between his nose and mouth. "Just warm it up," he said.

"Can I getcha anythin' else?" she asked, pouring coffee into his cup.

"No, thanks. I'm fine." She left the check and lumbered away to the next table.

He lifted the coffee cup to his lips. Over the rim, he watched a familiar figure cross the street and stop beside a fully restored cherry red '64 Impala parked at the curb.

The man was short and wiry with thick, curly brown hair that would be impossible to comb. He wore jeans and sneakers. His shoulders were hunched against the cold and his hands were crammed deep into the pockets of a green army field jacket that had definitely seen better days. He shivered, then looked in all directions before getting into the car.

A knowing smile curved Winward's lips as he tossed money on the table, pulled on his fleece-lined leather coat and left the café. He looked both ways for traffic before sauntering across the street. When he reached the Impala, he pulled open the driver's side door, revealing its white vinyl interior, then slipped behind the wheel and lovingly closed the door.

"You're late, Sterling," he said.

"Yeah, I know. Somethin' came up. Man, it's cold. Why don't you blast the heat so I can thaw out some."

The man's cocky tone made Winward grit his teeth. "Cut the crap and get on with it," he sneered. "If you're wasting my time, I swear you'll live to regret it." Their breaths began fogging the windows.

"Okay, okay." Sterling knew to respect Winward's threats. Five years behind bars should have at least taught him that much. "There's nothin' on the streets, but I talked to a newspaper friend of mine that had a pretty fascinatin' tale."

"Which was?" Winward drawled.

"He went to an art exhibit Saturday night to do a piece on this guy's grand opening," Sterling said. "There's a collection there that raised a few eyebrows."

Sterling paused for effect, but Winward's menacing scowl shattered the melodrama he'd hoped to create.

"You'd better not be jerking me around, Sterling," Winward said as he shifted a black gaze to the man sitting beside him. "What does an art exhibit have to do with eight murdered girls?"

"I'm gettin' there." Sterling huffed. "This friend of mine has a thing for missing children stories, so he was familiar with the case you're investigating. You've got to understand, this guy's a pretty tough character. So when he said he was floored by what he saw, I believed him."

Winward's jaw flexed as he ground his teeth. "Get to the point."

"Man oh man, Winward. I thought you'd have caught on my now. Geez."

Winward remained silent and fought the urge to hit Sterling as he rolled his watery blue eyes.

"The paintings, man." Sterling heaved a sigh, blissfully ignorant of how close he was to finding his face the target of the detective's brawny fist. "The whole collection was of missing children. Little girls, to be exact. The very ones you're lookin' for."

Winward felt the blood drain from his face. His head snapped around and he narrowed his dark gaze on the informant. "Where?" he ground out.

Sterling was either brave or stupid enough to toss Winward a smug smile. "Somehow I knew you'd ask me that." He dug in his coat pocket and pulled out a crumpled piece of paper. "In fact, I was so sure, I had him write down the address."

As Winward took the paper and silently read the scribbled print, the muscles tightened in his throat. 'Shear Gallery. 1122 Church Street.'

"Get out," he barked, starting the engine.

"Would you mind drop—"

"I said get out," he repeated with menacing calm.

Sterling fumbled for the handle of the door. He barely had time to plant his feet on the ground and shut the door before the engine revved and yanked the car from the curb.

Winward was five minutes away from the station, but he made it in four. He burst into the squad room, located Hayes, and motioned for him to follow. They entered Swainer's office without knocking and closed the door.

"We've got to talk to you," Winward said, ignoring the phone pressed against his chief's ear.

With drawn brows, Swainer motioned for them to sit. "Puckett, I don't give a rat's ass what he told you to do. I want that report on my desk now!" He heaved a frustrated sigh and slammed down the phone. "Okay, boys, as you can see, I'm not in the best of moods this morning. What've you got?"

"We can see that," Winward replied giving his chief a lopsided grin. "Maybe this will cheer you up." He handed Swainer the piece of paper with the address on it and sat back to watch the chief's reaction as he explained what it meant.

# CHAPTER FOURTEEN

Events from the night before replayed themselves for the thousandth time in Tom's mind. His mind had screamed warnings as she accepted the outstretched hand, but his frozen lips had refused to form the words. He'd felt immobilized, for all he could do was stand paralyzed as Kelly was led away.

Then, whatever controlled the vice holding him released its grip. Acute panic had shoved him forward and Kelly's name rushed from his lips as he sprinted into the foyer in time to see her cross the second floor landing. He'd found her dazed, gazing up at the closed attic door. 'She's inside me, Tom,' she had said to him.

Futile anger rose up once more and Tom opened his eyes to stare at the light rain tapping against the window of Kelly's bedroom. He'd forgotten to pull the shade. No matter. The early morning light was dim and gray; it made the lavender and rose of the bed seem faded. She was beneath the sheet and comforter and he lay on top fully clothed with her warm body cradled in his arms. He listened to the sound of her breathing and knew pure exhaustion had forced her into slumber.

As she stirred against him, he braced himself to, once again, soothe her frightened cries if she began struggling from the depths of another nightmare.

"What time is it?" she asked.

"It's early. Go back to sleep."

"What time do you have to leave for the university?"

"Not for a while. Go back to sleep," he repeated, giving her a gentle kiss. "I'll wake you before I go."

She rose up on her elbow to look at him and he hated the look of worry on her face. "Tom, what's going to happen now? I mean between us. I don't want you trying to protect me by sending me away."

"Sweetheart, that's probably the best thing I could do for you." He sighed. "I have to think of your safety. I can't let anything else happen to you."

"Well, I won't go, you know. I won't let you go through this alone. You'll just have to think of something else."

"Kelly—"

She silenced him by placing her fingers against his lips. "Kiss me," she whispered. "All I want right now is to feel safe in your arms."

Tom's heartbeat quickened at the thought of lying with Kelly's naked body against his as he aroused her flesh with a teasing tongue.

"I don't think that's such a good idea," he said, his voice husky. "You're vulnerable right now. Just holding you like this is driving me crazy. Besides, we're supposed to be taking things one step at a time, remember?"

"Consider it the next step." She leaned closer until she was a breath away. "Kiss me, Tom."

Desire surged through him as he gave in to her plea. A groan of longing rumbled in his chest as he gathered her up and saw the glow of passion in her eyes.

"Are you sure this is what you want?" he asked. He wanted Kelly with every fiber and knew if he accepted what she offered, he would be lost in her forever.

Her eyes fell to his lips. "Positive."

Tom rolled Kelly beneath him and slowly devoured her with one heated, possessive kiss. The seductive play of his fingers as he released the buttons of her nightgown made Kelly's body quake. Then he rose to his knees and pulled down the covers. His lust soared when he saw that her nightgown had risen to her hips during the night, revealing long, smooth, perfect legs.

Tom couldn't resist feeling her supple skin and started at her ankle. He felt his way up to the inside of her thigh and she groaned as she raised her knee, following his caress. Kelly's hips lifted and he heard her gasp as he boldly continued, giving the heated flesh between her legs one deliberate, gentle stroke. He pushed her nightgown up further and his breathing almost stopped at the sight of her neatly trimmed auburn V pointing the way to where he desperately wanted to be.

He raised her up and in one fluid motion, peeled the garment over her head. Tossing it aside, he urged her back down, hungrily devouring her body with his eyes. He began at her dainty, manicured toes, up her legs to her firm, flat stomach and narrow waist. Her breasts were perfect orbs and Tom barely contained a lustful groan as he watched her dark-pink nipples tighten as the cool air caressed her skin.

"You're so beautiful," he breathed, looking into her eyes, knowing that she had been watching his every move, his every expression.

The whispered endearment lingered between them as he lowered his head to place a kiss on the flat surface of her stomach, his morning stubble teasing her skin, before rising from the bed. He saw her shiver with the loss of his heat and raised his eyes to hers to watch them grow cloudy with desire as he stripped his clothes away. He was long, thick, and hard, and he felt his skin burn as her simmering eyes scorched across his smooth, sculpted torso, and then down, following the line of dark, fine hair beneath his navel to his throbbing erection. He leaned over her and captured her lips. Then, he slid down beside her and drew the covers up and around them. Pulling her close, he molded his body to hers and began ravaging her mouth until they were both breathless and aching with need.

Tom heard her purr as he nibbled his way to the nape of her neck and down to the erect peak of her left breast. He sucked and pulled with his mouth, then teased with his tongue, savoring the taste of her. When he turned to the other and started his play all over again, Kelly began to writhe beneath him. She was running soft, eager hands over him, raking his skin with her nails, testing each nuance of his body until a shiver of pleasure passed through him. When her exploring hands found and wrapped around him, Tom gritted his teeth as his stiff erection responded with a jerk.

"I can't stand it," he said, stopping the stroking motion of her hand. "I want you so badly it hurts." He pressed her against the mattress and kissed her long and deep. When he dragged his lips away, he met the scorching possession of her eyes.

"Good," she whispered. "I want you to want me."

Tom kissed her once more, proving his surrender. Then he became unrelenting in his assault. His touch was light and exploring – deliberate. He suckled and teased until the tiny hairs covering her body rose, tracing the path of his fingers, lips, and tongue. As his touch went lower, she opened her legs, urging him to find the slippery crease of her body. He stroked and circled until Kelly's moan sent him deeper and he slipped a finger inside of her. He massaged her clit with his thumb as he pulled his finger out and slid two in. Her hips rose to meet his next thrust. She was so wet, he had to taste her.

Tom positioned himself between her legs and pressed her knees to the sides, opening her up to his gaze. Her pink skin glistened and wept, waiting for his touch, and he obliged as he spread her open further and covered her with his mouth. He heard her gasp as he sucked her clit into a swollen, throbbing nub. Her orgasm tore through her and Tom felt her clenching spasms against his tongue as Kelly cried out and whimpered, thrashing her head from side to side.

When he finally lifted his head, Kelly was breathless. He pulled himself up and their fevered gazes fused until he pushed inside of her, slow and smooth and deep. Her second orgasm was instantaneous and he felt her body squeeze and release around him. His groan was torturous as he clenched his eyes and held himself motionless until he could trust himself to go slowly and not find his own release too soon. Then they began moving in an age-old rhythm that consumed his soul.

Tom drove to the university with thoughts of Kelly filling his mind. The passion they'd shared had overwhelmed him with its intensity. He had never felt anything like it before, and the thought of interfering forces destroying the most precious thing in his life made him seethe with self-preserving determination. He had to find a way to handle the apprehension that had settled in the back of his mind. If he didn't, he knew the experiences he and Kelly had had, and the circumstances surrounding them, possessed the power to destroy everything they held dear in life.

His preoccupation seemed to extend the day and Tom was relieved when it was finally over. As he drove home, the rain increased with every mile. It pelted against the roof of the Jag with the reverberation of a drum as the windshield wipers thumped from side to side, fighting methodically against the relentless onslaught. The sound began to blend until it gave way to fists meeting flesh.

*The man's face was scarlet and his eyes bulged. Shouts grew louder as he cursed the woman at his feet. Then, he turned the full impact of his attention on Tom. "What are you looking at, you little shit?" the man growled.*

*Tom shook with fear and turned to run. A sudden grip stopped him as vise-like fingers dug painfully into his bony shoulder. He was sent reeling by the back of his father's hand and barely heard the advancing man's words over the ringing in his ears.*

*"Where do you think you're going, slut? I've got something special in mind for you."*

A blaring horn shattered the image and Tom jerked the Jaguar back into his lane. His shaking hands gripped the wheel. He took a deep breath. The roar of traffic moving along Church Street was muted by the driving rain. What could be heard most was the swish of tires as they gripped their way through collecting water. Storm drains gurgled as they fought to keep the streets from flooding.

He clicked on his right turn signal and slowed as he approached his driveway. He turned in and pulled through the shelter of the colonnade. An immaculate red Impala was parked in the lot behind the house. He could barely make out two men sitting in the antique's dry interior through the blur of the torrential downpour. *Now what?*

Tom steered into his parking space and turned off the engine. After flipping his coat collar up, he got out of the car. Instead of admitting visitors through the kitchen's back door, he trotted to the shelter of the colonnade to the porch steps at the side of the house. He searched his key ring for the front door key as his steps thudded across the porch.

Tom heard two car doors slam and the sound of hurrying steps splashing their way toward him. A voice rumbled, "Damn puddle."

"Excuse me, Mr. Shear?" Tom inserted his key before turning to see two men crossing the porch toward him.

One of the men was black and huge: six foot four, two hundred and twenty pounds, all muscle, and in his early forties. The other was a well-built Caucasian: six foot, one hundred and eighty pounds, early thirties, dark-brown hair that brushed his collar, brown eyes that were almost black in a somewhat handsome, clean shaven face.

"Yes, may I help you?"

"I hope so," the smaller man replied. "My name's Detective Mark Winward." He removed his badge and held it up for Tom to see. "This is my partner, Detective Don Hayes. We'd like to talk to you if you don't mind."

"Not at all," Tom said. His curiosity developed an uneasy edge. "We can talk inside."

Winward smiled, showing straight, white teeth. "We'd appreciate that. It sure has turned out to be a nasty day."

"That it has," Tom agreed, leading them inside.

After deactivating the security system, he took their damp coats and hung them on the foyer coat rack along with his own. Tom had not failed to notice the shoulder-holster strapped to Detective Winward's chest securing what looked like a Glock 9 mm, or the hip-holster on Detective Hayes's belt holding the same make gun before the two men straighten their dress-coats.

"Now, what can I do for you, gentlemen? I must admit I'm puzzled by your visit."

"I'll come straight to the point, Mr. Shear," Winward said, taking in the polished wood floors, high crown molded ceiling, the wide curving staircase and the closed double French doors on either side. "It's come to our attention that you have a collection of paintings which could be vital to an investigation we're conducting. We'd like to see them, if we could."

"I fail to see how my paintings could possibly serve in an investigation. I create my work from my own imagination and feelings."

"I'm sure. But we'd still like to see them, if you don't mind," the detective persisted. So far, the giant by Winward's side had maintained a brooding silence.

"Of course, but I have several collections. If you can tell me which one you're interested in, I'll be happy to show you," Tom said, his tone casual.

Winward flashed a smile. "It's a collection of little girls."

Tom had expected the answer, but his heart thumped nonetheless. "That would be my collection of Rage."

"Collection of Rage, Mr. Shear?" Winward raised a challenging brow and pinned Tom with eyes the color of black steel.

Ice formed in Tom's stomach. "If you'll just follow me," he said, "I'm sure everything will be self-explanatory."

Tom saw the glance the two detectives shared and his mind whirled with questions as he turned toward the left side of the staircase and led them down the hall. *Why would they be interested in my paintings? How did they even know they existed?* His mind froze. *Emmy. Is this what you've been trying to tell me?*

"Right through here," he heard himself say. His voice sounded serene and yet, very far off like he was speaking through a tunnel.

Tom pushed the doors of the Rage gallery open and stepped inside. As he flipped the light-switch, he watched the two detectives enter the room and saw the involuntary widening of their eyes.

As Winward walked from painting to painting, scrutinizing each one, his insides twisted with a mixture of excitement and disgust. The resemblances were so familiar there was no need to refer to the pictures he carried in his pocket.

The only child missing was Kathy Packard. In her place was a face he didn't recognize, and the implications it presented chilled his blood.

He moved on and his heartbeat quickened as he stepped in front of a painting bursting with agony-filled faces. He counted seven all together; all were tormented and helpless within the confinement of the canvas. Their images were so clear, he could almost hear their moans mingled with desperate cries for help. Suppressing a shiver, he moved on.

"How long have you lived here, Mr. Shear?" Hayes asked. His voice rumbled low like the thunder outside.

"I moved in the first week of November; so, a little over a month."

"Have you always lived in the area?" the detective questioned while studying a painting filled with instruments of torture.

"Basically. I lived in Atlanta before moving up to Marietta."

"And how did you happen to find this particular house?" Winward asked, hoping to find a chink in the man's defensive barrier.

"By taking the usual steps, detective. I consulted a real estate agency."

A thick silence shrouded the room as Winward slowly turned from his perusal of the fake closet doors with their slide-bolt locks to face Shear's shuttered expression. "Mr. Shear, how did you come to paint these paintings? To create this setting?" he asked, motioning toward the doors. "And please don't try to tell me they came entirely from your imagination, because I wouldn't believe you."

Shear's smile was indulgent, softening the glint in his eyes. "Of course not," he said. "Even though the overall effect evolved from simple imagination, the root of the theme came from the very common source of newspapers."

"As simple as that."

"I'm afraid so." Shear looked from him to Hayes and back again. "May I ask what this is all about? Have I done something wrong?"

Winward turned the full force of his penetrating gaze on the man across from him. "Well now, that all depends, Mr. Shear. The girls hanging on your walls are missing and have probably been murdered," he explained, turning to one of the paintings. "We were lucky enough to find one of the bodies and the murder weapon, but I find something very strange."

"I fail to see your point, detective."

"It's just this, Mr. Shear. I have to ask myself, since a description of the murder weapon was never disclosed to the media, how could he, meaning you, possibly know so much about something that had never been revealed?"

Shear was silent as he met and held his gaze. "I'm sorry, sir, but you've lost me again," he said. "I haven't the faintest idea of what you're accusing me of."

"Am I accusing you of something?" Winward asked, feigning surprise. He cast a glance at Hayes and shrugged. "I'm merely speculating."

"All right. Then maybe you'll be kind enough to tell me why I'm the focus of your speculation."

Winward didn't bother hiding his smug triumph. He pointed to a painting where a dark, un-detailed assailant leaned over a nude male body, sufficiently hiding his victim's identity, with a glinting spiked ball and chain raised high above the his head in a brutal attack.

"Because, Mr. Shear, the weapon we found next to Kathy Packard's mutilated body happens to be identical to the one you've painted here." He turned to watch Shear's reaction. "Now, isn't it a coincidence that the murderer of that little girl and an impressive man such as yourself should have the same gruesome taste in weapons?"

Thomas Shear digested this bit of information in silence as his gaze turned to stone. "I assure you, sir, that's all it is."

"Yeah, I suppose so," Winward said, letting his disbelief ring in his tone. "Thank you for your time, Mr. Shear." He turned abruptly and moved toward the door. "Oh, you're not planning a trip anytime soon, are you?"

"No, I'm not," Shear stated, allowing Winward and Hayes to precede him from the room and lead the way back into the foyer.

"Good. I hope you won't mind if we call on you again in the future?"

"Of course not." Shear handed them their coats and opened the door to the driving rain. "If I can be any further assistance to you, just let me know."

Winward smiled. "You can count on that, Mr. Shear."

# CHAPTER FIFTEEN

The gloom of the day was held at bay by closed blinds, lights overhead, and the amber shaded lamp on Jonathan's desk. The room was large and elegantly appointed. Jonathan's prized maple desk was antique like the cabinets and tables arranged throughout the sitting area. The crème walls held a couple of Tom's paintings resembling his Life collection; an office warming gift when Jonathan had opened his own practice.

When the call waiting began to beep, Jonathan laid his pen down and gave the telephone an exasperated look. He was just finishing up and was eager to leave. He pressed the intercom button.

"Marilyn?"

"Yes, sir?"

"Tell whoever it is that I've left for the day and take a message, will you?"

"It's Thomas Shear, Mr. Fields. He said it was important."

"Tom? Okay. Thanks, Marilyn." He disconnected with Marilyn and took the call. "Hey, Tom, what's up?"

"I need to talk to you, Jonathan."

"Sure, buddy. Why don't you come over to the house tonight. I'm sure Marsha won't mind setting another place for dinner." His eyes shifted to the brass framed picture of Marsha and himself, grinning like fools that sat on his desk.

"Not tonight, Jonathan. I need to talk to you alone."

"What's wrong? Is it Kelly?"

"No."

Jonathan stilled. "Are you in some kind of trouble?" he asked.

"Yeah, I think so. I'm going to need your help."

"Legally?" Jonathan asked, surprised.

"Yes."

There was a pause as Jonathan took in the single word. "Okay. Let me finish a few things here and I'll come over on my way home."

"I appreciate it, Jonathan. I really do."

"I'll be there as soon as I can."

The subtle urgency in Tom's voice worried Jonathan as he hung up the phone. Any other person probably wouldn't have detected it, but he'd known Tom for too many years not to know his moods. Something was definitely wrong.

He leaned over the papers on his desk and tried to concentrate, but Tom's words, or rather the lack of them, kept getting in the way. Throwing down his pen, he shoved the papers into his briefcase and left the office.

The den of Tom's house was lit by a single lamp. Shadows loomed thick. The house was quiet except for the tick emanating from the clock hanging on the wall. It said the time was seven thirty. Darkness pressed against the glass of the window flanked by blue silk drapes.

Tom noticed Jonathan looking around as he waited. It was the first time he'd been in the room since Tom moved in. The entertainment center had been hooked up and set in place against one wall below the flat-screen TV. A bookshelf filled with everything from mysteries to artist instruction guides shared another wall along with a small bar. The leather sofa, two wrought-iron and glass end-tables with a matching coffee table, as well as the recliner in which

Jonathan sat, filled the remaining corner space. The reading lamp by his side was the single source of light.

Tom's black brow was knitted over turbulent blue eyes. He could feel the square line of his jaw flex with tension as he paced the carpet. Even though Jonathan appeared calm as he sat waiting, Tom knew his friend was growing more anxious as his curiosity mounted.

"Tom, what is it? It can't be all that bad. You're acting like a man who's about to be sentenced to death."

Tom stopped and stared at Jonathan. The arbitrary remark had made his blood run cold. Shrugging off the unnerving feeling, he shook his head and resumed his restless motion.

"Okaaay," Jonathan said, startled by Tom's reaction. "If you didn't have my undivided attention before, you certainly have it now. Now sit down and tell me what's happened. You're making me nervous." He pulled at the collar of his dress shirt, loosening his tie.

"I'm trying to find a way to explain the impossible."

Tom turned his back on Jonathan to stand before the dark, rain-splattered window and saw his own reflection. Because he was wearing a black pullover, his pale face was all that could be seen and it unnerved him to think of his own floating head staring back at him from the other side of the glass. He turned away and gave Jonathan his profile.

"It's all so fantastic. Sometimes I have trouble believing it myself."

His head ached with his turbulent thoughts. *Should I reveal Emmy's existence? Will Jonathan believe the incredible truth? Or will he think it's delusional insanity? Jonathan believes in hard facts. What facts do I have to offer as proof besides the obvious reality of my paintings?*

*And then there's Kelly. If I reveal the truth of Emmy and Jenny's existence, how can I possibly protect Kelly's involvement? Can I trust Jonathan to realize the destruction it would cause in Kelly's life if she were involved? There's no way I'm going to drag her down with me. No way.*

And what of the other secret he carried deep within himself, the deepest, darkest secret of all? The one so devastating and personal that he'd had to bury it for the sake of his own sanity. *What of it? Any good detective, and Winward certainly seems to be one, will surely uncover the truth. Its coincidence will undoubtedly be misconstrued. What then?*

*It's got to be told*, he decided. He had no other choice now. It could help save his life. *Or condemn it*. He suppressed a shudder.

"You'll probably think I'm totally deranged. But you're the only person I can trust."

"Tom I've known you too long to think any such thing," Jonathan said. "Just take your time and start from the beginning."

Tom shoved his hands into his jean pockets and took a deep breath. "It all started with this house. Somehow, I was drawn to it. The instant I saw its picture in the real estate office, I knew I had to take a closer look."

He turned to face Jonathan's calm expression.

"After I moved in, I began having nightmares. They were so vivid, I can still remember every detail."

"What kind of nightmares?"

"The first was of a little girl. She cried out to me for help, but as she came within reach, she was pulled away. All I could see was an arm that pulled her back before I could do anything to help her. Her screams were terrifying.

"The first night it happened, I went to my studio. The dream was still so clear in my mind, I knew there was only one thing I could do. So, I set up my easel and started painting. I could feel her presence all around me. I could hear her cries in my head. I could even feel their resonating vibrations beneath my feet. I felt as if I were being drawn up in her sorrow, like I was being possessed. I know it's a strong word, but that's how I felt. It's the only way I know to describe it."

"So that was the beginning of the Rage collection," Jonathan said.

"Yes," Tom answered, turning back toward the rain-streaked window, but at a different angle. "I thought, or maybe I should say, I hoped, that would be the end of it. I chalked it up to stress and an over-excited imagination. It wasn't. The nightmares continued and my collection grew."

Tom hunched his shoulders to contain a shiver. He eyed the decanters on the bar, then picked up the glass he'd been using and refilled it. "Want one?" he asked. Jonathan shook his head.

"I thought I was losing my mind," he stated. "Each time it happened, I became more and more disoriented. I'd find myself standing in front of a finished painting and realize I'd lost hours out of a day or night. Then, the night I began setting up the Rage gallery, something extraordinary happened." His brow creased as he lifted his glass to his lips. "I think this is the part you're going to have a hard time believing."

Jonathan watched his friend take a long pull from his drink. "Let me be the judge of that."

Tom nodded and carried his drink back to the window. "After I'd hung the first painting," he began, "the one of the first little girl, the room got cold. No, not cold, frigid; I could see my breath, and I had an eerie feeling that someone was watching me from behind." He hesitated and turned to see if there was a change in Jonathan's expression. Seeing none, he continued. "I turned around expecting to find an intruder. Instead, what I saw turned everything I believed in upside down."

Jonathan's brow shot up in incredulous disbelief. "Are you telling me you saw a—"

"A ghost? An apparition? A disembodied spirit? That's exactly what I'm saying," Tom stated, watching Jonathan rise to the edge of his seat. "It was the ghost of the little girl in the portrait I'd just hung on the wall. The same little girl who'd cried out to me for help on my first night in this house."

Jonathan stared, then blinked and shook his head. "Tom, you know I've never been a believer in the supernatural. I've always considered the mere possibility absurd. I don't know what to say," he confessed.

"There's nothing *to* say…yet."

"You mean there's more?"

"Oh, yes. I've just begun."

Jonathan seemed to leap from his chair as he made his way to the bar. After pouring himself a generous shot of bourbon, he took a fortifying swig and motioned for Tom to continue.

"You've got to understand something before I go on," Tom said, his voice firm. "There's no way I want Kelly involved in any of this if there's an investigation. She's been through enough."

"Kelly? What does Kelly have to do with this? And what do you mean by 'an investigation?'"

"Before I say anything else, you've got to promise me Kelly won't be involved. Anything I tell you concerning her has got to stay between us."

Jonathan searched Tom's determined expression. "I'm not sure I should do that." When it became clear Tom refused to say anything further, Jonathan heaved a resigned breath. "Okay, you have my word. Now, get on with it," he said, motioning with his free hand.

"Last night, after we left your place, we came back here to have dinner. I was putting on music when I heard breaking glass in the kitchen. Kelly was hysterical. After she calmed down, she told me a little girl had appeared and pleaded for help."

"Did you see her?"

"No," Tom admitted. His brow furrowed in thought. "At first, I thought it must've been Emmy."

"Emmy?" Jonathan's eyebrows practically hid themselves in his hairline.

Tom nodded. "The little girl who appeared to me."

"Somehow I knew you were going to say that." Jonathan's reply dripped with sarcasm as he met and held Tom's gaze. "We'll discuss how you came to know her name later. Right now, I want to know what you meant by 'at first' you thought it was Emmy."

"Kelly went into the Rage gallery. I followed. She stood in front of Emmy's portrait and very calmly told me Emmy wasn't the child she'd seen. That's when she turned and saw the other portrait." Tom stopped and swallowed hard. "I'm still having trouble with what happened next. It was terrifying."

"Just take it slow."

Tom tossed back the remaining contents of his glass. After a deep breath, he continued.

"As the temperature dropped, a frame of mist rose from the floor." He avoided Jonathan's incredulous expression by crossing to the bar. "It was the girl in the portrait. She walked over and took Kelly's hand, but there was absolutely nothing I could do as she led her from the room. It was like I'd been drugged and was paralyzed.

"After what seemed like an eternity, whatever it was holding me let go. When I found her, Kelly was standing dazed in front of the attic stairs. The way she looked scared the hell out of me and all I could think to do was to shake her. Then she started to cry, saying Jenny had entered her and that she couldn't stand the pain."

"What do you mean? Entered her how?"

"The same way Emmy entered me. Kelly absorbed the little girl's spirit, Jonathan. She feels all of the emotional pain Jenny felt before she died."

"Tom, do you realize what you're saying? It's incredible." He took a hearty gulp of his bourbon. Tears came to his eyes as it burned its way down.

"I know, Jonathan. But you've got to hear me out."

He wheezed, "I'm listening."

"Today I had visitors. They were detectives." He watched

Jonathan's eyes widen. "They wanted to know about the paintings in the Rage collection. Apparently, they're investigating a case of murdered children. The children were all little girls."

Jonathan let out a low whistle. "What kind of questions did they ask?"

"They wanted to know how long I'd lived in the house. How I found it. How I came up with the idea of the collection."

"What did you tell them?"

"I told them the main concept came from newspaper articles. I know it was a lie, but can you imagine what their reaction would've been if I'd told them the story I'd just told you?"

Jonathan nodded grimly. "Yeah, I see your point. Did they believe you?"

Tom's grave expression darkened. "I don't think so."

Jonathan stood very still and gave him a pointed look. "What makes you say that?" he asked.

"One of the detectives, Detective Winward, found something in one of my paintings that was pretty incriminating."

"Which was?"

"A weapon identical to one that was found along with the body of one of the little girls."

"How could that be incriminating?" He did a lawyerly wave with his empty glass and began to pace. "Something like that is circumstantial at best. I've seen your paintings. They contain weapons that could be found in most any household."

"Yeah, all but one. This weapon's unique because it's a mace, a spiked ball and chain."

Jonathan stopped and looked up at the ceiling as if seeking divine intervention, then ran his hand over his face. "You're kidding, right?" he asked almost hopefully, turning his pacing direction toward the bar.

"Believe me, I wish I were."

"Tom, this is unbelievable." Jonathan shook his head. "It's going to take me a while to digest what I've heard tonight. And I'll be honest with you. I'm going to have to do some heavy duty soul searching before I can even fathom the possibility that your ghosts are real. If I had heard this story from anyone else, I would probably have laughed in his face."

"I understand. I didn't expect you to be totally accepting. Any man in his right mind would have his doubts. But please, don't take too long. Winward said he'd be back. And I have a feeling it'll be sooner than expected."

Jonathan's brow lowered into a suspicious scowl. "Why?"

Tom heaved a sigh. "I've held something back from you, Jonathan, from everyone. Something very personal. Something that, until now, I'd always thought would remain buried forever."

Tom grew silent and turned away from Jonathan. He'd thought he had conquered the degradation of his past long ago. But as all of his repressed fears and anxieties came flooding back, he realized with sudden certainty that they had never been truly banished, only concealed from sight and mind. He wanted to cry out in anguished denial, but he knew the effort would be futile. The memories were seared into his being and would always be a despised, permanent part of his life.

When Tom finally spoke, his voice was strained and low.

"Up until I was twelve years old, I was the victim of gross sexual and physical abuse. I grew up in a house void of normal love and emotions, one dominated by the unnatural cruelties of an evil, overbearing father.

"At first, my mother did what she could to stop his advances toward me. But after being beaten to near death more than once, she finally gave up and started drowning my screams in a bottle. Don't get me wrong," he said, casting Jonathan a challenging glance, "she wasn't a weak person. Not in the beginning, anyway. I guess, after enduring so much physical and mental abuse, her spirit broke and she just gave up."

Jonathan was speechless. He sank to the edge of the recliner, his glass dangling in his hand. Compassion glistened in the tears he blinked back, and Tom rejected the pity he saw by turning away. Stronger now that the initial shock had been absorbed, he continued.

"Somehow, we'd all managed to keep the years of abuse a secret. That is, until the day my grandfather decided to pay us an unexpected visit." He lifted his glass and took a drink, then shook his head at the grim memory. "I can't even imagine what he must have felt when he came into our so-called 'home' and found my mother, his daughter, beaten and unconscious on the floor. Or what it must've been like to find my drunken father hurriedly pulling on his pants over a naked and bleeding little boy.

"I can remember looking up through a haze of pain to see him beating my father until his cries of outrage turned into whimpers. I remember the tears on his face as he looked down at me, and I can still feel the strength in his big, gentle hands as he picked me up."

Tom stared into his empty glass as if seeing it all again and sighed.

"He saved my life that day. I know without a doubt I would have died if I'd had to suffer my father's abuse much longer. I think that's why Emmy was drawn to me. Somehow she could sense my pain and saw that it matched her own to a certain degree. At first, I was confused by the fleeting look of pity I saw on her face, but now I think I understand. I think in some way, she's trying to help me cope with what happened to me just as I'm trying to help her. Now that I've thought it through, it makes perfect sense.

"So you see," he concluded, turning to look directly at Jonathan, "if Detective Winward takes the time to dig it up, which I'm sure he will, the coincidence of the situation will surely cause him to be more suspicious of me than ever. How could it not?"

"Yes. I see your point," Jonathan conceded. "If this gets out, which like you said, probably will, we've got a dangerous situation on our hands, my friend. And I'm afraid it'll take more than just me to handle it."

# CHAPTER SIXTEEN

By the time the morning sun breached the thinning clouds, Tom knew what he had to do. There was a connection between the house and the missing children, and he meant to learn what he could about them both.

When classes were over, he went to his office, sat at his desk and pulled up the internet. All he got was a message reading, 'Unable to connect to Internet.' He tried again, received the same message, and sat back in his chair perplexed and frustrated when there was a knock on his door.

"Come in."

A member of the main office personnel opened the door.

"Hey, Tom," she greeted and walked in to place papers on his desk.

"Hey, Stacey."

"What's wrong?" she asked. "You look disgruntled."

"I am. My internet's not connecting."

"It's been disconnected. Didn't you get the memo?"

"What memo?" he asked.

She smiled and shook her blond head. "I emailed it personally to all staff members a month ago and, then again last week." When he only gave her a blank look, she chuckled. "Our system's getting an upgrade. They began last night."

"Damn."

"Is there anything I can help you with?"

"No. I just wanted to do some research before I left."

"The library system is up. It was upgraded over the Thanksgiving Holiday while most of the students were gone."

"Thanks."

"No problem," she said with a smile as she left his office.

Tom debated just going home to search on his own computer, then thought about the time that would be wasted sitting in rush-hour traffic. He pulled on his coat, turned out his desk lamp, closed the office door behind him, and made his way across campus.

A deafening hush fell against his ears as he entered the library. Thousands of books were all categorized and neatly shelved. The sprinkle of students who sat crouched over open books in the glow of desk lamps ignored him as he made his way to the woman sitting behind a long, curved desk.

Her straight brown hair was pulled back into a ponytail, revealing high cheekbones. She was an attractive woman in her own way with one startling feature. Her eyes were an extremely light blue around the black pupil, then rimmed by a thin dark-blue ring. Long, thick lashes acted as a frame around a masterpiece.

She watched his approach. "May I help you?" she asked, keeping her voice low.

Tom smiled. "I hope so. I'm Professor Shear. I want to research a project I'm planning for my students, but the internet's down on my side of the campus."

"What kind of research? Maybe I can help you."

"It's a study on the mechanical mind structure of people who commit child homicides; particularly the kind preceded by abduction."

"What sort of material do you need?"

"There's a series of newspaper articles I'd like to start with."

"Our system is up and running, so you're welcome to use one of our computers. But for what you're suggesting, if you know the time frame, you might want to try microfilm. I'm sure we'll have what you're looking for."

"Yes, I'm sure you will," he said. "The articles I'm interested in are fairly recent. They involve a series of child abductions that occurred sometime last year around this area. The problem is that I'm not exactly sure when the abductions started. I do know they involved young females and that the police were unable to come up with many leads as to who the abductor was."

"I remember that," she said. "I think they started sometime around the end of last year and continued through the first part of this year. But if it's the one I'm thinking of, and I'm sure it is, you're wrong about the police not finding the abductor."

"What do you mean? I thought the case was unsolved."

She stood, shaking her head. "I don't think so," she said. "The police found the man responsible dead, with a confession. It made all of the major headlines." She moved from behind the desk. "I'll show you where you can find the articles you're looking for and you can see for yourself."

Tom did seem to remember something about what the librarian had just described, but the details eluded him. He followed her through a narrow corridor of books into a room lined with unusually tall filing cabinets. As she scanned the labels on the drawers, he noted several viewing monitors along the far wall. A young woman, oblivious to their presence, was taking notes from one of the screens.

"Here we go." The librarian extracted a roll of film. "You should find what you're looking for on this."

Tom followed her to a monitor and watched her insert the film. After giving him instructions on how to operate the system, she left him alone with his research.

He took off his coat and draped it over the chair beside him. Then he sat, took a deep breath, and forced his hand to the controls. He skimmed the pages until he caught sight of an accosting headline printed in big, bold letters. Goose flesh rose on his arms. Until now, his conclusions had been mere conjecture, but the unquestionable words on the screen wiped away any remaining doubts.

## STILL NO LEADS IN SECOND
## CHILD ABDUCTION

Vicki Martin, age 8, disappeared from Dillard State Park late last week only days after the abduction of Jennifer Miles, age 11, was reported. The fact that both girls disappeared from the same location give credence to the speculation of a connection between the two events.

....continued, page 3.

Tom swallowed hard as two small faces, so familiar in his mind, caught his attention. As he stared at the pictures of Jenny and Vicki, he wept inside for the naïve smiles that had been eliminated. Suddenly, his overwhelming sadness turned to bitter rage as he tore his eyes away from the pictures to continue his search.

## DILLARD ABDUCTOR CLAIMS
## VICTIM NUMBER THREE

Police have increased security at Dillard Park after a third abduction in less than two months. Amanda Sawyer, age 10, was last seen entering the park Friday afternoon on her way home from Crammer Elementary School. Her parents, Mr. and Mrs. Daniel Sawyer, contacted the Cobb County Police later that evening to report her missing.

A search is still underway for 11-year-old Jennifer Miles

and 8-year-old Vicki Martin. As of yet, the police refuse to comment on any leads. However, sources have revealed that police are investigating the strong possibility that this is the work of one man, now dubbed "The Dillard Abductor" by members of the press.

A reward is being offered by the families of the missing girls for information leading to the apprehension and conviction of the person

....continued, page 2.

## LITTLE GIRL DISAPPEARS
## FROM SHOPPING MALL

No trace can be found of Julie Dobbs, age 9, who was abducted yesterday morning from the Westside Shopping Mall on Barclay Street. The Cobb County Police Department conducted a thorough search of the premises, but no leads were found. A connection between the Dillard abductions and this case is not suspected.

## PANIC STRIKES AFTER FIFTH
## ABDUCTION

Citizens of the Cobb County community are terrified for the safety of their children. Parents are keeping boys and girls alike close at hand, fearing they may become the next victim in a frightening string of abductions.

The latest victim is 12-year-old Caroline Doltry. She was last seen exiting her school bus early yesterday afternoon. The police have, as yet, reported no leads as to her whereabouts and have offered no other comment.

Tom's eyes blurred against the screen as his hand dropped to his lap. He sat rigid in his chair as the horror of his confirmed suspicions sank to the pit of his stomach. Reluctantly, his hand returned to the monitor's control. Searching from page to page, he almost flinched as the next bold headline leapt up to meet him.

## HAS ANOTHER CHILD BEEN ADDED TO THE LIST?

Rachael Porter, age 10, was reported missing yesterday by her mother, Ms. Janice Porter, when she failed to return home after attending a neighboring friend's birthday party. A thorough search of the neighborhood and surrounding area was conducted, but no leads could be obtained. The Cobb County Police Department made no further comment.

## "SEARCH IS UNDERWAY," DETECTIVE SAYS

Police activity has reached a frenzied height after announcing the disappearance of Amy Monroe, age 9. She was last seen at her school bus stop early yesterday morning by neighbors who have come forward to be interviewed by police. During an early morning interview, the leading investigating officer, Detective Mark Winward, stated, "All I can tell you at this time is that a search is underway. I can not divulge any other information concerning this case for fear of compromising the ongoing investigation." When asked if his last statement meant there might be a connection between the last six disappearances and this case, Detective Winward's reply was, "No comment."

…continued, page 4.

## EIGHTH VICTIM SUSPECTED

The latest apparent victim of abduction is Kathy Packard, age 13. She was last seen leaving her home yesterday afternoon en route to Dillard Park to meet friends. When she failed to return home by the early curfew set by her parents, Mr. and Mrs. Stanley Packard immediately telephoned police.

After extensive interviews, the only comment officials made was that Kathy was apparently abducted shortly after leaving home that afternoon.

The Cobb County community is outraged over the apparent inability of the police to put a stop to the growing list of missing children. Even though numerous suspects have been held and questioned, no arrests have been made.

## ABDUCTOR'S BODY FOUND HANGING FROM RAFTERS

Early yesterday morning, police found the naked body of Mr. Theodore Chandler hanging by the neck in the attic of his rental property on Church Street in Marietta, with mutilating, self-inflicted wounds. Sources indicate a confession was found on the scene linking Chandler to at least four of the eight abductions that have occurred over the past six months.

Tom sat back in his chair, trying to take in what he had just read. "This can't be happening," he said.

*But it is*, a voice that was devoid of emotion whispered in his head. Seemingly of their own accord, his eyes returned to the screen and focused on the pictures of the four little girls. Pulling his eyes away, he continued reading.

Needless to say, the community is shocked by the outcome of this investigation. Chandler was a prominent businessman of Atlanta and surrounding cities. He was a respected citizen and leader in the community and was involved in numerous charities.

…continued, page 2.

Tom scanned the next page, reading Theodore Chandler's impressive resume, then moved on to the next day. As he read, his thoughts swirled in confusion.

## LITTLE GIRL'S BODY DISCOVERED IN WOODED LOT

Late last evening, ten days after she was reported missing, the body of 13-year-old Kathy Packard, the latest victim in a series of baffling abduction cases, was found in a wooded lot off US Hwy 41 by police.

When interviewed, Detective Mark Winward, the lead investigating officer, admitted the body's location was disclosed in the confession found at the suicide scene of Mr. Theodore Chandler. He would not comment on other evidence that might have been found on the scene. When asked about details concerning the victim's cause of death, the only response given by Detective Mark Winward was, "No other statement will be issued until the coroner's report has been received."

Tom scowled. "It doesn't make sense," he said under his breath. "Why just the last victim? What happened to the other seven?"

"Tragic, wasn't it?"

Tom's heart lurched. His engrossed mind had failed to register the quiet steps of the librarian as she walked up behind him.

He flicked off the monitor and stood up. "Yes, it was."

"Did you find everything you were looking for?"

"I think so." He shrugged into his coat and looked at his watch. "I didn't realize it was so late."

Her smile was warm with understanding. "You've been at it for quite some time."

"Yes," he responded. "I appreciate your help."

During the drive home along Interstate 75 North, Tom's mind reeled with what he had read in the viewing room. It was hard to comprehend a man of Theodore Chandler's caliber harboring the merciless killer instincts that were so grossly portrayed in the dreams he had experienced. He had been a man accepted in the most distinguished of circles. A man who had accomplished goals the average person could only imagine. *How could such a man, one who was held in the highest respect and trust of his peers, camouflage his true nature so completely? Well, I guess it* was *possible. Just think of the BTK killer in the seventies and eighties. He was admired and held a high position in his church. He had a wife and children. It took the police 30 years to catch him.*

His brain was on automatic and he barely registered steering the Jaguar onto the Hwy 41/Marietta exit that would take him home. As he stopped for the red light in front of Kennestone Hospital, questions filled his mind.

*If the abductor really was Chandler, then why were the police still investigating? Could there have been an accomplice? Or did they suspect more than one abductor? A copy cat, perhaps? Is that the reason they're looking at me?*

The sudden blast of a car horn snapped Tom's bridging thoughts. He glanced up at the green light and pulled through the intersection. As he cruised past the immense structure of the hospital, one question pushed to the forefront of his mind with ominous clarity. *Why wasn't there any mention of Emmy? Where did she fit into all of this?*

*There are too many questions.* Tom's frustration peaked. *Somehow I've got to find out more.*

As an idea began to form, he looked at the dash clock illuminated in neon-blue. Taking a left turn, he drove over to the one-way street heading in the opposite direction. Once he was turned around, he pulled out his cell and scrolled for a number.

Three heartbeats later Kelly answered. "Tom, hey." He could hear the smile in her voice.

"Hey, sweetheart. Where are you?" he asked.

"I'm still at the office. You just caught me. I was about to leave."

"Stay there, I'm on my way."

"Why?"

"I need to see you, baby. I'm about five minutes away."

There was a pause, then Kelly's voice saying, "Alright. I'll be waiting."

"I'll be there soon," he promised before disconnecting. He pressed the accelerator.

# CHAPTER SEVENTEEN

It had grown dark and cold. The sickle moon played hide-n-seek behind a thick bank of clouds, adding to the darkness, and making it somehow complete. The only illumination came from storefront lights, streetlamps, and automobile headlights passing on Sandy Plains Road.

The Remax Real Estate office, a brick, one-story building with dormer windows in a steeply pitched roof, could easily pass for an up-scale residence. The parking lot was empty except for a Ford Expedition and Kelly's white Lexus. Tom pulled into a parking space on the side and withdrew his key from the ignition. The dark hush caused a wave of memory to wash over him.

*His small body flinched with each muffled slap coming from another part of the house. He knew the quiet would bring his father and he would be forced to stand naked, shaking with fear and humiliation. Then his flesh would rip as his father's erection was shoved deep inside his tightened rectum. He had no doubt his father would find him, and his child-self quaked within the cloaking blackness of the closet.*

A sharp rap on the window made Tom start. The unexpected memory had left him trembling and his heart pounded as he took a deep, steadying breath. His controlled expression revealed nothing as he stepped from the car.

"Are you alright?" Kelly asked, snuggling her chin into the collar of her coat.

"Sure. I'm fine," he said.

"You were in another world. Were you thinking about Emmy?"

"Emmy, and other things. I've also been thinking of you," he said, filling his hands with her soft coat lapel to draw her closer.

"Well," she said, her face softening with pleasure. "I didn't expect to see you tonight."

Tom leaned down and kissed her warm mouth. "Surprise," he said against her lips. He kissed her again and she hummed a sigh when he pulled back.

"To what do I owe this unexpected pleasure?" she asked, smiling. "You almost missed me, you know. I was on my way home."

Tom heaved a sigh and caught the unmistakable smell of charbroil from the Burger King across the street. His stomach grumbled, but he ignored it knowing that he had inadvertently misled her into thinking that he had come here for the sole purpose of seeing her. Now he took a chance of pissing her off.

"I wanted to see you, please believe that. But I also need a favor," he said, waiting for the hurt to show in her eyes. Instead, what he saw was probing curiosity.

"What kind of favor?" she asked.

"I need your file on Mrs. Theodore Chandler."

Kelly squinted at him with a look of suspicion.

"Please, Kelly. I wouldn't ask if it weren't important."

"If I do this, will you tell me why?" she asked.

Tom hesitated. "I can't promise you that." He watched a play of emotions cross her face. "Please, Kelly. I need your help."

She studied his face a moment longer. "Oh, all right." She turned back toward the office. "Just because I'm agreeing to do this, doesn't mean I'm going to be satisfied until I know the reason why. You owe me for leading me on," she chided over her shoulder.

"I didn't mean to," he mumbled under his breath, not intending for her to hear.

"Uh huh," he heard her say.

Tom knew enough to keep his mouth shut as he followed her clicking heels along the concrete sidewalk, up the steps and into the familiar reception area. The lights had been dimmed and the monotonous drone of a copier, thumping rhythmically in the otherwise quiet suite of offices, sounded oddly forlorn to his apprehensive ears. It smelled nice though, like they had one of those air freshener dispensers with a timer that sprayed a mist of scent every so often.

"Wait here," Kelly said. "I'll be right back."

As she disappeared through a doorway, female voices drifted toward him over the noise of the copier.

"Kelly, I thought you'd left."

"I did, but I forgot a file I'd meant to take home. Aren't you leaving soon?"

"Yeah. I only have a few more documents to copy. Why don't you hang around a minute and we'll go to Louie's for a drink."

"I can't. I've got a date."

"A date, huh? He must be a real winner if you're taking work home to keep you warm."

Tom heard the woman's low chuckle and felt a smile curve his lips at Kelly's reply. "Oh, he's a winner, alright. But tonight, he might just have to beg for it."

The woman whooped and laughed. "I hear some juice in that story. Sure you don't want to go for that drink?"

"I'm sure. See you in the morning, Gloria."

"Yes, you will, and I'm gonna want details – lots of 'em."

Kelly reappeared and blushed beneath his grinning gaze.

"Not one word."

"Did I say anything?"

As they stepped from the warm office into the crisp night, Tom pulled Kelly close beneath an illuminated street lamp. He lingered in the warmth of her alluring eyes and let his warm breath betray his desire before lowering his mouth to hers.

When he lifted his head, he released a steadying sigh. Her eyes fluttered open to reveal passion simmering in their depths and he smiled, shaking his head in wonder.

"I can't get enough of you," he said, his voice rough with pent-up emotion. "If I have to beg, I will."

"Good. That's the way I like it."

Tom grinned and wrapped his arm around her shoulders as an arctic breeze rustled the leaves of shrubs and the needles of pines. He steered her past his Jaguar toward her car. When she pressed the unlock button on her remote, he opened the door and interior light spilled from the Lexus.

"Thanks for doing this for me, Kelly."

He lowered his head for another kiss and reached for the file she held in her hand. Her retreat was sudden as she took a step back.

"Hold on there, big guy," she ordered, clasping the file to her breast. "If you think I'm just going to hand this file over without an explanation, you're wrong, Thomas Shear. You're not getting anything until you've told me why it's so important."

Tom stood silent, holding his renewed frustration in check.

"Why won't you tell me?" she asked. "Why won't you confide in me? I trusted you by getting this file. Now I'm asking you to trust me." She waited for his answer and grew impatient with his brooding silence. "Is it Emmy? Has something happened to her?"

"Besides the obvious?" A sardonic grin twisted his lips. "No."

"Then what is it?"

"I just don't want you involved, okay?"

"Involved!" She stared at him. "Whether you realize it or not, I became involved the moment we met. I carry Jenny with me everywhere I go. I feel her pain as if everything that happened to her happened to me, and you have the gall to stand there and say you don't want me involved? I can't believe you!"

Kelly's words echoed in his brain and his anger evaporated. Seeing the tears she held at bay, he pushed common sense aside and gathered her in his arms.

"Okay. I'll tell you what I know. But not here."

She pulled away from him. "I want to go to the gallery."

Tom frowned. "I don't think that's wise," he said. "I think it'd be better if I followed you home."

Kelly's face softened under his worried gaze, and she raised her hand to his determined jaw. "I'm not going to tell you I'm not afraid, because it would be a lie," she said. "But I can't just walk away as if nothing happened. I can't pretend that Jenny, and what I feel of her, isn't real. It is and I have to find a way to deal with it, not hide from it."

Tom stood silent, watching her face as he debated his options. But he knew her determination would dismiss any argument he tried to make.

"My gut tells me I shouldn't let you do it," he said, "but I can see I have no choice. I don't suppose you'll let me have that file now?"

"You've got to be kidding," she said, sinking into the driver's seat of her car. "This file's my insurance."

Tom led Kelly to the brick patio at the back of the gallery. A free-standing gas-light at the far corner of the patio washed a tempered glass table with a closed umbrella and six cushioned chairs in its warm light. A large, black Weber grill stood in the opposite corner.

Kelly waited in silence as Tom opened the storm-door that had a sign reading "No Admittance. Use Front Door" and inserted his key in the lock. She preceded him into the dimly lit kitchen, the only source of light coming from the sixty watt bulb above the stove, and

Tom watched her scan the shadowed room as he reset security. She flinched as his hands came around her shoulders to take her coat. Smiling timidly, she took a deep breath.

"Are you okay?" he asked, hanging their coats on the wall mounted coat rack by the door. He flipped the switch to the chandelier above the table and the shadows dispersed.

"Fine," she said with a closed lipped smile.

Tom took Kelly's hand and led her across the kitchen to the back stairs. As her eyes traveled upward through the dark, she gave his hand an involuntary, nervous squeeze. Tom squeezed back in reassurance, turned on the stairway light, and led her up. At the top, a beacon of soft light spilled into the dark hallway from a single lamp in the den. As she entered, she released a relieved sigh before settling herself in a corner of his sofa. Tom went to the bar.

"Here," he said, handing her a snifter of brandy. "You look like you need this."

"Does it show that much?"

"Sweetheart, you're trembling all over. You know we don't have to stay here. I'm sure you'd feel better at your apartment."

Kelly took a sip of brandy then shook her head. "We're not going anywhere. Now, tell me what's happened."

Tom remained standing as he swirled the amber liquid in his own snifter, his brow knitted in thought as he watched its movement. He'd already decided not to tell her about Detective Winward's visit. There was no way he was going to voluntarily involve her in a murder investigation. If it came to that, he'd rather remove her from his life than subject her to that kind of situation.

"I went to the university library today and did some research. What I found was astounding." He lifted his gaze to her pale face. "I searched newspaper articles and found a series of missing children reports. The missing children were all little girls."

Tom weighed his words carefully. "Jenny was the first to be

abducted. Only one body out of eight was ever found. Her name was Kathy Packard. She was the last victim."

A heavy silence fell, then Kelly's voice was subdued as she said, "I don't know what to say. I remember reports several months back and I was shocked by the outcome, but I'm ashamed to say, as time passed, I gave the matter little consideration after that."

"I know what you mean," Tom replied. "I think it's only human nature to look the other way when something happens that doesn't affect your own life. But things have changed. It has affected our lives deeply and now we have to deal with it. That's why I went to the library today. I have to find out for myself what's happening to us and why."

Kelly looked thoughtful. "You said there were eight abductions," she said. "Weren't the police only able to link three or four together?"

"That's right. At least that's what the article said," Tom replied, remembering what he'd read about the confession found with Theodore Chandler's corpse.

"What do you mean? You sound as if you think there's more to it. You don't think all eight could possibly be connected, do you?"

Tom walked to the window and peered into the darkness. "I'm sure of it," he answered.

"How?"

"Jenny wasn't among the ones mentioned in the confession found on the scene of the abductor's suicide."

"I don't follow you."

"The abductor admitted to four cases. The last four," Tom explained, facing her. "Three of those four are on a canvas hanging in the Rage gallery."

Kelly stared at him without blinking as she considered the implication of Tom's statement. "What of the fourth?"

He held her gaze. "I've painted eight portraits and they're all hanging downstairs. With the exception of Emmy, I've portrayed seven of the victims. The only one I'm missing is Kathy Packard. Her body was discovered the day after Theodore Chandler was found hanging in my studio."

"What!" Kelly moved as if ready to leap, then slowly settled back against the sofa. She lifted her snifter and swallowed. After a fortifying breath, she met Tom's watchful gaze. "I knew Mr. Chandler committed suicide, but I had no idea it was here. You must've been overwhelmed when you found out."

"To say the least. That's why I need to look at that file. It might tell me something about the house that—" Tom's voice halted at the sudden expression of horror on Kelly's face. "What's wrong?"

"Mrs. Dempsey," she whispered.

Tom's brow creased. "What's Mrs. Dempsey got to do with this?"

Kelly looked startled. "I thought you knew," she said.

"Why does everyone say that to me whenever her name's mentioned?"

"She was killed in this house, Tom. She fell down the attic stairs and broke her neck."

Tom was stunned. "When?"

"It happened the day she showed you the house. She had some paperwork I needed so I drove over. The front door was standing open and her car was in the driveway, but I couldn't find her. I was just about to call the police when I heard a noise in the attic."

Kelly paused and took a deep breath to dispel the quaver in her voice.

"I don't think she recognized me, because my presence seemed to terrify her. She threw up her arms like she was expecting me to attack her and practically pushed me out of her way. That's when she stumbled and lost her balance. There was nothing I could do," she said, staring into the empty glass she held in her hand. "I reached out to her, but she was already falling."

Tom scowled as he took her glass and returned to the bar. The image of Mrs. Dempsey's broken body lying with dead, staring eyes at the bottom of the attic stairs flashed in his mind.

"The only thing I was told was that Mrs. Dempsey had been killed in an accident," he said, pouring more brandy for himself as well. "I assumed it was a car accident."

"Tom, I'm sorry. I had no idea you didn't know. I would've told you if I'd known. I hope you believe that."

Tom studied Kelly's face, then carried their drinks as he went over to her. He squatted in front of her, handed her a glass, and took her free hand. He gave it a gentle squeeze. "It must have been terrible for you."

"It was," she said. "But there's no excuse for you not being told the truth."

Ignoring her comment, he rose, turned back toward the window and stood swirling the brandy in his glass.

"Why was she in the attic in the first place?" he questioned, his gaze probing the darkness outside. "I had the distinct impression she was anxious to settle our business so she could leave. And what could've frightened her badly enough to make her bolt from the room?"

"I don't know."

"You don't remember seeing or hearing anything out of the ordinary?" he asked, turning in time to see a flicker of recognition in her eyes. "What?"

"It might be nothing, but as I climbed the stairs, I thought I heard a voice. And when I stood in the doorway, before she turned and ran toward me, there was a whimper. At first, I thought the sound came from Mrs. Dempsey. But now that I think about it, and considering everything that's happened since, it was definitely childlike."

"The voice you heard when you mounted the stairs, what did it say?"

"I don't know," she said. "It was muffled."

Tom's eyelids closed in weary thought.

"What are you thinking?" she asked.

Tom heaved a sigh. "I think Mrs. Dempsey was exposed to something she couldn't handle."

Kelly pondered her next question before she spoke. "Do you suppose there's a connection between what happened to her and Mr. Chandler's suicide? There's got to be more to it than mere coincidence that both deaths occurred in the same location."

"Oh, there's more to it, all right," he said in a rough voice as he began to pace. "I don't believe in coincidence anymore. Everything happens for a reason."

"What do you mean?"

"If I'm right, the attic above us is where the children were held captive. My gut also tells me it's where they died."

Tom's words poured over Kelly like iced water. Her face drained of color and her eyes grew wide with shock. Kneeling in front of her, he took her drink from her hand and placed both of their glasses on the coffee table before gathering her in his arms.

"We're going to find the truth, baby. We couldn't help them in life, but maybe we can help them in death. And when we do, maybe their souls will be set free."

Tom held Kelly close and she clung to him as she shook and nodded her understanding against his neck. His heart ached for her and only served to magnify the need to protect her from all that was happening.

Suddenly, the overwhelming realization of just how much she meant to him and what he stood to lose washed over him with a sobering effect. His determination to find the truth strengthened tenfold and he felt an uncanny calm fall over his emotions.

Kelly pulled away from Tom's embrace and wiped the tears from her face. "I'm sorry. I was just taken by surprise, but I don't know why. And I felt Jenny. What you said makes perfect since. Why else would Jenny have been here in the first place?"

"Darlin', you don't have to apologize. It's a lot to take in."

She shook her head. "When I see you calmly accepting things and moving forward to the next logical step," she smiled ruefully and shook her head again, "I must seem like a weak, sniveling female to you."

Tom harrumphed. "I've had weeks to come to terms with what's happening," he replied. "You've had, what, three days? I know you're a strong woman, Kelly. You don't have to prove anything to me."

"Yes, I do," she stated, holding his dark-blue gaze. "I want you to have the confidence to come to me, to know I'll stand by you, no matter what. I want to be your comfort and the one who helps you realize when you're screwing up. I want you to know, without a doubt, that I'm worthy and strong enough to be your woman." She held his gaze a moment longer, then her cheeks flushed and she lowered her eyes. "Maybe it's too soon to be saying these things, but it's the way I feel."

Tom was held captivated. He didn't know what to say. He'd hoped, but had never really expected, to hear such declarations from a woman he was falling, had already fallen, in love with. When she lifted her eyes to his, the longing they revealed made his groin tighten. The mere closeness of her body made his hands tingle with the urge to caress her smooth, bare skin.

"So, what can I do to help?" Her voice was husky with emotion.

"Just stand by me and be my sounding board," he answered. "If I had to deal with it alone, I'd probably go insane."

"What are you going to do now?" she asked, her question a mere whisper.

Tom's gaze fell to her soft lips and he breathed, "This," before smothering her gasp beneath his kiss. As her tongue moved in a slow, sensual dance with his, he pushed her skirt up, letting his fingers glide along the silkiness of her gartered thigh-high hose until he met bare skin. He then guided her legs apart, positioned himself between her thighs and pulled her close until he felt the heat of her crotch pressed against the hardness beneath his zipper. She trembled as he cupped her breasts, grazing their peaks with his thumbs, and his body grew rigid as her nipples tightened beneath her clothing in response to his touch.

"God, Kelly. I never knew I could feel this way."

His whisper was hoarse with longing as he nibbled a path from the mole at the corner of her mouth to the tender flesh of her neck. He pulled back, meeting her heavy lidded gaze, and slowly began freeing the buttons of her blouse.

"If this isn't what you want, baby, stop me now," he warned, his voice low and strained. "I'm aching to make love to you and it would be damned hard to stop if it goes much further."

Kelly's eyes had darkened and her moss-green gaze held Tom prisoner as she unbuttoned his shirt. She pushed it back from his shoulders and ran her hands across the broad expanse of his bare chest before shrugging out of her own gaping blouse.

"It's too late for either of us to stop now. Make love to me, Tom. Hold me in your arms. Love me."

The last command was lost in a breath as Tom found the front clasp of her bra and slipped his fingertips beneath the white lace to push it aside. At the sight of her naked breasts, his erection became like stone and throbbed. He cupped their weight in his hands and couldn't help a groan as his penis twitched with anticipation.

He gently pinched, then pulled her pink nipples, watching them tighten even more, begging to be suckled. "I do love you, Kelly. I always will," he growled. "God, you're beautiful." Tom lowered his head and licked her left nipple before pulling it into his mouth. As he sucked and rubbed with his tongue, his fingers found the right and began rubbing in circles, pinch-pulling with a gentle twist. Her nails scraped across his scalp, sending a sensual shiver over the back of his neck, across his bare shoulders, and down his back before she fisted his hair in her hands to pull him closer. Her back arched and she gave a low moan as her head fell back.

"That feels so good."

She then lifted her head and lowered her eyes to watch what he was doing as he moved to the other breast and began the process over again. Her lips parted and her breath quickened. Her eyes smoldered as she lay back on the sofa and pulled him down on top of her. His heart swelled as her whispered "always" caressed his lips.

As he deepened the kiss, his dazed mind ignored a gentle tug for his attention. The tug grew stronger and part of his brain registered the smell of roses. He lifted his head and realized the scent hung heavy in the air.

"What is it?" Kelly asked, holding herself very still.

Tom turned his head and scanned the room. "Don't you smell it?"

Her eyes widened and she followed his visual trail around the room. "Roses."

"Yeah," he said, lifting himself from the sofa. He gathered Kelly in his arms and picked her up. "Let's continue this in the bedroom, shall we?" At her nod, Tom left the room and the smell behind them.

Two hours passed without notice in the warm candle-lit room as they caressed and stroked in the redolence of the cocoon they'd created beneath the covers. Their cries and moans from pleasure-pain filled the bedroom as their orgasms ripped through them. Panting with pounding hearts and trembling muscles, they held each other close until the slick sweat that dampened their skin dried. Then, a look and a bold caress would fan their simmering passion and the ritual would begin again.

When their cries rang out once more, they collapsed in each others arms and their only movement was the rise and fall of their heaving chests. As Tom's mind began to settle, coherent thought was once again possible and he marveled at the intensity of their lovemaking, replaying every moment in his mind. When Kelly finally stirred against him, pulling out of his arms, he groaned. He sighed with deep regret, because he knew the world outside their haven was about to make an unwelcome intrusion.

Tom lounged on the bed with one arm beneath his head and the sheet pulled to his hips. He breathed in the aroma of sex lingering in the air mingling with the scent of the candles and watched Kelly's movements in the candlelight as she tightened the belt of his heavy, black terrycloth robe. When he wore it, the hem came to mid-calf. On her it grazed the tips of her toes and the sleeves swallowed her hands.

"I'm going to call Mrs. Chandler tomorrow and persuade her to see me," he said quietly, his eyes drinking her in.

She gave him a searching look then curled up beside him. "Even if she agrees to meet with you, what are you hoping to accomplish by talking to her?" she asked just as quietly, running her fingers down his bare chest to his navel.

"I'm not sure," he admitted, feeling his groin tighten valiantly once again in response. He gave his mind a mental shake. *It's like I'm eighteen again.* Suppressing a grin, he pushed the thought aside. "Maybe nothing. Maybe a lot. But it's the next logical place to look for answers. She might be able to point me in the next direction I need to go."

"Do you want me to go with you?" she asked, rising up onto her elbow to meet his gaze.

"I don't think so, honey. I'd rather you stay at your apartment and wait until you hear from me tomorrow night. The less you're involved, the better."

"But—"

"No buts, Kelly," he said. "I'm standing firm with this. There's no point in arguing."

"Then I wish you luck." She returned her head to his shoulder. "You're going to need it if you're planning to take on Merideth Chandler alone."

He lowered his chin and looked at the top of her head over the crest of his nose. "What do you mean by that?"

"It's a sad story, really," she mused, content in the circle of his arms. "Before her husband died, they were respected in the community. They had money to burn and she was the type who wouldn't think twice about lending her support to a worthwhile cause. She was a caring, generous person. She was also deeply in love with her husband. When his body was discovered, it devastated her. Her perfect world crumbled. People she thought were her friends started avoiding her. She turned into a recluse overnight and hasn't been out of her grand home since."

Tom was entranced with Kelly's story. Even though his heart went out to the person she described, his stomach knotted as he thought of the confrontation ahead.

"How do you know so much about her?"

"She and my mother worked charities together and were good friends before my mom was killed by a drunk driver. After the accident, she helped us get through the loss by taking me and Jason under her wing. I was fourteen when it happened. I was at an age when a daughter needs a mother's support and guidance. Merideth stepped in and helped fill that empty gap in my life. Since my father never got over losing my mom, maybe that's why I have a little understanding of what Merideth Chandler's going through. But, given the circumstances, I don't think anyone could ever really begin to imagine the extent of her pain."

"I'm sorry," Tom said, hearing how inadequate the words sounded. "I had no idea."

Kelly's expression softened before she pulled out of his embrace. "I'm hungry," she said, scooting off the bed. "Why don't I go down and see what I can find for a quick supper?"

She walked over to Tom's dresser, saw herself in the flickering light reflected in the mirror, and frowned in dismay. "Oh my." As she picked up his brush and began working the tangles from her long, thick hair, she glanced at his lounging image and saw him watching her, grinning with leering appreciation. "While we're eating," she said, administering the final strokes, "you can tell me what you know about the roses."

For an instant, Tom's body tensed and his eyes narrowed as he watched her. Shuttering his expression, he forced his body to relax. "Why do you think I know anything about *that*?" he asked.

She shifted her eyes to him and quirked her lips in a 'get real' gesture, then put the brush down and turned for the door.

"Wait. I'll help you." Tom threw back the sheet and swung his long legs over the edge of the mattress.

"You don't have to," Kelly replied, appreciating the display of his lean, muscled, naked body. "Besides, it'll give you a chance to read Mrs. Chandler's file. I'm sure I can manage alone."

"That's just it," he said, finding his jeans on the floor and pulling them on. "You'll be alone down there. Until this thing's resolved, you're not leaving my sight while you're in this house." He slipped his arms into a shirt, leaving it unbuttoned, turned on the bedside lamp, and blew out the two candles burning in the room before escorting her down the backstairs.

As Kelly searched the refrigerator, Tom settled at the kitchen table and opened the file. The house was quiet; the only sounds were the contenting domesticity of Kelly's movements and the soft shuffle of paper as Tom leafed through the file. He read each page, but there was little information that was pertinent or that he didn't already know. Frustration rose at the apparent dead end.

"Find anything interesting?" Kelly asked, placing a chef salad and a glass of iced tea on the table beside him. He noticed she'd rolled the sleeves of his robe up to her elbows.

Tom closed the file and pushed it away. "Not really. Besides Mrs. Chandler's address and phone number, the only thing I found of interest was that this house was built in 1903 by a man named Kramer. The problem is it has absolutely no bearing on the situation."

"If that's the case," she said, sitting down and tucking his robe around her legs, "tell me about the roses. And don't tell me you know nothing about it. Your reaction to smelling them tells me different."

Expecting the inquiry, Tom chewed slowly, pondering what to tell her. He'd smelled the rose scent often, felt gentle brushes against his hair or shoulders and knew she was around, but had only encountered her sexually physical, erotic touch twice. It had been weeks, as a matter of fact.

He swallowed and put his fork down. "I've had dreams of a woman. When I have these dreams, I smell roses. I've smelled them at other times, too. It's how she makes her presence known."

Kelly's own fork stopped in midair as she looked at him. "You've seen a woman in your dreams?"

"No," he answered, which was true. "I've heard her. She's spoken to me."

Kelly put down her fork and folded her hands in her lap. "What did she say?" she asked.

"She told me to help the children. She said they needed my help and that she would be here with me."

"That's it?" Kelly was watching him closely and Tom met her gaze without hesitation.

"That's it," he said, which was not true.

"Who is she?"

Tom shrugged. "I have no idea," he said, again truthfully, and forked another bite of salad.

"Do you think it could be Mrs. Dempsey?"

Tom's fork stopped midway as he looked at Kelly, remembering the woman he had met only briefly. Her prudish mannerism and lack of projecting anything remotely sexual had him shaking his head. "No. Definitely not Mrs. Dempsey." He resumed eating.

She nodded, accepting his certainty, then took a drink of tea. As she set her glass down, her brow furrowed in thought. "If you've had dreams of the children and they're trapped in this house, does that mean the woman's trapped here, too?"

"I don't think so," he said from the corner of his mouth.

"How do you know?" she asked, and waited for him to swallow.

"In my dreams the children are vivid. I haven't actually seen the woman. I've only heard her voice and smelled roses. It's like she's taken on the role of guardian." He took another bite.

"You mean like an angel?" Kelly asked, surprised.

Tom was amused and horrified all at once. He tried for nonchalance, but was afraid he only succeeded in staring at her like a startled owl. *Angels didn't do the things she's done, do they?* He swallowed and almost choked. "No," he said hoarsely, then cleared his throat, saying more calmly. "No, I don't think she's an angel."

Kelly lifted a brow and watched him for a moment longer, then thankfully, returned to her meal. They ate in silence, each deep in their own thoughts. Tom hoped his explanation about the woman was enough to curb Kelly's curiosity, but didn't count on it. He pushed the thought aside. He had to concentrate on the problem at hand.

He knew he had to convince Merideth Chandler to grant him a meeting. His instincts told him she knew more than had been revealed in the previous investigation, and he was determined to find a way to get her to open up to him.

"I don't know why I didn't make the connection before," Kelly said. She stood and gathered the dishes from the table. "I feel so stupid. I knew Mr. Chandler had killed himself in one of his rental properties. I just failed to put two and two together. I haven't been with the agency that long, so maybe that's why I wasn't told."

"I doubt that. Full disclosure goes against human nature. They needed to sell and knew that buyers wouldn't want a house where a violent death had occurred," Tom replied, admiring the sway of her hips beneath his robe as she walked to the sink.

"A good lawyer could probably get you out of the contract. The full disclosure law is there for a reason, you know," she stated, raising her voice over the growl of the disposal. "You were more or less coerced into buying this house and the agency knows it. I'd be willing to back you up if it came down to it."

"Believe me, the thought's crossed my mind," he admitted. "But the house suits my purpose perfectly. And the price—" He shook his head. "No. I think I'll stick it out a while longer and see what happens. If worse comes to worst, then I'll get out. For now, I'm staying put."

"I wouldn't wait too long, if I were you," Kelly stated, stacking the dishes in the dishwasher. "Tom?"

"Hmm?" he mumbled, pulling the file back in front of him.

"Why did you say 'with the exception of Emmy' when you were explaining about the little girls and the portraits you've painted?"

"There was no mention of her in the series I read today."

"That's odd. What do you think it means?"

"I'm not sure. There's no doubt she's connected in some way. The question is, how?"

The doorbell chimed, startling them both. Tom's gut tightened with the possibility of who the caller might be. He envisioned Winward and the hulking, yet stylishly dressed Hayes standing patiently on his front porch. Meeting Kelly's questioning gaze, he slid his chair away from the table.

"I'll get dressed while you see who it is."

"I'm not leaving you alone."

"I can't very well greet company like this, can I?" she asked with a wry smile. "I'm naked under this thing. Besides, it won't take me long and I promise I'll come right down as soon as I'm finished."

The bell chimed again.

"Go on. I'll be okay."

Tom hesitated a moment longer before leaning down to place a kiss on her lips. "Hurry," he commanded. She nodded, then disappeared up the back stairs.

His bare feet made a patting sound on the wood floor as his long strides carried him across the dark foyer. The insistent chime resounded once more. "I'm coming," he bellowed. He turned on the foyer and porch lights, pressed a code onto the security panel, twisted the deadbolt, and snatched the front door open.

Jonathan entered without preamble. The seriousness of his expression held Tom's relief in check.

"I need to talk to you."

Tom closed the door watching his friend. "Kelly's upstairs."

"I see." Jonathan glanced up to the second floor before leveling his gaze on Tom. "We can discuss details tomorrow. Right now, I have a few things I want to say."

"Can I take your coat?"

Jonathan shook his head. "This won't take long."

"I'm listening."

"I've thought it over. I've known you too long to doubt you. I'd trust you with my life, and I think you're trusting me with yours by telling me about what happened to you. I still think it's the most incredible thing I've ever heard, but who am I to judge? I believe in you and that's what counts. That's why I've made us an appointment with one of the best criminal lawyers in Georgia."

"Who?" Tom asked, feeling his insides twist.

"Russ Carson. We're to meet tomorrow afternoon. Two o'clock."

"Where?"

"At his office. I think you know the place."

"Yeah," Tom replied. "I know the place."

"I talked to Russ this afternoon and gave him a synopsis of what you told me. He was fascinated. He wants to discuss the case in detail. Can you make it?"

"How much did you tell him?" Tom asked, his voice steady.

"Enough to intrigue the hell out of him." Jonathan's cynical smile wavered as Tom's dark brow furrowed. "What's wrong? Why the hesitation?"

"I'm not sure, Jonathan," he admitted, startled by the truthfulness of the statement. He ran his fingers through his sex-tousled hair in agitation, the muscles of his bare chest beneath his open shirt responding impressively with the movement. "I guess it's the idea of being put under a microscope. It's infuriating."

Jonathan's expression was sympathetic. "I can only imagine. But, Tom, I'm not qualified to give you the kind of help you need. Russ Carson is. He's one of the best. If anyone can help you, he can." He paused to let this sink in, pushing his hands into the pockets of his gray wool overcoat. "Do you want to keep the appointment?" he asked, holding Tom's gaze.

"Is he going to do it?"

"What? Take the case?"

Tom nodded.

Jonathan's shoulders lifted in a quick shrug. "We'll find out tomorrow. Do you want to keep the appointment?" he repeated.

Tom's hands went to his hips and he released a discomfited sigh. "Yeah," he answered. "When do you want to meet?"

"Let's meet for an early lunch at Grady's and go from there. That should give us plenty of time to discuss—"

Kelly's curdling scream faded into eerie silence as Tom bolted up the staircase. He entered the bedroom at a full run and saw her standing fully dressed except for her gaping blouse. Her quick, shallow breaths were misty. The room was frigid. As he followed her wide-eyed stare, he shivered and his blood chilled as two little girls standing side-by-side came into view. His heart filled with trepidation to see Kelly the focus of their steadfast attention.

"My God."

Jonathan's choked whisper sounded distant behind Tom as he took a calculated step forward, his own sporadic breath puffing in front of him. Inhaling deeply to control his breathing, Tom positioned himself between Kelly and the little girls before lowering his knee to the floor.

"Hello," he said, swallowing hard to keep his voice from quavering.

His pounding heart lurched as their hollow gazes fused with his. He could feel Emmy's presence swelling within him, and had to blink back the flow of tears that rushed to his eyes.

"My name's Tom. Can you tell me yours?"

Silence hung over the room like a frozen shroud. When a small voice penetrated the thin air, its childish cadence was a piercing knife through his already aching heart.

"Amanda."

Tom was drawn to the uncanny sound and in one swift glance, he recognized the little girl who had spoken. Her eyes were blue and her short chestnut hair matched the hair he remembered in the photograph on the viewing screen, except now it was dirty and hanging limp. She was dressed in soiled white panties with yellow moons and stars and a torn, grimy blue t-shirt. Her feet were bare. With the bruises and abrasions marring her body, she stood exactly the same as portrayed in the portrait downstairs. He had to force his voice to remain calm, his body not to shiver.

"Who's your friend, Amanda?" he asked, almost flinching as he turned to the smaller girl by her side. The intensity of her gaze was shocking. The jet black of her long tangled hair and the bruises on her small, oval face only served to heighten the ferocity of her dark eyes. Their accusing stare made his skin tingle.

"Why are you here?" she hissed. Her eyes took on a look of suspicion and the temperature of the room dropped even more.

Tom fought the urge to clench his teeth against his body's reaction to the cold. His exhalations grew denser. "I'm here to help you," he answered with a sinking stomach. "Tell me what to do."

Their gazes shifted to look behind him and the dark-haired presence lifted her arm to point a condemning finger in Kelly's direction. Her meaning hit Tom like a tsunami and his body recoiled as if a striking snake had been placed in front of him.

"No," he demanded. "Kelly has nothing to do with this. Use me. I'll do anything I can for you. Leave Kelly alone."

The two girls took a step forward. Realizing their intent, Tom blocked their path and was seized by a numbing paralysis. He flinched against its tightening grip and watched in horror as the child specters penetrated his body. For a fleeting instant, their souls merged with his and a tremendous sorrow consumed him. He groaned beneath the oppressive weight, then his body sagged in humiliating relief as their forms emerged behind him.

Tom's paralysis vanished with Kelly's agonized scream and he spun around in time to see her crumble, unconscious, to the floor. Stumbling forward, he gathered her in his arms and looked up with bitter tears stinging his eyes.

"Why?" he ground out. "Why Kelly? Why couldn't you use me?"

The house remained silent.

Jonathan pushed himself from the doorway and knelt beside them. He looked at Tom with stunned, frightened eyes. "Is she--?" He felt Kelly's wrist for a pulse.

"Tom?"

Kelly's weak voice was like a caress.

"Kelly," he breathed. "I thought I'd lost you." His voice broke with a mixture of relief and sorrow. "I'm so sorry. I'm so sorry I let them hurt you again."

"They've joined Jenny, Tom." She wept in his arms.

# CHAPTER EIGHTEEN

As Tom entered the Fine Arts building and made his way to his office, he wasn't surprised to see Jonathan waiting in the corridor, leaning against the wall, out of the way of milling students. Neither spoke until they were inside with the door closed.

Tom's office was a few steps down the "posh scale" compared to Jonathan's. His desk was wood laminate. He had two filing cabinets and a prefab bookcase stuffed to capacity. There were chairs for visitors and a coat-rack that held a white smock stained with various colors of paint. One of his own paintings, a snarling blue panther – the university mascot – suspended in mid-jump with claws drawn, hung on the wall. The window blinds were half closed to reduce the glare from outside.

"How's Kelly?" Jonathan asked, sitting.

Tom let out a weary sigh as he pulled off his jacket and hung it beside the smock. He loosened his silver tie as he sank into his chair.

Running agitated fingers through his dark hair, he answered, "Depressed, scared, mentally drained."

Even though Kelly had recovered quickly from her shock, she had remained subdued and eerily quiet. Tom had driven her back to her apartment where she had been afflicted by nightmares. The sun had risen, putting an end to his vigil, only to find her sobbing in his arms.

"Tom?"

Jonathan's voice scattered Tom's thoughts. He looked up from the silver-framed photograph sitting on his desk that he'd been blindly staring at; a smiling group shot of six former students.

"I'm sorry, Jonathan," he said, rubbing his blurry eyes. "I don't think I'm going to be very good company today."

"Well, that's understandable." Jonathan's brow creased with worry. He leaned forward in his chair and put his elbows on his knees. "Did you get any sleep at all last night?"

"No."

Jonathan shook his head. "I still can't believe what happened. When I saw those little girls standing in the corner watching Kelly, my mind went numb. All I could do was pray and I haven't done that in years. When I think of the way you stood up to them and actually carried on a conversation--" he stopped and shook his head again. "I couldn't have done it. I was scared to death."

"And you think I wasn't?" Tom asked, picking up a polished white quartz paperweight and setting it down with a thud. "I did what I had to do, Jonathan. You would've done the same if it had been Marsha. The problem is, my so-called bravery had no effect at all. They still managed to get to her, and now Kelly's paying the price."

"You can't blame yourself, Tom. I was there, remember? I saw what happened. There was absolutely nothing you could've done."

Tom placed his elbows on his desk blotter and rested his head in his splayed hands. "I could've kept Kelly away from the house," he said, talking to the top of his desk. "If I had, none of this would've happened."

"Are you positive about that?" Jonathan asked. "I think they would've found a way to reach her no matter where she was. Maybe even through you. For some reason Kelly's their link to fulfilling a destiny we don't understand."

Tom sat back in his chair and met Jonathan's troubled gaze head on. "We're closer to understanding than you think."

He told Jonathan about the research he'd done the day before. He also told him of his plans to contact Merideth Chandler.

"This whole thing's incredible," Jonathan uttered, giving Tom a speculating look. "You're not going to like what I have to say, but I've given it a lot of thought. And what you just told me strengthens my resolve."

"I'm listening."

"I think we should have a talk with Detective Winward."

Tom looked at Jonathan like he'd just grown another head. "And tell him what?" he blurted. "That I'm up to my ears in his serial murder investigation because I just happened to buy the house where the crimes took place? That Kelly and I are being used as spiritual conduits by the victims to, and I quote, 'fulfill a destiny we don't understand'?"

"Something like that," Jonathan stated, sitting back in his chair.

"You're crazy, Jonathan. The answer's 'no'."

"Will you at least think about it?"

"No," Tom snapped. "It's a lousy idea."

"Then what about Marsha?"

Tom shook his head in confusion. "What about her?"

"Think about it, Tom. She's a criminal psychologist. Profiling criminals is part of her job. She's known you a long time. If you talk to her, maybe her professional analysis will help convince the police you're no murderer."

"I don't know, Jonathan. The fact that we're friends might cause the police to question her impartiality. Besides, my dirty laundry's being aired enough as it is."

"I understand. But I still think she can help, if not with the police, then with you."

"You think I need a shrink?" Tom asked, incredulous.

"My God, Tom, look at what you've been through? I think you need someone to talk to besides me, someone who has more to offer than just an ear. If not Marsha, then someone else, someone with a few emotional answers."

Tom's anger dissolved. His actions were slow as he rubbed his face before meeting the concern in Jonathan's eyes.

"I'll think about it," he said.

Jonathan put his hands on his knees and rose to his feet. "That's all I'm asking. Are we still on for this afternoon with Russ?"

"I suppose so," Tom said, following Jonathan to the door.

"Remember. Lunch at Grady's. Noon."

"I'll be there."

Tom opened the door to Marsha's smiling face.

"Well, well. What a nice surprise," she cooed, seeing Jonathan. "I was going to knock, but decided to wait when I heard voices. If I'd known who you had in there, Tom, I'd have interrupted and joined the party."

"You'd have been bored out of your mind," Jonathan said, smiling as he draped his arm across her shoulders and stepped out into the hall, "unless, of course, you have an opinion as to who's going to win the next World Series."

"You've got to be joking. Since when have the two of you been baseball fans?"

Jonathan shrugged and flashed a charming smile. "Since the Braves started winning, of course. I'd be glad to tell you all about it over coffee, if you'd like."

Marsha looked skeptical as she declined. "No, thank you. Besides, I have a class in fifteen minutes. I just came by to invite Tom to lunch this afternoon."

"Sorry. I've already made plans," he said, crossing his arms and leaning a shoulder against the doorframe.

"Oh. Well, how about dinner? I'll fix your favorite."

Tom smiled at her persistence. "Sounds enticing, but I can't do that, either, honey. Michael Raymond's coming this evening to pick up the paintings his father bought at the showing the other night." Her inquisitive stare made him uneasy, but he kept his emotions unreadable behind an expression of relaxed humor.

"Tom, are you okay?" she asked.

"Sure I am."

"Apparently, you haven't looked in a mirror lately. You look exhausted. Are you still having trouble sleeping?"

"A little, but it's nothing for you to worry about."

"Insomnia's nothing to laugh at, Tom. If you let it go, you're going to make yourself sick. Have you considered seeing a doctor?"

Jonathan groaned and rolled his eyes. "Leave the man alone, Marsha. He has enough on his mind without having to put up with your motherly harassment."

"Harassment! I was merely voicing my concern and if you were any friend at all, Jonathan Fields, you'd do the same. And what's this about having enough on his mind?" She looked at Tom. "Something's been bothering you for weeks. What's wrong?"

"Nothing." Tom leaned down and placed a kiss on Marsha's cheek. "Look, there's nothing to worry about. I'm fine. My gallery opens Friday, you know. Maybe we can get together then."

"Nice evasion, but don't think I'm going to let it slide." A sly smile replaced her frown. "And I haven't forgotten about Friday. I'm looking forward to seeing Kelly again. I really like her, Tom. I think she's good for you."

"Oh, for God's sake!" Jonathan heaved an exasperated sigh and took her by the arm.

As Jonathan steered Marsha away, Tom looked on in amused relief as their rallying voices blended with the slackening hubbub around them. The congestion in the hallway was thinning. Shaking his head, he shut his office door, straightened his tie and turned toward his awaiting students.

After morning classes, Tom sat in his office and called Kelly on her cell phone. He was relieved by her calm assurances. He made arrangements to meet her later that evening, then hung up and sat back in his chair. The sun shining through the blinds at his back was warm against his neck. His brow creased as he extracted a slip of paper from his shirt pocket. He picked the phone back up and dialed Merideth Chandler's number.

"Chandler residence." The voice that answered was male. It spoke precisely with a haughty demeanor.

"Hello. I'd like to speak with Mrs. Chandler please. My name's Thomas Shear."

"May I ask what this is regarding?" the disembodied voice asked drolly.

"It's concerning a property I purchased from her in September."

"One moment, please."

Tom sat forward with his elbows on his desk blotter gripping the receiver. He wondered if the man was really relaying the message or if he was standing by the phone an appropriate length of time to make him think he had. Tom ran anxious fingers through his hair and waited in silence until the same male voice came back on the line.

"I'm sorry, but the lady of the house isn't taking calls today. If you would like to leave a message, I'll see that it is forwarded."

His mind raced. *A message? Saying what? Tell madam, I need to speak with her concerning a bunch of little girl ghosts and her husband, their murderer?*

"It's very important that I speak directly to Mrs. Chandler. When will she be available?"

"I am unable to answer that, sir. If there's no message…?"

"Very well." Suppressing his impatience, Tom spoke slowly to soften the edge in his voice as he repeated his name and recited the numbers where he could be reached. "Please tell Mrs. Chandler that it's imperative I speak with her concerning the house I purchased at

1122 Church Street. If I don't hear back from her, tell her she can expect another call from me this evening."

"Yes, sir. Good day, sir."

Tom was startled by the abruptness of the disconnection. *Strike one.* He hung up. *Now what?*

Tom walked into Grady's and was met by a wall of conversation and testosterone filled laughter. He smiled at the hostess and waved her off as he pointed to where Jonathan sat in a booth along a plate glass wall. He passed pro jerseys displayed in Plexiglas frames along with photographs of famous and semi-famous sports professionals, but Tom had no idea who they were and didn't care as he registered Pink Floyd's "Money" at a tolerable volume from speakers overhead.

"Sorry I'm late," he said, sliding into the red-vinyl booth. "I had to make a few calls."

Jonathan signaled the waitress. When she left the table with their order of loaded burgers and two ales, he turned his attention to Tom.

"How's Kelly?"

"Keeping herself busy. She's showing property today."

"Good. Right now, that's probably the best thing for her."

"Yeah." Tom hesitated and met Jonathan's eyes. "I called Merideth Chandler."

"And?"

"And nothing. I couldn't get past the butler, or body guard, or whatever the hell he was."

Jonathan smirked. "Sounds dubious. Can't really blame her, though. I can only imagine how the press must've hounded her after her husband's death. Probably still are, come to think of it."

"My thoughts exactly," Tom said before taking a sip of the ale the waitress placed in front of him. "But I'm not giving up. I'll talk to her one way or another."

"Let me know if you have any trouble. Besides, I hope you know I'm going with you when you meet with her."

Tom's smile was grim. "Why not? I already have one tag-a-long."

"Kelly?"

Tom nodded and explained the situation between Kelly and the Chandlers. "She thinks their relationship might help break the ice," he said, "but I don't know. I still think the less she's involved the better."

"You have a point," Jonathan said, "but then, so does she. You have to accept the facts, Tom. She's already in this thing up to her pretty little nose. I can't see her meekly accepting a refusal."

"I know." Tom's grim expression darkened. "Have you talked to Russ Carson today?"

"No."

"Have you considered how much we're going to reveal during this meeting?"

"Of course I have," Jonathan answered. "We're going to lay it on the line. Tell him the truth."

Tom sighed and leaned back as the waitress approached with their burgers. "I was afraid of that."

Russ Carson moved behind his desk and motioned to the two red-leather wingback chairs across from him. "Please, gentlemen, sit down." The leather of his executive chair creaked expensively as he made himself comfortable.

His tall, thin frame was impeccably dressed in a custom made, dark blue pinstriped suit. Every hair on his white head was in place. His narrow face was clean shaven and he gave off a clean, spicy scent.

"I have to admit, Mr. Shear," he said, steepling his fingers in front of him, "I've been eager for this meeting. The conversation I had yesterday with Mr. Fields left me intrigued."

Tom regarded the man across from him with a wry smile. "I'm sure it did," he responded.

Carson smile was quick and closed lipped. "I can understand your reluctance at being here. It's a most unusual story." He observed Tom a moment before opening a drawer and withdrawing a small digital recorder. "I hope you don't mind if I record our discussion for future reference?"

"Actually, I do."

Tom ignored Jonathan's subtle throat clearing. A stilted silence followed and he held Carson's calculating, ice-blue gaze before the attorney relinquished by replacing the recorder and closing the drawer.

"Very well." Carson lifted a satirical brow. "Do you mind if I take a few notes?" he drawled.

Tom smiled at the attorney's mocking tone and replied smoothly, "Not at all."

Carson's expression darkened. As he picked up a pen and pulled a legal pad in front of him, he squared his gaze on Tom. "I take it everything started with the purchase of the house?"

Tom gave a slight nod and started from the beginning, intentionally leaving out two parts: his dream lover and Kelly's involvement. Even though the attorney's eyes flared several times with incredulous fascination, Tom silently applauded the man's ability to maintain a mask of indifference. Except for a few sporadic questions and the sound of his gliding pen, Carson sat stoically silent as Tom detailed the events of the past few weeks and remained so, even after he had finished.

The silence thickened and Carson cleared his throat as he looked from Tom to Jonathan and back again. "Well, gentlemen," he said, placing his pen in the exact center of the pad, "I have to admit that for once in my life, I'm speechless. It's an incredible story. If I hadn't heard it from such reliable sources, I would suspect the whole thing to be the plot of a spine-tingling novel."

Tom stiffened as his defenses fortified, but remained silent as he watched the man across from him consider the situation.

"The first thing I need to do is inspect this infamous collection of yours, Mr. Shear."

The corner of Tom's mouth lifted in a caustic smile. "And when would you like this tour?" He barely managed to hold his sarcasm at bay.

"Oh, right away, of course."

Carson's cold eyes reflected a momentary look of surprise as he entered the Rage gallery. He shifted his quizzical gaze to Tom as if to study the room's creator, then returned his attention to the paintings displayed on the walls.

"Incredible," he murmured, completing his inspection. "You are indeed a talented man, Mr. Shear. I'll have to give this matter a great deal of thought." His thin lips pursed as he took another look around the room. "I will say one thing. Mr. Fields was correct when he said the evidence is stacked against you. It'll be difficult proving you're not the serial killer the evidence makes you out to be."

Tom's apprehension mounted as his fears were brazenly put into words. "What exactly are you saying?" he asked, casting Jonathan a surreptitious glance to see his brooding frown.

"Look around you, Mr. Shear," Carson demanded, gesturing with lifted arms. "It's obvious you've freely given the police another avenue of consideration besides Theodore Chandler. The fact that they've taken advantage of your gift can only mean they're not satisfied with the outcome of their previous investigation. If this is true, and considering you're childhood abuse, they'll definitely call on you again. When that happens, you are to refuse the interview and call me immediately."

"Does this mean you're taking the case?" Jonathan asked.

It was then that Tom noticed the chill in the air and saw the faint outline of a little girl standing in the corner over Carson's shoulder. He could barely make out the pale yellow of her sundress against the dark red wall he could see behind her, through her. Her long blond hair was matted and stringy. Bruises looked like shadows across her face, shoulders, arms and legs. She stood barefoot, scowling, listening to their conversation with clenched fists. Carson's voice suddenly sounded too loud and abrasive.

"I'll have to look into a few things before I can answer that, Mr. Fields. In the meantime, I'll keep myself available for counsel."

As he turned back to Tom, Tom jerked his eyes away from little Julie Dobbs and met Carson's stare. The man's brow creased and he cast a glance behind him, but there was nothing to see. The little girl was gone.

As Carson turned back, he gave Tom a suspicious look, then crossed his arms in front of him as if just now noticing the cold. "I'm curious about something, Mr. Shear. How did the police find you? Did you advertise the collection?" he asked.

"No. In fact, I had decided not to open this particular collection to the public."

"Then why did you?"

"He was coerced into it, I'm afraid," Jonathan said with an apologetic smile, either ignoring or not noticing the slight, almost-not-there condensation of his breath. "If it hadn't been for a few friends' insistence, myself included, the collection would have remained out of the public eye."

"It seems you would've been wise to follow your instinct, Mr. Shear."

Tom bristled at the chiding, but was refrained from commenting by the resonating doorbell.

"I'm sorry, gentlemen, but I have to call an end to our discussion. I've completely forgotten about a buyer coming to collect today."

"That's quite all right," Carson replied, casting one last curious glance around the room. "We've covered enough ground for one day."

Suddenly, a woman's soft, melodious laughter filled the room.

The sound was gone in an instant, but was enough to raise the hair on Tom's body.

"What the hell was that?" Jonathan blurted. His wide eyes searched the rose scented air. "I thought the house was haunted by children. So who the hell was she?"

"I have no idea," Tom responded, refusing to say more.

"Remarkable." Carson seemed to give himself a mental shake as the resounding doorbell broke the spell.

As Tom led the way into the foyer, his attention was caught by the oscillating motion of the chandelier. Crystal prisms tinkled musically as the three men watched in stupefied fascination. The doorbell gave voice once again and the motion ceased as if by an invisible hand.

Tom took a deep breath and let it out slowly.

"You know, Tom," Jonathan said with a weak smile, "you really should look into having that fixed."

"I'll do that," he replied with a glance at Carson.

"Astonishing." The color was slowly returning to the man's face. "Maybe there is truth to your story after all, Mr. Shear."

Tom's face was expressionless as he held Carson's gaze. Without a word, he turned and opened the door.

The day was still bright and traffic moved ceaselessly southbound toward the square along Church Street, exceeding the 35 mph speed limit. But the day and traffic were subliminal to Tom as he faced the man standing on his front porch. Although this man was noticeably slimmer and still maintained a full head of thick russet hair, Tom had no doubt of his identity.

"Mr. Shear? My name's Michael Raymond."

Tom returned the man's relaxed smile, even though his own emotions rioted in his mind. "Mr. Raymond, yes, of course," he said, shaking the man's hand. "Please come in. I've been expecting you."

As he closed the door on the chilly draft that preceded the man from outside, he gestured toward the two men standing behind him. "May I introduce Mr. Jonathan Fields and Mr. Russ Carson? I'm sorry to say they were just leaving."

"Not on my account, I hope."

Carson's smile was indifferent as he shook the younger man's hand. "Not at all. Our business here is finished for the day."

"Russ Carson." Michael Raymond looked thoughtful. "Are you the Russ Carson of whom my father has spoken? His name is Craig Raymond. He owns several art galleries throughout the country and abroad. If I'm not mistaken, I think he said he was once referred to you by Theodore Chandler."

"You're Craig Raymond's son?" Carson responded in surprise. "I should have recognized the resemblance. Of course, I know your father. I helped him with a few financial matters before turning to criminal law."

"That's right. He's stated more than once that the financial world lost a very sly and clever man when you found you're true calling."

"Indeed." Carson gave a thin smile. "Well, it was very nice meeting you, Mr. Raymond. Please, give your father my regards."

"I certainly will."

Carson accepted the coat Tom retrieved from the rack beside the door. "Mr. Shear, I'll be expecting to hear from you," he said shrugging it on.

"Of course."

Jonathan took his own coat from Tom's hand then gave Michael Raymond a curt nod. "It was nice to meet you."

"The pleasure was mine, I'm sure."

"I'll talk to you later, Tom."

"Count on it."

Tom saw them out before turning back to Michael Raymond. The man was taking in his surroundings with a smile playing along his lips. He glanced at the closed French doors on either side of the foyer.

"I have your father's paintings wrapped and ready to go," Tom said, drawing the man's attention.

"Splendid. But before I rush off, might I impose on you for a tour of your gallery? I'm anxious to see what I missed the other night. After my father's ceaseless praise, I'm sorry I wasn't able to attend your showing myself."

"In that case, let me take your coat." Tom concealed the nervousness he felt with a smile. "Your father showed quite an interest in my Ice collection, so perhaps you'd like to start there."

"Actually, I've heard so much about your collection of Rage I think I'd like to start with it, if you don't mind. I've been told it's extraordinary."

Tom's smile remained fixed as he felt the familiar clenching of his stomach. "Of course," he replied hanging the man's coat. "Right this way."

He retraced his steps down the left hallway and stood aside to allow his guest to precede him as they entered the red gallery. Resisting the urge to look up at Emmy's portrait, he turned to watch Michael Raymond's reaction. Tom thought he detected a slight paling of the man's skin as his slow steps took him from painting to painting, but he was unable to read the man's thoughts beneath his controlled expression.

"Is it as you expected?" Tom asked, his voice slicing the unnerving silence. He watched Michael complete a full circle of the room as he waited for the man's reply. The only sound was the slow tapping of the man's footsteps.

"Yes and no."

For some reason, Tom felt, rather than heard, the hesitation in the other man's words.

"Yes, in the way of my father's description, but no, because I failed to realize the overwhelming effect it would have on my emotions. I am in awe, sir.

"If I may ask, how did you come upon such a concept and where did you find such worthy subjects? I feel as if I should know each of these children by name."

Tom was startled by the bluntness of Michael Raymond's questions. He couldn't help but feel they held more meaning than the mere words revealed and his smile became guarded as suspicion tinted his unease.

"I came upon the concept by a series of child abductions that occurred last year. Their familiarity is justifiable, since their pictures were distributed in every newspaper across the state."

"Tremendous," Michael intoned, apparently missing, or maybe ignoring, the connotation in Tom's voice. He cast a wistful glance around him and shook his head. "It's remarkable how you managed to capture the acute suffering they must have shared. I repeat, sir, I am in awe of your talent."

"In that case," Tom replied, stepping toward the door, drawing the man's attention away from the corner where Julie Dobbs stood once again beside her portrait, "perhaps you would care to see the rest of my collections." Her shadowed eyes were locked onto Raymond's back with drilling precision. Her small hands clenched and unclenched with menace.

Michael seemed to shiver and agreed readily, following Tom from the room. Tom continued the tour with Innocence, now on nervous alert, scanning with his eyes, dreading more surprises.

"You've done wonders with the house, by the way," Michael said as they made their way from room to room.

"You talk as if you've seen this house before."

"Oh, yes. Many times, in fact. I use to play here as a boy."

"Really," Tom said, veiling his shock.

"Indeed. Jacob Chandler and I used to be great friends when the Chandlers resided here." Mirth danced in his cobalt eyes as he chuckled under his breath. "We used to imagine the place being haunted."

Tom swallowed past the restriction in his throat and pasted an expression of humor on his face. "Is that right?" he asked, then let the man talk.

"Of course, we never told anyone of being tucked in at night by a woman smelling of roses whom we couldn't see. Who would have believed us? You know how fanciful children can be. Besides, Jacob had an image to uphold. He *was* Theodore Chandler's son. I was heartbroken by the news of his death a few years back. A swimming accident of some sort at Lake Lanier. Of course, his parents were devastated. He was their only child."

"That's terrible," Tom replied. "I had no idea. It must be doubly difficult for Mrs. Chandler since the unfortunate death of her husband."

"Oh, I'm sure. Poor woman. Nasty business, that was. I still can't believe Theodore Chandler was the kind of person who could do such a thing. I knew the man fairly well, and I've just failed to understand how such a person could change so drastically."

Michael paused as his face took on a look of revelation.

"I say, your Rage collection wouldn't by any chance be connected with the Theodore Chandler incident, would it?"

Tom hesitated before replying. "It has a connection, yes."

"Am I wrong in assuming the concept was conceived in this house where the Chandler tragedy took place?"

"That's right," Tom answered, his paranoia and suspicions growing.

Michael's gaze held him in speculation and his murmured "Fascinating" made Tom's skin crawl. Tom smiled congenially and turned away, eager to end the tour before further inquiry could be made.

He led the way into the last gallery room and watched Michael Raymond tour the dimensions of the room of Ice. After scrutinizing each painting with an experienced eye, Michael took in the interior of the room and smiled with pleasure.

"I have to repeat, Mr. Shear, I am in awe of your talent. Even the furnishings of your gallery reveal an artist's touch. I was especially impressed with the bean-bag chairs and throw-pillows in the gallery of Innocence. The décor matches the themes of your work to perfection. It sets the different moods very cleverly indeed.

"And keeping the temperature lowered helps preserve the art as well. Smart, very smart," Raymond replied, then seemed to reconsider. "On the other hand, you might consider raising it up a notch, especially in the Rage gallery, for your clientele's comfort, you know. While I was there, I could practically see my breath."

"I'll look into it." Tom wasn't sure whether he should be amused or alarmed. He decided to ignore it. "I'm glad you approve of my work, Mr. Raymond," he said. "A man of your status could be very helpful to a man in my position."

"Quite right," Michael agreed. "And I plan to be just that. After seeing for myself the talent you have to offer, I feel it necessary for our establishment to include your name in our list of distinguished artists. Of course, I'll need to consult my father on an appropriate proposal, but I see no obstacles standing in the way of a successful arrangement."

"I'm pleased to hear that."

"You'll be hearing from us in the next few days, I'm sure. My father mentioned discussing business over dinner, so be expecting an invitation."

"I'll be sure to accept."

"Splendid. Now, I'm afraid to say I must be off. I've already lingered longer than I expected. Have you by any chance a business card?"

"Of course," Tom said, leading the way out of the room. "They're on the table in the foyer. Take one for your father, as well. We'll gather his purchase on the way out."

"One moment." Michael Raymond stopped and cocked his head, listening. "We are alone in the house, are we not?"

"Yes, we are." The hair along Tom's neck began to rise as the familiar scent grew stronger. He could barely detect the tinkle of connecting crystal as the chandelier in the foyer began to sway.

"Do you not hear that?" Michael's voice took on a note of urgency. His eyes flared as a woman's voice chuckled with an ominous edge, then began humming the soothing melody of a child's lullaby that echoed softly through the gallery.

———·(())·———

Tom sat hunched over on the sofa in his upstairs den with his elbows on his knees and waited as another ring sounded in his ear. Suddenly, the same male voice he had spoken with earlier came through the receiver.

"Chandler residence."

Tom straightened his spine. "Hello. My name is Thomas Shear. I believe we spoke earlier this afternoon."

"Yes, sir." The voice was cool and emotionless.

"I need to speak to Mrs. Chandler. Is she in?"

"Yes, she's in, sir. But I don't believe she's receiving calls."

"Would you mind asking her, please? I wouldn't be bothering her if it wasn't important." Tom heard the man pause with indecision.

"Hold the line, please."

"Thank you." Tom heard a soft thump followed by silence and waited with building impatience.

"I'm sorry, sir. Mrs. Chandler is unable to take your call."

Tom's heart leapt at the man's abrupt reply. He expelled a sigh of frustration.

"Would you please tell Mrs. Chandler it's imperative that I speak with her and to expect another call from me tomorrow?"

"I'll make sure she receives your message."

"Thank you."

Tom hung up before the disconnecting click. With a deep sigh, he stood up and put on his leather jacket. He switched on one of the table lamps flanking the sofa, then headed for the door.

"I'm not giving up, Mrs. Chandler," he promised under his breath. "You'll be hearing from me again. And again and again if necessary." He descended the back stairs, flipped on the light over the stove as he passed through the kitchen, set the alarm, and closed the back door behind him.

# CHAPTER NINETEEN

The drive was excruciating. As he made his way up Shallow-ford Road toward Roswell, his mind whirled with the familiar faces that had stared down at him from the walls of the Shear Gallery. *The Shear Gallery. Now, that was a point to ponder.* He couldn't believe it. *They were all there. Every damned, last one of them. Even she was there.* The scent of her perfume, along with the sound of her voice, had almost been his undoing. *How could this happen?*

He thought he had covered his tracks. Chandler had been the perfect scapegoat. He had given the police enough evidence against Theodore Chandler to leave no doubt and the case had been closed.

*Damn Thomas Shear and his insufferable paintings. Does he realize the extent of damage those paintings are going to cause? If he doesn't now, he soon will. The man's harder to read than a closed book, but anyone could see he's not stupid. The evidence hanging on his walls is staggering. He's given a detective like Mark Winward everything he needs to re-open the investigation. That had to be the case. Why else would Shear be forced to consult with lawyers?*

The thought of Winward brought a sneer to his lips. He was like a cur sniffing out a bitch in heat during the investigation. He'd searched every cesspool in the city for the one responsible.

*But he didn't find me, did he?* His thoughts were taunting. *And he won't, either. Thanks to Thomas Shear.*

His quiet chuckle grew until it became almost maniacal in the confines of the car. The slamming of his brakes and blare of his horn as another vehicle brashly pulled out in front of him severed his laughter like a razor.

"Stupid bitch," he yelled, but of course the slanderous curse went unheard as the other car sped away.

"Women," he muttered as if tasting something foul. "They're all bitches. Every last one of them.

"They all look so innocent when they're little girls," he sneered, bringing his car back up to speed. "Cunning, manipulating, backstabbing, evil little girls that grow up to be cunning, manipulating, backstabbing, evil bitches! They make you love them then throw you away like garbage when something better comes along. They're nothing but boils on the ass of the world. Swollen, runny, disgusting boils. They should all be terminated at birth. Every last, slutting one of them." Laughter rumbled in his chest. "I started terminating a long time ago. And thanks to lucky Mr. Shear, it won't be long until I can continue the satisfying process."

A face floated across his mind's eye and his lips twisted in a nasty caricature of a smile. "Thanks, mother," he slurred, "for giving me such a satisfying goal in life."

He saw the beckoning neon of a bar sign and pulled into the parking lot. He needed time to think. The day had been so overwhelming that he needed to come to terms with what to do next.

*Thomas Shear is the key. There's no doubt about that. All the police need is a little nudge and Shear's house of gold will crumble around his ears.*

His grin widened as he stepped into the gloom of the smoke-filled bar and AC/DC met him at the door ringing "Hells Bells".

# CHAPTER TWENTY

Tom stood motionless at the bottom of the attic stairs. He looked up into the gloom and watched the door at the top swing open to reveal a shaft of light. Detecting the faint sound of a rhythmic creak emanating from the glare, he felt light-headed with the hypnotic effect it had on his mind.

As the sound grew louder with each pause in its rhythmic pattern, Tom felt himself being drawn further into the light under its entrancing influence. Its soothing cadence lured him up until he stood in the open doorway, bathing in the welcoming feel of the glow. He could feel his body begin to sway in perfect rhythm.

"No! You've got to run! Go back!"

Emmy's voice shrieked, jerking him from his hypnotic state. Tom's senses came alive and his heart pounded. The once enchanting light became oppressive, and the air was squeezed from his lungs by its crushing weight. Forced to his knees, he cried out in desperation.

"Emmy!"

The weight lifted from his body. Tom raised his head and saw nothing but the gloom of shadows surrounding him. Confusion muffled his mind as he rose to his feet and stared at the tiny shafts of light filtering through the shuttered windows.

Screeching hinges made him whirl and he could only watch as the attic door slammed shut. Hearing the rhythmic creaking resume,

Tom turned back and the mutilated body he suddenly saw hanging from the rafters made his blood run cold. Bulging, sightless eyes seemed to stare down at him in warning, but he could only stand in horrified silence as the bloodied hands dangling by its sides twitched.

Then, the tall silhouette of a man walked from behind the corpse and stood with obvious pleasure in front of it. Tom watched the assailant raise his featureless face to admire the desecrated body and felt weak with fear as the man's shoulders began to shake with laughter.

"I'm coming for you next, Tom."

The ominous words sent icy rivulets through Tom's veins. He could do nothing but stare at the expanse of the man's shoulders as the silhouette gained solidity. The menacing form threw back his head and cackled with blood-curdling laughter.

"You're next, Tom!"

With insane laughter ringing in his ears, Tom flung himself at the door and cried out in horror as the knob came loose in his hands.

Tom jerked awake, opened his eyes, and let go a startled, harsh yell. A luminous figure loomed over him, its face only inches from his. Its bulging eyes, reddened by hemorrhage, pierced him. Its swollen lips moved without sound. The stench of dead breath made him gag before the specter vanished and restraints encircled Tom's shoulders. Another harsh yell was torn from his throat as he thrashed against the arms holding him. He searched the shadows of the moon-lit room until the sound of Kelly's crooning voice penetrated his mind and reasserted reality.

"Tom, it's all right. I'm here. You're awake now."

"It was so real," he whispered, gathering her in his trembling arms. His heartbeat began to slow and he felt his tense muscles relaxing beneath her stroking fingers.

"Do you want to talk about it?" she asked.

"No. Not right now," he said, pulling from her embrace. "I have to go." He knew who the specter was. He was sure of it. Theodore Chandler was reaching out.

"What do you mean 'you have to go'?"

Tom rose from the bed to grope through the clothes that had been discarded on the floor. "There's something I have to do."

"What?"

When he failed to respond, Kelly got out of bed and turned on the bedside lamp. "It's three in the morning. What's so important that it can't wait a few more hours?"

By this time, Tom was dressed and pulling on his shoes. "I have to go home. I think Emmy's trying to tell me something."

"I'm coming with you."

"No, you're not, sweetheart. You're staying here. I'll call you as soon as I can."

"If you think I'm going to sit here and wait for the phone to ring, you're crazy, Tom." She picked her sweater up off the floor. "I'm coming with you." Kelly pulled the sweater on over her head and covered her naked breasts, daring him to refuse.

"Kelly, listen to me," he said, lowering her to the bed. "This is something I have to do alone. Besides, I want you where I know you'll be safe. The gallery is the last place you need to be."

"What's so important that you have to go back there now?" she asked, her voice and eyes pleading as she looked up at him.

"I have to paint."

———— «(O)» ————

"Where have you been?"

Tom squinted into the late afternoon sunlight and saw Jonathan standing on the porch. He motioned him inside.

"Marsha said you weren't in class yesterday and that you'd cleared today's schedule."

"That's right," he said, ignoring Jonathan's critical inspection as he took in Tom's worn jeans and t-shirt that were smeared with different shades of paint and looked like they'd been slept in. Dark stubble covered his jaws and chin. His eyes felt bruised and sunken. His hair was tousled, and it was obvious why as he ran his fingers through its ebony strands for what must have been the hundredth time.

"I've been painting."

"You need to have a phone installed up there. The least you could do is to keep your cell handy."

"Why?"

"Why? Because I've been trying to call for the past two days, buddy, that's why."

"Sorry."

Jonathan looked at Tom and shook his head. "You've been painting, huh?"

"Yeah."

"Not another missing child, I hope."

"No. Come on. You can see for yourself."

Tom led the way up to his studio and stood back to let Jonathan pass in front of him. The room was cavernous and their footsteps sounded hollow on the raw planks of the floor. Thick rafters and wall studs were exposed making one think he stood in the torso of the house where the skeletal bones of its ribcage surrounded him. Six dormer windows, four on the front side of the house and two on the back, did what they could to let in light, but the main source came from five large skylights overhead. A sink had been installed and a table stood next to it with an array of artist tools. A portable stereo and a rack of CD's sat on another table beside a folding director's chair. Dozens of past paintings leaned together in rows. A few left-over unpacked boxes were stacked along the far back wall. The air smelled of turpentine, oil-based paint, and aged, dusty wood.

Tom was silent as Jonathan stepped onto the drop-cloth and perused the three paintings perched on easels in the center of the room.

"Where did these come from?" Jonathan's voice sounded strained.

"From a nightmare."

Tom walked over and stood at Jonathan's shoulder. He looked at the painting in front of them and felt his frustration rise up once more.

The distorted face of the hanging corpse was clearly that of Theodore Chandler. Whether Jonathan recognized the resemblance, he couldn't tell.

His eyes shifted to the dark silhouette of the assailant standing by the corpse's side. Its dark face was raised and Tom could almost hear its mocking laughter. A ray of light shone down on them both, illuminating the scene with glowing reverence.

"My God. Is this you?"

"Yes," Tom answered, shifting his gaze to the next painting.

The assailant stood by the swinging corpse and pointed a condemning finger at Tom's retreating likeness. The fear expressed on the miniature's face as it glanced over its shoulder was startling and Tom's chest constricted with the feelings it evoked.

Tom wrenched his eyes away as Jonathan moved to the next painting. This was a portrait of the assailant wrapped in silhouetted darkness. The face was ominously blank.

"I can see you've been busy," Jonathan said, glancing at Tom over his shoulder. "When did this particular nightmare occur?"

"A couple of nights ago."

"No wonder you haven't been sleeping well. With dreams like these, it's amazing you sleep at all."

Tom snorted and turned away. "The thing is, I feel like I should know him. The corpse is obviously Theodore Chandler. But I'm not sure of the assailant."

"Theodore Chandler?" Startled, Jonathan looked back at the first painting. "How do you know?"

"Because of the articles I read the other day. His picture was plastered all over the front page."

Jonathan's incredulous gaze riveted to Tom. "Do you realize what you're saying?"

"Perfectly."

Jonathan shook his head. "Must I remind you that a confession was found on the scene? Chandler's confession, I might add."

"Consider this," Tom said. "What if Chandler was a convenience? All the assailant would've had to do is stage a suicide and plant a confession. It would've been a gamble, but consider the publicity pressure surrounding the case. He would've had to rely on the police being in such a state of frenzy they would have jumped on anything plausible. And they did. All accept one, that is."

"Winward."

"Winward," Tom concurred with a slow nod.

"Intriguing." Jonathan studied the dark portrait of the assailant. "And you feel like you should know him?"

"Yes." Once again, Tom ran his fingers through his hair. "The voice I heard in my dream was familiar in some obscene way. And the build of the man is familiar. I just can't place it. I've tried to picture the scene as it must have happened." He looked up at the rafter above his head. "From the position of the body in my dream, it must have hung from there. I can imagine how the assailant walked around the corpse with admiring satisfaction and my stomach turns with the smug expression he must've had on his face. I can even hear his laughter, a high-pitched, cackling, insane sound." Tom grimaced at his maddening inefficacy. "The scene is so clear in my mind; everything except his damn face."

Jonathan raised his eyes to the rafter, then shuddered and turned away. "Under the circumstances, I can't see how you can work up here," he said with a frown. "Just thinking about it gives me the creeps."

Tom shrugged.

"What's this?" Jonathan walked over and lifted the cover from a painting that stood alone in the corner. "Pretty," he said, admiring the woman it portrayed. Her long, dark wavy hair was parted slightly off center and hung loose over one bare shoulder. The thin ribbon that pulled the neck of the white peasant blouse closed had been left undone to reveal the alluring flesh of her slender throat and chest and dipped low to entice the observer with the swell of firm, full breasts. Whiskey colored eyes sparkled with seductive mischief. "Who is she?"

"I don't know. But I think she's the woman we heard the other day. She performed for Michael Raymond as well."

"That's what the cold means, that a spirit's present?" Jonathan asked.

"I wondered if you noticed the chill. But the woman didn't bring the cold. Julie Dobbs did. She stood in the corner and listened to our conversation with Carson. And she looked pissed. I think the cold comes when they're upset or angry. Apparently, she didn't like what she was hearing. It was the same thing with Michael Raymond when he was glibly talking about how their pain and suffering affected him."

"I saw your distraction and caught a glimpse of her before she disappeared, just as Carson turned to look over his shoulder."

"Thanks for keeping a cool head," Tom said with a smirk.

"Just following your lead, buddy. But I do have to admit I had to work at being nonchalant. I almost peed myself." Jonathan's smile was self-deprecating as he shook his head. "I swear, Tom. I don't see how you can stay here. When I heard that woman's voice, every hair on my body came to attention. You must have the balls of a rhino."

"I admit it was startling, but she wasn't exactly new to me. She'd made her presence known before."

Jonathan gave Tom a sidelong glance then looked back at the portrait leaning against the wall. "She is a luscious looking woman. Hot." He looked back at Tom and seemed to bite off whatever he was going to say next. He cleared his throat. "I'm not even going to ask."

Tom's smile was sardonic. "Good. Come on. We'll go down to the den and you can tell me why you've been trying to get in touch with me."

Jonathan stood still, staring at the portrait. "Is she connected with what's going on?"

"I don't know."

"What? You think she's just hanging out watching the show?"

"I don't know," Tom repeated, turning for the stairs. "But I do think she wants help for the little girls."

"Huh, another baffling twist."

"Tell me about it."

"You know," Jonathan said, descending the narrow stairs, "if I were you, I don't think I'd show those paintings to just anyone. I mean, how would you explain knowing the details of a murder scene unless you'd actually been there? It would probably raise more questions than you could reasonably answer."

"I know. I've already thought of that."

They entered the den and Tom walked to the bar to pour them both a drink. Jonathan pulled off his coat and sat back on the sofa crossing one silk clad ankle over one tailored knee.

"Now," Tom said, handing Jonathan a glass. "What did you want to see me about?" He remained standing.

"I wanted to know if you'd had any luck with Merideth Chandler."

"No. I tried phoning yesterday, but I got the same runaround. I guess I'm going to have to go and knock on the woman's door. Which is probably what I should've done in the first place," he said gesturing with his glass before taking a drink.

"Let me try getting through before you do that. Since I'm an attorney, maybe I'll have better luck."

Tom's gaze narrowed. "Why? What's happened?"

"My secretary, Marilyn, told me a couple of detectives named Winward and Hayes stopped by to pay me a visit today. Luckily, I was out chasing you down."

"Tom's brow creased as he swirled his drink. "I'm not surprised. You know as well as I do it was inevitable."

"I'll have to talk to them," Jonathan stated.

"Of course. Just put on that lawyer face of yours and answer their questions. They can't do anything to you." Even though Tom's voice was confident, he knew if Winward and Hayes found out Jonathan knew more than he was willing to tell, he could be considered an accomplice. It could mean disbarment. Or worse.

"I'm sorry I got you into this mess, Jonathan," he said, shaking his head. "I should never have told you."

"You know I wouldn't have had it any other way. I can take care of myself."

"You have to tell them the truth, you know." Tom looked his friend in the eye. "I don't want you lying to cover my ass. You know what it would mean if you were found out."

"I know. But if they don't ask--" Jonathan shrugged his shoulders.

The phone rang, and the two men exchanged looks before Tom reached for the receiver.

"Hello?"

"Tom? Marsha. Would Jonathan be there, by any chance? I tried his cell but it sent me straight to voicemail."

"Hey, Marsha. Yeah, he's right here."

Tom's mouth quirked in a humorless grin as he met Jonathan's gaze. "Brace yourself," he warned, watching Jonathan's scowl darken as he pressed the receiver to his ear.

"Hey, babe. What's up?" Jonathan looked at Tom as he listened.

"What did he ask you?" he asked and grew silent, still holding Tom's gaze. "What did you tell him?" After a moment, Jonathan shook his head as if Marsha could see him. "Don't worry about it. You did fine." He shook his head again. "No, I can't tell you what's going on right now. I'll have to talk to you later." Jonathan cast Tom a disquieted look as he ended the call and put down the receiver.

"Let me guess," Tom said, turning toward the frost-etched window. "Winward and Hayes just left Marsha's office."

"Yeah, but just Winward. Hayes wasn't with him." Jonathan took a long pull from his drink. "She said he asked general questions, at first. How she knew you. How long she had known you. How long you'd lived in the house. Where you lived before moving in. That sort of thing. Then he got more specific and started asking about the Rage collection. Thank heaven she didn't know anything. She couldn't tell him anything besides the obvious. She said, at first, she was only puzzled by the interview. But when he started asking about your moods and how you had seemed lately, she got downright worried."

"What did she tell him?"

"She told him you were acting normally. A little preoccupied maybe, but that that was understandable considering the strain you've been under with the opening of your gallery and handling prospective buyers while maintaining your scheduled classes."

Tom shook his head and sighed. "What a mess. This thing's getting more complicated by the minute."

"You know I'm going to have to do some explaining when I get home tonight."

"I know."

Tom turned from the window. He dropped to the sofa and leaned his head back. He closed his eyes and began massaging his temples to ease the tension.

"We'll have to tell Russ what's going on," Jonathan said. "He'll need to be kept informed. Are you going to be home tonight? He'll probably want to talk to you."

"No. I've got a business dinner with Craig Raymond tonight at seven o'clock to discuss featuring some of my work in his galleries. I'm not sure when I'll be home."

"Okay. I'll talk to Russ and one of us will give you a call in the morning. In the meantime, I have to go," he said, pulling on his coat. "I've got a stack of paperwork on my desk a mile high."

He paused in the doorway and cast Tom an appraising look. "Why don't you try to get some sleep? You look like hell."

# CHAPTER TWENTY-ONE

In the city of Buckhead, a community skirting Atlanta and known for its nightlife entertainment, restaurants, artisan exhibits and museums, was the Magnolia House Restaurant. The centuries-old mansion had been transformed into an oasis of fine dining. Glowing candlelight created an air of privacy as the hum of quiet conversation mingled with the clinks of china and the chimes of crystal resonating through the large, open rooms. Dimmed crystal chandeliers hung suspended from fourteen foot ceilings. Tables were draped in white linen. Lavender orchids in crystal bud vases adorned each table next to the glowing candles. Soft jazz drifted through the rooms. Delectable aromas created by five-star chefs mingled with the scents of candle wax, perfumes, and colognes.

Tom followed the maitre d' into the left front parlor room where his hosts sat waiting and watched Craig and Michael Raymond rise from their seats at his approach. Dressed similarly in dark, pen-stripe suits, the two men held an uncanny resemblance. The only noticeable differences were the robust thickening of Craig Raymond's midriff and his rapidly thinning gray hair. Michael Raymond had a tall, lean frame. His reddish-brown mane was thick and well-kept. They each had the characteristics of cobalt eyes, straight and narrow Norman noses, and thin lipped mouths that seemed to lift at one corner with an indulgent hint of mockery.

"Ah, Mr. Shear," Craig Raymond greeted, offering his hand, "so glad you could make it."

"It's my pleasure," Tom responded, shaking Michael's hand in turn. His own suit of dove gray wool contrasted boldly with the other men's dark dress. With his thick raven hair and dark, chiseled features, he cut a striking, handsome figure. "I hope I haven't kept you waiting."

"No, no. Not at all. We've only just arrived ourselves," Raymond declared, taking his seat. "Would you like a drink?"

Tom voiced his preference to the hovering waiter.

"I hope you don't mind my joining the party, Mr. Shear." A congenial smile graced Michael's lips. "But since our talk the other day and seeing your work first hand, my interest in the business transpiring between you and my father has grown."

"I'm flattered, Mr. Raymond. Why should I mind?"

"Capital." Michael's smile widened. "I must also apologize for my hasty departure. I'm afraid the talk we had of childhood fancies had a disarming effect. I'm sorry to say I let my imagination run away with me."

"Think nothing of it," Tom replied.

"What's this?" Craig Raymond asked, looking from Tom to Michael.

"It's nothing of consequence, Father. It's only being inside Mr. Shear's gallery brought back a few forgotten memories."

"Indeed," Raymond interjected with a chuckle. "As I recall, Mr. Shear and I had a discussion along those same lines. It would appear your gallery affects people in more than the usual way, Mr. Shear."

"But shouldn't that be a goal for any artist?" Tom countered as the waiter placed his bourbon on the rocks in front of him.

"It should be, yes," Raymond answered. "But you, my friend, have mastered the concept. As a matter of fact, Michael seems to be quite taken with your Rage collection, Mr. Shear. Even more so than I, it would seem."

Tom's brow rose with a mixture of surprise and amusement. "That's hard to believe. You drove a pretty hard bargain yourself."

"But to no avail," Raymond admitted. "Have you by any chance reconsidered?"

"No. I'm afraid not," Tom answered with the hint of a smile.

"Would it make any difference that, with deep consideration and a little arm twisting from Michael, I've decided to raise my offer?"

Tom gave a low laugh at the man's audacity. The sound was deep-throated and rich. "Like I said before, you drive a hard bargain. But the answer is still no."

Craig Raymond eyed Tom. "I can't decide whether you're just being stubborn, Mr. Shear, or very shrewd. You're tactics could very well be considered clever. Very clever, indeed."

Tom returned the man's probing gaze. The corner of his mouth lifted at Raymond's insinuation. "You're certainly entitled to your opinion, sir."

"Indeed." The older man seemed to be fighting a smile. "Let's order dinner, shall we?" He shifted a quick glance at Tom before opening his menu. "Only if you're ready, of course."

"Certainly."

After they placed their order, Raymond wasted no time in broaching the subject of business. Tom listened, maintaining a mask of indifference he had perfected at a very early age.

"Mr. Shear, I think you're aware of our profound interest in your work. It is my intent, with your permission, of course, to feature several pieces of each of your themes in exactly the same way you have presented them in your own gallery. The settings you've created are superb. I was very impressed. And that means the art lovers of the world will most certainly be impressed as well. It would mean a phenomenal amount of recognition. But let me stress the point of what I just said to waylay any misunderstandings. When I said several pieces of each of your themes, I was also including several pieces of the Rage collection. The publicity would be astronomical from those particular pieces alone."

"Father, you can't be serious," Michael spouted, revealing as much surprise as Tom kept hidden. "What I mean is…well…" His face flushed above his tight collar. "What I meant to say is, Mr. Shear has already stated his opinion of selling the Rage collection and I think we should honor his decision. To suggest dividing the collection just to own a few pieces would be close to sacrilege, to which I'm sure Mr. Shear will undoubtedly agree."

Craig Raymond turned a baleful eye on his son. "I wasn't suggesting our buying a few pieces of the collection, Michael. Of course, it would be beyond consideration to split such work. All I'm suggesting is for Mr. Shear to allow part of the collection to be shown in one of our choice galleries."

Tom kept his eyes discreetly lowered as Michael's lips tightened and the flush on his face deepened. Turning his attention back to Tom, Raymond missed his son's malevolent stare as he picked up his drink to wash down the bitter humiliation his father had caused.

"Of course, I wasn't implying what my son just suggested, Mr. Shear. My main objective is only to proudly present what you've created to gain the publicity and recognition it deserves. I'm sure a man of your intelligence and skill can appreciate that. And naturally, considering the circumstances, I would also hold the exclusive for purchasing the entire collection when the time comes for you to sell."

Raymond watched casually for Tom's reaction. When none came, he continued, withdrawing a contract from the briefcase beside his chair.

"Now, since the particulars have been discussed and agreed upon, I see no reason why we shouldn't conclude our business by signing the contract I took upon myself to bring and be done with it. Dinner should be along any moment and I do hate conducting business over anything as delectable as Beef Wellington. Bad for digestion. Don't you agree, Mr. Shear?"

"Excuse me, sir," Tom said, ignoring the papers Craig Raymond held out to him. "But our business is far from being discussed or agreed upon."

"Oh?" Raymond feigned surprise, raising his salt and pepper brows. "Is there something you would like to add?"

"As a matter of fact, there is," Tom said, returning Raymond's stare. His calm exterior concealed his rising anger. "First of all, I'm not an adolescent who can be bullied into a situation against his wishes. Secondly, the Rage collection is mine to decide whether it should or should not be exhibited. And at this time, my decision is to keep the entire collection at my own gallery to exhibit when and however often I like.

"So therefore, gentlemen, if the terms of our agreement have to include the Rage collection, I'm afraid we have nothing further to discuss. If my other work hasn't enough merit on its own to establish a business relationship between us, then I apologize for wasting your time."

Tom forced a gracious smile and gathered his napkin from his lap. Laying it on the table, he looked from one speechless man to the next and gave each a polite nod.

"Gentlemen, I want to thank you for your hospitality." He began to rise. "Come by the gallery anytime. My door will always be open to you."

"Mr. Shear, please. Let's not be hasty," Raymond protested with a modest chuckle. His heated blush began to recede. "Surely, an arrangement can be made."

"Of course your other work has merit, Mr. Shear," Michael interjected, enjoying the sight of his father's discomfort. The hostile glance he received only seemed to heighten his mirth. "I'm sure my father never meant to imply otherwise."

"Forgive my insensitivity, Mr. Shear," Raymond stated, mastering his emotions. "I was aware of your attachment to the Rage collection, but apparently I was unaware of exactly how deep those attachments run. Of course, I'm interested in your other work. Very interested, in fact. I'm sure arrangements can be made which will sufficiently satisfy your needs as well as my own."

He paused to eye the waiter approaching their table.

"But first, let's enjoy our dinner, shall we? We can resume business over coffee later."

"An excellent idea." Michael picked up a claw of his steamed lobster. "I was surprised to meet Russ Carson at your gallery the other day, Mr. Shear. I didn't realize he was an art connoisseur."

"Russ Carson," Raymond exclaimed. "I've known Russ for years. I was unaware he was an acquaintance of yours, Mr. Shear."

"We were introduced through a mutual friend," Tom responded with a nonchalant shrug, severing a slice of perfectly prepared prime rib.

"The other man present was a lawyer as well, wasn't he?" Michael asked casually. His brow creased in thought. "I'm ashamed to admit his name escapes me at the moment."

Tom wondered how the man knew Jonathan's profession. It wasn't mentioned during the introductions before the two attorneys left the gallery that day. His initial reaction of suspicion toward the man grew.

"Jonathan Fields." Tom's expression cloaked his growing apprehension. "And yes, he's an attorney, also."

"Fascinating. Is he a specialist in criminal law, as well?"

"No. His specialty is domestic disputes."

"Fascinating."

Tom shrugged again and turned his attention to Craig Raymond, ignoring the sharp look he received from Michael for his subtle dismissal.

"You said you'd known Mr. Carson for years. Is he a close friend of yours?"

"I'm not sure you would exactly call us close," Raymond replied. "I haven't seen Russ in years. No, that's not quite true," he corrected himself, raising his napkin to his lips. "The last time I saw Russ was at a funeral we both attended several months ago. But we spoke very little. It wasn't exactly the right atmosphere for a jovial reunion."

Tom felt the hair rise on his forearms and the back of his neck. "No. I shouldn't think so."

"I remember that miserable day," Michael said with a distasteful turn of his lips. "It rained in sheets. Actually, it was quite befitting considering the circumstances surrounding Chandler's death."

"Quite," Raymond agreed, forking a bite of Beef Wellington as he turned to Tom. "I'd known Theodore for a long time. We met in college. In fact, he's the one who introduced me to Russ." Raymond lifted the bite of food to his mouth, chewed, and swallowed before continuing.

"Russ handled the legalities concerning my first gallery. And later on, as business flourished, he helped with my expansions. Of course, this was before he turned to criminal law."

"You might consider giving Mr. Carson a call, Father. It might not be wise to let such a friendship fall by the wayside." Michael looked at Tom with an innocent eye. "Wouldn't you agree, Mr. Shear?"

"My opinion doesn't matter. The decision is your father's," Tom answered, paying close attention to his plate.

"For once, I agree with you, Michael," Raymond said, studiously watching his son. "I'll give the matter some thought." He turned his speculating gaze back to Tom. "But right now, I want to know more about you, Mr. Shear."

"Such as?"

Raymond smiled at Tom's evasiveness. "I recognize a Southern-bred gentleman when I meet one. Have you always lived in the South?"

Tom returned Raymond's wry smile. "Yes. I was born and raised in the small town of Kingston. My grandfather was a farmer and my parents worked in the mills."

"Have you traveled?"

"A bit."

"And what about your artistic talents? How did they evolve?"

Tom digested the inquiry with calculated patience as an indulgent smile formed his lips. "From a vivid imagination and years of practice," he replied.

He was saved from further explanations by the appearance of the waiter. During dessert and coffee, business was resumed and a satisfactory deal was made. No mention of the Rage collection was offered.

"I'll have the contracts drawn up and deliver them personally," Raymond stated, causing the ice cubes in his drained water glass to tinkle as he placed it on the table.

"That's not necessary," Tom said. "I'd be happy to meet with you at your convenience."

"Nonsense. Besides, it'll give me another chance to look over your work and decide which pieces to exhibit."

"Very well," Tom agreed. "When shall I expect you?"

"It shouldn't take more than a couple of days to have the papers drawn. Don't worry. I'll be in touch very soon."

"Oh, I'm not worried, Mr. Raymond," Tom replied. "I just like to know what to expect."

Michael released a smug laugh. "A sentiment I agree with, Mr. Shear."

"Well, gentlemen, it would seem our business is complete." Tom rose from his seat. The two Raymonds pushed away from the table and stood as if on cue. "I want to thank you both for dinner. It was exquisite."

"My pleasure, Mr. Shear," Raymond said, accepting Tom's hand. "I'll admit it's been entertaining."

"Yes. Quite entertaining," Michael replied with a smile.

Tom could not dismiss Michael's smile and knew the man's keen gaze followed him out.

# CHAPTER TWENTY-TWO

The squad room was alive with a cacophony of noise and motion. Telephones rang, papers rustled, file drawers opened and closed while detectives and staff tapped on keyboards. Voices, some loud, others engaged in mumbled conversations, competed with the chattering hum of fax machines and printers. Hayes's deep baritone rumbled across the adjoining desks as he faced Winward with the phone pressed against his ear, pen in hand, filling out a report form.

Winward looked up from the file on his desk as the glass doors of the squad room flew open. He watched as Ronny Keppler, a departmental snitch, also known as Cracker—a nickname derived from his love of crack cocaine—was hauled in for questioning by Detective Jack Morrison.

"I already tolt ya, man," Keppler whined. His dark skin glistened with nervous perspiration as Morrison led him to the desk across the isle from Winward. "I don't know nothin'. I wuten even dere when dat ho was kilt."

"That's not what we heard, Cracker," Morrison said. "We've got eyewitnesses who said you were there smokin' crack. They also said you were coming on pretty strong with the lady."

Keppler's jaundiced eyes glinted with defiance as he straightened his bony spine. "Maybe I was dere. But I neva kilt no ho, man. I was dere foe da drugs. Dat's all. If anybody says differnt, they's lyin'."

"Okay, Cracker. Just relax and have a seat. I've a feeling it's going to be a long day." Morrison gave him a gentle push, causing his skeletal frame to collapse into a chair.

"Hey, Winward."

Cracker's voice was beginning to shake with a mixture of fear and the need of his addiction. Winward looked up from his file on Thomas Shear and returned the sweating man's darting gaze.

"Tell 'im, man. Tell 'm I neva kilt no ho. You've knowd me foe a long time, Winward. Tell 'm I don't have nothin' like dat in me. He'll believe you, man."

"Can't do it, Cracker." Winward laced his fingers behind his head. "For one thing, I wasn't there. And for another, it's not my case."

Ignoring obscenities insulting certain members of his family, Winward returned his gaze to the file open on his desk. It was frustratingly thin. He had read its scanty contents over and over hoping to find something he might have missed the time before. Name, social security number, date of birth, names of mother and father, previous addresses since childhood. Mother – deceased. Father's whereabouts – unknown. Raised by grandparents since age twelve. Six years of college – mastering in both business and creative arts.

*No prior record whatsoever. Not even a damn parking ticket. According to this, Thomas Shear's practically a saint.*

"There's got to be a connection," he murmured. "It's here. It's got to be."

"Are you Detective Winward?"

Winward looked up to see a wiry young man with an acne-blotched face. With a sigh, he pushed the file away and leaned back in his chair.

"Yeah. I'm Winward."

"Got a package for you. Sign here." The youth held out a clipboard and pen.

Winward signed his name and looked at the envelope the courier dropped on the desk. "Who's it from?"

The youth smirked. "How would I know?" He retrieved his clipboard and turned for the door. "Have a nice day, officer."

Winward scowled at the squad room door as it swung closed. "Asshole," he muttered, tearing open the envelope. He pulled out a single piece of paper and read, "111 Redding Road, Kingston."

His scowl deepened as he fingered the gold-embossed Shear Gallery business card that had fallen from the envelope onto the file lying open on his desk. Comparing the address he had just received with one listed in the file, Winward jumped to his feet.

"Hey, kid," he shouted, slamming through the squad room's glass door. "Wait up!"

The courier quickened his pace and Winward soon lost sight of him as the kid turned into a corridor leading to the main entrance. Pushing his way past officers escorting a couple of thugs in handcuffs, Winward made his way out the door and onto the street.

"Damn," he swore.

A swift glance in all directions confirmed his fear. The courier had vanished.

⸺ ((◉)) ⸺

The day was crisp and bright. Wispy clouds floated over the distant panoramic view of Atlanta seen from his office window. Turning away, he no longer felt the need to suppress the laughter growing within him.

*So, Shear thinks he's going to be a great artist.* A rumble began building in his chest. *I wonder what the critics on Death Row will think of his work.* His laughter increased as he settled behind his desk. *By now Winward should be looking into the incentive I sent him this morning.* His eyes gleamed with amusement. *A few inquiries in the right places and he'll be dancing in the streets. He'll consider himself a bloody hero.*

His smile faded as a child's image floated across his mind. Her eyes were dark and sunken. Her dark hair hung in disarray, stringing across her shoulders and down her back. Her dress was soiled and torn. Ugly bruises marred her small body. He shook the unsettling vision from his mind.

He had been shocked to see the portrait of his half-sister hanging on Shear's wall. He had known then that something would have to be done about the collection.

*I can't allow it to be shown. Too many people know about the damn thing already. Tomorrow, Shear's going to open his gallery to the public and unless something is done to prevent it, everything I've worked so hard for will be ruined.* His brow creased. *Mr. Lukin won't like that.*

A sardonic smile flitted across his narrow lips. *But that's not going to happen, is it? By the time I'm finished, Mr. Thomas Shear won't know what hit him and Lukin will be none the wiser.*

*Emmy. Stupid little bitch.* His hatred seethed. *If it weren't for you, none of this would be happening. If you'd never been born, I wouldn't have had to throw you down that well. But I had no choice.*

*Conniving, backstabbing, stupid little bitch! Even in death you stole mother's love from me. When they found your body, they said it was accidental. That you must've slipped and fell. I couldn't have been more pleased. But then I realized that mother knew. Somehow she'd known what I'd done.*

The buzz of his intercom sounded dimly within the upheaval of his thoughts.

*Stupid, manipulating bitch. You deserved to die. Both of you deserved to die. Stupid, backstabbing, whoring bitches!*

The persistent buzz was like an annoying, sadistic mosquito. He slammed his fist against the intercom button. "What!"

There was a maddening pause before a hesitant voice sounded through the speaker.

"I'm sorry to disturb you, sir. But there's a call for you on line two. You also wanted me to remind you of your three o'clock appointment."

"Yes. Yes, of course," he said. "Thank you."

He picked up the phone and pressed it to his ear. "Yes?"

"It's me."

"You fool," he snarled. His brows drew together in outrage. "Why are you calling me here? I thought I'd made myself clear—"

"Winward's suspicious."

"How do you know?"

"Because he chased me out of the police station, that's how."

"Did he catch you?" he asked.

"No."

"Then what are you worried about?" He paused, then asked, "I trust you've kept your afternoon open?"

"Sir?"

"Be at the Grant Park Zoo at five o'clock, in front of the reptile exhibit. There's something else I need you to do for me."

"Yes, sir."

"Oh, and one more thing."

"Sir?"

"Don't ever call me here again," he growled. "Is that understood?"

"Yes, sir."

He replaced the receiver and checked the time on his watch. *No use in stalling. It's got to be done. A pity, though. He's really a very talented artist.*

He released a whimsical sigh as he stood to retrieve his briefcase. Pausing before the mirror hanging on the wall, he ran a smoothing hand over his hair and smiled.

# CHAPTER TWENTY-THREE

The day was bright and cold as Winward and Hayes drove north on Interstate 75. Once they left the cities of Marietta and Kennesaw behind, businesses along the north and south bound lanes began falling away. Forests stretched along the roadway, pines still green, hardwoods bare, just waiting for spring.

"So, how'd it go last night?" Winward asked, turning down the volume of Bob Seger's "Night Moves".

Hayes lowered the pages they'd printed from Map Quest. "Hmrrghm." The sound resembled a disgruntled bear. "I didn't like him," he said.

"Why not? Did he pick his nose at the table?" Winward inquired, grinning.

That noise again. "That's just it. He was well mannered. Spoke respectfully to Violet and me. Going to Georgia Tech, studying architectural design. Smart kid. Good looking. He even cracked a couple of pretty funny jokes. Made Violet laugh, anyway."

Winward's grin widened. "Oh, okay. Let's see if I have it straight. The kid's intelligent, working toward an affluent career, respectful to the in-laws and has a sense of humor. Hmm, I see your point. The kid's definitely a looser. Might as well take him out and shoot him."

Hayes turned a hostile eye toward Winward. "He's after my Tory, man. My baby!"

"Isn't she seventeen?"

"Like I said, a baby."

"What did Violet have to say about him?"

"She liked him." He screwed his big, dark face up in a not to be comical, but was, imitation of his wife. "Thought he was sweet," he said in his best feminine voice, which would have been perfect for a cross-dresser named Butch. He let the face fall. "Liked the way he treated Tory. Reminded me that Tory will be eighteen next month, and that *she'd* been eighteen when *we* got married." That noise again. "I told her point blank 'my girl's going to college to make something of herself'. Luckily, she had sense enough to agree, although I didn't like the indulgent expression on her face while she did it. Pattin' me all lovey-dovey in the process like she was puttin' a child at ease." That noise again.

Winward was astounded as he glanced over at his partner. His amusement showed plainly on his face. That was the most Hayes had ever said in consecutive sentences. He cleared his throat to keep from laughing.

"You're really having a problem with Tory growing up, aren't you?"

That noise again.

"I can't speak from experience, but I can imagine how tough it must be. Sometimes I wish I'd had kids."

"You still can," Hayes stated. "You're still young. Just because things didn't work out with Kathy doesn't mean your next relationship will end badly."

Winward made a noise of his own.

"What about that sweet, young thing you took out last week? What was her name? Sonya? Sharon?"

As Winward exited at the first Cartersville exit and picked up Highway 41 North in town, he replied, "Becky."

"Yeah, that's right. Becky. What's up with her?"

Winward shrugged. "Becky's great. Her kids are another subject."

"How many kids does she have?"

"Two. A boy and a girl. Ten and eight."

"What's wrong with'em?"

"They miss their dad. Having a rough time with mom dating. The usual."

"Well, they'll have to get use to it. Eventually."

Winward braked for a red light. "That's reassuring." He looked around remembering when this was nothing more than your typical small country town. The courthouse used to be the largest building around. Now he could see signs for a Super Wal-Mart and a Home Depot. Texaco, Quik-Trip, and BP convenience stores stood at three corners of the intersection. They had already passed a Long Horn Steak House and a Ruby Tuesday's. There had even been a Red Lobster. He gave a mental sigh. Progress.

The light turned green and he watched the traffic in front of him accelerate through the intersection. As he picked up speed, Hayes referred to the map.

"Turn-off should be up ahead."

At the junction of Hwy 293, Winward took a left at the light and headed north-west toward Kingston. They watched the houses grow further apart as green pastureland stretched on either side of the two-lane highway.

Livestock dotted the rolling landscape, some grazing while others huddled together beneath leafless, forlorn trees. A chestnut horse caught Winward's eye as it galloped across a field, and he silently admired the grace of the animal before speeding by.

"You know," Hayes said after a companionable silence, "in a way, you're kind of lucky."

"How do you figure that?"

"You get to play with the babes, man. Granted, they're usually divorced with kids, but still. You can handle that. And you get to spend your money the way you want. You have a nice house in the 'burbs. Not to mention this kick-ass automobile. Yes siree, kick-ass," he embellished, referring to the cherry red, mint condition '64 Impala in which they rode.

"I can see how you could think that, but you're forgetting something,"

"Which is?"

"Family." Winward let the word hang for a heartbeat. "Now don't get me wrong," he said, giving the dashboard a loving pat. "I do love this sweet, rumbling machine of mine. But I think you're the lucky one. My advice? Ease up on Tory. At least a little bit."

Hayes regarded Winward with a thoughtful scowl. "You're feeling needy, aren't you?" he asked. "I know just the thing. Home cooking. That's it. I need to invite you over for dinner more often, don't I?"

Winward chortled as he took a left onto Redding. A mile later, he slowed the car to a crawl and parked at the grassy curb in front of the small, single story white-frame house at 111 Redding Road. The property had been well-maintained and boasted a profusion of shrubs and flowering gardens that, at the moment, were lying dormant until spring. Vines of prickly roses were trellised between windows and on each side of the front door.

As the two detectives watched, a little girl, bundled in a blue coat and pink toboggan, burst from the side door and raced toward the swing-set in the fenced back yard. They could hear her squeals of delight as she kicked off and pushed higher while holding tight to the chains supporting the swing.

Winward pulled his eyes away and looked at the neighboring house forty yards away. It had been there for years. Its trees were old with enormous canopies. The house looked like it had risen from the ground with its stone pillars supporting an open front porch and wood siding the color of sand, trimmed out in a dark forest green. Its peaked tin roof was streaked with rust. A rock chimney rose up the side of the house and over the tin's edge.

*Close enough to be aware,* he thought. It *was* a small town, after all. Long time residents knew pretty much what was going on with their neighbors. It was his experience that new residents usually kept to themselves, so the house on the other side would be a waste of time. It was big and new, two hundred yards away, at the least. Spindly, hand planted trees dotted the yard.

"Let's go," Winward said, switching off the engine. They got out of the car and made their way up the gravel driveway to the front door of the small white house.

At Winward's knock, the door was opened by a young woman with soft, inquiring brown eyes. Her long brunette hair was pulled back in a ponytail with bangs fringing her brow. The dusting cloth in her hand was momentarily forgotten.

"Yes?"

"Hello, ma'am." Winward held up his badge. "My name's Detective Winward. This is my partner, Detective Hayes. We're with the Cobb County Police Department. We're sorry to disturb you, but we need to ask you a few questions."

Her eyes grew wide. "I can't for the life of me think of why police detectives would want to talk to me," she said. "We haven't done anything wrong."

Winward displayed a coaxing smile. "Of course not, ma'am. What we need to discuss with you concerns the former owners of this house."

"Oh." Her obvious relief turned to surprise. "The former owners? I don't really know what I could tell you. I never met the woman who lived here before. We bought the house from her son about a year after she died. I think her name was Shear. Betty, Betsy, something like that."

"Had the house remained vacant after Mrs. Shear's death?"

"As far as I know."

"Did the realtor give any details about the house or Mrs. Shear's death, Mrs....?"

"Francis. Joleen Francis," she said with a shy smile. "Yes, I believe she said something about cancer. As far as details of the house, we only had to use our eyes. The yard was really something to see. It was spring and everything was bloomin'. It looked glorious. Especially the roses. They were breathtakin'. I think that's what finally persuaded us to buy the place."

"There's nothing else you can tell us about Mrs. Shear or her son?" Hayes asked, his deep voice drawing the woman's timid gaze.

"No, I'm afraid not."

"Mrs. Francis, I want to thank you for your time. We appreciate your patience," Winward replied.

"That's quite alright. I was just doin' a little cleanin'," she said, brandishing the remembered cloth.

Winward smiled as he and Hayes turned to go.

"You might want to talk to my neighbor. Mrs. Padgett's lived here for years. She probably knew Mrs. Shear pretty well."

"Thank you. We'll do that."

As Winward and Hayes walked along the road toward the house next door, sounds of the romping little girl drew Winward's attention. He paused to watch her play and the image of a slender little boy with raven hair and ebony-rimmed, dark blue eyes filled his mind. Frowning, Winward followed Hayes up the cool rock steps to Mrs. Padgett's shaded porch, and knocked.

"Mrs. Padgett? We're with the Cobb County Police Department. My name is Detective Mark Winward. This is my partner, Detective Hayes," Winward stated when the inner door opened.

They held up their badges for the old woman to see. She stood behind the frail security of a screen door and peered at what they offered with quick, flashing eyes, then her small head lifted and her alert, scrutinizing gaze searched their faces.

"Yeah? So what do you want with me?" Her voice was strong, without quaver. She was petite with a slight, delicate frame. Her face was lined with wrinkles. Silver-white hair was pulled back into a bun and she wore a dress with a daisy print, a thick, white sweater, orthopedic hose, and pink, fuzzy slippers.

"We'd like to talk to you about the previous owners of the house next door."

"Betsy Shear?" The old woman's cornflower blue eyes sparkled with mischief and her cackle of amusement brought a smile to Winward's lips. "Betsy's been dead fer three years! What could she've done to you?"

Hayes's laughter rumbled. "You're feisty, aren't you?"

Mrs. Padgett's eyes narrowed as she craned her neck to meet Hayes's gaze. "I've been called worse," she replied, releasing a chuckle. "You're a big'un, ain't ye?" Her amusement drained away. "What do you want with Betsy? She never hurt nobody."

"No, ma'am. We didn't mean to imply that she had," Hayes stated. "We just need to know her as a person. What kind of family life she had. That sort of thing."

"What fer?"

"I'm afraid we can't tell you that, ma'am," Winward said. "We just need some information."

"Infermation my foot," she quipped. "I know why yer here, young fella. I might be old, but I ain't deaf, dumb, or blind. It's about that no account husban' a her's ain't it?" She searched the men's guarded expressions and heaved a sigh. "You might as well come in out a the cold. I've a feelin' this is gonna take a spell."

Concealing their surprise, Winward and Hayes followed the old woman's spry steps through the aged house and into the kitchen. The house was warm. Almost too warm. The den was furnished with a worn, cozy sofa and matching chair. The ottoman had a patchwork pillow. A large picture of Christ beseeching the heavens graced the mantle.

The kitchen looked like its last renovation happened in the '70's. The refrigerator was green and Winward knew that if he opened the freezer he would find it covered with fuzzy looking white ice that had to be defrosted by hand. A tea kettle simmered on top of an electric stove that was the same outdated green. He glanced out the window over the double sink and saw Joleen Francis's house next door.

"Go ahead and sit yerselves down," she directed, pointing a bony finger to the slat-backed chairs gathered around the scarred oak table. "We'll have our talk over coffee. Don't get much comp'ny any-more. Seems everybody I know's done gone and kicked the bucket." Her cackle of laughter filled the spacious, outdated kitchen, bringing amused smiles to the men's faces.

"How well did you know the Shear family?" Winward asked, accepting the chipped mug of instant coffee she placed in front of him.

"As well as anybody, I expect. We were neighbors for nigh on thirty years."

Winward's brow rose in surprise. "How long have you lived here?" he asked.

"Sixty-three years come spring. Married when I was fifteen. My husband, Charlie, God rest his soul, brought me here right after the weddin' and I ain't left since."

Winward shook his head in awe. "Do you ever have regrets?"

"Regrets!" She eased herself into a chair between the two men. "What'n heavens fer? I raised nine children within these walls, young fella. Ain't got time fer regrets with that many babies pullin' yer apron strings. Course, they're all grown now. Two's even passed on. But regrets?" She shook her head. "No. I've had nary a one."

"What about Betsy Shear?" Hayes asked. "Do you think she had regrets?"

"Betsy? Oh, sure. Lots of'em. The only things Betsy ever had in her grown life to be proud of was her son, Tom, and that garden of hers over there."

"I saw the garden," Winward replied. "I bet it's beautiful in full bloom."

"Yep. That Betsy sure was blessed with a green thumb. She loved perdy things. Couldn't afford to buy'em, so she just up an grew'em herself." She stared into her cup as a sad smile curved her wrinkled lips. "It filled her last days with peace ta look out her winder an see all the beauty she'd created. Lord knows she deserved it. She passed of cancer, you know."

"Yes. Mrs. Francis next door mentioned it."

Winward settled himself more comfortably in his chair. If there was one thing he'd learned during his years as a detective, it was when to keep his mouth shut and let a responsive person talk. A gold mine of information could be obtained by just listening. All that was needed was a few coaxing questions in the right direction.

"What did you mean by 'she deserved it'?" he asked.

"The peace and beauty, a course."

"What do you mean?"

"Lord knows she had precious little of either in her life. That sorry, good-fer-nothin' husban' a hers made sure a that."

"Was Mr. Shear abusive?"

"Abusive! Son, he was the devil himself."

Winward's brow shot up. His pulse began to race as he exchanged a quick glance with Hayes.

"Treated her and that little boy like trash," she continued. "I seen her many a day out in her garden all black and blue. Course, she tried to hide it. But I could tell. Tom, too. An him no more'n a mite. Poor child. If his granddaddy hadn't a come by that awful day, that boy wouldn't a lasted much longer."

"How do you know that?"

"Cause I seen him carry the child out in a blanket an put him real gentle like in his car. Poor thing was limp as a dishrag. An bloody, too. He'd took a beatin', that's fer sure."

"What about Mrs. Shear?"

"Her daddy went back in an pulled her out, too. Same condition as the boy. Course, hers was mainly due to the bottle. She'd suffered so over the years that it drove her to drink. No help to the child, a course, but it's the only way she had to cope."

"Why didn't she take the boy and leave?" Hayes asked.

"Son, things were differ'nt back then here in the country than they are now days with the cities growin' like they are. Places to go was scarce. 'Specially when ye didn't have money and a way ta git there. Don't get me wrong. Betsy weren't no weaklin'. She tried to leave. More'n once, in fact. But he'd just find'em an drag'em back."

"What about Betsy's father? Didn't he know what was going on?"

"The Abernathys lived down south somewhere. Savannah, I think it was. Anyway, they didn't get up this way much. It was only blind luck that brought her daddy out this way in the first place. He was a farmer, ye see. Couldn't get away much. He'd only come up to check on some equipment that was bein' sold at auction.

"Lord, that man was fit ta be tied when he found out what'd been goin' on all those years. Run that devil son-in-law a his plumb out of town. Least-wise that was the story bein' told. People around these parts tended to believe the other version and, because I witnessed the raw emotion a that day, I tended to believe it, too. Ain't seen hide ner hair a the man since. Good riddance, if yer askin' me."

She shook her silver head in disgust and took a cautious sip from the hot mug in her arthritic hands.

"After a while, Betsy came home," she continued, easing the steaming mug back onto the table. "She'd left Tom with her daddy so's he could be raised proper like. Course, Tom made regular visits. Even after he was grown, he never missed a visit with his mama. He was there at the end, too. She didn't pass alone and I was mighty grateful fer that. Nobody should have ta face the dark shada a death without a carin' soul ta hold ther hand. Yep. He was always a good boy, that Tom. Strong, too. And I'm not meanin' with no muscles, either, even though he had more'n his fair share after he was grown. I mean in spirit. He never let his daddy break'im, and that says an awful lot about a man."

"Mrs. Padgett, have you told anyone else about this? Has anyone been around asking questions?"

"Ain't nobody's business if they did. Only told you 'cause of them fancy badges you was wavin' around. But if it'll help put that no-account away for good, if he's still livin' and that's what yer here fer, then I'm glad to do it. He deserves to be punished, even though it ain't near enough justice for what he did to those two."

Winward left Mrs. Padgett's house with mixed emotions. "Why am I not thrilled?" he asked Hayes as they returned to the car. "This is the break I've been praying for. A good prosecutor, hell, even a bad one would have a field day with what we're heard today."

"Yeah, but everything we have so far is circumstantial."

"Don, you know as well as I do that people are convicted every-day with less than what we have on Shear. If a shrewd prosecutor used the supposition that Shear was acting out his revenge on in-nocent little girls to get back at his mother for not protecting him from his father's abuse, he would have no problem building a case." He turned the key and the Impala rumbled as he pulled away from the curb.

"What if it's true?" Hayes asked. "You have to admit it fits."

As Winward steered toward the highway, his nagging doubts persisted. "It fits all right," he said in disgust. "If you ask me, it fits a little too well. I've got this menacing little voice in the back of my head that keeps reminding me that not everyone who was a victim of abuse turns out to be a serial killer."

He shook his head in consternation. "Someone wanted us to find out about Shear's abuse. It's like that confession found on the scene of Chandler's suicide. Crucial evidence was dropped into our laps, wrapping everything up like a Christmas present for us." He pulled onto the highway and pressed the accelerator.

"I think the first thing we need to do is find out who sent that telegram this morning and why. Hopefully, the lab will find someone else's prints besides mine. After that, maybe we'll have something to celebrate."

# CHAPTER TWENTY-FOUR

Ella Fitzgerald, accompanied by Louis Armstrong, played low from the stereo in Kelly's apartment. The lamps were dimmed, their merlot shades glowing softly. Vanilla and peach candles were lit and sat in decorative holders throughout the den and on the table in the dining area where Tom and Kelly sat.

Tom frowned as he watched Kelly push her barely touched dinner plate away. There were circles beneath her eyes, and her shoulders slumped under the weight of her depression. Feeling his watchful gaze, her eyes lifted over the rim of her iced tea glass and his heart wrenched at the forced smile he received.

"Come on," he said, pushing away from the table. "You need to relax. Go on into the den. I'll clean up."

"That's sweet, but unnecessary. I'm fine."

"Like hell you are." He pulled her to her feet and steered her toward the sofa. "You look beat, Kelly. Now, get in there and lie down." He kissed her on the lips and her arms came up to wrap around his neck. As her body molded to his, swaying to the slow beat of the music, Tom groaned deep in his throat and lifted his head. "You need rest, baby," he said, matching her steps.

"I'm not *that* tired," she replied, pulling his head back down. "Besides, if I let you have your way with me, all I have to do is lay there and revel in the delicious way you make me feel."

His chuckle was deep and throaty as he tasted her lips and took the lead in their slow dance. His hands slid around her back and pulled her close. Goose flesh rose on his skin as she raked her nails down his back before slipping her hands into the back pockets of his jeans.

Deepening the kiss, his fingers traced a tantalizing trail down her spine. No bra. He molded her hips in the palms of his hands and pressed her against him. Her white flannel pajamas were soft against his inquisitive fingers and told him she wore no panties underneath. The summons of the doorbell stilled their rising passion and Tom reluctantly released his hold.

"Saved by the bell." His voice was husky.

"Who needed saving?"

"We both did," he answered, giving her a gentle swat on her shapely, flannelled behind. "Go lie down. I'll see who it is."

Tom opened the door and was staggered when he saw Detectives Winward and Hayes standing on the threshold.

"Mr. Shear. We thought we might find you here." Winward smiled. "Mind if we come in?"

"Actually, I do," Tom said, blocking the doorway. "Kelly's resting and I don't want her disturbed."

"Ah, yes. Miss Stafford. Now, that's one lady I'd like to meet. Feeling a bit under the weather, is she?"

"You could say that."

"Oh, well. It's really you we came to see, anyway."

"Tom? Who is it?" Kelly asked, coming up behind him.

Tom stiffened at her appearance. "This is Detective Winward and Detective Hayes, Kelly. They're from the Cobb County Police Department. Gentlemen, Miss Kelly Stafford."

"We're sorry to intrude, Miss Stafford. Mr. Shear mentioned you weren't feeling well. I hope it's nothing serious?"

Kelly's smile was hesitant as she shook Winward's hand. "Just fatigue, detective. What can we do for you?"

"Well, ma'am," Hayes responded. "We were wondering if we might be able to talk to you and Mr. Shear a moment."

"About?"

A complaisant smile curved Winward's lips. "May we come in? It's a bit chilly out here. Besides, we're letting all of your heat out."

Kelly looked at Tom as his eyes narrow at the detective. Taking his hand, she stepped away from the door.

"Certainly."

"Detective Winward," Tom said, stepping into the man's path, "this is neither the time nor the place. I'll be happy to talk to you, but I'd prefer not to have Kelly involved. She has nothing to do with what we have to discuss."

"Is that right?"

"Tom, what are you talking about?" Kelly questioned. Her hold on his hand tightened.

"Kelly, please. I'll explain later."

"No. Not later. Now."

Tom's dread deepened with her stubborn response. He looked into her eyes and his heart thumped with remorse before his expression turned hard and unreadable.

"Please, Tom," she pleaded, keeping her voice soft. "Whatever it is, don't shut me out."

Tom released a sigh of resignation. Stepping from the doorway, he followed the two detectives and Kelly inside.

Winward surveyed the dinner dishes on the table. He took in the candles and soft music as well. "It looks like we disturbed your dinner," he stated without apology.

"We'd just finished," Kelly replied. "Can I offer you anything? Coffee perhaps?"

"No, thanks," Winward declined. He focused his gaze back on Tom. "We made a most profound discovery today, Mr. Shear."

Tom went to the stereo and turned off the music, severing Louis's trumpet solo. "And I'm sure you're just dying to tell me all about it."

The detective gave Tom a tolerant smile as he walked to the den window, parted the sheer curtains and peered out.

"We took a drive up to Kingston this morning. We had a very enlightening visit with an old acquaintance of yours, Mrs. Emogene Padgett. I believe she used to be your next-door neighbor."

Tom felt his chest constrict with fear. He had anticipated Winward discovering the truth. He had also expected a confrontation, just not this quickly, and certainly not in front of Kelly.

"Yes, she was," he acknowledged. "I've know Mrs. Padgett for a long time."

"It would seem she knows you pretty well, also."

The hair stood up on the back of Tom's neck. "I'm sure. She lived next door to my mother for thirty years.

"Yes. She mentioned something to that effect. In fact, we had quite an interesting chat. We learned all kinds of things about you today, Mr. Shear."

Tom ran his fingers through his hair and let out a disconcerted sigh. "Detective, let's end the cat and mouse game, shall we?"

"Fine with me."

"Tom?"

Tom was alarmed to see that Kelly's pale face had grown chalky. He watched her sink to the edge of the sofa and clamp her hands between her knees.

"Are you all right?" he asked, kneeling in front of her.

"Tell me what's going on, Tom." Her voice was small and beseeching, her eyes wide with bewildered fear. "I need to know what's happening."

Tom held her cold, clenched hands in his palms and lowered his head in defeat. "Damn you for this, Winward," he said, before raising his eyes to hold Kelly's apprehensive gaze. "I was going to tell you. But in my own time. In my own way. Please, believe that."

"Tell me what?"

"My father. He was an abuser. He abused my mother and…me."

Tom watched shocked pity flash in Kelly's eyes before her expression calmed.

"For how long?" she asked. Her voice was strong and steady.

He released her hands, rose to his feet and turned away.

"The verbal abuse was always there," he stated in a flat, detached voice. "The beatings started when I was five. The sexual abuse started a few years later. It continued until I was twelve."

Winward and Hayes had remained silent throughout the exchange. At the mention of sexual abuse, however, they exchanged a quick glance as Winward's brow shot up. He let out a quiet breath.

Kelly's brows were knitted in thought as she watched Tom's back. "So that's why you feel so strongly about the Rage collection. You were able to bring them to such revealing life because you know their pain."

"I believe so, yes," he said, turning back to face her. Their gazes held until Winward spoke.

"You know, Mr. Shear, painting those portraits was your undoing. I can't for the life of me think of why you would do such a thing. Unless, of course, you wanted to be caught. You knew word of them would spread. It was only a matter of time."

"What are you talking about?" Kelly demanded. Her eyes darted from Tom to Winward. "What are you accusing Tom of doing?"

"He thinks I'm responsible for the deaths of those little girls, Kelly," Tom explained. Her eyes grew wide with shock. "He's been suspicious of me ever since the opening."

"But that's absurd!"

"Is it?" he asked, taking on the countenance of a counselor facing a jury, or a teacher lecturing his class. "First, I've created portraits of seven missing and presumed murdered little girls. Second, there seems to be incriminating evidence in one of the paintings concerning a unique weapon, a mace with a spiked ball and chain that no one could possibly have known about except the murderer. Third, I was abused as a child to which could only mean that I became an abuser myself and committed the same brutal act on innocents of about the same age. A good psychologist could undoubtedly come up with the reason why I chose to perform my revenge on little girls, but that's beside the point at the moment. Fourth, and here's the kicker, I'm now residing in the house where the crimes took place."

"I hope you realize, Mr. Shear, that you've just added another nail to your coffin," Hayes stated.

"What do you mean?" Kelly asked, piercing him with her gaze.

"Well, Miss Stafford, I have to ask myself how Mr. Shear could possibly know where the crimes took place. Only the one responsible would know that."

The corner of Tom's mouth came up in a derisive smile. "That, detective, is a long story."

Hayes returned Tom's stare with an indulgent grin. "Mr. Shear, we have all the time in the world."

Kelly stood and placed her hand on Tom's arm. "I don't think you should say any more without a lawyer, Tom. Call Jonathan and tell him what's happening. Maybe he can help."

"Jonathan already knows. So does Russ Carson," Tom replied.

"Russ Carson?" Winward's brow rose in surprise. "You've made a good choice, Mr. Shear. Carson's one of the best criminal lawyers this side of the Mason-Dixon."

"So I've heard," Tom said, not bothering to hide his sarcasm.

"How long have they known about this, Tom?" Kelly asked. "How much does Carson know?"

"After Detective Winward and Hayes's visit last week, I knew I was in trouble. I called Jonathan. Since criminal law is beyond his field of expertise, he made contact with Carson. They know everything."

She looked at Tom. "Everything?"

"Everything," he stated. He watched her face and saw her thin, sculpted brows knit in thought.

"Then why didn't you call him? You obviously knew why these men came here tonight."

"I'm not sure. I guess I wanted to see what they would do." He turned to face Winward. "Out of curiosity, detective, considering everything you know, why haven't you placed me under arrest?"

Winward hesitated before answering. "We still have a few questions that need to be answered. It's totally within your rights to have a lawyer present, so if you feel the need to call Carson before this interview goes any further, please do so."

Tom guffawed. "You don't mean that. He'd only tell me to keep my mouth shut."

Winward allowed a small smile. "It was my duty to inform you of your right for representation as a citizen of our great nation." He shrugged. "Part of the job."

Tom's eyes narrowed in speculation. For some reason, he was hesitant about calling Carson. His gut told him to call Winward's bluff.

"I'll wait."

"Tom, no. He needs to be here," Kelly said in alarm.

"Kelly, I want to hear what these men have to say."

Hayes looked at Tom with interest. "Mr. Shear, I'm curious about something. Why haven't you claimed your innocence? Most people in your position, whether they were innocent or not, would have stated as much from the start."

"What good would it have done?" Tom asked, shrugging his shoulders. "I can see the way things stand as well as you can. All of the evidence points to me. In order to proclaim my innocence, I have to be able to prove it."

"Can you?" Winward asked. "Prove it, I mean."

"At the moment, no. But I think I know someone who might be able to shed some light on the subject."

"Who?"

"Merideth Chandler."

Winward was silent a moment, then he asked, "How? She was interviewed during the initial investigation and could tell us nothing."

"Maybe she wasn't asked the right questions. Maybe she knows more than you think."

"What do you mean?"

"Everything that's happened seems to stem from the house I bought from her. Wasn't it a rental property?"

"Yes."

"Who rented it before Theodore Chandler's death? How long was it in their possession? Did Chandler make regular visits to make sure it was being maintained properly?"

"Those questions have already been answered," Winward replied. "The house remained vacant for several years before it was rented to a man who made his permanent residence overseas. He'd only planned to use the house once or twice a year when he came to the U.S. on business. Unfortunately, he died of an apparent heart attack before his first visit."

Tom looked thoughtful as he started to pace. "So, the house was never actually occupied," he said. "Who handled the arrangements? Did Chandler have the rental contracts drawn up or hire a broker?"

"I'm not sure," Winward admitted studying Tom's absorbed expression. "Why?"

Tom stopped pacing to face the detective. "The answer to that should be obvious, detective. If the house was to stay vacant, but under contract, it would give the killer the perfect opportunity to commit and conceal his crime."

"How are you so sure that that house is where the crimes were committed?" Winward asked.

Tom stopped and impaled Winward with a measuring look. "Because of what's happened to me since I moved in."

"Which is?" Winward's eyes followed Tom into the kitchen and watched him gather a brandy decanter and glasses. Then his gaze fell to Kelly, where she sat motionless in the corner of the sofa. Her legs were curled beneath her, her head lowered in thought. She released a silent sigh and closed her eyes, but not before a hint of morose knowledge could be seen in their troubled depths.

"If I answered that question, detective," Tom replied with a hint of a smile, "you'd be ordering a straightjacket before I had a chance to finish my drink." He handed a snifter of brandy to Kelly and winked encouragingly. He then filled two other glasses and presented them to the detectives.

Hayes took the offered drink and swirled the amber liquid under his nose. Winward declined.

"No thanks. I don't drink on duty."

Tom snorted in mocking amusement. "Take it and screw duty. If I tell you what you want to know, you'll be glad you have it. You might as well have a seat while you're at it. Apparently, you're not going to be leaving anytime soon."

Hayes gave truth to Tom's last statement by pulling a chair away from the dinner table and turning it to face the den. He sat, sampled his brandy then placed the glass on the coffee table. He crossed his arms over his immense chest and leveled his dark, steady gaze on Tom.

Winward smiled indulgently. He accepted the glass, but refrained from sampling its contents.

"Mr. Shear, because of my profession, I'm well beyond the point of being shocked by anything." He watched Tom raise his own glass and take a slow sip. "But I have to inform you that anything you say can and will be held against you in a court of law."

"Are you making a formal charge?" Tom asked. He leveled his inquiring gaze on Winward.

"Not at the moment. I just wanted to make you aware of my position here."

"Oh, I'm fully aware of your position, detective. The thing is, something is happening to me that I don't fully understand. It goes beyond everything I was ever taught or believed in. The only thing that hasn't been turned upside down by this experience is my gut feelings, my instincts. And right now, only God knows why, they're telling me to trust you."

"Why? Because I haven't placed you under arrest?"

"Partly," Tom answered. "But I have to ask myself, why? There's certainly enough evidence against me to warrant the action. So, why haven't you? I must've asked myself this question a dozen times tonight. Then it occurred to me. I remember reading where the commissioner himself made the announcement that officially closed the investigation after Chandler's suicide. That being the case, it could only mean one of two things. Either that announcement was only a ploy, or you're working a renegade mission.

"Now I'm thinking, if it was a ploy, why are you hesitating about performing your civic duty? You could've at least taken me down to the station for questioning. Your actions speak for themselves, detective. Obviously, you weren't satisfied with the way things turned out, so you decided to do a little investigation on your own. Am I right?"

"Mr. Shear, your deductive reasoning is admirable." Winward sat in the overstuffed chair and made himself comfortable. He placed his glass on the table beside him. "You're correct in assuming that we weren't satisfied with the way things were wrapped up. As far as I was concerned, there were too many unanswered questions. There still are."

"Such as?"

Winward gave Tom a wry smile. "I thought we were the ones asking the questions, Mr. Shear."

The corner of Tom's mouth quirked. "Still playing cat and mouse, are we?"

"Not at all," Winward replied. "I'm just waiting to hear why you're so sure the house is where the murders took place."

Seconds passed before Tom began to speak. He started at the beginning and told them everything. He watched Winward's expression turn from passive interest to incredulity, then from incredulity to disbelieving humor. Hayes had shown no emotion at all.

Winward remained silent, pursing his lips in thought. After a moment, he sighed deeply and looked up to study Tom's cool demeanor.

"Mr. Shear, there was a portrait omitted from your collection."

"Kathy Packard."

Winward nodded and held Tom's gaze. "Can you tell us why?"

"No, but I can guess. I think it's because her body was found."

"So, you think that's the reason behind the…hauntings? They can't rest until their bodies are found?"

Tom shrugged. "Can you think of a better reason? Besides revenge, that is."

"I might."

Tom chose to ignore the provoking remark. Instead, he held his silence and watched the detective over the rim of his glass.

Winward acknowledged the challenge in Tom's eyes with a shrewd smile. "There was a portrait in your collection I didn't recognize. I take it that's the little girl you referred to as Emmy?"

"Yes."

"And she was the first to appear?"

"That's right."

"So you're saying we have nine victims instead of eight."

Tom shrugged once again. "Maybe. Maybe not. I don't have all the answers, detective. I can only tell you what I know."

"What you know." Winward shook his head and spouted an incredulous chuckle. "You actually expect us to believe that story?"

"It's true." Kelly voice was a mere whisper. She had remained motionless until this point.

"We ought to know," she said. Her eyes glistened with tears. "We're the ones they've chosen. I have to live with their presence every agonizing moment. I can't sleep because of the nightmares." A tear slid down her cheek and she swept it away in rising anger. "Of course, you don't believe. You haven't seen. You haven't felt what we've felt. But it's true."

Kelly visibly struggled to remain calm. "Tom didn't commit the crimes you're accusing him of, Detective Winward. Everyone who knows him can tell you that. Even the victims."

Clearing his throat, Hayes rubbed the stubble on his chin, making a raspy sound. "Mr. Shear? Who would have had access to your business cards?"

Tom's heart had constricted as he'd watched Kelly go head to head with Winward. He wanted to hold her, but turned to Hayes instead. "I had them printed before the opening. Any number of people had access to them," he said. "Why?"

"Detective Winward received an interesting note this morning telling him to check out your Kingston address. The envelope also contained a Shear Gallery business card."

Tom's eyes narrowed and his jaw grew hard.

"The fact that I grew up in Kingston is no big secret. My grandparents and Mrs. Padgett are the only ones who know first hand about the abuse. That is, until I was forced to tell Jonathan Fields and Russ Carson. The only other people I can think of that might have an interest keen enough to dig it up are Craig and Michael Raymond. They're a father and son team who own a string of art galleries throughout the U.S. and Europe. I had dinner with them last night to discuss a business proposition, and Craig Raymond seemed very interested in my background.

"They've also been very adamant with their interest in the Rage collection. They offered to buy it twice, each time raising their offer considerably. Another thing, is that they both knew Theodore Chandler."

"Really?" Winward smiled in pleasant surprise. "Now, these are the kinds of facts I can believe in, Mr. Shear." Disregarding his earlier statement, he picked up his brandy glass and raised it to his lips, leveling his shrewd gaze on Tom.

"I don't blame you for not believing me, detective. I know how it sounds," Tom said. "Jonathan didn't believe me, either. Oh, he said he did, but I knew he didn't mean it. He only said it because he knew I believed." Tom chuckled with humorless mirth. "Seeing the spirits of Vicki Martin and Amanda Sawyer took care of that."

"I think it's time to have a chat with Mr. Fields."

"I'll make it easy for you. I'll have him meet us at the gallery. That is, if you'll trust me enough to allow me to do so. I've got something to show you that you might find interesting."

# CHAPTER TWENTY-FIVE

The bright, chilly day had grown cold and overcast with the lowering sun. Dampness hung in the black, night air and seeped to the bone if one was exposed too long. As Tom pulled into the driveway, a light mist began to fall. It grew into drops and pinged against the car with a mixture of frozen precipitation. He moved slowly forward, then felt Kelly's hand upon his arm. He drew to a stop and turned on the Jag's wipers, making the minute ice crystals melt as they were pushed to the sides. Then, he followed her transfixed gaze to the house.

The long, narrow windows flanking the front door were softly illuminated from within by the foyer lamp. The remainder of the house was dark. It seemed to have an air of alertness, like it was waiting for its living occupants to return and stir the life within it.

"It feels like it's been waiting for us," she said, verbalizing his thoughts.

As they sat in the warmth of the Jaguar, all was quiet except for the freezing rain and purring engine. Suppressing a shiver, Tom pried his eyes away, pulled beneath the colonnade, and turned off the engine. Lights stained the rearview mirror as Winward and Hayes pulled in behind.

"Why aren't you parking in back?" Kelly asked.

"It's raining."

"So?"

"You don't need to be out in this mess. Besides, that's what this thing's for, to protect damsels. I might as well get some use out of it."

She gave him a knowing smile and ran her fingers along his sandpaper jaw. "You're sweet, Tom."

He scoffed, then gathered her hand in his and pressed her fingers to his lips. "Speaking of protecting, I still don't like the idea of you being here," he said, watching the headlights behind him blink into darkness.

"Tom, we've been over this."

Kelly pushed her door open and stepped from the car before he could say anything further. With a sigh of resignation, he escorted her to the front door as the two detectives followed. The icy rain grew heavier and the ticks and taps as it fell on objects in its path grew louder.

"Jonathan should be along any minute," he said, inserting his key. "He's already seen what I'm about to show you, so there's no reason to wait."

Winward gave a silent nod and entered the house behind Kelly and Hayes. Tom closed the door then started to punch in the security code to deactivate the alarm. The alarm wasn't activated. He looked at it perplexed.

"I know I—"

"Tom?" Kelly's voice shook.

Dreading what he might find, he turned. Hayes and Winward stood motionless. Tom's scalp crawled as he followed their transfixed gazes and looked into bruised, sunken eyes.

The sight of a juvenescent image staring at him from the somber darkness of the hallway made his heart lurch and he was momentarily spellbound as a small arm lifted to motion him forward. Her short, honey blond hair was stringy with sweat and grime. She wore purple shorts and a violet print white t-shirt, both spotted and smeared with blood. The left side of her small pixie face was swollen where she'd been beaten. Blood trickled from her nose and oozed from her left thigh. Ugly reddish-purple bruises blotched the delicate skin of her arms and legs. Her dirty feet were bare.

Tom swallowed past his restricted throat and forced his feet to move. "Stay here, Kelly," he ordered, keeping his eyes leveled on the little girl. "You two stay with her. Don't let her out of your sight."

Obeying the silent summons, Tom stepped forward and watched the little girl turn into the oppressive shadows beside the main staircase. He was vaguely aware of Winward being beside him and, for once, was glad of the man's presence. The darkness deepened as they approached the looming kitchen door. Tom's heart pounded as the little girl peered at him over her shoulder, then stepped through the closed door and vanished.

Tom pushed the door open and saw the light he'd left on over the stove. The little girl stood in the corner watching. As he stepped through, hissing reached his ears just as a sickeningly sweet smell filled his nostrils. His eyes widened in horror.

"Gas," he said. "Hayes! Get Kelly out of here, now!"

Tom rushed for the controls of the stove as Winward shoved open the windows. They headed for the back door and left it open to help ventilate the gas-filled room. Standing on the stoop, gasping cold, clean air, they peered back inside.

"Look," Winward said, pointing to a small device on the table. "I'll know more after I get a closer look, but it looks like it's rigged with a timer. Someone knew what they were doing."

Tom glowered over Winward's shoulder. "What is it?" he asked, his voice calm, almost monotone.

"My guess is that it's some type of detonator. With the gas, one spark from that thing would have leveled the place. The guys in the lab will be able to tell us for sure, though.

"Come on," he said, moving across the patio toward the walkway to make his way around the house. "Hayes needs to know what's going on."

"You go ahead," Tom said, propping the glass storm-door open. "I'll open a few more windows and meet you out front."

"You shouldn't go back in there until the gas has cleared."

"I'll hold my breath," Tom said with a smirk. "That detonator thing, will it explode?"

"I don't think so. I didn't see any explosives. I think its purpose was to create a spark to set off the gas."

"You don't think so," Tom repeated. "Great. That's just great."

Gathering his resolve, he stepped back inside. He used a chair from the kitchen table to hold open the interior swinging door to help disperse the gas, then slid the window's open in the room of Ice.

Hurrying across the hall beneath the main staircase, Tom entered the darkness of the Rage gallery and was stunned as a sudden blow to the back of his head sent him to his knees. He instinctively threw up his arm to avert the next strike which turned his body in the assailant's direction. Deflecting the attack, Tom growled in fury and heaved himself forward, tackling the man to the floor. A grunt was forced from his aggressor as the full impact of Tom's superior weight came down on him, then the man began to choke as Tom gripped his throat with one hand and dealt several brutal punches before being forced off balance and shoved to the side. Scrambling to stop the man's retreat, Tom made it to his feet before his reeling senses drove him back down to his hands and knees. Panting, with his head hanging limp, he was dimly aware of running feet thumping across hardwood, then a shout from outside. He flinched at the popping sound of gunfire.

"Tom! Where are you?"

Kelly's frantic voice had barely penetrated the buzzing in his ears when the red room was suddenly flooded with blinding light.

"Kelly! Marsha! In here!"

Trying not to vomit, Tom squinted against the harsh brightness as Jonathan helped ease him back against the wall. His scowl darkened when he saw that his paintings had been replaced by bad imitations. The original, frameless canvases were stacked against the wall, ready for transport.

Kelly was by his side in an instant. "Are you all right?" she asked, rubbing the tousled hair from his brow.

"I'll be okay." His voice was a hoarse whisper. "Just give me a minute."

"Marsha, I need a towel," Jonathan said, kneeling down to examine Tom's bleeding scalp.

As Marsha sprinted from the room, Winward entered. His grave expression deepened at the blood soaking Tom's dark hair and collar.

"Are you okay, Shear?"

"I'll live."

"What happened?"

Tom's scathing gaze met Winward's. "You tell me," he snarled.

Marsha rushed in and Tom winced as the towel was pressed against his head. Drawing in a deep breath, he exhaled slowly to control his anger.

"Someone jumped me. I don't know what he hit me with," he said more calmly and flexed his right hand, barely glancing at his bruised and abraded knuckles. "We fought. He got away. That's all I know."

"You've received quite a blow, but it doesn't look like it needs stitches," Jonathan stated. "You're going to have one hell of a knot, though. You should probably see a doctor."

"Let me see," Kelly said as she nudged Jonathan to the side. She examined the cut, then placed her palm over the wound.

"I don't need a doctor. What I want is to know how that guy got past the security system," Tom demanded, feeling warmth suffuse his scalp.

"The average burglar wouldn't have," Winward stated, glancing around the room. "But for this guy, your system was probably nothing more than a nuisance. He had a specific purpose for being here and he obviously knew what he was doing." Winward looked pointedly at the paintings stacked against the wall.

"What do you mean?" Kelly asked, following his gaze. "Why would he go to the trouble of switching them?"

"It's obvious his plan was to steal the Rage collection and blow up the house to cover his crime. Any evidence would have been consumed in the resulting flames."

"But in order to accomplish this," Jonathan continued, deducing Winward's train of thought, "he had to put something in their place; something that could be found in the rubble, but burnt beyond recognition."

"Exactly. Placing the fakes in the original frames only served to divert suspicion." Winward cast Tom a toothy smile. "It would seem, Mr. Shear, you screwed up his plans by coming home earlier than expected."

"I hadn't planned on coming home at all. I'd intended to spend the night at Kelly's."

The detective walked over to where an abandoned painting rested face down on the floor. As he lifted it up, Caroline Doltry's huge, soulful blue eyes gazed back at them from the canvas.

"I heard gunfire," Tom said, tearing his eyes from the portrait.

"Yeah." Winward pulled his eyes away and gently rested the canvas against the wall. "The assailant had a gun. We had no choice."

Sirens sounded in the distance.

"Dead?"

"Yeah."

The sleeting had ended and was now only a steady, cold sprinkle. Tom stood leaning against the railing of the porch out of the drizzle and watched the coroner's van pull away, its tires whooshing on the wet asphalt. He saw Winward speaking with a uniformed officer and watched as the officer flipped his note pad closed before heading toward the patrol car where his partner stood waiting. A cluster of die-hard, looky-loo neighbors stood shivering across the street and Tom wondered if he should smile and wave. Feeling Kelly's presence beside him, he turned and took her in his arms.

"Tom, come inside." Her voice was soft and edged with worry. "It's cold and it's late. You need to rest."

"Not yet. I need to talk to Winward."

"Can't it wait?"

"No, it can't."

She watched his face. "I wish you had gone to the hospital. What if you have a concussion? It's not wise to let something like that go untreated. You need to take better care of yourself."

He gave her a weary smile. "I don't have to anymore. I've got you to do it for me now."

"Are you being snide?" she asked affronted.

Tom chuckled. "No. I'm not."

"Tom, I'm serious."

"So am I." He captured her gaze and peered deep. "How did you do it, Kelly? When you placed your hand on my head, I felt heat, then the bleeding stopped and the pain practically disappeared. I barely have a headache now."

Kelly bit her lips and met his intent gaze a heartbeat longer. Uncertainty clouded her eyes before she looked away.

Marsha appeared beside them. "Things are finally winding down. How are you feeling?"

Tom smirked as he pulled his eyes from Kelly's face to meet Marsha's worried frown. "In what capacity are you asking, doctor?"

"Right now physically," she said, ignoring his sarcasm. "Any blurred vision? Dizziness?"

"No. Just a slight headache. What are you doing here, anyway?"

"After what Jonathan told me, did you really expect me to be anywhere else?"

"I guess it would depend on how much he told you."

Marsha's eyes narrowed as she studied him. "Enough to know that you were in serious trouble. I had to extract a few teeth for details, though. My guess is he's leaving that part up to you."

"How's the head, Shear?" Winward asked, walking toward them.

Tom heaved a sigh and corralled his annoyance. "Ask me in a couple of days," he replied, obeying Kelly's tug as she led the way into the house.

Winward grinned at seeing how the two women hovered in concern. "How many times have you been asked that question tonight?"

Tom saw Winward's smile and his expression darkened. "Too many."

Winward tried to curtail his grin and cleared his throat. "Understood. Where's Hayes?"

"I last saw him in the Rage gallery. Or what's left of it."

"You might be interested to know we found the guy's van parked around the corner. Empty, of course."

"Will you be taking my paintings back with you?"

"Not tonight. It depends on the investigation if we'll need them in the future or not. If it turns out the perpetrator acted alone, we'll have no use for them. But, if we find there's someone else involved, we'll need them as evidence for a trial. In the meantime, we'll use them as bait."

They entered the Rage gallery and saw Hayes talking with Jonathan.

"Were you able to identify the guy?" Tom asked.

"Yeah," Winward answered. "We checked the van's registration. His name's Roger Wilson. Ring any bells?"

Tom shook his head. "No."

"He's also the courier who brought us your Kingston address and business card this morning."

"Which means he was working for someone else," Jonathan said.

"Probably."

Hayes turned to Tom. "Mr. Shear, we saw the paintings in your studio. Is that what you brought us here to see?" he asked.

"Yes."

"Do you mind if we take another look?"

"Not at all."

Tom led the way up to his studio in the attic. As he uncovered the paintings, Kelly gasped.

"I've seen this man," she whispered, "in my nightmares."

"Do you know who he is?" Tom asked, watching her.

"No. His face is always shadowed."

"Mr. Shear, how did you come to paint these?" Hayes inquired.

Tom noticed that he scrutinized the painting of Chandler's hanging corpse and heaved a weary sigh. "Nightmares, detective."

"Do you know the man you've painted here?"

"Yes, I do," he answered. "It's Theodore Chandler. And he didn't commit suicide, Detective Hayes. He was murdered."

Winward and Hayes exchanged glances.

"Do you realize how this looks, Mr. Shear?"

"Yes, he does," Jonathan interrupted. "And I don't think he should say anything else without consulting his attorney."

"Jonathan's right, Tom," Kelly acceded. "Maybe you should call Mr. Carson."

Tom leveled his gaze on Winward.

"You have every right to do so, Mr. Shear," Hayes stated.

"Are you going to arrest me?" Tom asked, holding Winward's gaze.

Winward turned to the paintings. "Let's think logically about the situation, shall we? First of all, you purchase a house where a suicide takes place. The victim is assumed to be responsible for the abductions and murders of four out of eight little girls. Next, you create a series of paintings. In that series, you have portraits depicting seven of the little girls who are missing and presumed dead. One of your paintings displays a number of weapons, one of which was found on the scene of the only body recovered. Then, our investigation tells us you were also abused as a child. And finally, you lead us here and show us paintings with explicit details of something you couldn't possibly have known about unless you had been a witness to the act itself."

Tom's patience was wearing thin. "Are you going to arrest me?" he repeated.

The detective met his level gaze. "No."

"Why not?"

Winward rubbed his bristled chin. "I'm going to be honest with you, Shear. While I had a few officers at my disposal, I had them conduct a full search of this house for a device that might've cast an image of that little girl while everyone of nonofficial capacity was kept sequestered in your den tonight."

Jonathan's brow creased with deprecation. "That was illegal, you know."

"I'm aware of the technicalities, Mr. Fields."

"What did they find?" Tom asked, ignoring the exchange.

"Nothing."

Kelly looked from one detective to the other. "Do you believe us now?" she demanded.

"Miss Stafford, you've got to understand our position," Hayes said. "As officers of the law, we deal with cold, hard facts. You have to admit, what's being suggested here is—"

"Ridiculous? Fantasy? Hysteria?" Her green eyes flashed with anger. "You saw that little girl yourself, detective. You saw her lead Tom to the gas. And you," she said, unleashing her fury on Winward.

"You said yourself that the man who attacked Tom was the one who delivered the package to you this morning. What more do you need?"

Tom embraced her, pulling her close. "Sweetheart, they just need time to sort things out. I think we need to give them the chance."

"Tom's right, Kelly," Jonathan replied. "If they haven't arrested him by now, that means they have more questions than answers. I don't think they're totally convinced he's guilty. In fact, when you think about it, there's quite a bit of evidence pointing to his innocence."

Tom released his hold on Kelly and moved to cover the paintings. "Are we finished here, gentlemen?" he asked, breaking the thought-filled silence. "I don't know about the rest of you, but I've had one hell of a day."

"Come on, Kelly," Marsha said, placing a comforting arm across her shoulders. "We'll give you a ride home."

"I'm not leaving."

"Yes, you are," Tom said. She turned to him with a worried frown and he leaned down to give her lips a tender kiss. "Sweetheart, I'll be alright. Nothing else is going to happen tonight."

"Then there's no reason I can't stay. I don't want to leave you, Tom."

"I know." His smile was gentle as he gazed into her pleading green eyes. "But I don't want you here, Kelly. The only way I'll be able to sleep is to know you're safely away from this house."

"He's right, Kelly." Jonathan took her hand and turned her toward the stairs. "He'll be okay after he gets some well-deserved rest."

Tom brought up the rear as everyone trooped down the attic stairs so he could turn out the lights and shut the door. He saw everyone to the front door and gave Kelly a long, warming kiss before she was ushered out by Jonathan and Marsha. He watched her until she was safely in the backseat of their car, then turned to the departing detectives.

"Is my system busted?" he asked.

"No," Winward answered, stepping out onto the porch. "He was wearing a backpack with the tools he needed to do the job when he ran. He had a device that retrieved your codes. You'll want to change those as soon as possible, but your system should still function properly."

"Good to know."

"Get some rest," Winward said as he followed Hayes down the porch steps.

"That's the plan," Tom confirmed before closing and locking the door. As he activated the alarm, the Impala's motor rumbled to life. With sore muscles and a slightly aching head, he went through the house, securing locks and turning out lights. Then he climbed the stairs longing for a shower, his bed, and a healing, dreamless sleep.

⸻ «◍» ⸻

Winward and Hayes didn't speak as they got into the Impala. Winward backed out of the driveway and headed south on Church Street toward the station. The only sound was the swish of the tires on wet pavement, the low rumble of the engine, and the methodical thump of the wipers.

"I don't think we should've left things the way we did," Hayes said, breaking the silence.

"What do you mean?"

"If we couldn't arrest him, we should've at least taken the paintings as evidence."

"I don't agree. We'll need them as bait. They'd be no use to us locked up in the station's evidence room."

"At least they'd be protected. And what do you mean by 'bait?' You think Shear's innocent?"

"I'm not saying that."

"Then what *do* you think?"

Winward heaved a sigh. "Hell, I don't know." His grip tightened on the steering wheel. "I was there. I saw that little girl. I followed her to the gas and watched her walk through a solid wood door." He glanced over at his partner. "Don, she was waiting for us on the other side. You talk about freaky, that was freaky." He shook his head and from the corner of his eye, Winward saw Hayes's shoulders shift like the big man was suppressing a shiver. "I do know one thing, though. If we'd been ten minutes later, that place would've gone up like a roman candle."

"Don't you think Shear could've set the whole thing up?"

"The thought crossed my mind. But my gut tells me no."

"How can you be so sure?" Hayes asked. "What if he paid Roger Wilson to do his dirty work? That delivery could've been to point our suspicion in another direction, to make us wonder why anyone guilty would lay a bombshell like his own abuse at our feet to be used against him in our investigation. And don't you think it's ironic how we happened to arrive at the house, just in the nick of time, before it blew? And how Shear just happened to be alone when Wilson attacked? The fact that Wilson was killed couldn't have been more convenient. The only other witness that could've done him harm has been eliminated."

"And those paintings of Chandler and the mystery man." He stopped and shook his head. "Mark, he had details of Chandler's suicide that only a handful of people know about. Did you see the stiletto knife lying against the baseboard in the exact position it was found? Hell, it was depicted perfectly, right down to the pearl handle. I just can't believe he got such detail from a nightmare. My dreams aren't that explicit. Are yours?"

Winward cast Hayes a sidelong glance, his mouth quirking w' amusement. "Down right chatty today, aren't we? I'm impress<sup>r</sup>

Hayes gave Winward a scathing look.

"Okay, okay. No need to get testy." Winward heaved another sigh. "Look. Believe me, I know what you're saying, Don," he conceded. "Everything you've said makes sense. But aren't you forgetting something important? I've looked at the file photos enough to know that the little girl we saw was Caroline Doltry, the fifth victim."

"Agreed. So what's your point?"

"My point is this. If the whole thing was staged, how'd he do it?"

"He would need a recorded image and a projection device," Hayes said.

"Then why wasn't that device found? The men knew what they were looking for. The place was thoroughly searched. Hell, we even had detectors and still couldn't find anything."

"So you're suggesting what we saw was an actual ghost?" Hayes asked, his tone incredulous as he watched his partner.

Winward gave the question some thought as he braked for a red light. "Yeah," he answered. "I guess that's what I'm suggesting."

Hayes's laughter rumbled in his broad chest. "The chief's gonna have a conniption. You know that, don't you?"

Winward's lips curved into a grin as he pulled through the intersection.

# CHAPTER TWENTY-SIX

C hief Swainer rested his bony elbows on his desk as he leaned forward in his chair. He eyed the two detectives.

"You actually expect me to believe that cock-n-bull story?"

Winward stood at the rain dappled window, watching the encroaching clouds through the thin plastic slats of the open blinds. He shoved his hands deep into the pockets of his jeans and shrugged, barely noticing as the movement tugged on the shoulder holster that kept his Glock 9 mm strapped securely against his ribs.

"I know what I saw last night, chief." He looked at Swainer and held his stern gaze.

"Mark, listen to what you're saying." Swainer pushed himself up from his chair. "You're telling me you saw a ghost, for Christ's sake." He propped himself on the corner of his desk and pierced Winward with his eyes. His hand automatically patted his empty breast pocket and he let out a low, heartfelt curse.

"Chief, all I'm saying is, if it was staged, I can't figure out how he did it."

"You're sure the search was thorough?"

"Yes. I led the search myself. The place was clean. There was nothing whatsoever that could've projected that little girl's image."

"And you're sure it was Caroline Doltry," Swainer probed, looking at Hayes.

The big man sat back in his chair, his arms crossed over his immense chest, and nodded.

Swainer shook his head as he contemplated the situation. "What about Roger Wilson? What'd you find on him?"

"He was a jack-of-all-trades," Hayes said. "His rap sheet reads like a dictionary, but his only conviction was for stealing a car when he was fourteen; spent six months in juvie. After that, he got smart and learned to cover his tracks. Even though he was brought in numerous times on suspicion, he was never charged."

"And Shear? What about him?"

Winward stepped away from the window. "He's clean. Not so much as a parking ticket." He began a slow pacing. "Besides, I'm not totally convinced Thomas Shear is the kind of man capable of murdering eight little girls."

"And what are you basing that on?" Swainer asked, watching his man closely.

"My instincts," Winward replied, halting his motion to meet Swainer's eyes.

Swainer shook his head and sighed. "Your instincts aren't good enough, Mark. We need proof." He looked at Hayes. "What do you think?"

Hayes shrugged. "Mark's got some legitimate doubts. I think we should consider the possibility that someone else might be involved. But everything we have so far points to Shear. I don't think we should dismiss him as a suspect."

"I agree," Winward stated.

"So, what are you suggesting?" Swainer asked, looking from one detective to the other.

Winward and Hayes exchanged glances. At Hayes's affirmative nod, Winward made their proposal.

"We need to put Shear under surveillance and spread the word of his attack and the attempted theft. If someone else is involved, maybe we can spook him into making his next move."

———※《●》※———

"It would seem we have competition for Shear's Rage collection."

Michael Raymond's muscles tensed at the sound of his father's voice. He'd been lost in thought and was unnerved that he'd been caught off guard. Feeling his pulsating anger begin to seethe, he maintained his stance facing the rain-streaked window until his emotions could be fully mastered.

"Yes," he replied, keeping the malice from his voice. "I was just informed by Detective Winward and his giant sidekick."

"I know. They came to me first."

Michael turned from his office window and let a satirical smile curve his lips. "Of course, they did." He walked over to the executive chair behind his desk and sat down. "I wouldn't worry, if I were you."

"Why?" his father asked, suspicion in his narrow-eyed gaze. "What are you up to, Michael?"

Michael leaned back and steepled his fingers over his mint-green tie. "The Rage collection, of course. It's what you want, isn't it?"

"Yes, but—"

"Then leave everything to me," he avowed. "The less you know, the better off you'll be."

He met his father's doubtful gaze and rose to his feet. Moving back to the window, he masked his contempt by turning his gaze to the brooding, morning sky.

He had grown uneasy during the exchange between Shear and his father at the restaurant. The thought of his father obtaining only part of the collection had been unthinkable. His emotions had spiraled until Shear's blatant rejection had offered a settling resolve.

The thought of his father's bungled attempt filled him with disgust. Thomas Shear was no idiot. It had been foolish to underestimate the man. Apparently, his father had relied upon Shear's eagerness for recognition to cause him to roll over and accept whatever was offered. His inward laugh rang with disdain. *Stupid move, daddy dear.*

"Michael, I want to know what you're planning and I want to know now."

His mind churned with loathing. As his hands began to shake, he clasped them behind his back and clenched his teeth until he was able to control his voice.

"Since your attempt at dinner the other night failed, let's just say, I think it's time to take a more direct approach."

"You'd better not be planning anything illegal," Raymond demanded. "I've worked too hard building our future to have it destroyed by your stupidity."

Michael's face paled in reaction to his father's insult, and his insinuating threat. His body began to tremble with rage and he had to fight to maintain his steady breathing. Keeping his malevolent stare focused on the turbulent sky, he barely managed to suppress the scorn from his voice.

"Stupidity?" He emitted a low, grinding laugh. "Father, your endearments astound me. Do you think I've added treasures to our stock by being stupid? You've never questioned my methods before. Don't start now."

"What are you planning, Michael?"

When his son continued to stare through the window and did not answer, Raymond shook his head. "If only your mother was here, maybe she'd—"

Michael whirled. "Well, she's not, so don't speak to me of mother."

He went back to his desk and sat down. "In answer to your question, Shear's gallery opens to the public this afternoon. I, for one, intend to be there."

# CHAPTER TWENTY-SEVEN

Jonathan relaxed in Tom's recliner with the footrest extended as Tom stepped to the front window of his den and parted the blue silk drapes. He peered up the street through the drizzling rain to the residential side street and watched the white sedan pull away as another car pulled in behind.

"Are they still out there?"

"I think they've just changed shifts," Tom answered, watching the second car. "Two men in a brown Buick pulled up and the white Chevy left."

"Are they doing anything?"

"No. They're just sitting there." As he rubbed the back of his neck to ease the tension, his broad shoulders flexed beneath his dark-blue, long-sleeved t-shirt. "Maybe I'm just being paranoid. There are a dozen homes and businesses along this street. Those men could be there for any number of reasons."

Jonathan looked skeptical. "You can't honestly believe that after what happened here last night."

Tom gave a harsh laugh. He turned from the window with a bitter grin, letting the drape fall back into place. "Isn't it great? My gallery opens in two hours and I have an unmarked police car parked in front of the house."

"They're not right in front of the house, Tom. In fact, I doubt if anyone will even notice."

"We noticed."

Jonathan shrugged. "Only because we halfway expected it. Especially after Winward mentioned using the collection as bait." Mischief glinted in his eyes. "If anyone asks, you can always tell them they came with the motion detectors you had added to your security system this morning."

"Yeah, right."

Swirling the ice cubes in his glass, Jonathan cracked a smile at the sarcasm in Tom's voice. He watched his friend's preoccupied pacing and pursed his lips in thought.

"You need to get back into regular workouts again. A rough and tumble sparing match would help with that tension you're dragging around. Besides that, you don't want to get rusty, lose your edge."

"Trust me," Tom said, "last night drove that lesson home. If it hadn't been for my training and fast reflexes, that guy would've bashed my brains out. And if I'd been in top form, I might've subdued and held him for Winward. Then, maybe we would know who we're dealing with by now. It was stupid of me to go running blindly into a dark room knowing someone had broken in and could still be there. So, yeah, I'll start training with you again. I need to get my head out of all the shit it's mired in and get my focus back."

"Good. Glad to hear it. Besides, you're the only one who can keep up with me properly. The guys I've been dealing with are pansies. I hardly break a sweat before they're lying prone on the mat."

Tom chuckled. "Right," he drawled. "Don't worry, buddy, I'll be kicking your ass before long, then you'll be the one lying prone on the mat."

"You can try," Jonathan replied with a mean grin.

Tom smirked, resuming his pacing. Jonathan's expression turned pensive before he said, "You and Kelly seem pretty tight."

"I'm in love with her," Tom said straight out. "She's the one."

Jonathan's grin nearly split his face. "Blindsided you, didn't it?"

Tom guffawed and nodded. "Right upside the head. Knocked me flat on my ass."

Jonathan's chuckle turned into a gleeful snicker. "Now you know what it feels like. I'll be able to get in a few well placed jabs at your mourned bachelorhood like you've given mine."

Tom grinned. "I guess you're entitled. I've had a lot of fun over the last four years at your expense."

Jonathan's smile dimmed. "Is she coming today?"

Tom's vanished altogether. "I hope not. I talked to her on the phone this morning. I told her I didn't want her here. I'm supposed to go to her place later on."

"And she just meekly accepted that?"

Tom grimaced. "Hardly. I had to threaten to go over there and lock her in the bathroom."

"That was considerate of you. She would've at least had a place to pee."

Tom grinned and shook his head in wonderment. "I don't know where she finds the courage. The things that have happened to her in this house have been devastating, and yet, I can't keep her away. She's amazing."

"She's in love."

"Yeah well, she shouldn't be," Tom said with a rueful smile. "Look where it's gotten her."

Jonathan collapsed the footrest, rose to his feet and strolled to the bar. "She's a strong-willed woman, Tom," he said, ice cubes clinking as he filled his glass. "You need her now and she knows it. If I were you, I'd be counting my blessings."

"What about Marsha? Do you count *your* blessings?"

"Everyday," Jonathan stated, helping himself to Tom's cranberry juice and a splash of vodka.

"I was a little surprised to see her here last night," Tom said, taking another peek out the window.

"Why? You knew after Winward's visit I'd have to tell her what was going on. Did you really expect her to stay away?"

"No, of course not," he said, turning from the window. "I guess I was just hoping you'd gloss things over. Leave out a few of the more damaging details."

"Believe me, I tried. But you know Marsha. She saw right through it. I told her as much as I thought was my place to tell. The rest I said she'd have to get from you."

"Great. Thanks a lot."

Jonathan raised his glass in salute. "You're welcome." His lips curled in a smile. "She was outraged when I told her you were a suspect. You can do no wrong, you know that, don't you?"

"That's not a very professional stance."

"On the contrary. She knows you better than you think. Hell, she knows me better than I think, and I don't think I like it much. Living with a psychologist can be a pain in the ass."

"I'll bet. What about the rest of it?"

"You mean the haunting?"

Tom nodded.

"To tell you the truth, she wasn't all that surprised." Jonathan shrugged. "She's always had a spooky sort of intuitiveness. She knew something wasn't right the day we helped you move in."

"What do you mean?"

"While you were with the carpet guys, Marsha and I had a look around. When we reached the attic stairs, she refused to go up. Something about it really scared her. I'm telling you, man, her reaction gave me the willies."

"Why didn't you tell me?" Tom asked in surprise, watching as Jonathan returned to the recliner with his drink and raised his feet.

"And what?" Jonathan asked, crossing his ankles. "Bust your bubble? I don't think so. Besides, just because there are aspects of the paranormal she doesn't question, that was before you and I were believers."

"Yeah, well, I'd better not hear the suggestion of a séance," Tom stated, going to the bar for a drink of his own then rejecting the idea. "Just the thought of it gives me the creeps."

Jonathan's grin widened. "Don't worry. I've already nipped that one in the bud."

Tom smiled with amusement. "Not exactly your conventional psychologist, is she?"

"Maybe that's what makes her so good at what she does," Jonathan said as Tom resumed his pacing.

"By the way, I called Russ this morning to fill him in on what happened last night. He was in a meeting, so I left a message for him to call here."

"Fine." Tom looked at his watch. "Are you going to be here for a while?"

"I'd planned to be," Jonathan answered, eyeing Tom with suspicion. "I'm supposed to meet Marsha here. Why?"

Tom snatched up his leather jacket and put it on.

"Where are you going?"

"To do something I should've done a long time ago. I'm going to pay Merideth Chandler a visit."

Jonathan set his glass on the sandstone coaster beside him and started to rise. "I'm coming with you."

"You can't," Tom replied, heading for the door. "You've got to meet Marsha. Besides, someone has to be here when Carson calls."

"But—"

Tom stopped in the doorway and looked back. He raised a brow. "You're not afraid to stay in the house alone, are you?"

Jonathan looked like a worried fish as he opened his mouth, closed it, opened it, then straightened his spine. "Hell no. You're spooky old house don't scare me."

Tom grinned. "Glad to hear it," he said, chuckling as he left.

Tom was marveled by Merideth Chandler's prestigious Roswell home as he pulled into the long, circular driveway. The house was secluded on several acres and could barely be seen from the road because of the trees and shrubs surrounding the property, even though most of the trees were leafless. Impressive white marble columns stretched to the second floor, supporting a spacious portico. A multitude of tall windows lined the front of the house. Their appearance gave him the impression of guarding sentinels, peering through the gray drizzle over spacious lawns, in search of visiting intruders, like him. Taking a deep breath, he faced the beveled mahogany door and pressed the lighted doorbell. Its haunting cadence echoed within the huge red brick structure.

The door was opened by a tall, thin man of about sixty with critically trimmed, gray hair. He wore the stereotypical black and white butler uniform, complete with tails and a black bow tie, all pristine and crisply pressed.

"May I help you?" he asked, regarding Tom with an imperious, bored expression.

"Yes. My name's Thomas Shear. I'm here to see Mrs. Chandler."

"I'm sorry, sir, but Mrs. Chandler is presently unavailable."

"Please. I've called several times and left messages. It's imperative that I speak with her."

"I'm sorry, sir."

The butler took a step back in dismissal. As the door began to close, Tom pressed his palm against it.

"Please, wait." He pulled an envelope from the inner breast pocket of his jacket. "Will you at least give her this?" he asked, holding it up for the man to see. "It's very important."

The man remained silent as he studied Tom with keen, assessing blue-gray eyes. "Very well," he said, taking the envelope from Tom's hand.

She watched the sleek, black car receded into the distance as the butler's soft knock pulled her away from the window. Releasing the curtain, she turned and called admittance.

"Was it the same young man?" she asked, watching as he laid Tom's envelope on the table beside her chair.

"Yes, ma'am. He's been very adamant about speaking with you."

"Thank you, Peter. That will be all."

"Yes, ma'am."

She watched his silent retreat before picking up the envelope. She withdrew the note and her breath quickened as she read.

*I know your husband was innocent. Please. I need your help.*

***Thomas Shear***

"Thomas Shear," she whispered as a tear slid down her cheek.

"We've got visitors," Tom announced, turning from the den window.

Jonathan looked hopeful. "Marsha?"

"No. Don't worry. She'll show up."

"Who is it?" Jonathan asked, following Tom downstairs. Lit candles cradled in sconces along the foyer walls were giving off their vanilla scent while soft, bluesy instrumental music drifted throughout the gallery rooms.

Tom's grin broadened as he crossed the foyer. "Jason Stafford.

And it looks like he's brought the entire student art committee with him."

Tom opened the door and Jonathan's eyes danced with amusement as Jason bounded in.

"Hey, Mr. Shear. I bet you're surprised to see us." He gave Tom's hand an enthusiastic shake. "We thought you might need a little support, this being your first day and all."

"Thanks, Jason. I can use all the support I can get." A smile played along Tom's lips as the young man surveyed his surroundings in awe.

"No problem. I think you know everyone…" Jason said, his voice trailing off as he turned in the direction of the Ice gallery.

Tom instructed the students where to hang their coats and stepped back as the group dispersed in different directions. Pursing his lips, he exhaled a deep breath as he watched Mary Ann Cooper hurrying in pursuit of Jason.

"Am I ready for this?" he asked.

Jonathan grinned. "Do you have a choice?"

The doorbell chimed and both men were startled to see Russ Carson standing on the threshold. His dark expression gave warning of his mood.

"Gentlemen, we need to have a talk."

Tom cast a glance at the students mingling through his gallery. "Now?"

"Now."

Tom curbed his irritation. "Very well. Jonathan, will you escort Mr. Carson up to my study while I excuse myself from my guests?"

"Certainly."

Jonathan led Carson upstairs as Tom went in search of Jason. He entered the gallery of Ice and his lips twitched when he saw him standing with a captivated Mary Ann while explaining his own unique impression of the painting before them.

"Excuse me. I hate to intrude, Jason, but I need to ask a favor."

"Sure thing, Mr. Shear."

"I'm going upstairs to take care of some unexpected business. I need you to keep an eye on things down here while I'm gone."

"No problem."

"Thanks."

"Uh, Mr. Shear?" Jason said as Tom began turning away. "I just wanted to tell you, I'm really impressed with what you've done here. This whole place is awesome." The young man's smile was sheepish. "It kinda gives a man hope for his own artistic future. You know what I mean?"

A subtle grin curved Tom's lips. "Yeah, I know what you mean. And thanks."

Tom gave the younger man an appreciative pat on the shoulder, then turned and made his way upstairs. As he entered his study, he saw Carson standing at the window between forest-green drapes, staring out with his stiff back facing the room. The silence was almost palpable as he looked at Jonathan and received a noncommittal shrug before closing the door.

The room was furnished so business could be conducted in stylish comfort. Three of Tom's paintings hung on the walls. The first was of his grandfather's farm in autumn at sunset. The second was an abstract with the same autumnal colors that reminded the observer of fallen leaves carpeting the ground. The third, also an abstract, depicted an old farmer in blue over-alls with his thumbs hooked in side loops, leaning toward a young boy with raven hair. Even though their features were blurred, one could still see humor in the old man and adoration in the boy as he stood with his face tilted upward.

"Now that we've all assembled," Carson said, sarcasm edging his voice, "I want to know why I was not informed of last night's attack." His eyes were filled with indignant anger as he turned from the window to face the two men. He was impeccably dressed in a dark-blue three piece suit and his white hair shone like a beacon above it.

Jonathan shrugged and eased himself into a chair. "Obviously, you failed to receive my message this morning."

"That's irrelevant," Carson remarked, standing erect with his hands locked together behind his back, looking from one man to the other. "The point is, gentlemen, I should've been informed immediately. You should've called and waited for my arrival before allowing yourselves to be questioned. I can't possibly be expected to build a defensive case if this kind of behavior continues. You're an attorney, Mr. Fields. You should know that."

"Don't blame Jonathan, Mr. Carson," Tom said, meeting the man's stern, icy gaze. "I'm the one who made the decision not to call you last night."

Carson's eyes narrowed. "Apparently, you've failed to realize the extent of your situation, Mr. Shear. We're talking about the death penalty. And that's exactly what you'll get if you continue withholding pertinent information."

Anger flared in Tom's eyes. He stood with his feet apart and crossed his arms over his chest. "I'm fully aware of my situation, Mr. Carson. I don't have to be reminded."

"Obviously, you do. I'm your consulting attorney. I should've been prepared for Detectives Winward and Hayes this morning. Instead, you made me look like a fool and I don't appreciate it."

"They came to you?" Jonathan asked. "Interesting."

"Of course, they came to me. Why shouldn't they?" Carson said. His keen gaze sharpened. "What are you thinking, Mr. Fields?"

A pensive smile appeared on Jonathan's face as he returned Carson's stare. "Doesn't it make you wonder what they're up to?" he asked. "Something tells me Tom played the right game last night by not calling you."

"In what way?"

"His actions seemed to establish a kind of truce. He answered their questions and, in return, managed to ask a few of his own. And, I must say, the answers he received were quite candid.

"May I ask what your meeting consisted of this morning?"

Carson gave a quick, agitated shrug. "They merely wanted to inform me of last night's assault. After we discussed the details, they left."

"Interesting," Jonathan repeated, stroking his chin as he pondered the possibilities. "The question is, why come to you at all? It should've been mine or Tom's responsibility to fill you in on what happened."

"It sounds to me like they're spreading the word," Tom said. "Maybe they've decided to take the possibility of someone else's involvement seriously."

Jonathan nodded. "That would be my guess. So much has happened, how could they not?"

"Indeed." Carson looked thoughtful. "Mr. Shear, perhaps I misjudged you."

Tom held the man's gaze as a soft knock sounded on the study door. Pushing aside his resentment, Tom turned toward the door and called admittance.

Kelly's smile was defiant as she stepped into the room and met Tom's gaze. She wore a fuzzy, pale green sweater that made Tom's fingers tingle with the urge to stroke it, to stroke her. Her hair was pulled back from the sides, revealing dangling jade teardrops that enticed him to nibble her dainty earlobes while rubbing the fuzzy sweater. He clamped down on his control.

"I'm sorry to intrude, Tom," she said, "but Detective Winward's downstairs. He wants to see you."

"Does he now?" His expression softened as he took her hand. "When did you get here?"

"A few minutes ago."

"Kelly, have you seen Marsha?" Jonathan asked.

"She's downstairs. We rode together."

"You did?" he asked, his brow rising in surprise.

Kelly nodded. "I picked her up. It didn't make sense the both of you having a car here."

"You're a brave woman, Kelly," Jonathan said, his eyes shimmering with mirth. "Marsha's been chomping at the bit with curiosity about you and Tom. I'm glad to see you survived."

"That's mean, Jonathan." Her shining green eyes betrayed her repressed smile.

Jonathan laughed and shook his head, lacing his fingers across his stomach. "Not mean, just realistic."

Tom led Kelly into the hallway. Pulling her close, he murmured against her ear, "What are you doing here? I thought we agreed—"

She silenced his protest with a kiss. "There's no way I could stay away," she said against his lips. "I just couldn't." She leaned back in his arms and searched his eyes. "Is everything alright?"

Tom sighed. "I'll answer that after I hear what Winward has to say." He ran a caressing finger across her cheek. The soft, musky scent of her was intoxicating. He reluctantly released his hold. "As long as you're here, you might as well send him up."

She nodded and started to turn.

"Kelly?" He took her hand. "Don't think I've forgotten about what you did last night."

She started shaking her head. "Tom, I didn't do any—"

He cupped her jaw in his palm and forced her to meet his gaze. "Please. Will you talk to me about it later tonight? Will you trust me?"

She searched his eyes for a long moment then nodded. "Tonight," she said and turned away.

Tom's brow was drawn as he re-entered the study leaving the door open. "It would seem our meeting's getting cozier by the minute, gentlemen. Detective Winward's on his way up."

"Are you going to mention your little excursion this afternoon?" Jonathan asked, keeping his tone casual.

"Probably."

Carson looked from one to the other, settling on Tom. "More secrets, Mr. Shear?"

Before Tom could reply, Winward entered the room.

"Good afternoon, gentlemen. I hope my appearance isn't an inconvenience."

"Of course not, detective," Carson replied. "Why on earth would you say that?"

"Mr. Carson. I wasn't expecting to see you twice in one day."

"Nor I, sir. I can't exactly say it's a pleasure."

Winward dismissed the attorney with an indulgent smile and turned to face Tom. "I noticed the paintings in your Rage collection have been returned to their proper places, Mr. Shear. Did you work through the night or take the day off to ready your gallery?"

"Surely, you must know the answer to that, detective," Tom said. "The men you've had watching must've given you their report by now."

"Ah. I see you've noticed my surveillance team. That's quite astute of you."

"Not really. As Jonathan commented earlier, 'it was halfway expected.'"

"May I ask what you're hoping to accomplish by putting my client under surveillance, Detective Winward?" Carson asked. "You couldn't possibly believe he'd be stupid enough to commit some grievous crime while you're breathing down his neck, could you?"

"Your client was attacked last night, sir. Or have you forgotten?"

Carson stiffened. His cold eyes narrowed as he stared at Winward. Jonathan cleared his throat, drawing attention, defusing the electric tension filling the air.

"Detective, is there a purpose for this meeting?" he asked.

"I came to inform Mr. Shear of the team I have stationed outside, but apparently there was no need."

"Let me ask you something, detective," Tom said. He leaned back against his desk and crossed his arms. "Is the one car all you have, or are there more?"

"Don't worry, Mr. Shear. My men are very experienced."

"Were your men supposed to be watching me or the house?" Tom continued, ignoring for the moment that Winward had failed to answer his question.

"Both, actually. Why?"

"Because I drove out to the Chandler residence this afternoon and was surprised no one followed."

Winward glanced at the door. The men watched as he raised a ceasing hand and stepped into the hallway. "Why, Mr. Raymond," he said. "Isn't this a surprise? May I ask how long you've been standing there?"

Michael Raymond stepped into view, sputtering with outraged embarrassment. "How dare you suggest such a thing? I can assure you, sir, I am no eavesdropper." He took a visible hold on his composure before stepping into the room.

"Please, forgive my intrusion, Mr. Shear. Things are not as they appear. I merely dropped by to deliver the documents we discussed over dinner the other night. My father was unable to get away, so I offered my services. I apologize if my boldness seems offensive."

Tom forced a smile. "No apologies are necessary, Mr. Raymond. If you'll allow me a moment, I'll be happy to look over the documents you've brought."

"Gentlemen, Mr. Raymond's arrival reminded me that I've neglected my guests downstairs long enough. If you have anything further to discuss with me, I'll be available after my gallery closes this evening."

"There are still a few matters that need to be clarified, Mr. Shear." Carson cast Tom a meaningful stare, bristling at being dismissed.

"I'm aware of that," Tom replied, ignoring the implied command in Carson's voice as he escorted the men from the room. "In the meantime, I'm sure Mr. Field's will be able to answer any questions you might have."

Tom caught Jonathan's eye as Carson and Winward turned toward the stairs. "I need you to take care of Carson," he murmured. "He's going to ask about Merideth Chandler and I want you to play it down. Tell him as little as possible. I don't want him interfering if she grants me an interview."

"Right. What about Winward?"

"I'll take care of Winward. You just smooth things over with Carson."

"I'll do what I can."

When Tom returned to the study, Michael Raymond was standing in front of the painting of his grandfather's farm. Tom motioned to a chair.

"Have a seat, Mr. Raymond."

"Thank you."

Michael sat and retrieved documents from his briefcase. He handed them over as Tom propped his hip on the corner of his desk.

"I must tell you, Mr. Shear, I was appalled to hear of last night's assault and attempted theft. Nothing was damaged, I hope."

Tom glanced up from the papers in his hand and met Michael's level gaze. "News travels fast," he replied.

"Especially when it's delivered to your door by two detectives. That Detective Hayes is an intimidating sort, isn't he?"

"They visited your office?"

"Indeed, they did. They interviewed my father, as well. It's rather worrisome they even thought to come to us."

"They were only doing their job, Mr. Raymond. They asked me who might have an interest in my Rage collection. Considering your father's adamancy about my selling, I mentioned your names.

I wouldn't worry, if I were you, however. Unless, of course, you have something to worry about," Tom said, holding the man's gaze.

Michael's eyes grew wide with indignation. "Surely, sir, you're not insinuating my father and I could possibly have had anything to do with what happened here last night. The mere suggestion is offensive and—"

"Relax, Mr. Raymond," Tom told him. The tight rein he was holding on his patience was beginning to slip. "You have to understand my position. I was attacked last night. They tried to steal my collection and destroy my home. Do you actually think I'd withhold information that might help apprehend the people responsible? Think, man. My very life was at stake. Of course I'm going to do whatever I can."

"Yes, of course," Michael conceded.

Tom returned his eyes to the contract in his hand and tried to focus. The realization that he had let a virtual stranger glimpse his emotions was unsettling.

Michael cleared his throat. "Forgive my curiosity, Mr. Shear," he said, "but I couldn't help overhearing Merideth Chandler being mentioned earlier. Have you by any chance spoken with her?"

Tom remained silent as he lifted his eyes and impaled Michael Raymond with his stare.

"Please, don't take offense. It's just that I spent quite a lot of time with the family when their son Jacob and I were boys. I grew to care for them greatly and my heart goes out to the poor woman."

Tom moved behind his desk and sat down. "What's your point?" he asked.

"I'm merely interested in her welfare, Mr. Shear. If you've spoken with her, I was hoping you'd be kind enough to tell me how she's faring."

"I haven't had the pleasure, yet, Mr. Raymond. If, or when, I do, I'll be glad to relay your concern."

"Thank you. I would appreciate that."

"Now, shall we get to business?"

"Certainly."

The details of the contract were discussed. Satisfied, Tom penned his signature to the documents.

"It would seem, Mr. Raymond, we've made a very optimizing arrangement," Tom said, rising from his chair.

"Yes. I want to thank you for your indulgence, Mr. Shear. I think we've both prospered here today." Michael smiled as he placed the contracts in his briefcase. "I'm sure my father will be pleased."

"I'm sure he will," Tom said, following Michael from the study. "Would you care to stay and join me for a drink of celebration?"

Michael chuckled as he descended the stairs. "I wish I could, but I really must be heading back. I've taken enough of your time as it is." He retrieved his coat and umbrella from the foyer stand. "But I'll take a rain check. Father hated that he couldn't be here today so he'll probably want to join us." He slipped into his coat and flipped up the collar.

"Anytime," Tom replied, opening the front door. "Please, give your father my regards."

"I will. Have a good evening, sir."

The smile faded from Tom's face as he watched Michael Raymond open his umbrella and hurry toward the black Lincoln parked in the wide driveway.

"Well?" Jonathan asked, appearing at his side.

"They offered a good deal. They'll be back in a few days to look over my inventory."

"Congratulations." Jonathan smiled and clapped Tom on the shoulder. "Just think, I'm going to know someone famous."

Tom's lips twisted in a cynical grin. "How'd it go with Carson? Is he still here?"

"No. But you were right. He questioned me about Merideth Chandler."

"What'd you tell him?"

"I told him she was a shot in the dark. That you had been refused a meeting and had given up on the idea of talking to her."

"Did he believe you?"

"I think so. But I got the impression he might pursue the idea."

"Why?"

"Because he's a good attorney, Tom. A good attorney will do almost anything if it'll help his case."

"Well, let's hope I get to her first. What about Winward?" Tom asked, watching an older couple, walking arm in arm, emerge from the room of Life and disappear down the hallway into the room of Ice. He lifted an inquiring brow and Jonathan followed his gaze.

"Oh, yeah. They showed up while you were upstairs. Said they saw your advertisement in the paper. There're a few others floating around somewhere who said the same thing."

"At least something's going right. What about Winward?" he repeated.

"He left after we came downstairs. He said to tell you he'd be back."

"I have no doubt of that."

Tom glanced up and smiled as a pair of students crossed the foyer. "I was told a tidbit of information you might find interesting," he said, leaning close. "It would seem Winward and Hayes had a busy morning. Carson wasn't the only one who received a visit. Craig and Michael Raymond were on their list, as well."

"Really?" Jonathan's brow rose in speculation. "That *is* interesting."

"That's not all. Michael Raymond admitted overhearing our conversation as I mentioned Merideth Chandler. He asked if I'd spoken with her."

Jonathan's brow rose a little higher. "And what reason did he give for wanting to know that?"

"He told me he had grown to care for the family as a boy and was only concerned for her welfare."

"Did you believe him?"

Tom shrugged as he cast a glance over Jonathan's shoulder. Marsha approached with a scolding smile.

"Well, well, if it isn't the elusive Thomas Shear." She sidled up to Jonathan and watched Tom with appraising eyes.

"Sorry, sweetheart. I had some business that took longer than expected."

"How's the head?"

"The headache's gone, if that's what you mean."

"And if it's not?" she asked.

He met the concern in her eyes. "Then you might as well give it up," he said. "I went through therapy a long time ago. I'm really okay."

"I know that. But you still might need to talk. I just want you to know that I'm here for you."

Tom watched her a moment longer then heaved a sigh. His smile was soft as he kissed her cheek. "I appreciate your concern. I really do. But now's not the time. If you really want to help, then help us figure out who's doing this and why."

"I intend to."

"Damn! What a team," Jonathan said, giving them an enthusiastic grin. "This guy doesn't stand a chance."

"Speaking of the team, where's Kelly?" Tom asked, looking around.

Marsha's eyes glistened with mirth. "She's in the room of Innocence with Jason. That brother of hers is something else. He has women all over him."

Tom grinned. "This, I've got to see."

"I'm not a bit surprised," Jonathan said, draping his arm over Marsha's shoulders as they followed Tom across the foyer. "There's just no escaping the charismatic charm of a virile man, darlin'. Haven't you learned that by now? You've certainly been exposed to the phenomena often enough. Hanging out with Tom and I should've taught you the warning signs."

Marsha rolled her hazel eyes and laughed. "When I start needing a club to fight my way through a throng of drooling women, I'll buy one."

"Christmas is right around the corner, you know."

"If I find a club under the tree, Jonathan Fields, the first thing I'll use it on is your head to deflate that delusional ego of yours."

Tom's smile widened as he entered the room of Innocence. He realized Marsha's description wasn't far off as he watched the women of the student committee, and a couple he didn't recognize, gathered around Jason with mooning eyes. He almost laughed to see Mary Ann Cooper's hostile stare daring them to venture too close.

"Quite the lady's man," he replied as Kelly came to stand beside him, wrapping her arms around his waist.

"He has a good teacher." Her smile turned impish as she watched his surprise. "You're his role model, you know."

"I am?"

Jonathan smirked with amusement. "Be careful how you tread, Tom. It would appear you hold the fate of either success or failure for that young man's sexual future in the palms of your hands."

"Jonathan?"

"Yes, Tom?"

"Shut up."

# CHAPTER TWENTY-EIGHT

As daylight descended, the temperature dropped, transforming the day-long drizzle into crystals of sleet which fell in a soothing pitter-pat rhythm. He closed the heavy drapes against the winter night and tightened the belt of his blue silk robe. Lifting a snifter to his lips, he leveled his gaze on the brown leather album lying open on a low table.

He knew he should've gotten rid of it. But its beckoning power overrode his self-preserving instincts. Instead, he kept it hidden, taking it out only when his reminiscent urges became too overpowering to resist.

It was his one true weakness, the one indulgence he had allowed himself over the years. Leafing through the album's stiff pages, each one a bittersweet reminder of the budding lives he had so ruthlessly extinguished, filled him with swelling triumph. Their individual lives had meant nothing to him each time he'd focused his Polaroid camera, but their suffering had; that's what he saw whenever he permitted himself to peruse the pages.

He sipped from his snifter once more and took a step closer. As he looked down into the bruised, swollen eyes of Amanda Sawyer, his expression grew smug before his gaze shifted to the corresponding newspaper clipping.

"You shouldn't have been born a girl, you know," he said, stroking the tiny, terror-stricken face in the photo. "I had to do it. If I hadn't, you would've grown up to be a deceitful, slutting woman like all the rest. I couldn't allow that."

His eyes grew glazed as a memory of a touch whispered in his mind. The memory solidified and his heartbeat quickened. His skin began to tingle beneath its gentle caress as he remembered his mother taking him into her bed to begin his lessons by letting him suckle at her breast as she stoked his hair, pulling him closer. At first, her coaxing moans had frightened him until she laughed softly and explained that what he did made her feel good in the way only a man could make her feel. His ten year old ego soared at being thought of as a man. And as time went by and he grew bolder, she began to teach him the giving, and taking, of sexual pleasure. The feel of his mother's smooth, warm skin beneath his fingers as she encouraged his tentative explorations had been exciting. Fascinated by her soft moans and the reaction of his own inexperienced body, he quickly became a willing, eager student.

But as he grew older and became more demanding, her attention began to wane. When she began seeing other men and became pregnant as a result, he was enraged. He loathed the sight of her extended belly and the way she waddled when she walked during her last trimester.

After the baby girl was born, he expected things to return to the way they had once been, but they didn't. Instead, he became an outcast. His mother doted on the child constantly. He could feel the love that rightfully belonged to him slipping through his fingers. He could do nothing to stop it and his resentment deepened as he watched the child flourish.

"Emily," he sneered. His eyes grew wild as he hurled his glass against the wall. He watched it shatter into a thousand glittering shards and began to pace as its contents trickled like tears.

"Damn you!" His nostrils flared as he breathed deeply to maintain his self-control. "I was twenty. I was a man. I needed her! Can't you see I had no choice?"

He paced to the bar and filled another snifter with cognac. He took a long pull, wiped his chin with his sleeve, and laughed.

"It was so easy," he whispered, staring with unfocused eyes. A contented smile played along his lips. "You followed me so trustingly. Even as I picked up the brick and raised it above my head, you watched with wide, trusting eyes."

His musing gaze clouded with suspicion. "Why didn't you cry out?" he asked. "I crushed your skull and you didn't make a sound. Why?"

He remembered her whimpering moans as he carried her to the well. He had been glad she didn't die instantly. She was going to suffer as he had suffered for six long years, and the thought had filled him with bitter satisfaction.

After Emily's death, he had anxiously awaited the return of his mother's affection. Instead, she had grown more withdrawn, sitting for hours in silence, pinning him beneath her stare. Somehow, she had known.

"It took them only hours to find your body," he said, his voice hardening. "Two weeks later, I found hers."

He ran his hand across his face as if to wipe the memory away and drank deeply before refilling his glass. His gaze returned to the album and his body quaked with the thought of the paintings still hanging in Shear Gallery. He'd planned it all so carefully. Now everything had been ruined by a smart-ass punk.

"Idiot!" he shouted, slamming his glass down. "You deserved to die for being so stupid. Those paintings should be mine now, and Shear should've been left in ruins. Now, thanks to you, dear Roger, he'll become more challenging than ever."

He began to pace as his mind raced with calculating precision.

"Shear's a clever man. If he talks to that bitch Merideth Chandler, he'll realize the truth. And when he does, I'll be ruined. I can't let that happen."

He stopped abruptly and his eyes fell to the album. *I've got to get rid of it. It's the only piece of damning evidence there is. Everything else would be circumstantial at best.*

A smile curved his lips. As an idea began to take form, his smile broadened until he was cackling with laughter.

———— ◆ ————

The last car pulled away and Tom closed the door. Leaning against it, he watched Kelly smile sympathetically and felt her fingers slide through his black hair.

"You look worn out."

"I am," he answered, triumph shining in his eyes, a smile playing on his lips.

"You should be," Jonathan said while holding Marsha's coat as she slipped her arms into the sleeves. "There were people in and out of here all day. And they were all clamoring for your attention. Especially the women." He waggled an eyebrow. "I can tell you, it was a sight to see."

"You're not kidding," Marsha said, straightening Jonathan's coat collar. "There's still a small town mentality about this place, you know. Before long Thomas Shear is going to be a household name."

"I think it already is," Kelly said. "The drama that played out here last night has the gossip grapevine sizzling. One conversation I overheard had Tom pegged as an international spy working with the police to break an underground art smuggling ring. According to one source that no one could actually name, there were bodies strewn all over the yard after the gunfight with the police."

Jonathan laughed outright. "I know what you mean, Kelly. I had one woman sidle up to me, her eyes blazing with curiosity, and ask in a conspiratorial whisper, 'Is it true?' and I whispered back, 'Is what true?', and she answers, 'That Thomas Shear is a playboy secret agent.'"

"No!" Marsha gasped and laughed. "How did you answer that?"

"I leaned down, because she was shorter than me, you know, and whispered in her ear, 'Yes. But you can't tell anyone.' Then she drew back fanning herself and said, 'I understand,' before making a bee-line to a group of women watching us."

Tom chuckled shaking his head as he walked around the foyer snuffing the ensconced candles. The smell of burnt wick and wax filled the air. The two floor lamps standing in the corners were left on. "Great. Just the reputation I was hoping for. I actually had a man, a neighbor from across the street, come up to me and ask me point blank 'what happened here last night.' I told him a burglar triggered the alarm and the police shot the guy before he could shoot them."

"Regardless," Kelly said, pride shimmering in her eyes as she watched him, "you should be proud of yourself. Even with all of the intrigue, you managed to sell a couple of your paintings, didn't you?"

"I did. But it was probably *because* of the intrigue."

Ignoring Jonathan and Marsha, Tom pulled Kelly into his arms. His grin faded as he lowered his head and gave her a languid kiss.

Jonathan smiled crookedly. "I think that's our cue to leave."

"Jonathan, darling, have you looked outside? We should've left an hour ago."

"Come on," Tom said, keeping his eyes on Kelly. "I'll follow you home before this weather gets any worse."

"I left my coat on your bed. I'll run up and get it."

Her voice was husky as she met his gaze with soft, alluring eyes. She turned away, and Tom's smile grew lazy as he took a moment to admire her heart-shaped, jean-clad bottom.

"You guys wait a minute. We'll walk you out," he said. "Kelly, wait. I'll come with you."

She opened her mouth to protest then clamped it shut as she cast a hesitant glance to the top of the stairs. The only light sources illuminating the landing were lamps emanating from the den and bedroom doorways down the hall. Tom was filled with remorse at the apprehension he saw in her eyes.

Before he had a chance to move toward Kelly, a knock resounded through the quiet house. Peering over his shoulder, Tom stared at the front door in disbelief.

"Now what?"

Tom jerked the door open and watched as Detective Winward stepped inside.

"Oh please, do come in," he said, closing the door with an irritable thud.

"You don't seem happy to see me, Mr. Shear." An amused grin flitted across the detective's face.

"That's very perceptive. I'm impressed." Tom crossed his arms and leaned his shoulder against the doorframe. His eyes narrowed as he took in Winward's appearance. "How long have you been out there?"

Winward ran his hand over his wet head and grimaced. "Long enough. Next time I'm wearing my parka."

Jonathan looked dubious. "Where's Detective Hayes? You didn't leave him shivering in the cold, did you?"

Winward flashed a grin. "As a matter of fact, I did."

"Why didn't you come in sooner?"

"I didn't want to be interrupted, or overheard, by pesky neighbors. You had a busy day today, Shear. Congratulations."

Tom ignored the compliment. "Can't it wait? I was just about to see Kelly home."

"I'm not worried about Miss Stafford hearing what I have to say."

Jonathan raised a challenging brow. "Wait a minute. You're not getting rid of us that easily."

"Look, detective," Tom said. "Anything you have to say can be said. Everyone here knows what's going on."

Winward hesitated and then shrugged. "All right then. I lied this afternoon, Mr. Shear. I knew you went to see Merideth Chandler."

The corner of Tom's mouth lifted in a forbearing smile. "I expected as much. Even though I didn't see anyone following, I knew you wouldn't just let me come and go as I pleased. But why the game? I really don't think your little deception fooled anyone. Everyone in the study today, with the exception of Michael Raymond, knows I'm considered a suspect."

"That's right. But I think you're overlooking one important point."

"Which is?"

"The break-in. It's obvious Roger Wilson bungled the job by getting caught, so therefore, his only accomplishment was to throw doubt on any suspicions we might have about you. His accomplice, if there is one, will know this. Odds are he'll accept the idea that the surveillance team you saw is the only one watching you and this house."

Tom remained silent, his brow furrowed in thought.

Winward continued. "I had a hunch everyone connected with the case would find an excuse to be here today. I'm proud to say, Mr. Shear, you played your part to a tee. You couldn't have asked better questions if I'd coached you myself."

"Do you mean you wanted your men to be seen?" Kelly asked.

"The one team, yes," Tom responded. "He'll probably let the men sit for a couple of days and then move them to another, more discreet, location to make the person responsible think they've been removed altogether. If he takes the bait, maybe he'll make his next move."

"Precisely," Winward acclaimed. "And when he does, we'll have him."

"How many men do you have on surveillance, detective?"

Winward shrugged. "Enough."

"Aren't you forgetting something?"

"What do you mean?"

"Everyone was here today, like you said, with the exception of Craig Raymond."

Winward's dark eyes glinted. A small smile raised the corner of his mouth. "I'm not overly worried about Craig Raymond. I'm gambling his son will inform him of the day's developments."

"Are you saying you think Michael Raymond overheard the entire conversation?" Jonathan asked.

"Oh, I made sure of it. Michael Raymond pulled in as I entered the house. By sending Miss Stafford up to announce my arrival, I bought the time I needed to make sure he saw me. I knew he'd be curious enough to follow. All I had to do was commence with a little chit-chat until he had time to position himself outside the door."

"You sound pretty sure of yourself, and of Michael Raymond," Tom replied.

Winward dismissed Tom's misgivings with a wave of his hand. "I want to hear about your visit to Merideth Chandler. Did you speak to her?" he asked.

"No. But I was allowed to leave a note. I was assured she'd receive it."

"What did your note say?"

"That I knew her husband was innocent and that I needed her help."

Winward looked at Tom in surprise. "That was a pretty gutsy statement, Mr. Shear, considering the position you're in."

Tom gave Winward a dead-pan stare. "I'm aware of that, detective," he said. "I can only hope she'll take me seriously enough to respond."

"If she does, I want to be informed."

"You and everyone else."

"What's that suppose to mean?"

"Nothing."

"I'm serious, Shear." Winward held Tom's gaze. "If she makes contact with you, I want to know about it."

"You will, detective," Tom said, his voice flat. "As soon as I talk to her, if I talk to her, I'll tell you all about it."

Winward shook his head. "That's not good enough."

"What do you mean, 'that's not good enough?' What more do you want?"

"You don't really expect me to let you go alone do you?"

Tom bit off a reply. His jaw clenched as his gaze fused with Winward's. "I guess not."

Satisfied, Winward gave a small smile and nodded.

"Detective Winward, may I say something?" Marsha asked, drawing everyone's attention.

Winward turned to face her. "Of course, Miss Webster. Say away."

"You know that Tom's not the man you're looking for, don't you?"

"And what makes you think that?"

"For one thing, the candid way you're talking with us. For another, you wouldn't be much of a detective if you did. You know as well as I do he doesn't fit the profile."

"And on what are you basing your opinion?"

"Experience, detective."

"Miss Webster, you've known Mr. Shear a long time. Is that correct?"

"It is."

"Then couldn't it be possible your professional judgment is clouded by your emotional attachment?"

Marsha gave Winward a thin smile. "Don't patronize me, detective. I've researched and performed enough case studies to strongly suspect the person you should be looking for is a psychopath."

"I agree. But we also have to look at the evidence, and the biggest majority of it is pointing to your friend here."

Marsha released an impatient sigh. "Look, detective. A psychopath has one defining feature that sets him apart from others engaged in criminal activities. He's cold, heartless. He lacks emotional response. He feels nothing for the pain he causes. You have to understand. A psychopath's brain doesn't function like those who are non-psychopathic. MRI brain scans show a dramatically different processing between normal men and psychopaths while observing emotionally provocative events.

"The scan of a psychopath displays very little color in the brain stem area where the scan of a normal man reveals striking color patterns radiating toward the temporal lobes, thereby indicating extensive brain activity. In other words, a psychopath has no conscience. No remorse. Only a person lacking those abilities could've performed the brutal crimes that have been committed here. There's also a probability, considering the type of victims he's chosen, that sexual abuse by an adult female when he was a child triggered his murdering instincts."

"You are aware that Mr. Shear was a victim of abuse as well, aren't you?"

"I am. But there's a huge difference. Tom exhibits none of the traits I've mentioned. He shows no signs of the characteristics indicative of a psychopathic personality. More importantly, Tom's no longer a victim. He's a survivor. With the help of therapy, he was able to come to terms with what happened to him. He accepted who he was, therefore enabling himself to begin the healing process and move on."

"You're sure of this."

"I'd stake my professional reputation on it."

"I wouldn't be so quick to say that, if I were you. That could be exactly what you're asked to do."

Winward held her gaze until she gave a sharp nod of acknowledgement, then turned to Tom.

"Mr. Shear, I believe you said you were about to see Miss Stafford home."

Tom felt dazed as he tore his gaze from Marsha's face. "That's right," he said. "I'd hoped to be out of here before the weather worsened."

"Don't worry. It hasn't begun to stick on the roads, yet. You have time," Winward replied. "Are you coming home, afterward?"

Tom's lips twisted roguishly as he looked at the detective. "Probably not, mom," he answered and watched Winward's mouth twitch.

"Mind if my men tag along?"

"Do I have a choice?"

"No. But don't worry. You won't be expected to share your pillow. They know to bring their own."

Tom grunted with ill humor and opened the door. "In that case, I would suggest you tell your men to bundle up. As you well know, it's a nasty night."

Winward's eyes glimmered with amusement as he gave a curt nod.

Jonathan cuffed Tom's shoulder before following the detective out. "We'll talk to you two later. Be careful tonight."

"Count on it," Tom said. He caught Marsha's hand before she could precede Jonathan through the door. "Marsha? Thank you."

She smiled and shook her head. "Not necessary."

Tom closed the door and sighed.

"Marsha pushed a strong point tonight," Kelly said, her voice soft.

"Yeah, she did. I hope Winward heard her."

"He was listening."

Tom's look lingered as he gave Kelly a gentle smile. "Come on," he said, squeezing her hand. "Let's get our coats and get out of here."

"You know, I think I might actually like that man," she said, leading the way upstairs and into the bedroom.

"You've got to be kidding." Tom scowled as she slipped her arms into the coat he held up for her.

"He's just doing his job, Tom. Isn't that what you told me?"

Tom grunted, unimpressed. He watched a smile play along her lips, then draped his arm across her shoulders, pulling her close to nip the lobe of her ear with his teeth.

"Let's just hope he's on our side, likable or not."

They stepped into the hallway and watched two small vapors solidify in front of them. The regret Tom saw in their bruised, sunken eyes made his blood run cold.

"No," Kelly moaned, backing away. "Please, no."

Caroline Doltry and Julie Dobbs took a unified step forward. Scooping Kelly into his arms, Tom ran for the main staircase. When the two little girls materialized below him, he stopped and spun around, only to see Rachel Porter and Amy Monroe emerging from the attic stairs to block his path. As the four little girls moved in converging unison, Kelly's scream split the eerie silence.

Tom bolted into a headlong descent. The familiar paralysis weighed heavy in his limbs, causing his fear to escalate as he struggled to keep Kelly sheltered in his arms. He fell against the banister in an attempt to keep his balance, but his knees buckled and he was only able to stumble a few steps lower before he collapsed back upon the stairs.

Suddenly, the unnaturally cold air turned frosty as the lights flickered and then flared with blinding brilliance, shattering random bulbs throughout the house with popping, hissing explosions. Kelly's screams crescendoed and her body convulsed as the girls stepped close and seemed to melt, one by one, into Kelly's chest. As the last little girl merged and disappeared, Kelly fell limp against him and a sob shook Tom's body. He gathered her close, tightening his hold, ignoring the two detectives standing wide-eyed just within the open doorway, silhouetted by the ambient light outside. A gust of wet, arctic wind rushed in behind them.

The surveillance officers advanced and Winward cast Hayes a warning glance. With the hint of a nod, the huge man filled the doorway then stepped outside, closing the door behind him, leaving them in darkness.

The chandelier came on, its light dim with only a few bulbs left intact, before Tom felt a hand press against his shoulder. His face felt like stone, but his eyes burned and he saw Winward flinch when he looked at him.

"They've won." Tom's voice was disturbingly calm. "They took her and there was nothing I could do to stop them."

Winward cleared his throat. "I know. I saw what happened." He avoided Tom's eyes by checking Kelly's pulse. "We should get Miss Stafford to a hospital."

"No."

"She needs help, Shear."

"Not that kind of help."

"What do you mean, 'not that kind of help'?" Winward snapped. "Look at her."

Kelly's face was ashen. Tears slid from beneath her closed lids and Tom tenderly brushed them away.

Winward's expression was grave as he rose to his feet. "I'm calling an ambulance."

A whispered "no" stopped him.

Winward turned to see Kelly watching him. Her eyes shimmered with tears and her voice was weak, but she had regained control.

"Doctor's can't help. Tom's the only one who can help us now," she said, shifting her gaze to the man who held her. "He knows what to do."

Tom's heart lurched. "Kelly, I—"

She shook her head and her eyes fluttered shut. A shiver passed through her body.

———•((●))•———

Tom helped Kelly into her nightgown before putting her to bed. She struggled to keep her sagging eyelids open, but she seemed powerless against the weariness which weighed her down.

"Will you stay?" she asked. Her eyes flickered open and met his gaze.

He sat down beside her, tucking the purple sheet and floral comforter more snuggly around her shoulders like a cocoon. "Sweetheart, a garrison of troops couldn't drag me away."

His smile was tender as he bent to kiss her. He rubbed the furrow that creased her brow with his thumb and watched her eyes close once more before reaching for the bedside lamp.

"No," she said in a breath. "Leave it on."

His next kiss lingered as he swallowed the thickening in his throat. Rising to his feet, he blinked hard to clear his vision before leaving Kelly's bedroom to face the man waiting in the next room.

"How is she?"

"Sleeping."

Winward turned from the window where he stood with the lace sheer pulled aside watching the sleet tapping against the panes. He shook his head. "I still think we should've taken her to the hospital. They could do a hell of a lot more for her than we can."

Tom rubbed a weary hand over his face. "Could they?" he asked, meeting Winward's dark, brooding gaze. "What could they do? All of the tests in the world wouldn't be able to explain what happened to her. She would probably be confined to some mental ward with the diagnosis being acute depression." Tom gave a harsh laugh.

"Drugs and weekly visits to a shrink is not what she needs, and I'll be damned if I'll let that happen to her. So, unless you want to try and explain what caused Kelly's collapse, and make them believe you," he said, "I suggest you give the matter some thought."

Winward scowled as he turned back to the window and looked out. Heaving a sigh, Tom went into the kitchen and returned with brandy and glasses.

"Where's Hayes?"

"He went home."

"Why? Too much for the big guy to handle?"

Tom's lips took on an acerbic curve when he saw the detective's noncommittal shrug. "Here," he said, handing Winward a glass. "And don't give me any of your duty crap. I think we're will past that by now."

Winward sniffed the brandy, then lifted his glass in saluting agreement before tipping it to his lips. As Tom began a restless march around Kelly's den, picking up nick-knacks then replacing them and studying family photos on the walls, the detective sank into a chair.

"What'd she mean when she said you were the only one who could help? She used the term 'us' when she said it. She also said you knew what to do." Winward paused as Tom's sullen expression darkened. "Do you?"

"I think so."

"Well, would you mind explaining? I'm not stupid, but this supernatural shit's a little beyond my field of expertise."

"And I suppose you think I know all about it."

"You know a hell of a lot more than I do."

A knock on the door postponed Tom's reply. Looking at Winward, he lifted a questioning brow. "Expecting anyone?"

Winward shook his head. "Not me."

Tom opened the door to a brooding Hayes who stood hunched and shivering in the frigid wind.

"What are you doing here?" he asked, stepping out of the man's way. "Winward said you went home."

"Huh. To do what?" Hayes rumbled. "Sleep? Not bloody likely."

Tom glanced at Winward and watched a knowing smile lift the corners of the detective's mouth.

"Curiosity got the better of you, I see," Winward said, settling himself back into his seat. "I thought it might. Once you had time to think things over, that is."

Hayes gave a loud snort as he took off his coat and slung it over a chair at the dining table. Accepting the glass Tom held out to him, he gave an appreciative nod and eased his bulk onto the sofa before offering Winward his skeptical regard.

"I suppose that means you've completely reconciled yourself to the impossible?"

Winward shrugged and sipped his brandy. "Maybe not completely. But I'm a man of facts, Don, like you. And the fact is, I really saw what I saw tonight. I didn't make it up and I didn't imagine it. Neither did you. Kelly Stafford's proof of that. Besides, who are we to say what's truly impossible or not?"

"How is she?"

With his anger flaring, Tom cut Winward off before he could say anything. "How do you think she is?" he snarled. "She's being torn apart." He tossed back the remaining brandy in his glass and ran an agitated hand through his hair.

After a short, uncomfortable pause, Tom looked at Hayes. "I'm sorry," he said. "I had no right to speak to you that way. It's just that Kelly's very important to me."

"Mr. Shear, I saw what happened. At least, I think I did, and I don't think there was anything any of us could've done."

"You're wrong. I should've found a way to keep her from that house. I knew what could happen. It's happened before."

Winward's expression grew pensive. "I remember you mentioning a paralysis that overtook you whenever the spirits appeared to Miss Stafford. It happened again tonight, didn't it?"

"Yes. I'm surprised you didn't feel it."

"I did," Winward said. He turned to Hayes. "What about you?"

"I felt something, but I thought it was a reaction of being scared shitless."

"That admission must be monumental for a man like you, Don." Winward held up his glass. "I salute you for admitting you're human."

"I thought you'd left after we'd all said our goodbyes," Tom said, watching Winward get up to refill his glass. "What made you come back?"

"Don and I were discussing tomorrow's arrangements when the screaming started. For a second, I thought it was the wind," he admitted and took a fortifying drink. "But there was something strange about it. It was too damned eerie. Luckily, the door was unlocked or Hayes here would've broken it down."

"How much did you see?"

"Enough to grab our attention if that's what you want to hear," Hayes replied, meeting Tom's eyes with a scowl.

"Enough to make you believe?"

"Believe?" Hayes grunted. "There's still the possibility of fraud, Mr. Shear. We have devices nowadays that can do all sorts of things. I would imagine someone with the know-how would have no problem staging what Detective Winward and I saw tonight. But then again, I'm no electronic wizard. Are you?"

"And what about Kelly?" Tom asked, trying not to grind his teeth.

"Miss Stafford? Well now, that is a little puzzling. But experience has taught me that a woman, no matter how intelligent, will do almost anything for the man she loves if she's handled right."

Tom was momentarily speechless. Passing Hayes a scathing look, he turned to resume his pacing as he struggled to control his seething temper.

"Right now, detective, I really don't give a damn what you think. Kelly's the only person who matters now."

"Which leads me back to the question I asked earlier," Winward said. "What exactly did she mean when she said you were the only one who could help them?"

"It should be obvious, detective. Especially to a man like yourself."

"Humor me."

"Nine little girls are dead and the man responsible is still out there. Obviously, they expect me to find him."

"What do you mean 'nine little girls are dead'?" Hayes growled. "At last count, Mr. Shear, there were only eight."

"That's by your estimate, detective, not mine. There's one you haven't accounted for yet: Emmy."

"Ah, yes. The little girl you first told us about." Hayes stared at Tom with dark eyes. "There's only one problem with that, Mr. Shear. If you're so sure she's connected with this case, maybe you can explain why no missing person's report was ever filed? Surely, someone would've reported her disappearance to the authorities."

"I can't answer that. Maybe she lived in a different area or a different state."

Hayes shook his head. "Not likely. I checked police records. I went back several years and there was no one fitting her description in the system."

"What do you expect me to say? Regardless of what you might think, I don't have all of the answers. All I'm working with right now is instinct, and my instincts are telling me she has the main role in all of this."

"What do you mean?"

Tom heaved a sigh. "If I answer that, Detective Hayes, you'll only say I've added another nail to my coffin."

"Try me."

Tom regarded the man in silence, then shook his head with a

humorless smile. "What the hell. Things can't get much worse, can they?"

"That all depends."

Ignoring the remark, Tom walked to the window Winward had vacated earlier and peered into the darkness.

"I think she was the first to be murdered," he said. "I also think she knew the man responsible."

Hayes cleared his throat, but said nothing.

"What makes you think that?" Winward asked.

Tom shrugged. "It's just a feeling. Maybe it's because she was the first to appear, I don't know. But she seems more confident than the rest. Stronger somehow. In some way, she holds the key. I think if we could find out who she is, that knowledge would lead us to the killer."

Tom turned, letting the sheer curtain fall back into place and saw Kelly standing in the doorway. He stepped over and gathered her in his arms.

"Baby, what are you doing up?"

"I thought you'd left."

He looked into her eyes as he caressed her cheek. "I'm not going anywhere. Come on, I'll take you back to bed."

"No," she said breathlessly. "I don't want to sleep. I don't want to dream anymore."

Her imploring eyes had assumed the sunken, haunted characteristics of the portraits in his gallery and the sight filled Tom with dread. Pulling her close, he stroked her sleep tousled hair.

"Okay," he said. "At least come and sit down." He steered her toward the sofa and covered her with the lap blanket draped across its back.

"Maybe we should continue our discussion at another time," Hayes suggested, giving Tom a denotative look.

"No. I have a right to hear what you have to say." Kelly looked from one man to the other before resting her green gaze on Tom. "I want to know what you're planning to do about Emmy."

"I'm not sure. I do know she's connected with the house in some way. Maybe I'll start there."

"I'll help you."

"Kelly, no. You're going through enough as it is. I don't think—"

"Tom, you can't do it all by yourself. What about the university, your gallery? When will you find time to sleep?"

"I'll manage."

"How?"

"By taking a leave of absence until this thing's resolved."

"But what if it takes too long? Tom, you could lose your tenure."

"Kelly, I stand to lose a lot more than that if I don't," he said. He watched her lower her eyes to the hands she held fisted in her lap.

"You seem to be forgetting something, Shear. Winward and I are the detectives here. Maybe you should let us handle things. Chances are you'll just get in the way."

Tom's eyes narrowed on Hayes. "So far, detective, you've shown me nothing but your closed mind. If you think I'm just going to sit around while you ignore what's right in front of you, you really are as incompetent as you seem."

Hayes's face grew rigid and Winward quickly rose to stand between the two men. He cast his partner a warning glance. "I think that's enough for one night. Don't you agree, gentlemen?"

Hayes rose stiffly to his feet and Tom met the man's impaling gaze without flinching. As the two detectives donned their coats and moved toward the door, Winward stopped. A smile tugged at his lips as he regarded Tom with a mingling of admiration and curiosity.

"We'll be watching," he said, letting his smile spread. Then, with a shake of his head, he followed Hayes out.

# CHAPTER TWENTY-NINE

Tom watched the bleak sunrise with red, staring eyes. Its dim rising did little to dispel the darkness of the long, sleepless night. It left only a shroud of eerie, gray gloom that robbed the quaintly furnished bedroom of color, enhancing his feeling of encroaching doom.

The chime of the doorbell made him blink. With weary movements, he pushed himself from his chair and stood by the bed, where Kelly thrashed from side to side. She was now locked in a world of torment. Once she succumbed to sleep and its darkness, she had remained there, unable to free herself from the nightmare that held her.

Over the course of the night, her appearance had taken on a dramatic change as well. Bruises had begun appearing. Her eyes were sunken and ringed with discoloration. Her cheeks had grown hollow. He had been stunned to see how perfectly she mirrored the portraits hanging in his gallery. She had taken on the very essence of the little girls, and even as his heart swelled, his skin crawled each time their chorus of whimpers combined with Kelly's moans, jarring the still night. It was like they were all in the room with him, like they were all crying out at once, each one needing help to ease their suffering and using Kelly as her outlet. It all seemed so cruel to him, but he knew being angry at the little girls was futile. He had a more tangible, corporeal person to focus his anger on. The one responsible for it all.

Tom turned away as the doorbell rang again. By the time he opened the front door, Jonathan could barely contain his impatience. He stepped through and assessed Tom's appearance in one quick glance.

"I got your message," he said, following Tom into the den. "How is she?"

"Not good."

"I don't have to ask how you're doing. What happened?"

Tom recounted the events of the night before. When he finished, Jonathan could only shake his head.

"This thing's getting more bizarre by the minute. You said Winward and Hayes saw the whole thing?"

"I think they came in just before the electricity went haywire and the lights exploded. They saw enough."

"I don't suppose you've told Russ."

"No."

"I'll take care of it. This is something he'll definitely need to know. Just think what it would mean in a trial to have the two star detectives testify for the defense."

"Jonathan, I could care less about a trial. It's Kelly I have to worry about now. If something's not done, I don't think she's going to make it."

Jonathan looked startled. "What are you talking about?"

Tom turned away and rubbed his hands across his beard shadowed face. When he turned back, his distress was striking.

"I think she's dying."

"What! You can't be serious."

"See for yourself."

Tom led the way into the bedroom. Kelly was in constant motion. Tears stained her pale cheeks while her quiet sobbing alternated between frightened whimpers and deep, mournful moans layered underneath by multiple child voices.

He took the damp cloth he had used during the night and gently wiped the moisture from her bruised face. Then Tom leaned close and caressed her cheek with a reassuring hand.

"I'm here, Kelly," he whispered. "I'm here, sweetheart. I love you." His voice broke. Tom hid his face against her shoulder and her motion ceased, her sobs quieted. She turned her face to his and he continued his tender stroking until her breathing grew slow and even.

Jonathan knelt by the bed and felt Kelly's pulse with an awed, horrified expression. "My God, Tom, why isn't she in the hospital?"

Rising, Tom shook his head and motioned Jonathan from the room. When they reached the den, Tom crossed to the window and looked out, feeling Jonathan's eyes on his back.

"She looks like she's been beaten up. Where did the bruises come from?"

Tom shrugged. "I think from the little girls. They're sharing their physical, as well as, their mental pains. She's not cut, though. She's not bleeding, thank God."

"So, I repeat. Why isn't she in the hospital?"

"Think about it, Jonathan. What could they do? How could you possibly explain the bruises and the voices and make them believe you? The last thing she needs right now is to be placed in some psych ward while she's being pumped full of antidepressants. Not to mention the examination they'd put her through for being assaulted. Then they'd probably lock me away for being the one that hurt her, because there's no way they'd believe the truth."

Jonathan lifted his palms in frustration. "I don't know, Tom. I'm no doctor and neither are you. It may be the only way to help her."

"I don't believe that."

"Why?"

"Jonathan, I'm truly convinced the only way to help Kelly is to find the killer."

"How?"

"That's where you come in."

"Tell me what you need."

"I need you to start a full background check on the house. Find out everything you possibly can about former owners, renters, whatever. I also need someone I can trust to stay with Kelly."

"I take it you have someone in mind?"

"Marsha."

Jonathan nodded and reached for the phone. "I'll give her a call." He punched in the number as Tom picked up his coat. "Where are you going?"

"To shower, change, pack a bag, then beg for a leave of absence."

⚫

Winward was livid. "You had to do what?"

Swainer released a noisy sigh and took a draw from the cigarette clamped between his fingers. "Look, Mark. Someone tipped the commissioner. He was breathing down my neck as soon as I walked in this morning. I had no choice. It was a direct order."

"Chief, our investigation depended on those surveillance teams."

"What can I say?" Swainer said behind a screen of smoke. "You'll just have to think of something else."

Winward threw up his hands and stormed out of Swainer's office. There was a can of citrus scented air freshener sitting on the corner of Swainer's desk and Hayes gave it a pointed look before meeting Swainer's narrowed, I dare ya, eyes. With a sigh and a shake of his head, Hayes left, closing the door behind him.

"Who do you think tipped him off?" he asked, easing his bulk into the chair across from Winward's desk.

Winward flipped open the Shear file and thumped a list of names. "Take your pick."

"What about the guys on surveillance?"

Winward rejected the idea with a shake of his head. "No way. I hand-picked those guys myself. They knew what was at stake. They wouldn't have gone behind our backs. It had to be someone connected with the case."

"Who?"

"When we answer that, Don, we'll have our killer."

---

Tom entered the apartment and was met by silence. Panic reared in his chest until he saw the purse sitting on the dining table and the coat that was draped over one of the chairs. He entered Kelly's bedroom and was stopped short by the sight of Marsha sitting on the bed holding Kelly's head in her lap while she stroked her hair. Marsha's eyes glistened as she met Tom's gaze. She crooned words of comfort in Kelly's ear then eased herself from the bed. Kelly curled into a fetal position and quietly sobbed.

Tom swallowed hard as tears stung his eyes. He watched Marsha tuck the covers around Kelly's shoulders, then turned and left the room. He stood in the den like he wasn't sure what he should do next. In a moment, he felt Marsha's presence behind him.

"Did Jonathan explain?" he asked, turning to face her.

"Yes. Oh, Tom, it's unbelievable. How could this happen?"

"I stopped asking myself that a long time ago," he said, shrugging out of his jacket. He tossed it into the chair Winward had claimed the night before. "The question is, how do we stop it?"

Marsha shook her head. "I don't know. But I'm here for as long as you need me."

"Thank you. You already seem to have done more for her than I was able to do all night."

"That's because one of the girls thinks I'm her mother."

"Her mother?" he repeated in surprise.

Marsha nodded. "I'll tell you, Tom, it gave me the woolies. As soon as I walked into the room and spoke, a little girl's voice started calling for her 'mommy'. She almost became hysterical when she couldn't find her, so I assumed the role and she became instantly subdued."

Tom closed his eyes and ran his hands over his face. When he removed them, his expression was chiseled with determination.

"Where's Jonathan?"

"He's meeting with Russ Carson. He said he was going to start researching the house after that."

"Good," he said as he began rubbing his temples. "Where was he going to do his research?"

"I'm not sure."

He walked into the kitchen and took a bottle of Tylenol from a shelf over the stove. As he filled a glass with water from the tap and washed down four caplets, Marsha shook her head.

"How long has it been since you've eaten?" His absent-minded shrug was the only answer she needed. "I'm going to fix Kelly some soup. I'll fix you something while I'm at it."

"Don't bother. I'm not hungry."

She searched the lower cabinets until she found the pots and pans, then began another search of the pantry. "You'll eat. I'm mother, remember?"

He opened his mouth to protest, but the ringing phone stopped him. He answered before the second ring.

"Hello."

"Thomas Shear?"

"Speaking."

"Mr. Shear, Craig Raymond here. You certainly are a hard man to track down."

Raymond's jovial chuckle was like sandpaper against Tom's raw nerves. He had ignored several calls from the man earlier on his cell phone and let voicemail pick up the calls. Now, as he stood with Kelly's land line pressed to his ear, he unclenched his fist and took a deep, slow breath before saying calmly, "What can I do for you, Mr. Raymond?"

"I've been calling your gallery and cell phone all morning. I also called the university and was informed you've taken a leave of absence."

"That's right."

"Could it be you're planning to lock yourself away in that studio of yours to create another masterpiece collection?"

"Not quite." Tom bit back his impatience. "My reasons are strictly personal. As a matter of fact, I've decided to close my gallery altogether for a few days. If a matter of importance arises, you should be able to reach me here or on my cell phone."

"This is beginning to sound quite serious. Is there anything I can do?"

The man's curiosity was tangible, but Tom was in no mood to play games. "I appreciate your concern, but no, thank you. I'm sure you didn't go to the trouble of tracking me down to chit-chat. Is there something I can do for you?"

There was a moment's pause, and Tom could almost see Raymond patting his ruffled feathers.

"You're quite right. My reason for calling was to congratulate you on the contract you negotiated with my son, Michael, yesterday. I was also hoping to set up an appointment with you to begin selection of the paintings to be placed in our galleries."

"We both should be congratulated. But as far as scheduling an appointment, I'm afraid it will have to wait a few days. I hope that's not going to be a problem."

"No, no. Not at all."

"Great. Until next week then."

"Mr. Shear, before I ring off, please let me reiterate that my services are open to you. If there is anything I can do, please don't hesitate to call."

"Thank you, sir. I'll keep that in mind." Tom hung up and stared at the phone as if expecting it to move. Then he picked the receiver back up and dialed the number he'd memorized.

"Chandler residence."

Tom could see the man behind the voice. His starched butler's uniform and imperial disposition were hard to forget.

"Hello. This is Thomas Shear. I was hoping to speak with Mrs. Chandler. Is she available?"

"One moment, please."

Tom began to pace as he awaited the butler's return. Marsha's movements in the kitchen as she prepared lunch had become sub-liminal background noise.

"Mr. Shear? This is Merideth Chandler."

Tom straightened to attention. His heart pounded with excite-ment until he realized he was suddenly at a loss for words.

"Mr. Shear?"

"Yes, ma'am. I'm sorry, but you took me by surprise. I wasn't re-ally expecting you to take my call."

"Am I going to regret it?"

"I hope not," he said. "For both our sakes."

The silence on the line seemed to stretch forever.

"What do you want from me?"

"A moment of your time and your knowledge."

"My knowledge? Mr. Shear, I've already told the police every-thing I know. I'm sorry, but I can't help you."

"Mrs. Chandler, please don't hang up," he said. "Everything I hold dear is hanging in the balance, and you're the only person I can think of to turn to."

"Why me?"

"Because something has happened since your husband's death. I'm convinced he was murdered and I think you may know of the person responsible."

"That's impossible."

Tom heard the break in her voice and could only imagine what this conversation was costing her.

"Mrs. Chandler, please," he said, gentling his voice. "Please talk to me."

After a moment, she spoke. Her voice was strong and Tom knew she'd won her inner battle.

"You're a very persistent man, Mr. Shear."

"I have to be. I'm not the only one this has affected."

"What do you mean?"

Tom swallowed the lump rising in his throat. "Someone I love very much is being torn apart by what's happening, and I have to find a way to help her. She's someone you cared about once. I'm hoping you still do."

"Who?"

"Kelly Stafford."

"Kelly?" Merideth sounded breathless. "How did Kelly get involved?"

"By falling in love with me," he answered. "Please, Mrs. Chandler. I need your help. Right now, you're my only hope."

"Why should I trust you? How can I know you're telling the truth?"

"Meet with me and decide for yourself. I swear to you, I mean you no harm. If at any time you feel the least bit threatened, you can always have that bodyguard butler of yours throw me out."

"Oh, I intend to."

"Does that mean you'll grant me a meeting?"

"Tomorrow morning. Nine o'clock sharp."

"Yes, ma'am. Thank you, ma'am."

The conversation ended with the resounding click of a quick disconnection. Tom withdrew the receiver from his ear and lowered it to the cradle. He sank to the sofa with his elbows on his knees and held his head in his hands.

"Well?"

Tom felt like he was in a daze. He looked up to find Marsha standing over him.

"That *was* Merideth Chandler, wasn't it?"

"Yes. I have a meeting with her tomorrow morning."

"Tom, that's wonderful. Do you think she'll really be able to help?"

"I don't know. I hope so."

He got up and stepped to the window. The surveillance car that had been there the night before and early this morning was missing. He released the curtain and put on his coat. As he went to the door and stepped outside, Marsha was on his heels.

"Where do you think you're going?" she asked, hugging herself in the cold doorway. "Lunch is ready."

"I'll be right back. You stay with Kelly."

Tom walked the perimeter of the building, but found nothing resembling a replacement team. As he returned to the apartment, his frown deepened when he glanced up and saw that the cloud cover had condensed into a heavy white blanket tinged with grey. It seemed to press the air, trapping it against the earth. Sounds had become muted and there was a sense of expectation, like fate was holding her breath. He climbed the steps, unable to suppress the shiver that crept up his back, along his arms and across his scalp.

Marsha carried a tray with a bowl of soup toward the bedroom, but stopped in mid-stride when she saw him.

"What's wrong?"

His shoulders bobbed in a dismissing shrug. "Probably nothing," he said. "Is that for Kelly?"

"Of course."

"I'll take it."

"No, you won't. I'll take care of Kelly. Your lunch is on the table. Now, eat."

"Later. Right now, I want to see Kelly."

"She's okay, Tom. I checked on her a few minutes ago. She was sound asleep."

Tom followed Marsha into the bedroom to find Kelly curled in the same fetal position as before. Her breathing was sound and regular. A soft flush stained her cheeks. He smoothed the hair away from her face, and his touch brought her eyes open. His relief was immense when he saw recognition in their bruised depths.

"Tom."

Her voice was hoarse, but it was the sweetest thing he had ever heard. "Welcome back."

She gave him a weak smile then gestured for an embrace. Tom gathered her up and squeezed tight. She felt warm and alive, and his mind rebelled at the thought of ever losing her.

"I love you, Kelly. Please, don't ever leave me." His whisper was a caress against her ear, and he felt her arms tighten around his neck.

"Okay, you two. Are you going to make me stand here and hold this tray forever?"

"Nope," Tom said, releasing Kelly. "As a matter of fact, I'll bring my food in here and we'll have a picnic."

He helped Kelly sit up and plumped the pillows behind her back.

"Please," she croaked, "I really don't think I can eat."

"Honey, at least try. If nothing else, something warm might soothe your throat."

She agreed with a hesitant nod and Tom trotted from the room. A moment later, he returned with chicken noodle soup and a grilled ham and cheese and positioned himself on the bed facing Kelly. Tom watched as she took a minuscule sip of broth, before taking a long, noisy slurp of his own. His heart rejoiced when his childish antics brought a smile to her lips. He managed to coax her into taking a few more spoonfuls before her eyelids began to droop, begging for sleep.

"I'll get these out of the way."

Marsha stacked the dishes on the tray. When she was gone, Tom helped Kelly back beneath the covers, then stretched out beside her. He gathered her in his arms and held her while her breathing took on the steady rhythm of a deep sleep, lulling him into dozing.

When the doorbell rang, Tom came awake with a start and saw that Kelly was still sleeping. He eased himself from the bed and heard Jonathan's voice as he closed the bedroom door.

"Where's Tom"

"He's resting with Kelly."

"Tom's right here," he said, smiling.

"Hey, that's a genuine smile," Jonathan stated, pulling off his coat. "I take it Kelly's improved?"

"She has. She even managed a little soup."

"That's great."

"What are you doing here? I thought you were out researching the house."

"Things didn't exactly turn out the way I planned. You wouldn't believe the day I've had. Things were getting so bad I threw up my hands and came home."

Marsha took his hand and led him to the sofa. "What happened?"

Jonathan sat down with a thankful sigh and placed a possessive hand on Marsha's jean clad thigh as she sat beside him, tucking her socked feet beneath her. "To begin with," he said, "things took longer with Russ than I expected. After I told him what happened, he had me looking through case files for anything that might strengthen his defense. He was astounded that he might be able to use Winward and Hayes as defense witnesses."

Tom's laughter was condescending as he sat down in what he now thought of as Winward's chair. "I'll bet. What did he have to say about Kelly?"

"Not too much, actually. Only that he doubted he'd be able to use her because of her mental state."

Marsha gave a dainty snorted and rolled her eyes. "How sweet. That just positively oozed with sensitivity."

Tom refrained from commenting.

"He's not paid to be sweet, darlin'," Jonathan replied.

"Maybe not, but he could at least show a little compassion."

Jonathan hung his head as if he were counting to ten, then lifted his face with a pasted smile. "Where was I?"

Tom hid a grin. "You were just leaving Carson's office," he said.

"Thank you. As I was saying, I left Russ and headed toward the County Registrar's Office. I was sitting in bumper-to-bumper traffic when the car starts overheating and I have to beat my way to the curb. Can you believe it? Thirty degree weather and my car overheats.

"Well, thank the man above for cell phones because I had no trouble calling a tow truck. The only problem was that I had to wait almost two hours for the nitwit driver to show up. He hauled me to a garage and an hour and a half later, another nitwit that called himself a mechanic showed me a busted radiator hose. He told me the part would have to be ordered and that it'd be a couple of days before he could replace it. By then, I only had an hour before the registrar's office closed, not enough time to do any real digging, so when it started spitting snow, I got out while the getting was good and paid a cab driver forty bucks to bring me here."

Marsha's brow was knitted with skepticism. "How could you have a busted radiator hose? The car's practically brand new."

"The mechanic, if I may be so loose with the term, said it was probably cut by road debris."

"It was cut?" Tom knew he was being paranoid, but the fact that Jonathan was kept from reaching the registrar's office made him uneasy.

"Road debris can be nasty stuff." Jonathan held Tom's gaze. Tom gave a nonchalant shrug and let it drop.

"I guess this means we'll have to carpool for the next couple of days," Marsha said.

"Nope. I intend to reserve a rental. We can pick it up on the way home. If the weatherman can be trusted, we might need a four wheel drive. We're supposed to get several inches of snow in the next couple of days, if you can believe that. Which I can," he said with a disgusted scowl. "What I want to know is what happened to global warming? It feels like January out there. We haven't needed heavy coats this time of year for over a decade." He shook his head looking like a sullen little boy. "I hate cold weather."

Tom chuckled, watching his friend's animated expressions. "I can't help you with the weather, but you can always use my car," he offered. "It's the least I can do, considering you're out forty dollars because of me."

"But what about Merideth Chandler?" Marsha asked. "How would you keep your meeting?"

"I'd use Kelly's Lexus if I had to. But hopefully you'd be back by then. Unless of course, taking the time off is going to cause a problem for you."

She dismissed Tom's concerns with a wave of her hand.

"Meeting? What meeting?" Jonathan's ears had perked at the first mention of the elusive Merideth Chandler. "Why didn't you tell me?"

Marsha smirked. "And what, interrupt your rant about the weather? He hasn't exactly been given the chance, now has he?"

"When is it?" Jonathan asked, ignoring the woman by his side.

"Tomorrow morning. Nine o'clock."

"Do you want me to tell Russ?"

"No," Tom stated emphatically, shaking his head. "I intend to handle this one solo."

"Not without me, you're not."

"Jonathan—"

"Look, Tom. I'm already into this thing up to my receding hairline. If you think I'm going to miss a meeting with Merideth Chandler, you'd better think again. Besides, you may need a witness to the conversation. Can you think of anyone better?"

Tom heaved a sigh and rose from his chair. He paced to the window and looked out.

"You didn't happen to see our watchful friends outside, did you?"

"Come to think of it, no," Jonathan answered as he stood and walked over to stand beside Tom. "Why?"

"Because, unless they've changed tactics, they're gone."

# CHAPTER THIRTY

The crowd in Towne Center Mall was growing thinner. Everyone around him were either customers hurrying to make last minute purchases or clerks in a rush to ring up last minute sales. Some of the smaller merchants had already engaged metal security gates across store entrances with the lights behind them dimmed. Colorful vender carts lining the mall avenues were closed down and empty, their merchandise put away until morning. No one bothered to notice the dark-haired, bespectacled man wearing white coveralls, a blue Atlanta Braves baseball cap, and latex gloves pushing a broom.

He scanned the people around him and saw a frazzled woman pull a stroller to a stop. The blond bangs fringing her brow barely concealed the frown between her eyes. As the child inside the stroller wailed, she searched the contents of a diaper bag. The blond haired, blue eyed little girl by her side squirmed as she pulled on the woman's sleeve. His gaze turned to the child with incisive precision.

"Mommy, please," the little girl begged. "I have to pee."

"Shush. Do you want everyone to hear?" The woman looked around to see if anyone was watching. "You'll have to wait until I go into this store and buy the shirt for your daddy that we saw earlier."

"I can't," she whined, squeezing her knees together as she bobbed up and down. "I have to go now!"

"Brenda, please. In a minute."

"Why can't I go by myself? I know where it is. I can see the sign."

The woman looked up and realized the child was in true distress as a melodious male voice came over the mall's P.A. system announcing mall hours. Glancing around, she too saw the restroom sign pointing the way down a mall corridor a few feet away.

"Oh, all right," she said. "I'll pay for the shirt and wait for you right here. But hurry up. The mall's about to close."

"Yes, ma'am," the little girl said, performing one last squeezing bob before scampering away.

"Be sure to go in the right one," the woman warned. "And don't forget to wash your hands." She watched until the child disappeared around the corner, then inserted the nipple of a bottle between the lips of her disgruntled infant.

Repressing a smile, he strolled past the unsuspecting woman as she and the stroller entered the store and traced the little girl's steps into the corridor. He returned the broom to the janitor's closet and remained behind the cracked open door as voices reached his ears. The clap of multiple heels on tile grew louder and a woman's laughter echoed hollowly in the deserted corridor. He listened as they passed, hearing the heavy metal door to the employee entrance a few feet away clang open and then click shut as the two employees left the building. Making sure he was once again alone, he removed the chloroform bottle from his pocket and soaked a handkerchief with a small amount. He positioned himself against the wall beside the women's restroom and watched the door open. As the little girl stepped out, he covered her face with the handkerchief. She fell limp against him without making a sound.

Seconds later, he was through the employee door, jogging through freezing wind and stinging snowflakes toward a nondescript gray Chevrolet. He was alert for mall security and curious onlookers, but the few people he saw hurrying to their vehicles were either wrapped in scarves or had their chins buried in coat collars. No one noticed as he got into the backseat with the child, closed the door, bound her with duct tape, and hid her small body under a blanket. Then he climbed over, slid into the driver's seat and started the engine. His cackling laughter rang out as he eased his way from the mall parking lot through accumulating, sludgy snow and into merging traffic.

"Tom, Tom, Tom, Tom," he repeated in a sing-song voice. "I'm going to enjoy seeing you squirm with this one. You'll never have the chance to meet with Bitch Chandler and learn the history of the house. I'm even going to make sure you lose your pretty little plaything. That itself will be a joy. Almost orgasmic, I guess you could say." His laughter exploded and then quickly died. His expression turned snarled and ugly. "Oh, yes. Making that bitch pay will be sheer pleasure."

As he neared Shear Gallery, he extinguished his headlights and pulled into the driveway in darkness. He drove to the back of the house, away from prying eyes, and checked his sleeping passenger before opening the trunk. He replaced the latex gloves he wore with a clean pair, then repeated the process, double gloving his hands. Two pair of shoe covers went over his size eleven tennis shoes to help hide their tread and another went into the pocket of his coveralls along with a third pair of gloves. He put a chisel and a small hammer in another pocked, then retrieved bolt cutters and a flashlight and made his way to the shed. The frozen grass crunched beneath his steps and a red flag went up in his brain. He looked back at the path he'd taken and then up to watch the increasing snowflakes dancing in the air as they fell to the ground. He grinned with renewed confidence and turned back to face the shed.

With a grunt, he removed the padlock securing the doors and stepped inside. He avoided shining his light on what was hidden in darkness beneath the wide work table, and located an extension ladder.

At the back of the house, he extended the ladder, climbed to the second floor, and used the chisel and hammer to pry the molding from a pane of glass. It wasn't long before he had full access to the house. He then returned the tools to the trunk of his car and lifted the little girl to his shoulder.

At the top of the ladder, he passed the child threw the window then removed the outer layer of gloves and shoe covers, replacing them with the clean pairs from his pocket. He climbed through, closed the window to prevent any trace of moisture from entering, and wiped the area dry before lifting the child and following the beam of his flashlight up to the attic he recalled so well. After securing the shutters, he turned on the light, put the flashlight in his pocket, then removed the tape binding the little girl's tiny wrists. The tape securing her eyes, mouth, and feet he left in place.

He stood for a moment, admiring the little girl at his feet and then sneered. "Count your blessings, bitch. You'll be leaving here with your life. The others weren't so fortunate."

The thought of having to set her free was maddening. Resisting the urge to lash out, he pressed his clenched fist against his sides and turned his back. His attention was immediately drawn to a partially covered canvas, and he stepped over to remove the cloth. His breath quickened and his nostrils flared as he removed another, and then another.

He studied the painting of Chandler's hanging corpse and recognized the man standing before it. As with the painting of the dark silhouette, the resemblance was remarkable, but the fact that the faces in both paintings were obscured only made him smile.

"Why, Tom. Aren't you a clever boy. Your imagination is astounding."

His eyes shifted to the painting of Tom cowering in fear and his smile widened. He couldn't believe Tom had predicted his own future. He was unable to control his laughter as it shattered the silence. He scanned the attic more closely.

"What other treasures have you got hidden away, Rabbit? Anything

I might find interesting?" He pulled the cover from a canvas leaning against the wall and felt as if he'd been punched in the gut.

The face of the woman was flawless. Her brown eyes danced with mischief as her full lips curved in a seductive smile. Her soft, dark hair draped one bare shoulder in waves. The white peasant blouse dipped low, revealing the cleavage of firm, full breasts.

His hand trembled as he stroked the canvas with a lover's touch. "Mother," he breathed, and drank in the sight he thought he'd lost forever.

A movement caught his eye. He looked over to see the waking child struggling to sit up. He smirked when he heard her muffled whine.

"There, there now," he said in a magnanimous voice, carrying the canvas with him as he approached. "Didn't anyone ever tell you no one likes a whiner?"

As she began clawing at the tape covering her eyes, he jerked her hands away and gave her a rough shove.

"Tsk, tsk, little Brenda. That is your name, isn't it?" He waited, but the child only quailed and began inching her way backward.

"Isn't it?" he growled, bringing his palm down hard across her cheek. The blow sent the child reeling and her head hit the wall with a resounding thump.

"Mind your manners, bitch! I asked you a question and I expect an answer!"

As she struggled to push herself into an upright position, he took a moment to regain his composure. When he spoke again, his voice was calm and controlled.

"Now. Shall we begin again?"

The dazed little girl began crying in earnest and he released an explosive sigh.

"Shut up," he bellowed, "and answer the question. Is your name Brenda?"

The little girl jerked and began nodding her head vigorously up and down, as if she sensed his hand rising to deal another blow.

"That's much better. Now, Brenda, I'm going to remove the tape from your mouth. If you cry out, I'll hurt you. Is that understood?"

Cringing, she pressed herself against the wall and nodded. As he stepped forward, her small body flinched with each footfall and he grinned before ripping the tape from her tender lips Her pain filled whimper was swallowed behind a sob as her small hands jerked up to cover her mouth.

"Now, bitch, how old are you?" he asked, setting the canvas aside.

She hiccupped, holding back another sob, and croaked, "Eight."

He grinned once again at her ready response. "Well, bitch, my name is Thomas Shear. Can you say Thomas Shear?"

She gave a faint nod.

"Then say it!"

"T-Thom—"

"Thomas Shear!"

"T-Thomas Sh-Shear," she stammered.

"Again." He began a pacing march across the floor.

"T-Thomas Shear."

"Again."

"Thomas Shear."

"One more time."

"Thomas Shear."

"Excellent! Give the bitch a cigar." He clapped and squatted in front of her, reveling at the way she cringed. "Now, what's my name?"

"Thomas Shear."

"Wonderful!" He rose to his feet. "You're an astute pupil, Brenda Bitch. And as a reward—" He drew back his fist and punched her in the face. She went sprawling and began wailing hysterically.

"Shut up," he said softly as he examined the blood on his gloved knuckles from her split lip. "I said, shut up!"

She gulped air, trying to control her crying and curled into a ball on her side.

"Now. I have to leave for a while," he said, retrieving the portrait as he made his way toward the door. "I want you to be a good little girl until I get back. Do you understand?"

"Y-Yes." Her little girl voice had grown tiny.

He pulled the flashlight from his pocket, started down the stairs, then stopped and looked back. "If you want to remove the tape from your eyes, that'll be okay," he said. "But you have to count to one hundred very slowly before you do. Is that understood?"

"Yes, s-sir."

"Good," he drawled and continued his way down the stairs.

He was almost at the bottom when hands shoved him from behind. He fell hard to his hands and knees and his head exploded with pain as he crashed into the opposite wall.

Snatching the flashlight from the floor, he scrambled to his feet, searching wildly, the beam of light jumping sporadically from wall to wall. Seeing nothing, he grabbed up the canvas and ran, then bolted through the study door and screeched as searing pain burned across his torso.

Holding back a sob, he shoved the window open and hauled himself outside, securing the canvas between his knees and the ladder. He leaned back in, retrieved the pane of glass and molding he had left on the floor, then lowered the window and secured the lock with shaking hands. Once the glass was back in place, he returned the ladder to the shed and drove away.

During the drive home, his eyes were wild as he took slow deep breaths to ease his pounding heart. Then he cackled insanely and rubbed the gouged scratches along his chest. He was still chuckling as he stepped into the shower to wash the black dye from his hair.

Brenda's sobs subsided as she began listening to the silence. When it only deepened, she peeled the tape from her eyes and struggled with shaking hands to remove the tape binding her feet. She stood, scanning the room, then froze, riveted by the frightening paintings in front of her. Carefully sidling around them, she eased downstairs, listening to every nuance of the settling house.

A dim light shining up from the foyer served as a beacon as she crept along the dark hallway toward the staircase. On either side, black, gaping doorways enhanced the image looming in her mind of a pouncing stranger that wanted to hurt her again. The unseen threat made her small body tremble as she ran the last few yards. She stopped to search the shadows before slowly descending, and her heart was nearly bursting by the time she reached the front door and pulled hard on the knob.

When the door refused to open, her choked whimpers began to build. Her small fingers fumbled to release the locks and as the last tumbler jarred into place, the door sprang open aided by a blast of frigid, stinging wind.

———◦《◉》◦———

A man eased a van down the street and parked, then cursed when he saw the door of Shear Gallery standing open. Suddenly, blue lights flashed toward him and the wail of sirens grew in volume. Too late, he threw the vehicle in gear and tried to make his escape.

———◦《◉》◦———

Winward stared at the ceiling above his bed listening to the gusting wind outside. He had always found the sound soothing, but tonight the sleep he longed for eluded him. Instead, his mind churned with the events of the past few days.

His stomach knotted as the telephone suddenly shrilled. He took a deep breath and answered.

"Winward."

"Detective Winward, it's Alan Johansen from dispatch. The security at Shear Gallery just went wild. We've tried to make contact, but got no answer. I've already dispatched a couple of cruisers to check it out."

Winward was already pulling on a pair of jeans. "Call Detective Hayes and tell him to meet me there," he barked. "And tell the responding officers not to touch anything until I get there."

# CHAPTER THIRTY-ONE

Scattered snowflakes glistened in the flashing blue lights of several cruisers as Winward pulled to a stop and got out of his car. Hunched beneath the hood of his parka, he showed his badge to an approaching officer.

"Are you the leading officer?"

"Yes, sir. Name's Hendricks."

"What have you got, Hendricks?"

"A man was apprehended fleeing the scene in that van," the officer said, pointing to a black commercial type van at the curb. "He maintains his innocence of any wrongdoing."

"ID?"

"The name on his license is Robert Manning. He had a bag containing everything he would need to complete a successful break-in."

"Where is it?"

"Over there, in the trunk of that cruiser."

"Did you find anything in the van?"

"No, sir. The van was empty. Its registration said it's owned by a company named Marcel Enterprises. We're running the plates."

"Good. What else have you got?"

"When we arrived, we found the front door standing open. There's been no movement within the house that could be seen and no one's gone in per your instructions. The exits and perimeter have been secured."

Winward tilted his head toward a handful of pedestrians braving the elements to watch the commotion. "What about those people? Have they been interviewed?"

"No, sir, not yet."

"Get someone on it. If they're curious enough to withstand freezing temperatures at eleven o'clock at night, then one of them might've been curious enough to have seen something."

"Yes, sir."

"Has Mr. Shear, the owner, been notified?"

"Not yet."

"Good," Winward said, moving toward the police car where Manning was being detained. "I'll take care of it once we find out what we're dealing with." He lifted the trunk lid and searched the bag's contents.

"Tell the men you have at the exits to stand ready. We'll go in through the front to secure the inside. And stress extreme caution, Hendricks. There's already been an attempt to stage a gas explosion at this location. To find some sort of booby-trap wouldn't surprise me a bit."

"Yes, sir."

Winward turned to approaching headlights as Officer Hendricks began speaking into his walkie. The car pulled to a stop, and Detective Hayes got out, pulling the brim of his fedora low and the collar of his coat more snugly around his neck. Hayes rammed his gloved hands into his coat pockets and surveyed the scene.

"What's going on?"

"That guy over there was apprehended while fleeing the scene. His name's Robert Manning, and apparently, he's not your average burglar. He had a bag containing an assortment of burglary devices. I found a set of security system deactivators that would've impressed James Bond."

"Was anything taken?"

"The van's registered to Marcel Enterprises and it was empty. No one's been inside the house, yet. Only the outside's been secured."

"Have you talked to the guy?" Hayes asked.

"Next on my list."

"Let's go."

Winward opened the back door of the police cruiser and gave Manning an amiable smile as he crowded him over to the middle of the backseat. He pulled his door closed enough to block the wind, but not enough to engage the one-way lock. As Hayes did the same on the other side, minus the amiable smile, Winward detected the faint aroma of vomit underneath the pine scented air-freshener hanging from the rear-view mirror on the other side of the Plexiglas partition.

"Mr. Manning, I'm Detective Winward. The man on your left is Detective Hayes. We'd like to talk to you for a minute, if you don't mind."

Manning had expertly trimmed dark brown hair and a long, slim nose above thin lips. The first thought that came to Winward's mind was aristocratic. He couldn't tell the exact color of his eyes in the dim light, but decided on a gray.

"I'm not saying anything without my attorney."

The man's speech was articulate. Winward thought he detected a slight British accent. He also noticed the man was dressed entirely in black.

"All right. Obviously, you're a man who knows his rights. So, I'll tell you what. You just sit there and listen. I'm going to lay it on the line for you, Mr. Manning. Detective Hayes and I happen to be conducting a serial murder investigation. And guess what? You just jumped in with both feet." Winward took a second to let his comment sink in.

"You probably already know this," he continued, pretending not to notice the man's widening eyes, "but this just happens to be the scene where we suspect the murders took place. You also probably know that someone tried to blow the place up the other night. You look like a smart man. You know anything about explosives? Or maybe you could give us a hint as to the location of the bodies. That would be a tremendous help."

Winward tilted his head and staged a look of remorse. "Oh, sorry. I forgot. You're not answering questions, are you?" He waved a dismissing hand. "That's okay. Hayes and I have great imaginations. We'll figure something out."

Winward eyed the sullen man with interest. "You know, with the way you're dressed and your little bag of goodies, I bet you could get in and out of almost anywhere undetected. And then there's your choice of vehicles; a van that size would hold quite a bit of loot. A certain collection of paintings would be no problem. You do know the collection I'm talking about, don't you?" he asked, leaning close. "It's a collection of portraits. Portraits of the same little girls we're looking for."

Winward's brow furrowed in thought. "What do you think, Don?" he asked, looking across Manning. "Don't you think that collection would make one hell of a trophy for the killer?"

"Now, wait just a minute," Manning erupted. "I don't know anything about any murders. You're not going to pin your mess on me."

Winward feigned surprise. "Oh, sure we will. Besides, we have to pin it on someone, don't we? You're just as good a candidate as anyone else."

Hayes grunted affirmation and compressed Manning with his stare. Cold sweat glistened on the man's forehead, but he quickly regained his composure.

"Look," he said calmly. "I know what you're trying to do and it's not going to work. I had nothing to do with your murders and you'll not find any evidence to prove otherwise."

Winward gave a nonchalant shrug. "Maybe, maybe not. But you shouldn't underestimate our abilities, Mr. Manning. If we can't get you for the actual murders, we can always charge you with accessory. Either way, you'll be in a shitload of trouble."

Manning clamped his mouth shut and fixed his eyes on the seat in front of him. Winward sighed and shook his head.

"You know, it's too bad, really. All you have to do is tell us who sent you. Was it someone from Marcel Enterprises, or someone else? Just give us a name."

When no reply came, Winward gave another shrug. "Okay. Have it your way." He pushed the door open and moved to get out of the car. "Officer Hendricks, could you step over here a minute?"

"Wait."

Winward turned back at the command and met Manning's unflinching gaze.

"When I pulled up, that door was standing wide open. I didn't even get out of the van. I was leaving when the police stopped me. That's all I know. I swear it."

"It's obvious you came for the paintings. Who sent you?"

Manning shifted his gaze back to the seat in front of him. "I refuse to say anything further until I'm advised by my attorney."

"Fine," Winward replied and got out of the car. He shut the door on Manning's stoic profile. "Hendricks, call back-up. I want this man taken to the station and booked; charges pending."

"Yes, sir."

Winward looked up at the dark house and his gut tightened with apprehension. Reaching beneath his parka, he removed his Glock from its holster and released the safety with his thumb.

"Do you think he's telling the truth?" Hayes asked.

Winward heaved a sigh. "Yeah, I do."

Hayes surveyed the scene once more. "I don't like it, Mark."

"Huh, neither do I," Winward said. "If we had our damn surveillance teams, we might at least know what we're dealing with."

Hayes pulled his 9 mm from his hip-holster and pointed it down in the traditional two hand hold, resting his right fist in his left palm. He kept his eyes on the house.

"Maybe it's time we found out," he said.

Winward was the first inside, followed by Hayes. Hendricks entered next, trailed by four other officers. All had guns drawn. Winward motioned for Hendricks to send his men upstairs. Within minutes, each room was cleared, the house declared secure. An inspection of the premises was soon underway.

"Detective Winward?"

Winward stopped in the foyer and turned to face two approaching officers. Hendricks was behind them giving each man a gimlet eye.

"What is it Hendricks?" he asked.

"Robert Manning's gone. Somehow he escaped."

"What! How?"

"We don't know, sir," one young, red-faced officer answered looking Winward in the eye. "While the house was being cleared, we arrived to transport the prisoner to the station. When we approached the first cruiser to make the transfer, we saw that it was empty. I opened the back door to make sure, but there was no one inside."

Winward heaved an exasperated sigh and stepped to the front door. When he looked out, he saw the cruiser that had contained Manning sitting at the curb. The back door was open.

He turned to the young cop. "Did you leave that door open?"

"Uh, yes, sir."

"Are you sure both doors were secure before they arrived?" he asked Hendricks.

"Yes, sir. Both doors. The prisoner was secure," he answered.

Winward heaved another sigh and shook his head. "He didn't

CYNTHIA H. WISE

just vanish," he said, throwing up his hands. "Make a search. Put out an APB. That's all we can do for now."

He sucked in a deep breath to curb his frustration and turned away to continue his search. After scanning the rooms of the first and second floors, Winward found himself in the attic studying strips of discarded duct tape. His expression remained drawn as he stood and turned at Hayes's approach.

"Anything?"

"Not yet," Hayes said.

Winward huffed in disgust. "No forced entry, no sign of the place being searched, nothing stolen. If it was, it was something very specific, nothing we would notice."

"Maybe it's time to call Shear. If anything's missing, he'd be the one to know."

"Not yet."

"Why not? He could tell us if anything's been disturbed."

"Oh, something's been disturbed, alright. I have no doubt about that. And it's here in the attic," he said, looking over the attic more closely. "I've got a feeling in my gut that I'm missing something."

Suddenly, he realized what had been bothering him. "It's the shutters," he said. "They're closed. They were open when we were up here the night of the break-in. Apparently, someone wanted privacy.

"Another thing is these paintings," he continued. "Shear was very meticulous about keeping them covered."

Winward pointed to the strips of used duct tape lying on the floor. "And take a look at those. They have smears that look like blood. A couple of drops are on the floor in the corner as well. There's colored fiber attached to the adhesive on a couple of strips. And it looks to be cloth, not paper. On one of the shorter strips, I found strands of blond hair. I also found what appears to be facial hair; like eyelashes, or maybe hair from a brow."

"They were used as bindings," Hayes stated.

"That's my guess. And if we're right, maybe whoever set off the alarm wasn't coming in, but going out."

Hayes squatted to examine the tape and his scowl deepened. "Could be. That would explain the front door being left open. If someone was in distress, the last thing they would worry about is closing the door."

"My thoughts exactly."

Winward met Hayes's speculative gaze before calling down for Hendricks.

"Were any of the people outside able to tell us anything?" he asked when the officer appeared.

"Just one. A man who lives down the street said he'd just stepped outside to walk his dog when he saw Manning pull up in his van. He swears the guy never got out before the police arrived. Other than that, they all reported the same thing. They all came out when they heard the sirens. No one saw anything before that."

"Then we'll have to do a door-to-door of the immediate neighborhood. If there is a witness, he or she was smart enough to stay inside."

Winward's concentrated gaze surveyed the attic once more. When he returned his attention to the officer, there was a crisp decisiveness to his instructions.

"Call in and see if there's been any reports of missing persons or abductions. Start with little girls. Next, bring Jenkins in with his kit. I want fingerprints, and I want this tape and the front door tested first."

Winward's brow knitted in thought as he took it a step further. "I assume the upstairs windows have been inspected for forced entry?"

"Yes, sir. No glass has been broken and all of the locks are secure."

"Do it again. And make sure they're given more than a cursory glance. The person we're dealing with isn't stupid. He'd find a clean way in. He'd also want privacy, so focus on the ones that would give him that."

"Yes, sir."

Hayes watched Hendricks hurry from the attic before turning to study his partner. "What are you thinking?"

"I think we're dealing with two different crimes. Someone was in this house tonight, but it wasn't Manning. He just happened to come to the right place at the wrong time."

"How can you be sure?"

"Because of the timing. It's all wrong. It's obvious Manning's an expert at his chosen trade. There's no way he would've come here knowing the police were on their way."

"Meaning we have more than one person interested in the Rage collection."

Winward nodded. "But for different reasons."

"Okay," Hayes conceded. "I'll buy that. But if you think about it, it doesn't really change our current situation. I still consider Shear our main suspect."

"Of course. But I can't stop asking myself, 'Why would he do it?' Why create such an elaborate hoax?"

"To redirect the blame."

Winward shook his head. "I just can't believe it's that simple."

"Mark, listen to me. If there's no evidence of forced entry, a key would've had to have been used. Who else besides Shear would have a key? Not to mention the security code. Why won't you just admit the possibility that Shear's guilty?"

"I'm not marking Shear off our list, Don. I'm just exercising other possibilities."

"Such as?"

"Consider this. After the first break-in, Shear had his security upgraded to a topnotch system. The thing is, because the foundation and high ceilings put the upstairs windows twenty feet off the ground, he only beefed up security on the first floor. He knew the chance of someone using an upstairs window as a route to gain access was slim.

So, he gambled by placing security stickers in every other one with hopes that the stickers along with the sign posted in the front would be enough to deter anyone from trying an unlawful entry.

"Now," he said, holding up a finger, "if the silent alarms and motion detectors weren't triggered by someone coming in, but by someone going out, the question is, if it wasn't Shear, how'd that person gain access in the first place? If they had no key or deactivation code, the only logical answer would be an upstairs window. And that means they knew enough about the system to call his bluff. How else would they know the upstairs windows were vulnerable?"

"That's all fine and dandy," Hayes said, "but I think you're over thinking things. There are no obvious signs of forced entry, no destructive surprises were found, and nothing was stolen."

"Maybe he didn't come here to destroy or steal. Maybe he wanted to leave something."

Hayes glanced at the tape on the floor before his eyes focused on his partner. Winward could see the calculating thoughts flying and waited on Hayes to make the next move. He didn't have long to wait.

"Are you suggesting someone kidnapped a little girl, bound her with duct tape, brought her here, carried her through a twenty-foot-high window, placed her in this attic, and left through the front door to set off the alarm so she could be found by police, just to frame Thomas Shear?"

"That's one possible scenario."

Hayes stared at his partner in complete astonishment. "You can't be serious." When Winward didn't respond, his dark expression turned stormy. "I think you're crazy. Somewhere along the line, you sailed right off the deep end."

"I haven't, but the man we're dealing with has."

"Mark, what you're suggesting is really out there. I'm sorry, but this time I just can't go along with you."

"I suppose you've got a better idea?"

"Yeah, I do. Maybe, just maybe, Shear's been our man all along. Maybe he kidnapped a little girl, bound her with duct tape and brought her here. You have to remember. He's been out of circulation a long time. His urge to kill must be overwhelming. But he knows he can't be out of sight of someone for any length of time. He would need to establish an alibi, right? So what does he do? He leaves her with full intentions of returning later to finish his dirty deed. But his plan's spoiled because she manages to free herself. She runs downstairs and out the front door, thereby tripping the motion detectors and alarm."

Winward stood over the duct tape and stared down at it, as if his steely gaze could extract the answers they needed.

"I think your scenario's as crazy as mine," he stated, turning to face Hayes. "You're forgetting that Shear doesn't know the surveillance teams have been called off. For all he knows, he's still being watched. If he is our man, why would he jeopardize everything he's tried to do by taking such an enormous risk?"

"It wouldn't be such an enormous risk if he's the one who tipped the commissioner," Hayes said. "Mark, you know as well as I do we're not dealing with a totally rational human being. In a psychopath or sociopaths mind, he can rationalize anything. Especially if a certain urge is strong enough. I don't think he would hesitate with risk. He'd find a way around it."

"Okay. I agree with that. But if he really wanted to keep someone here, don't you think he would've done a little more than bind her with duct tape? I don't care how irrational he is, the guy's not stupid. He would've taken measures to make sure escape was impossible. Hell, at the very least, he would've locked the attic door."

Footsteps on the stairs brooked further comment. The two men turned to see the wiry form of Lonny Jenkins enter the attic. His blond features looked grim with discontentment. It was obvious he was not a happy man.

"Déjà vu, gentlemen," he grouched. "I want you to know I was cozy as a bug under the blankets, snuggled up to Miriam's glorious butt, sleeping like a baby. I'll tell ya, guys, I had a hard time answering my damn beeper. This place is quickly becoming a pain in the ass."

"At least you've got a glorious butt to snuggle up to," Winward replied.

"You know what your problem is, Mark? You have no social life. You're married to the bad guys of society."

"No. Just one. And he was here tonight."

"Hendricks told me about the front door. I've got my people on it. He also mentioned duct tape."

Hayes pointed. "It's over there. There's also traces of what we think is blood in the same area."

Jenkins set his forensic case down and opened the lid. "After I take some photographs, I'll see what I can find. Then I'll bag and tag everything for more extensive testing at the lab."

"Great," Winward said. "And when you dust, don't forget the shutters and those paintings. Also, concentrate on the windows on the second floor at the back of the house. I have a hunch that's how he got in." He ignored the sharp glance he received from Hayes.

"Gotcha."

"Thanks, Lonny. Let us know if you find anything. We'll be outside checking the grounds."

"No problem."

Hayes followed Winward down the stairs, but they were stopped by Hendricks on their way out.

"A call came in a few hours ago. Brenda Kellerman, age eight, disappeared from Towne Center Mall around nine o'clock tonight. A full-scale search is underway."

Winward rubbed his brow. "Damn."

"Do you think there's a connection?" Hendricks asked.

"It's too early to tell," Winward replied, but his expression had grown dark and solemn. "We'll have to wait and see what Jenkins comes up with, if anything."

The two detectives continued outside. Pulling flashlights from their pockets, they cast their halogen beams in a slow, sweeping search of the snow covered ground as they made their way around the house. Flakes tapped coldly against their exposed faces and tickled their eyelashes.

"It's cold as a witch's tit out here," Hayes grumbled. "I don't know what you're hoping to find, Mark. The ground's frozen solid. This snow's not helping things, either."

"I know. And it looks like the flakes are getting bigger, like it's getting heavier."

"It is. The forecaster said we could get up to four inches tonight." Hayes lifted his face into the cold air and then tucked his chin into the scarf around his neck. "At least the wind's dying down."

Winward slowed his pace as they rounded the corner to the back of the house. He looked up, then cast his beam on the ground several feet from the foundation. After a careful search, he took several paces further on and repeated the process.

"If you're looking for footprints, take your pick," Hayes said sweeping his light out and over the churned snow. "People have been back and forth all evening." The accumulation of falling snow was already filling in the crevices.

"I'm not looking for footprints," Winward replied. "I'm looking for ladder prints."

"Hmrrghm." The disgruntled bear noise. "Of course you are," he growled.

Ignoring his partner, Winward moved on then squatted. Two shallow dips could be seen in the freshly fallen snow. He took out his camera phone and snapped several pictures from different angles. Then he carefully brushed away the collected snow before concentrating the beam from his flashlight for a closer inspection.

"What about this Brenda Kellerman thing?" Hayes asked. "I heard what you told Hendricks, but do you think it's connected?"

Winward looked up to meet Hayes's gaze. "My gut says yes. What does your gut say?" He held Hayes's eyes long enough to make his point, then returned his attention to the ground in front of him.

"Don, take a look at this," he said, fingering a tuft of stiff grass. "I think we just found a needle in a haystack."

He took more pictures as Hayes crouched beside him and directed his light.

"See how the frozen grass is crushed? And look at this." Winward aimed his light further on. "Same thing. I'd say that's about the width of a ladder, wouldn't you? Also, whatever did this had a slight back and forth motion. I would guess the same motion a ladder makes whenever someone climbs the rungs."

Hayes turned a speculative eye on his partner. Following Winward's gaze, he realized they were directly beneath the study window. He shook his head.

"Mark, you know as well as I do that those marks could've been made any number of ways. The ground's been trampled by officers, for heaven's sake."

Undeterred, Winward stood and shined his light around the perimeter of the backyard. Seeing the double-garage sized shed, he made his way toward it.

"You know I can't buy into any of this supernatural shit, don't you?" Hayes asked, following Winward inside.

"There's nothing supernatural about someone using a ladder to reach a second story window, Don."

"You know what I mean. If I buy this theory of yours, it would mean I'd have to buy the rest of it, too. I'm not saying we didn't see something last night, but I have to believe there's a plausible explanation for what happened."

Winward shined his light around the twenty-by-twenty shed. "I understand. I'm not sure I'm buying it all, either. All I'm asking is for you to try and be a tad bit more open-minded. We wouldn't be detectives if we failed to investigate an avenue open to us just because it went against the grain."

"If I try to open my mind a little bit, will you try to keep a level, rational head?"

Winward held his flashlight beneath his chin and presented Hayes with a ghoulish grin. "Absolutely," he said in a bad imitation of Bela Lugosi.

"You're a real comedian." Hayes shook his head and turned his attention to the contents of the shed. "He does is own lawn maintenance," he stated, casting his light over a weed-eater and leaf-blower hanging from hooks attached to a peg-board wall. His light traveled lower and rested on a brand-new red riding lawn mower. "I wonder how much that puppy cost."

Winward gave him a dubious look.

"What? I'm in the market," he said with a shrug.

"The important thing is, he owns an extension ladder," Winward replied, holding the item in question in a beam of light. He walked over to where it rested on its side against the wall and inspected its feet. "Well, well, what do you know? It still has a few blades of grass attached." He snapped more pictures then examined the crushed blades. "They're still moist."

"That still doesn't prove anything, Mark."

"Yeah, yeah."

An officer appeared at the door. "Detectives, Jenkins needs to see you right away."

Winward and Hayes left the shed. They found Jenkins waiting for them in the attic.

"Things don't look good, gentlemen. I thought you should know we found a child's fingerprints on that tape and the front door. We also used laser and found shoe impressions on the hardwood. Picked them up with an electrostatic dust lifter for the lab to analyze. Several sets are adult males and I'm guessing they're yours from when you entered the house for a search. We'll need a comparison print to take back to the lab. The child's print we found looks like a child's tennis shoe. Is that the kinds of things you were looking for?"

Winward looked grim and heaved a sigh. "It's what we hoped we wouldn't find."

"One more thing. All of the child prints were leading out and down the attic stairs. There were none coming in."

Hayes's black scowl intensified. "She was carried in."

"Then left to find her own way out," Winward said.

"Also, the trace found on the tape tested positive for blood. The lab will compare the blood and hair to see if they match." Jenkins picked up his forensic tool box. "Well, we're finished in here," he said. "What little other trace evidence we found will be analyzed at the lab. I have a hunch your perp is either a resident, or wore protective clothing while he was here such as shoe booties and gloves. Probably even a hat or hair net."

"I'm betting on the resident," Hayes stated.

"Maybe," Winward replied. "Lonny, work the study, will you? And don't forget the window, inside and out. Check to see if a pane of glass has been tampered with. There's an extension ladder in the shed out back that you can use. Before you do, though, it'll need to be processed. There's fresh grass in the tread of its feet that needs to be bagged. Samples need to be taken from the two marks on the ground beneath the study window, as well. I want them analyzed to see if that ladder made those marks and, if it did, when. I took pictures before and after I disturbed the snow. There on my cell. We'll download them later."

"I'll get right on it."

The two detectives were silent as they listened to Jenkins's footsteps recede down the attic stairs. The knowledge of another child being taken filled them both with seething anger.

"I think it's time for a door-to-door."

Hayes gave a jerking nod. "The sooner the better."

Back-up was called in and a residential search soon began. While officers woke residents to be interviewed, others, along with Winward and Hayes, worked methodically, moving from house to house, searching the surrounding grounds for signs of the missing girl. Increasing snowfall made the hunt difficult, but it served to strengthen their resolve to find the child before the weather worsened. Time was working against them and they knew it.

Minutes passed as the night wore on. Their radio crackled with life as individual search teams checked in, but there was no news of a child being found.

"If she was snatched from inside the mall she probably wasn't wearing a coat. Do you think she could've made it this far?" Hayes asked, shining his light beneath a row of snowcapped shrubs separating two properties.

Winward blew hard on his gloved fingers, trying to warm them, frustration etching his face. "I doubt it. Not in this cold."

"Maybe we should start working our way back."

"And pray someone else finds her before we make it."

"Yeah, if she's here to be found. She could've gone in any direction."

Winward played his light in a wide arc of the area before following Hayes across the deserted street where slush churned up by earlier motorists had refrozen creating a lumpy crust of ice. He lowered the beam and the hair on his body stood on end. It had flickered across the porch of a neighboring house and there, huddled in the corner, wedged between the wall and a stacked cord of firewood, was the curled-up form of a child.

Winward shouted for Hayes as he ran across the frozen, snow

covered lawn. He bounded up the porch steps and kept his light level as he dropped to his knees in front of the still form. Her blue lips stood out from her ghostly complexion and his heart chilled at the coldness of her skin as he felt her neck for a pulse.

"Paramedics are on the way," Hayes huffed, vapor clouds forming around his head as he crouched beside Winward. "Is she--?"

"She's alive, but just barely. We have to get her inside."

Winward peeled out of his parka and wrapped it around the child's body. He then cradled her against the warmth of his chest and waited impatiently as the locked storm-door rattled in its frame with the urgency of Hayes's pounding.

Lights flooded the darkness. A gruff voice answered the summons in angry, muffled tones. "Who the hell is it and what the hell do you want?"

"Police," Hayes shouted. "We have a medical emergency. Open up."

The front door cracked open and the ruffled man's eyes widened at the sight of Hayes's dark, burly form pressing his badge against the glass of the storm-door.

Thick iron-gray brows, bristling like exotic tentacled insects, drew together suspiciously. "What kind of medical emergency?"

"A child with hypothermia."

"How do I know you really—"

The door swung open and a thin woman in her fifties appeared. She was wrapped in a thick robe and her short bottle-blond hair was slightly flattened on one side of her head. She took one look with quick, assessing blue eyes and immediately unlatched the storm-door lock.

"Out of the way, Luther. Let 'em in. Can't you see the poor child needs help?"

Hayes snatched the door open and pushed past the man as he followed Winward inside.

"In here," the woman directed, taking charge. She led them into a living room to the right of the foyer that was decorated in floral pastels. "Lay the child on the sofa while I get some blankets. Luther, fix up your hot water bottle. The child needs it."

Hayes pulled the coffee table out of the way as Winward laid the little girl down. She was soon buried beneath several layers of warmth.

"Her pulse is getting weaker," Winward announced, keeping his fingers pressed against her fragile neck to monitor the rhythm of her heartbeat. "Where are the damn paramedics?"

"They're on their way, Mark. Just stay cool. It's up to us until they get here."

"Damn it," Winward growled. "She's in cardiac arrest."

He pulled the little girl from the sofa and laid her on the pink carpet where Hayes began compressing her chest.

"Don't do this, Brenda," Winward demanded. "Come back to us, honey. Your mamma's waiting for you."

Hayes counted, "One...two...three...four." He watched the small chest rise with the air Winward forced into her lungs.

The process continued until sirens screamed to a halt in front of the house. Paramedics rushed in and soon had full control of the situation.

"How long was she exposed?" one asked, assessing vitals.

"Two, two and a half hours," Winward answered.

"How long has she been in cardiac arrest?"

"Three minutes. What took you guys so long?" he demanded. "The hospital's ten blocks away."

"Come on, Mark," Hayes said, pulling Winward back. "They're here now. Let'em do their job."

The paramedics worked to regain cardiac rhythm. "I've got a pulse!"

"Let's get it stabilized."

Everyone in the room let out a collective sigh. Minutes later, Brenda Kellerman was lifted onto a gurney. A sea of policemen parted as she was wheeled outside and placed inside the ambulance. Reporters had been kept on the periphery, but at the sight of the little girl and the sudden activity, their voices rose in a wave of vocal noise as cameras began to flash.

"I'm going with her," Winward said, climbing inside the ambulance.

"Okay," Hayes agreed. "I'll take care of things here and meet you there."

He slammed the doors shut and the siren began to wail as the vehicle pulled away.

<hr />

Winward rubbed his grit-filled eyes as the sun began to lighten the crisp, cold morning. The blanket of snow would soon reflect its glare, but he stood shielded behind the tinted glass of a hospital window as he looked out at the growing mob of reporters.

"Here," Hayes said, handing him another cup of coffee. "Have another jolt."

"Another jolt might just send me careening off the walls," he said, accepting the hot paper cup anyway.

"Hear anything?"

"Not yet."

"You know it's a zoo out there," Hayes commented as he lowered his big, tired body onto a padded blue-vinyl chair that was connected to a row of identical blue-vinyl chairs lining one sand colored wall.

"I know. I've been watching. Has the family been bothered?"

"No. Not yet, anyway," Hayes replied. "Hospital security's doing a good job keeping the press contained outside the building.

"Have you talked to Swainer?" he asked, taking a slow sip from the cup in his big hand.

"Yeah." Winward raked his fingers through his dark hair to ease the caffeine jitters that tingled across his scalp. "He wants us to bring Shear in for questioning. He said the commissioner's having a tantrum because he thinks the blame's going to be put on him for pulling surveillance."

Hayes grunted in disgust. "Don't be surprised if he passes the buck," he said. "To us."

Hayes blew on his coffee in silence before taking another hesitant sip. "What about Manning?" he asked. "We're going to take some heat for that, you know. Legally, we had nothing on him, but still."

"I know," Winward replied then guffawed. "How the hell did he do it? How the *hell* did the man get out of a locked police car?" He shook his head. "That one's driving me nuts."

"Someone screwed up. That's all there is too it."

"Yeah well, that someone could only have been you or me. We were the last one's to confront him. I shut my door securely when I got out. Did you?"

"Yeah, I did." The big man shook his head and scowled. "What can I say, Mark? The man's a Houdini."

"And smart. He'll be long gone by now. We won't catch him. Not anytime soon anyway. But I've been giving it some thought. We need to know who owns the company the van was registered to: Marcel Enterprises. I don't believe Manning was working alone. If that's the case, who else besides our killer would have an interest big enough in the Rage collection to attempt stealing it?"

"My first guess would be the Raymonds."

"Mine, too. But why?" Winward asked. "I mean, I don't know that much about art, but it's not exactly like it's a collection of Picassos. And since it'd be stolen, the only way Raymond would be able to unload it would be on the black market. Even then, I couldn't see it pulling a price that would make the risk worth his while. Besides, I don't think Craig Raymond's involved with illicit trading. Our investigation has shown nothing shady whatsoever about the way he does business."

"Maybe there's a player we don't know about."

"Maybe. After we take care of Shear, let's research deeper into Raymond's competitors and known associates. Maybe we'll get lucky."

A heavy double door swooshed open. "Detective Winward? Detective Hayes?"

Brenda's doctor walked toward them. His five foot five inch frame was covered by green scrubs and a white lab coat with his name stenciled on a breast pocket. Slight bags drooped beneath his red-rimmed blue eyes. His smile was tired as he offered his hand.

"It's been a long night, gentlemen."

"Yes, it has," Hayes replied. "How is she?"

"She's awake and alert. She's not completely out of the woods yet, but her prognosis is good. Barring complications, we expect her to make a full recovery. You two saved that little girl's life last night. Without your quick thinking and CPR, she wouldn't have made it. I'm sure the family will want to thank you."

"No thanks are necessary," Winward stated, feeling as if an enormous weight had been lifted. "When will we be able to talk to her?"

"Not for a while. I want her as sedate as possible right now. I don't want her upset."

"We understand."

"There is one thing, though. I don't know if it will help you, but I thought you should know."

"What's that?"

"As she regained consciousness, she kept repeating a name."

"What name?"

"Thomas Shear."

# CHAPTER THIRTY-TWO

Tom awoke to the sound of Kelly's sobs and his stomach sank. In the darkness, he could feel her movements and knew her delirious state had worsened. He turned on the bedside lamp and his throat clenched. Her face was pale, her cheeks, tear-stained. Her brow was drawn and troubled. The bruising around her eyes, along her jaw and on one side of her forehead, had darkened. There were also new bruises around her throat that resembled large, squeezing fingers.

He smoothed the damp hair from her face and crooned, "I'm here, Kelly. I'm right here, baby."

He looked at the clock and his vision blurred from lack of sleep. Six-thirty. Almost sunrise.

Suddenly, the doorbell seemed to shout through the apartment. Tom snatched on his jeans and was at the door when the pounding started.

"Thank God, you're here," he said, stepping out of Jonathan's way. "I think Kelly's getting worse." He held the door open and looked out. "Where's Marsha?"

"She's on her way. Look, Tom, you've got to get out of here."

"What?" Then Tom noticed Jonathan's frown and the urgency in his voice. "Why?"

"Because the police will be here any minute. I'm surprised they haven't shown up already." He began propelling Tom toward the bedroom.

"Why?" Tom stopped and turned to face his friend. "What's happened?"

Jonathan heaved an impatient sigh. "Carson called. He said he heard on the radio that a little girl was abducted last night. She managed to escape and is now in the hospital suffering from exposure."

"And the police think I'm responsible, no doubt."

"Yeah well, they have good reason to. I listened to the news on the way over here. The alarm went off at your gallery last night and the police found the door standing open. A couple of hours later they found the little girl a few blocks down the street. They think she left the door open while escaping."

"What!"

"Carson wants you to turn yourself in."

"The hell I will."

"That's what I thought you'd say," Jonathan said, shoving Tom forward. "That's why you have to hurry."

They entered the bedroom and Tom began pulling on the rest of his clothes. Jonathan's frown deepened when he saw Kelly.

"Here," he said, handing Tom a set of keys. "You take the rental. I'll take your car and park it in the Crosswind apartment complex about a mile up from here. Then I'll find a way to Merideth Chandler's house and meet you there."

"What if you're stopped on the way?"

"I'll say you let me borrow the car because mine's in the shop. They can even check if they want, because it's true."

"I'm not leaving Kelly until Marsha gets here."

"Tom, you don't have a choice. You have to meet with Merideth Chandler. How can you do that if the police come and carry you away? Look, I know you're worried," he said, "but Kelly's not going anywhere and Marsha will be here any minute. When I left, she was packing a bag in case she had to spend the night. I told her we'd leave the key under the mat, so hurry up. We have to get out of here now."

"Damn it!" Tom sat on the bed and pressed his forehead to Kelly's. "Marsha will be here soon," he said, then kissed her lips. "I'll be back. I love you, Kelly."

———◉———

He saw the garage door open and watched Jonathan back out into the snow and drive away. A few minutes later, the other door opened and a second car began slowly backing out of the garage. He noticed snow-chains on the tires and grimaced. *Who, besides me, would think to keep snow-chains at the ready in the simmering South?* He shook his head in disgust. *Pathetic, pussy-whipped man brainwashed into protecting his prized whore.*

He waited until she'd driven away, then followed, staying back but keeping her tail-lights in sight so she wouldn't panic too soon. He didn't want her harmlessly slipping off the road; he wanted to break her. As she drew closer to a stretch of road with a steeply cut embankment, he sped up. The instant before his Suburban made contact, crashing into her back bumper, he watched her eyes flash wide with fear in the rearview mirror that was illuminated by his headlights. He made contact again and pushed hard, pressing his foot against the accelerator. The car in front of him veered and began to fishtail. As it began to spin, he hit it broadside and saw her horrified face through the window just before it shattered. His SUV rolled to a stop as the other car disappeared over the edge of the road and he quickly got out.

He stood with his long, black coat dancing around his legs while looking down the steep embankment at the crumpled metal of the woman's car and his cold laughter echoed eerily in the pre-dawn darkness. The trees surrounding the stretch of deserted road seemed to absorb and embody the evil in their midst as they swayed creakily in the sharp, penetrating winter wind. Their bare limbs rubbed and clacked together, like a multitude of rough, scaly voices speaking a forbidden language, applauding the vicious malevolence they'd just witnessed.

It'd been so easy. What he hadn't counted on was the thrill of watching the car roll as her muffled screams rose in pitch before abruptly dying.

"Sorry, bitch. But I couldn't have you getting in the way, now could I?"

Using his booted feet, he worked to disguise the snow-entrenched tire tracks until the sound of an approaching vehicle urged him back into the SUV. As he drove away, he watched the headlights appear and pass by the section of road he'd just left. A sneering smile split his lips.

"Now, bitch Kelly. It's your turn." His voice held a menacing edge. "I'm going to get rid of all of you, once and for all."

He looked at the green light of the digital clock in the dash and pressed the accelerator, causing the back tires to break traction on the slick, snow-coated blacktop. Time was running out. He needed the cloak of darkness to accomplish what had to be done. As he drove on to Kelly's apartment, he only hoped the other participants played their parts as he had planned.

When he pulled up to the security gate, he punched in the code he'd received the day before. His smile was predatory as the gate swung open. He wound his way through the complex and parked in time to see two apartment doors open almost simultaneously. His smile grew smug as he watched Jonathan and Tom exit one of the apartments, descend the stairs, and get into separate vehicles. He waited as Kelly's neighbor kissed his wife goodbye, got into a Ford F-150, and left before backing into the space Jonathan had just vacated. Snow and ice crunched beneath his feet as he walked to the back of the Suburban to unlatch the two rear doors, leaving them cracked open. When he reached Kelly's second floor apartment and tried the locked door, he smiled. As he lifted the mat and saw the key, his smile broadened.

"Thank you, gentlemen. I knew you wouldn't let me down."

He inserted the key and gave a surreptitious look around as a distant motor revved. Hearing a door open and close on the floor above, he replaced the key under the mat and slipped inside. He listened as steps receded down the outside stairs, then he stood quietly, rubbing his gloved hands together as he surveyed his tasteful surroundings. He moved from room to room until he stood in the doorway of Kelly's bedroom marveling at her condition as she moaned and strained against invisible bonds. Her face was gaunt and the bruises and welts on her exposed arms and chest stood out in vivid color against the whiteness of her sleeveless, low-cut nightgown. Her forehead was beaded with sweat and the fear induced, pain-filled furrow between her brows seemed to deepen as he stepped closer.

She was weak and incoherent, and this made his job extremely easy as he rolled her in a blanket and hoisted her onto his shoulder. On his way back through the apartment, he took the phone off the hook. When he reached the door, he froze.

Opening the door just enough to peer out, he listened as the voices outside subsided. He cursed under his breath for not getting away completely unnoticed as a man carrying a briefcase gave the unlatched, open rear doors of the Suburban a curious look before getting into his car. He watched the Camry drive away, its tires crushing the frozen top layer of snow, then scanned the area outside before leaving the apartment. Once Kelly was secure in the back of the Suburban, he closed the rear doors with a soft click. Smiling, he slid into the driver's seat and casually exited the complex. His next stop: Shear Gallery.

"Still having a hard time believing he's our man?"

Winward kept his eyes on the slushy, tire-trenched, snow covered road. "Right now, Don, I don't know what to think."

"Why is it so hard for you to admit you're wrong?"

"When I know for a fact that I am, I'll admit it."

He pulled in front of Kelly's apartment and stopped. Two following patrol cars pulled in behind.

"Shear's black Jag isn't here," Winward said.

"No, but Miss Stafford's Lexus is. She can probably tell us where
to find him."

Hayes sent two officers around to the back and gave them time
to get into position before ringing the doorbell. He waited, knocked,
and rang the bell again. Motioning to an officer standing ready with
a hand held battering ram, he instructed, "Break it down."

"Wait," Winward ordered, stepping over to the apartment
next door. "Let's see what we can find out before we destroy Miss
Stafford's door."

He rang the bell and waited until the door opened to reveal an
attractive woman in her thirties roasting her honey brown hair in
hot rollers. Her black-lined, blue eyes widened when Winward held
up his badge.

"Yes?"

"Excuse me, ma'am. I'm Detective Winward from the Cobb
County Police Department. I was wondering if you could help us.
Are you acquainted with your neighbor, Miss Stafford?"

"Kelly?" she asked, surprised. "Sure I am. She's a sweetie. I hope
she's not in any trouble."

"No, ma'am. We just need to talk to her."

"Well, you'll have to wait until she gets home. They left about
forty-five minutes ago."

"They?"

"Kelly and Tom."

"You know Thomas Shear?"

"Not exactly. I've seen him with Kelly, but I haven't actually met the man. Kelly sure seems to like him, though."

"You know for a fact that they left together?"

"No, not for a fact," she said crossing her arms and leaning her shoulder against the door-jam. "It's not like I stand at my window spying on my neighbors, you know."

"Of course not. But why did you say 'they?'"

"Because when my husband, Joe, left for work this morning, I opened the door to walk him out and heard Kelly's door close. I saw the top of Tom's head as he went down the stairs to the parking lot. He wasn't alone because I distinctly heard two sets of footsteps. Then I heard two cars crank up."

"Two cars."

"Yes, sir."

"You're sure about this?"

"Positive."

"Thank you, Mrs…?"

"Reeves. Susan Reeves."

"Thank you, Mrs. Reeves. You've been a big help." He took a step away, then turned back as she began closing her door. "Mrs. Reeves," he said.

"Yes?"

"I see you're getting ready for work."

"That's right."

"You might want to take the day off, or at least wait a few hours until the sun's had time to melt some of the snow from the roads. They're pretty treacherous right now."

"That's what Joe said, too." She heaved a sigh and nodded. "You're right. I have no business being out in this stuff. Better safe than sorry, huh? My boss won't like it, though."

"Tell him he can pay the deductible on your car when you wreck it," Winward replied and smiled.

"Yeah, right," she said and closed her door.

"Good deed for the day?" Hayes asked, making his way to the stairs.

"Why not?"

The two detectives walked back to Winward's Impala in silence. Hayes radioed the attending officers back in, then turned his frustrated gaze on Winward.

"He knows," he said, then slammed his fist against the roof of the car. Winward winced, but said nothing. "Damn it! He knew we would be coming for him. We should've been here an hour ago. He's probably on his way out of the state by now."

"No, he's not," Winward said.

"He ran, didn't he?"

"Of course, he did. If he's trying to clear his name, he knows he can't do that locked up in a jail cell."

"So you still think he's innocent."

"Innocent or not, we have to look at what we've got. Now, Mrs. Reeves said she heard two cars. Since Miss Stafford's Lexus is still here, that would mean they had help."

"Jonathan Fields."

"That's my guess."

"So, let's pay a visit to Mr. Fields."

Winward motioned the officers over. "Clark, you and Ramsey drive to Jonathan Field's residence. See if anyone's home. Hayes and I are going to his office. Let us know what you find."

"You got it."

On the way to Jonathan's office, Hayes called in an APB for Thomas Shear and Kelly Stafford. When they reached the office and Jonathan's secretary told them he was out for the day, his name was added to the list.

"Now what?" Hayes asked, getting back into the car. As if in answer, the dispatch radio crackled to life.

"Detective Winward, this is Ramsey. Do you copy?"

"Winward here. What have you got, Ramsey?"

"It's a no-go at Field's residence. No one's home," he said, raising his voice to be heard above a wailing siren.

"What's happening?"

"An ambulance. We were flagged down by a ditched motorist who was on foot. He noticed another vehicle off the road. A woman apparently lost control and rolled her car down an embankment. She's hurt pretty bad."

"Okay, Ramsey. Do what you can, and thanks for the help."

"So, I repeat," Hayes said. "Now what?"

"Get on the phone. Call Marsha Webster's office and the university. Check to see if she's at either place. Then call Russ Carson. Maybe we can get a little help from one of them."

"What are you going to do?"

"I'm going back inside to use the facilities. I drank too much coffee this morning."

Winward walked back across the slushy parking lot and found the public restrooms inside the building. On his way out, he veered back into Jonathan's office and smiled at the secretary as she looked up.

"Hey, there. It's me again," he said. "I decided to leave a message for Mr. Fields."

"Certainly, detective," she replied, reaching for the ringing phone. "I'll be with you in a moment."

"No problem."

"Fields, Attorney at Law…Good morning, Mr. Jones. We've been waiting to hear from you…Yes, sir. That's right…I'll be glad to."

Winward's eyes shifted as she wrote on a pad, the initials M. C. jumping out at him. Averting his gaze, he pretended to study a painting on the wall. He smiled as she hung up.

"I'm sorry to keep you waiting, detective. I believe you said you wanted to leave a message?"

"I've decided to wait until I see Mr. Fields in person. Thanks anyway."

"Certainly."

Winward left the office at a casual pace. By the time he reached the car, he was jogging.

"No luck," Hayes announced as Winward slid behind the wheel. "Everyone's out. And no one seems to know where they are."

"They're in Roswell. They're meeting with Merideth Chandler."

Hayes's head snapped around as Winward started the car. "How do you know that?"

"I went back inside to have a more in-depth chat with Field's secretary."

"Now I suppose you're going to tell me your natural charm had her purring like a kitten and she just happened to mention it."

Winward's cocky grin broadened as he gave Hayes a sidelong glance. "Not exactly."

———— «()» ————

Tom sat in Jonathan's rental car and watched through the rear-view mirror as his friend got out of the yellow taxi that had pulled in behind him. Jonathan scanned his surroundings as he walked forward and opened the passenger door.

"I'm glad you waited," he said, getting into the car.

"Yeah well, if you'd been much longer, I wouldn't have. It's almost nine o'clock. What took you so long?" Tom asked. He put the car in gear and started up the long drive that led to the Chandler house.

"I paid for the scenic route to make sure I wasn't being followed. There're quite a few people out there who wish they'd stayed home this cold, slippery morning. I've also been trying to reach Marsha, but the line's been busy, and her cell sends me straight to voicemail. So I called the office to see if Marilyn had heard from her. Marilyn couldn't talk. Winward was there."

"How do you know?"

"Because she called me Mr. Jones. I asked her to keep trying to get in touch with Marsha and when she did to have her call me. I also told her where we'd be and gave her Merideth Chandler's number, as well, just in case."

"In case of what?"

"Who knows?" Jonathan asked, throwing up his hands. "A magpie could swoop down and snatch my cell out of my hand because it's shiny. Or I could fry it by dropping it in a toilet. Anything's possible. The point is, I want Marsha to be able to reach us no matter what."

Tom's heartbeat sped up with heightened concern, but said, "Maybe Kelly's better. Maybe she's sleeping and Marsha took he phone off the hook so she wouldn't be disturbed."

"Probably."

The two men exchanged glances and Tom saw the foreboding he felt looking back at him.

"Hell, who are we kidding?" he growled, pulling to a stop in front of the manor house. "I don't like it, man. Something's not right."

"Yeah well, the sooner we get this meeting over with, the sooner we can find out what it is," Jonathan said as he opened the car door and got out.

Tom led the way to the door and rang the bell. It soon opened to reveal the same starched gentleman.

"Mr. Shear, please come in. Mrs. Chandler's expecting you."

"Thank you."

Tom stepped inside and was instantly awed. In one quick glance, his artist's eye took in the high dome ceiling painted to depict a celestial sky. The hand carved alabaster crown and chair-rail moldings surrounding the cavernous foyer contrasted sharply with the rich hue of the wide mahogany staircase. A massive crystal chandelier hung suspended in the center of the entranceway and cast a soft, prismatic glow on the black veined marble floor beneath his feet.

As Jonathan followed Tom inside, the butler eyed him with suspicion before motioning toward a set of open double doors.

"You may wait in the drawing room. I'll inform Mrs. Chandler of your arrival."

Tom nodded and followed Jonathan into the drawing room where they stood absorbing the wealth around them. He knew the formal furnishings were meant to impress, but Tom felt nothing except lonely despair as he gazed around the antique room that could have been a display in a museum depicting another era.

"Wow, what a place," Jonathan remarked under his breath.

"Yeah. Quite a lavish prison, isn't it?"

"Prison, Mr. Shear? You are Thomas Shear, aren't you?"

Startled, Tom turned to see a woman in miniature standing ram-rod straight in the doorway. Her elegant, silver-white hair was worn in a loose chignon and she was immaculately garbed in an ankle-length, long-sleeved dress the color of peaches made from the costliest silk. Her watchful eyes were the bluest of blue, and Tom felt penetrated by their challenge. Her very presence demanded respect and Tom complied as he stood humbled before her. The only crack he detected in her perfect façade was her tightly clasped hands.

"Yes, ma'am. I'm Thomas Shear. And I beg your pardon. I meant no disrespect."

"Is that how you see me?" she asked. "Locked away in my 'lavish prison'?"

"Yes, ma'am," he said. "But I also believe you were forced here by the ignorance of others."

She stepped further into the room and seemed to consider his words. A slight smile creased her lips.

"You're very candid, Mr. Shear. It's a strength I have found lacking in most people."

Her smile lingered as she closed the distance between them. "Even though I'm sure you know who I am, allow me to introduce myself. I'm Merideth Chandler." She held out her tiny hand and Tom took it in a firm, but gentle hold.

"I'm honored to make your acquaintance, ma'am. May I introduce my good friend, Jonathan Fields?"

Jonathan offered his hand and gave a slight bow as she placed her hand in his. "As Tom said, Mrs. Chandler, it's an honor. I want to thank you for accepting me into your home without invitation."

"Whether or not you are accepted, Mr. Fields, will soon be determined. I was under the impression Mr. Shear would be coming alone. Please do not think of me as being ungracious, but would you mind explaining why you are here?"

"Allow me, Mrs. Chandler," Tom replied. "Jonathan is more than just a very good friend. I have also found it necessary to obtain his services as a lawyer. He has been with me throughout this whole ordeal and has even been witness to some of its more bizarre occurrences. Without Jonathan and Kelly as my anchors, I'm afraid my reaction to everything that has happened would've been devastatingly different."

She eyed the men in silence. "Very well," she said. "Please, gentlemen, do sit down."

She perched herself in a chair and Tom noticed the chair she chose had a ledge in front. When he saw that her small feet sat securely on the ledge and not the floor, he understood why. Once she was seated, he and Jonathan sat together on a sofa obtained more for its antiquity than for its comfort.

"Mr. Shear, before this discussion goes any further, I must be candid with you, as well. Because of a news report I heard this morning, I almost refused you admittance."

"But you didn't. Why?"

"I need to hear what you have to say. I may be a foolish old woman for allowing this, but let me assure you I have not done so without taking precautions. Peter is standing with his hand on the telephone prepared to make the appropriate call if necessary."

"I can assure you, ma'am, he'll have no reason to do so. As far as the report you heard this morning, all I can say in my own defense is that I had nothing to do with that little girl. I was with Kelly all night and knew nothing of what had been happening until Jonathan came this morning to roust me from her apartment. If the police think she escaped from my gallery, then she must have, but I swear to you I have no idea how she got there."

Merideth Chandler did not speak as she scrutinized every nuance of Tom's expression. Her remarkable blue eyes seemed to delve into the very pit of his thoughts. Tom remained motionless beneath her deciding stare.

"You're either an excellent liar, Mr. Shear, or you're telling the truth."

She looked from one man to the other before settling her watchful gaze back on Tom. Then she bowed her head and took a deep breath. When she raised her eyes once more, Tom saw an anguish-laced determination in their depths.

"I want to know why you think my husband was murdered."

"Because of the nightmares I began having soon after I moved into your house."

"Nightmares are not evidence, Mr. Shear."

"No, ma'am," he said and heaved a sigh. "However, you have to understand, Mrs. Chandler. I'm an artist, a painter. That's my life. All I want is my own gallery, to teach my classes, and to continue painting. And I bought your house with the intention of fulfilling those desires. I'm sorry if this sounds crass, but the assumed circumstances surrounding your husband's death were just pieces of news to me that

I paid little attention to. When I bought that house, I had no idea it was where his body was found. You also have to understand that I was never a believer or disbeliever in anything paranormal. But as soon as I saw that house, inexplicable things started happening to me. I was drawn to it, and soon after I moved in, the nightmares began."

"What did these nightmares consist of?"

"At first they were of a particular abused little girl. I thought if I painted her, put the nightmare on canvas, I could vanquish the dreams. But as soon as I did, others began taking her place. I began experiencing lapses in time. I would find myself standing in front of a finished portrait and have no memory of painting it. Before I realized it, I had a series of abused children hanging on my gallery walls. I needed to know why, so I began researching newspaper archives. It was then that I realized I knew explicit details of an actual crime I'd known absolutely nothing about. The little girls I painted had not merely been abused, they had been abducted, tortured, and murdered. And I was stunned to realize that my brush had not been guided by imagination, but by the tangible spirits of those children."

Tom watched the demure widening of her eyes. "I know what you're thinking."

"Do you?"

"You're thinking 'this man's insane.'"

"If I thought that, Mr. Shear, Peter would be on the phone right now making that call. Is that all you have to tell me?"

"No, ma'am."

"Then press on."

"After my grand opening," he continued, "the police came to question me about the series. When it became obvious they were looking at me as a suspect, I called Jonathan."

Merideth Chandler's chin lifted a fraction higher confirming her conviction. "My husband did not murder those children, Mr. Shear," she said.

"No, ma'am," Tom replied. "I don't believe he did. Things have happened that only a living, breathing man could've instigated. And I think that man murdered your husband to put the blame on him."

Mrs. Chandler's intertwined knuckles whitened as she blinked back tears. "What of Kelly?" she asked in a firm voice. "How does she fit into all of this?"

"Kelly's the realtor who closed the deal on the house for me. Just before my opening, we became reacquainted and began seeing one another. Soon after, the spirits began manifesting. Maybe it was because she was a woman and could better understand their plight. I don't know. But it was like I'd served my purpose by bringing them to life through my paintings, because then, Kelly became their focus."

"How do you mean?"

"All but one invaded her body, forcing her to absorb their spirits. Now she's host to their torment and sorrow. Her nightmares are horrendous and because of it, she's slipping into a state of delirium. She's even begun to take on the physical characteristics of their abuse."

"Have you seen her?" Mrs. Chandler asked, turning an alarmed frown on Jonathan. "Is it true?"

"Yes, ma'am," he said, his expression somber. "What Tom has been telling you, Mrs. Chandler, is true. And Kelly's rapidly deteriorating because of it."

"Is she in the hospital?"

"No, ma'am."

"Why not?" she demanded, looking at Tom.

"Because I truly believe there's nothing they could do."

"Are you God, Mr. Shear? From the way it sounds, you're gambling with Kelly's life."

Her words cut deep and Tom struggled to control his anguish. "I love Kelly, Mrs. Chandler, more than anything in this world. And I will do whatever it takes to bring her back. But I refuse to watch her wither away in some mental ward."

He took a deep breath to help smother his emotions, and when he continued, his voice was controlled and calm.

"Before she slipped away, she said I was the only one who could help them, that I was the only one who knew how. But the only way I know is to find the man responsible for the deaths of those little girls. If I can do that, maybe their spirits will be freed and Kelly will be released. I do know everything stems from that house. That's the connection. And that's why I'm here. I need your help."

Unseeing, she stared at the Persian rug beneath her feet. "It's evil," she said, as if to herself, her voice tight with dread. "So many terrible things have happened there, and it has absorbed them all."

"I don't think it's the house that's evil, Mrs. Chandler. I think the evil lies in the person responsible for the terrible crimes that were committed there."

They were interrupted by the chime of the doorbell. Tom and Jonathan shared a glance of alarm.

"Expecting company, gentlemen?" Mrs. Chandler asked, observing the exchange. "The police perhaps?"

As if in answer, Peter materialized in the doorway like a starched harbinger of doom. "Excuse me, madam, but Detectives Hayes and Winward would like a word with you and your guests."

"Thank you, Peter. Show them in."

Tom and Jonathan rose as Winward and Hayes entered the room. Their eyes clashed and Tom shuddered to see the raw smile on Hayes's face.

"Good morning, detectives," Mrs. Chandler replied. "Please, do come in."

Winward gave her a quick smile of recognition. "Thank you, ma'am."

"Well, gentlemen, I must say, I really hoped I'd never see the two of you again."

"Considering the circumstances," Winward replied, "I can understand why."

Her shoulder's squared as her smile grew tight. "I don't mean to seem rude, but may I ask why you thought it necessary to pay me this visit?"

Hayes gave a slight bow and kept his eyes on the lady in front of him. "Actually, ma'am, it is Mr. Shear we want to see. We're here on official business."

"I suppose that means you've come to arrest him?"

Hayes cleared his throat. "Yes, ma'am."

"Well, it will have to wait. Mr. Shear came here for my help and I intend to give it to him."

"Mrs. Chandler, I don't think you understand. Mr. Shear is being charged—"

"Detective Hayes," she interrupted. "Mr. Shear is being railroaded. Anyone can see that."

Hayes straightened his spine and cast Tom a baleful look. "I suppose that means Mr. Shear's had time to tell his story," he said.

"Yes, he has."

"Did he include the part about the ghosts, nightmares and…" He was momentarily pensive. "Oh yes. Possessions?"

"Yes, he did."

Hayes sighed and presented her with a look of bewilderment. "Excuse me, ma'am, and please correct me if I'm wrong, but you seem awfully content with the idea. You don't actually believe all of this, do you?"

"I happen to be a firm believer in the paranormal, detective. During my life, I have seen things that could not be denied or explained. I was forced to believe. Now, detectives," she said, gesturing toward Tom and Jonathan, "if you don't mind, I would very much like to continue my conversation with these two gentlemen."

"And I, for one, would like to hear this conversation," Winward said.

"Mark," Hayes began, "I don't—"

"Detective Hayes, I'm right here," Tom said. "I'm not going anywhere. A few more minutes isn't going to matter."

"Come on, Don. Let's play along. It might be interesting. I might even have a few questions of my own," Winward replied.

"In that case, detectives," Mrs. Chandler stated, "you might as well sit down."

As Winward chose the embroidered Chippendale chair across from the sofa of the same vintage that Tom and Jonathan shared, Hayes eyed his partner thoughtfully and shrugged. Then he leveled his dark gaze on Tom and held it there. He did not sit down.

Satisfied, Mrs. Chandler returned her attention to Tom. "Now then, Mr. Shear, I believe you wanted to ask me about the house."

"Yes, ma'am," he said, resuming his seat. "I need to know its history. Anything you can tell me of its former owners, renters, or anyone else who might have a connection."

"How far back do you need me to go?"

"Begin with the most recent. The abductions began last year so let's start there. I believe the house was rented, but never occupied?"

"Yes, that's right. The man was from Europe and had business interests in Atlanta. He intended to use the house whenever he was in the states. Even though the account that had been established for the house received consistent and timely payments, months went by without so much as a word from the man. I remember Theodore commenting on how it was the easiest money he'd ever made. Then news came that he'd had a heart attack and died. A few days later, Theodore was found."

"Do you remember his name?" Tom asked.

"James Messer," Winward answered. "We ran a check on the guy during the initial investigation. He did reside in England and he did have periodic business in Atlanta. We even got a copy of the contract from Russ Carson. Everything checked out."

"Did your husband ever handle the contractual agreements?"

"Oh, no. Even though we had several rental properties, Theodore never wanted to be bothered by them. He had too many other things to deal with, so he left all of that type of business in Russ's hands."

"What about the time before Mr. Messer?"

"The house was vacant for several years before that. After we moved out, Theodore kept the property up, but never seemed motivated in the direction of renters."

"How long did you live there?"

"Twenty-two years. It's where we raised our son, Jacob."

"Are you acquainted with Mr. Craig Raymond and his son, Michael?"

"Certainly. Craig, Theodore, and Russ had business dealings for years. Jacob and Michael became great friends. Michael spent more time at our house than he did his own."

"So, he actually was very close to your family."

"Oh, yes. When things got bad at home he'd come to our house and stay days at a time."

"What do you mean 'when things got bad'?"

"Have you ever met Craig Raymond, Mr. Shear?" she asked.

"Yes, ma'am, several times."

"Then you know what a dominating personality he has. He was extremely authoritative. He controlled every situation and Michael hated it. His mother was his only bright spot and when she left, it devastated him."

"Do you know if Michael Raymond was ever physically abusive?" Jonathan asked.

"Angela would never have allowed Michael to remain in his father's custody if that had been the case. She left because of Craig's tyranny. And the many infidelities she'd had to endure over the years. Craig was an insatiable womanizer."

"Did any children ever result from his affairs?" Tom asked.

"There were rumors, of course. Apparently, a little girl had been born. It was said he supported the child even though he never acknowledged her publicly."

"Did anyone know who the child was?"

"Not with any certainty. Everyone had an opinion, of course."

"Did you?"

She held Tom's gaze. "I had my suspicions, yes. But to voice them would have been nothing more than gossip."

"Would you mind voicing them to me?"

"It all happened a long time ago, Mr. Shear. How could any of this have relevance to the situation at hand?"

"It might have none at all," Tom admitted. "But it might help give us a better understanding of the people involved."

She was silent a moment, watching Tom. The other men seemed to be forgotten.

"There was a tragedy. A mother and daughter died. Soon after, Angela left. Craig had become impossible to live with. Michael was only nine at the time, but he gained understanding of what had happened through his parents' arguments. Of course, he blamed his father for the divorce. And when Craig refused to relinquish custody to Angela, Michael's resentment only became more embittered. But as he grew older, I think he learned to accept things for what they were. He learned his father's business, and from what I understand, he's become quite the entrepreneur."

Tom fell silent. He could feel Emmy's presence swelling inside of him and wondered why. Then he remembered a statement Merideth Chandler had made earlier.

"Well, I think that just about wraps things up," Hayes said while taking a menacing step forward. "It's time to go, Shear."

"Mrs. Chandler, you told Detective Hayes that you're a firm believer in the paranormal," Tom said, ignoring Hayes's stolid advance. "Twenty-two years is a long time to live in one place. Did anything happen to you in that house?" From the corner of his eye he saw Hayes stop, put his hands on his hips, and hang his head.

Merideth Chandler looked down at her entwined fingers before meeting Tom's eyes with a direct gaze. "There was a presence. I could feel it. Lights would turn themselves on and off. Objects would be moved from where I'd left them. And I heard things when I knew I was alone in the house. I told Theodore, but he didn't believe me, so I never mentioned it again."

"What things did you hear?" Winward asked.

"Crying. A child's sorrowful crying." Merideth Chandler took a deep breath and began to study the hands she held clasped in her lap. "She only appeared to me once. But she was always there."

"Did you ever know who she was?" Tom asked and held his breath.

"Oh, yes," she stated, looking up. "I knew exactly who she was. The woman Theodore bought the house from had a little girl who died tragically when she fell down the well at the back of the property."

Tom's brow furrowed. "Well? What well?" he asked.

"It was no longer used and an obvious hazard, so Theodore sealed it with a slab of concrete and built that large out-building over it. He intended to have it filled in, but never did."

Tom exchanged a questioning glance with Winward. "What else can you tell us, Mrs. Chandler?"

"There's nothing left to tell, really. After her little girl's death, Mrs. Carson just gave up. She sold Theodore the house and then committed suicide."

An electric shock seared the room.

"Did you say 'Mrs. Carson'?" Winward asked. Excitement brought him to the edge of his seat.

"Yes."

"Would this be Russ Carson's mother?"

"Yes, detective. He found her body. The poor boy was completely traumatized. His hair turned white overnight."

"Was the little girl named Emmy?" Tom ventured, already knowing the answer.

Merideth Chandler looked startled. "Yes, that's right. Her name was Emily, but her mother called her Emmy. She was Russ's half sister. How did you know?"

Tom bowed his head. When he looked up, Winward was watching. An understanding passed between them. Then he looked over at Hayes. The big man stood staring at Mrs. Chandler, looking shell-shocked.

Jonathan shook his head in astonishment. "I can't believe it. I worked side by side with the man. I'm the one who fed him information. I told him everything. The only thing he didn't know about was this meeting. And if you hadn't refused him knowing—" he said, looking at Tom.

"Then he would've kept it from happening, just like he kept you from the County Registrar's Office."

"He also knew about our surveillance teams," Winward replied.

"I noticed they were missing."

"Yeah, well. Someone tipped the commissioner. He had them withdrawn."

Winward rubbed his bristling chin. "Did Carson know you were staying with Miss Stafford last night?" he questioned.

"Yes, he did," Jonathan stated sourly. "I called him when Marsha and I got home last night around seven o'clock to give him a status report. The son of a bitch acted genuinely disappointed because I'd failed to reach the registrar's office."

"Did he also know what type of security system Mr. Shear had installed in his gallery? And that only the first floor was wired?"

"Yes," Jonathan said, disgusted. "I remember the conversation. It was the afternoon after the first break-in. The day he came to the gallery after the two of you paid him a visit at his office. Tom was still upstairs with Michael Raymond."

"So he knew the house would be empty and he knew the safe way in. It gave him the perfect opportunity to abduct Brenda Kellerman and stage it so everyone would think you did it, Shear." Winward looked at Hayes. "Don, I think we need to locate Mr. Russ Carson."

Hayes's expression had turned lethal. He gave a sharp nod, turned on his heel and stalked out.

"What are you saying?" Merideth Chandler looked to each man. "Surely you're not suggesting Russ Carson is responsible for all of this. If you are, you're saying he's a murderer. That he killed Theodore." She gave her head a vigorous shake. "That's impossible. Russ was one of Theodore's oldest and dearest friends. Theodore mentored him after his mother's death; he helped Russ through college."

"Mrs. Chandler," Tom said, his voice gentle. "It has to be Russ Carson. He's the only common link."

# CHAPTER THIRTY-THREE

An insistent chirp drew everyone's attention as Jonathan stood and extracted his cell phone from his jacket. Tom paid close attention and rose to his feet as the blood drained from Jonathan's face.

"I'm on my way," he said.

"What is it? Is it Kelly?" Tom asked, barely breathing.

"No. It's Marsha." Jonathan began searching his pockets, the concern on his face chilling. "Marilyn said the hospital called. Marsha was in a car accident this morning. They're taking her into surgery. I have to go. Damn it! Where are my keys?"

"Here," Tom said, tossing them over. "Go."

With a jerking nod, Jonathan rushed from the room. Tom watched him go before turning to face Winward. His voice was thick with urgency.

"Marsha was supposed to stay with Kelly today. If her accident happened this morning on her way there that means Kelly's been left alone. Will you take me to her?"

"Hayes and I were there this morning. No one answered the door."

"She couldn't answer the door, detective. Her condition has gotten worse."

Winward's frown deepened. He gave a quick nod. "Let's go."

"Mr. Shear?"

Tom felt a hand on his sleeve. He looked down to see Merideth's lovely face marred by worry.

"My prayers are with you."

He looked deep into her shining blue eyes. "Thank you, ma'am." He squeezed the delicate hand on his arm. "Thank you for everything."

He turned away and caught up with Winward in the foyer as Peter pulled the front door open. Hayes stood outside beside the Impala and watched them exit the house at an urgent pace.

"What's going on?" he asked, slipping his cell phone into his pocket. "Fields just tore out of here like a bat out of hell."

"Marsha Webster was in an accident this morning," Winward said, almost leaping down the steps and trotting toward the Impala one step behind Tom. "She's in the hospital. We have to get to Miss Stafford pronto."

He jumped in the driver's seat as Tom took a place in the back. Then the engine roared to life. Hayes had barely made it inside before they lurched forward, Winward throwing the car in gear and fishtailing, slinging a rooster tail of grimy slush.

"Did you have any luck locating Carson?" Winward asked, barreling down the long, slick drive toward the intersecting residential street.

Hayes attached a police emergency light to the roof of the car, then pulled his arm back in and rolled up the window. He flipped a switch and the siren began to wail. "No," he said, securing his seatbelt and bracing himself for the harrowing ride. "He wasn't in his office, and if he was home, he wasn't answering his phone. I left messages at both places saying we needed to speak with him concerning his client, Mr. Shear."

Winward tapped the brakes at the end of the drive and jerked his head in both directions looking for oncoming traffic. He jammed the accelerator and made the turn with whining tires fighting to gain traction. "Good," he said, coming up fast on a slow moving car. "Hopefully, he'll think it's all routine." He swerved around the car as it began to pull toward the shoulder of the road and pressed the accelerator even further.

Hayes cleared his throat. "Mr. Shear, if all of this works out the way I think it will, then I'll owe you an apology."

Tom sat in the backseat with his arms splayed to keep himself from being thrown from side to side. "Detective," he shouted, trying to be heard over the screaming engine and ear splitting siren, "that's the last thing on my mind. Just get me to Kelly."

At Highway 92, Winward came upon a red traffic light and a row of vehicles waiting their turn to cross the intersection. He slowed and pulled into the oncoming lane. "Shit. I hate doing this. I'm going to get hit head-on one of these days."

"You mean you do this often?" Tom asked from the backseat, emitting a nervous snort.

"No, thank God, I don't." Nosing his way to the front of the line, he inched his way into the intersection and a woman talking on her cell phone narrowly missed taking off the front end of the Impala. "Shit," he repeated, slamming on the brakes at the same time the woman slammed on hers, causing her minivan to slide sideways, blocking the intersection. Winward began gesturing rudely and yelling for her to move her vehicle. Her eyes widened even more and she dropped the phone. With a death-grip on the steering wheel and a muddled nod, she pulled the minivan forward at a creeping pace. Winward pulled around her back-end and sped up through the intersection, turning west on Highway 92. He handled the Impala perfectly as it slid across the slippery asphalt in a graceful arc that ended in the direction they wanted to go. All of the other vehicles had stopped as their drivers watched the drama unfold.

The six-lane highway narrowed into a divided four-lane as they approached the northern city limits of Marietta. Winward once again proved to be an expert driver as he swerved around late morning traffic and bullied his way through intersections. As they crossed over Hwy 5 in Woodstock, traffic congested considerably. Forward motion was slow and tedious, but they soon pulled onto Interstate 575 and headed south at an alarming rate of speed considering the condition of the roads.

Tom peeled his fingers from the gouges he imagined he'd left in the vinyl backseat when Winward finally pulled to a stop in front of Kelly's building. He sprang from the car as soon as a door opened and raced up the stairs two at a time to the second floor apartment.

He tried the doorknob, then lifted the mat to retrieve the key. "I left it this morning for Marsha," he said, his adrenalin spiking as he unlocked the door and pushed it open. When he reached Kelly's bedroom, he was stunned to see the bed empty.

"She's not here. And her blanket's missing." Tom turned to Winward. The fear on his face was gripping. "There's no way she could've made it out of here by herself."

"Are you sure about that?"

"Positive. She couldn't even get out of bed, detective, much less leave the apartment."

Suddenly, Tom's expression turned wrathful. "Carson," he sneered. "He called Jonathan this morning to tell him about last night knowing he would come here to warn me. He knew we would run. And if he caused Marsha's accident—"

"That means he wanted her out of the way as well," Hayes finished.

"He knew we'd leave Marsha a way in and he took advantage of it."

"Okay," Winward said. "It all fits. Our problem is where to start looking. He could've taken her anywhere."

"No." Tom's eyes reflected the deadly edge in his voice. "He has all of his victims collected together. He'd take them back to where it all began."

⋙⋘

Carson drove around Shear Gallery to the back of the house and parked like he did the night before. He got out of the Suburban, unfolding a tall, lean body shrouded in long, black wool. Combat boots encased his feet. Closing his eyes, Carson lifted his face to the sun and stood motionless for a moment. The crisp air was alive with the drips and gurgles of snow as it melted from foliage, trees, and power lines and ran from roofs into gutters and drain pipes. When he opened his eyes and looked around, he was pleased to see how much the hedges lining the property had grown during the past year. They obstructed the view from neighbors and his confidence soared as he opened the rear doors of the SUV.

Kelly's blue-tinted eyelids fluttered open in the glaring light, but her green eyes remained unfocused. She let out a low guttural moan and he took a lung-filling, elated breath. He let it out in a satisfying huff, then un-wrapped the blanket from around her body. He watched gooseflesh rise on her skin in the cold air and grinned as her nipples hardened and pushed against the thin fabric of her white, cotton gown.

"Ah, is the bitch cold?" he asked with mocking concern as he took each nipple between a thumb and forefinger, twisting as he squeezed, relishing the moan of pain he received. "They really are beautiful, you know. I bet Tomboy creamed himself when he first saw them." Malicious desire filled his cold, gray eyes and he bent lower until his hot breath caressed her ear. "Don't you wish you had his mouth on them right now, sucking and biting until you squirm, until all of your inhibitions are ripped away?"

Carson's expression became a sneering leer as he straightened and grabbed a roll of duct tape. "Forget about it," he said. "That's a sensation you'll never have to worry about again." He bound her wrists with a long strip of tape, then repeated the process on her ankles. As he placed a strip over her mouth, he looked into her green eyes and saw a moment of intense clarity in their depths before they rolled upward, her lids closing. He shook off the cold finger of unease that traced his spine as he gathered her in his arms and lifted her from the Suburban.

He found her feeble attempt to struggle amusing as his long stride carried them across the snow-patched back lawn. At the double doors of the out-building, he pulled a door open and carried her inside where he laid her down on the hard-packed, cold dirt floor. Instead of turning on the overhead florescent lights, Carson opened the double doors wide so they could lend their late morning light to the two large windows in each of the long walls. Turning back, he stood over Kelly where she lay shivering. He watched her eyes open and saw lucidity; it thrilled him to see them widen with glazed fear.

"Well, welcome back, Bitch Stafford. Are you among the living now? You've been with the dead so long I was beginning to wonder if you would ever come back."

Kelly pulled at her bonds and he smiled. "Please, excuse the tape. I'm afraid it's a necessity. I couldn't have you regaining your senses and trying to escape, now could I? As far as the tape on your mouth, well, I must admit, your mewling began to get on my nerves."

He crossed his arms and looked down at her with musing curiosity. Then he began to pace, his boots thumping against the hard-packed dirt with each step. As he traversed the building's perimeter, he took stock of tools hanging in racks on the wall. Shovels and rakes leaned together in a corner. A red metal wheelbarrow held worn gloves, a gardening trowel and shovel, clippers, and a partial bag of potting soil. When he looked to where the extension ladder should've been, he stopped, a scowl darkening his face. With a shake of his head, he resumed his pacing.

"You know, you've been having some hellacious nightmares. Or should I say memories?" Carson chuckled.

"I would never have believed anything like this could happen. But when I heard how your voice changed to sound exactly like little bitch Jennifer Miles when she called for her mommy right before she died—" He stopped and looked gleefully impressed. "Well, I have to tell you, it sent shivers up my spine. To think someone can actually be possessed by spirits and forced to relive death over and over again is astounding. But don't worry," he said, his face splitting with an evil grin. "Soon you'll be living your own death and it'll all be over. I'm going to put you out of your misery, Kelly Bitch. I'm going to get rid of all of you, once and for all. And you know what the best part is?" he asked, raising his unnaturally light brow as if expecting an answer. "Your boyfriend is going to be blamed for everything."

His cackle reverberated off the metal walls making Kelly cringed in terror. When her eyes rolled back and her lids began to flutter, he gave her face a blistering slap.

"Oh, no you don't, bitch. Don't you go drifting off again. I want you to know exactly when it's time to die."

Carson shook his head in agitation. "It could've been over with by now if we hadn't had to wait. Police are such a nuisance, aren't they? Tacking their yellow crime scene tape everywhere, standing around drinking coffee and eating pastries, totally oblivious that they're being watched. I thought they'd never leave. It's enough to make a person retch," he said, screwing up his narrow face in disgust as he removed his long, black wool coat and hung it on a sturdy wall-hook installed to hold a heavy tool.

He rolled up the sleeves of his blue-on-white flannel shirt and walked over to the ten foot long, four foot wide worktable. He stood for a moment with his hands on his hips, then began clearing its surface. When he was finished removing all of the paint supplies, he ran a caressing finger along its sanded edge.

"A fine piece of work, don't you think? I made it myself. You'd never know there was a death pit underneath, would you?"

He heaved the table out of the way to reveal a masonry ring capped by a concrete slab. Three heavy metal eyelets had been inserted into the slab's edge to ensure easy removal.

Carson retrieved three hanging chains that were threaded into a pulley attached to a supporting roof joist. He hooked each one to a matching eyelet, then went to a crank mounted to the wall and began turning the handle. As the slab lifted, it made an abrasive, scraping noise and the ominous sound sent a delicious chill over his body. He turned back to Kelly with an ironic smile.

"Smell that?" His eyes glinted with insanity. "It's the stench of death. Deliciously aromatic, don't you think?

"It must be an awesome feeling to know the exact moment you're going to die," he said. "My little sister knew. All of the others knew, as well. You can see it in their eyes, you know. It really is amazing to watch. I wish I could've seen my mother. But I found her after she was already dead. The bitch committed suicide just because her precious Emily was dead. She knew I did it. She knew I threw that stupid little bitch down the well and it ate her up.

"And you want to know why? Because she knew it was her fault. She made me!" He growled and his eyes grew wild. He thumped his chest hard with his fist then swung his arms wide. "She created me and when I became old enough to make my own demands, she became frightened. It was her fault because she decided she didn't want me anymore. She stopped loving me and took another man. Then she had the *gall* to get pregnant!"

His eyes were blazing and his nostrils flared. His long, agitated strides took him back and forth as he raved.

"Bitch!"

He returned to his hanging coat and took a revolver from its pocket. He slammed it down on the table. He stared at it for a long moment before pointing at it with a steady, condemning finger.

"That's what she used! She blew her brains out with it." Carson gave his head an incredulous shake. "Not a pretty sight."

He resumed his pacing, then threw back his head and let out a howling, scornful laugh. It careened off the metal walls and seemed to become a living thing. Cowering, Kelly drew her knees up to become as small as she could and covered her head with her bound hands.

"The bitch deserved to die for what she did to me!" he said, his voice rough and menacing. He turned to Kelly with a wondrous, wide-eyed expression as if he were talking to a sympathetic, captivated audience. "Can you believe she sold everything right out from under me? She took the money and waved it in my face. Then she threw it in the fire! I couldn't believe it. All of that money, and I had to sit there and watch it burn. I was left with absolutely *nothing*. I had to scrimp and beg just to stay alive! Can you even fathom in that little brain of yours how absolute my humiliation was?" Carson shook his head again and turned away.

"And then Theodore Chandler took *pity* on me." His voice was mocking. "He helped me get into college. Wasn't that generous of him?" he asked, contempt dripping from each word. "Hell, he's the one who ruined my life in the first place. He's the one who bought the house and paid my mother the money I had to watch burn! But I got him back. I made sure that sanctimonious bastard paid dearly for taking everything away."

Kelly struggled with her bonds. Catching the motion, he looked at her as if he'd forgotten she was there. He smiled and something cold flickered in his eyes.

"Have you ever cut yourself and watched the blood ooze from the wound? I find it fascinating, don't you? If we only had more time, we could explore the possibilities together. I'd love to give you the proper attention you deserve."

He lifted Kelly off the ground. She squirmed in panic and tried to scream, but the adhesive covering her mouth muffled the sound.

"You know, I'm really going to enjoy this," he said. "You have very expressive eyes."

"Freeze!"

Carson whirled with Kelly in his arms and saw Winward and Hayes standing in the doorway. Their guns were drawn and aimed at his head.

"Put her down, Carson," Hayes directed. "It's over."

"It's not over," Carson scoffed. "They're still alive."

"It's over!" Winward demanded.

Letting Kelly's feet fall to the ground and holding her against him like a shield, Carson snatched the revolver from the table. He fired a shot in Winward's direction, but missed as the two detectives flung themselves inside, diving for cover.

"Stay away! You can't stop me," Carson yelled, dragging Kelly toward the well.

A deep, blood-chilling growl gave warning as Tom suddenly appeared in the doorway, stalking hungrily toward him. His predatory stare held the promise of death, and Carson cringed as he raised his gun and fired. His maniacal laughter rang out when Tom spun and hit the ground.

Suddenly, Tom jerked. A vapor lifted from his body and Carson's eyes widened. As it took form, his muscles went slack, letting Kelly slip from his grasp to crumple on the ground. He cried out as her body began to writhe with seizures.

One by one, seven more vapors appeared and took shape. Each one was of a different little girl, and Carson stood in awestruck horror as he watched his victims gather around him, unaware that Tom crawled on his belly to where Kelly lay motionless.

The long, florescent light tubes overhead suddenly flared and shattered, spraying razor shards of glass. Objects were lifted and flung through turbulent air. Windows shook in their frames. Metal stretched and screeched as the structure around them flexed with the force growing within.

"We've come for you, brother." Emmy's little girl voice was hollow and surreal. Her accusing eyes pinioned him with their stare. "We want you to join us. Join us, brother."

"Join us."

"Join us."

"Join us."

Their hollow voices blended into a haunting chant; overriding the chaos around them. As the girls stepped close, the chant grew in volume causing Carson to press his hands over his ears. His eyes grew wild with confusion as he began to shake.

"No!" he screamed, raising his gun. "You're all dead. I killed you!"

Sound exploded as bullets ricocheted off the steal walls, and Carson shrieked as the unscathed circle closed in around him. He slung his arms wildly to force them back, but only managed to throw himself off balance. Lurching forward, he took a step toward the open door as Emmy's image lengthened then narrowed and became arrow sharp. Her spirit penetrated between his shoulder blades with lightening speed and he threw his arms and head back like he had been dealt a solid, hard blow. The next little girl made him stagger, and as they took possession one by one, his convulsions intensified, becoming more violent until he finally collapsed to his knees.

Deep gashes began to appear, dripping blood over darkening bruises. The mass of his body withered while breaking bones crackled and impaled muscle to create gaping, grotesque wounds that soaked his clothes in blood. His face swelled with infection as putrid sores erupted, and the smell of burnt flesh reeked as invisible fire seared his skin. His body, contorting in agony, fell to its side, and his rasping screams grew deafening before they began to gurgle. After a moment that seemed to stretch forever, the terrible sound abruptly ended along with the impotent clicking of his empty gun.

Tom looked up from where he laid on the ground with Kelly beneath him and saw Carson lying prone and unmoving. He was turned toward him and Tom shuddered to see wide, hemorrhaged, dead eyes staring back at him from a mutilated face.

Kelly shifted and Tom looked down to see her watching him with clear, lucid eyes. He smiled as he carefully peeled the tape from her lips.

"Is it over?"

"Yeah," he said, holding her close. "It's all over."

Winward appeared and eyed them critically where they still lay on the ground. "Are you two all right?"

"We're okay."

Tom sat up and began removing the tape binding Kelly's wrists and ankles, and her eyes widened in alarm.

"Tom! You're bleeding."

"I'll be okay."

"Here, I'd better take a look," Winward said, squatting.

Kelly helped Tom out of his ruined leather coat. Winward opened the buttons of Tom's bloody shirt and pushed it back from his shoulder.

"It's a shoulder wound. And it appears to be clean. The bullet went straight through. You're lucky he was a lousy shot," he said, peeling out of his own coat and wrapping it around Kelly's bare shoulders.

Tom grimaced with the pain and controlled his breathing. "I don't think luck had anything to do with it," he said, watching Hayes pass Winward a stack of clean rags and a roll of tape he'd found on a shelf against the wall. He gritted his teeth as Winward pressed the rags against his wounds.

"Do you know what happened?" Tom ground out.

Winward glanced up and then back down at Tom's wound as he began to tightly wrap the tape to hold the pads in place. "Yeah, and I wish I didn't. I've never seen anything like it and I hope to God I never do again."

"You know, that was a pretty dumb stunt you pulled," Hayes said, rising from his inspection of Carson's ravaged body. "Courageous as hell, but dumb. You could've been killed."

Tom's shoulder was throbbing. Grinding his teeth, he carefully shrugged back into his coat. He pulled Kelly against him and held her close to shield her from the sight of Carson's corpse. He felt her hands slip up his back and chest beneath his coat and press gently against his shoulder wounds. Heat began seeping into his muscles.

"And what would you have done, detective, if someone you loved were in danger?"

Hayes grunted. "Something just as courageous and equally stupid, I suppose. I saw you get hit. That shoulder must hurt like hell."

"Is that all you saw?" Tom asked, breaking into a cold sweat as he slowly rose to his feet, bringing Kelly up with him.

Hayes scowled. "No. I guess I'm like Merideth Chandler. Even though I don't understand it, I've been forced to believe. But I bet she ain't never seen nothin' like that." He cast a glance over his shoulder, then looked at Tom and Kelly and shook his head.

"Come on, little lady," he said, pulling Kelly away from Tom and lifting her into his massive arms. "I think it's time we got you out of here."

"Tom's losing blood. He needs a doctor."

Winward slipped beneath Tom's good arm to help support his weight. "Don't worry. Your man will be well taken care of."

They all froze as the disembodied melody of a familiar lullaby suddenly teased the silence. The woman's lilting hum rose and fell with haunting gentleness as if soothing a sleepy child.

"Mama?" The little girl's voice was heartrending with innocence.

"Come, my angel. It's time to go home."

# EPILOGUE

Tom pulled Kelly against him as they reached the door of Marsha's hospital room. "I love you," he said.

"I love you, too."

Ignoring nurses in their cheerfully printed smocks gliding past soundlessly on rubber soles, he lowered his head and kissed her with slow deliberation. When the door opened, they were still in each other's arms.

"I thought I heard kissing out here." Jonathan's grin broadened. "And here I was, thinking Marsha and I were the only ones allowed."

"Shows how much you know," Tom replied.

"Nice sling, man. Do they come in designer colors?"

Tom chuckled and eyed his friend. "What's gotten into you? You're certainly in a good mood."

"I have excellent reason to be. Come see for yourself."

Jonathan led the way into a private room that was bright with sunshine and splashed with color. Floral bouquets of every variety took up the horizontal space and, in the center of it all, they found a smiling Marsha, sitting upright with the bed in its raised position.

"Hey, sweetheart, how're you feeling?" Tom asked, kissing her upturned cheek.

"Much better, thanks. The doctor said I was lucky. My injuries aren't as bad as they could've been. I'm already up and slowly walking the halls. I had my first real shower today and it was glorious. I just hope it doesn't take too long for these damn bruises on my face to disappear."

"It won't," Kelly said, taking Marsha's hand, careful of the IV taped to its back. "You just have to give yourself time to heal. It's only been a week."

"That's what I've been telling her. But does she listen to me? You'd think two days in intensive care would teach her something." Jonathan shook his head. "She's still as impatient as ever."

"Oh, hush." Marsha waved a shooing hand in Jonathan's direction as she eyed Kelly. "I'm glad you came," she said, squeezing Kelly's abnormally warm hand. "It seems like every time you do, I feel better." She chuckled. "And every time I see you, you're looking more wonderful."

Kelly flashed a smile. "I feel wonderful. It's amazing what a few days rest and a generous portion of tender loving care can do."

Marsha grinned and winced as she stretched a healing split lip. Turning her attention to Tom, she fingered the sling supporting his arm. "So, hero, how's the shoulder?"

"The shoulder's fine." He cast Kelly a secretive smile. "And getting better everyday."

"It'd better be," Jonathan said. "I'm going to need your services as soon as Marsha's better."

"My services," Tom repeated. "To do what?"

"To be my best man."

"You're kidding." Tom's face split with a comical grin. "So, you're finally taking the plunge?"

"With both feet and the rest of me following."

"He'd better," Marsha declared. "After everything he said to me when he thought I was dying, there's no way I'm letting him worm his way out this time." She blew Jonathan a kiss, then turned to Kelly. "I'd love it if you'd be my maid of honor."

Kelly's surprised look transformed into a smile of pleasure. "I'd love too."

"Great. Just let us know when you want us to return the favor."

Tom draped his good arm across Kelly's shoulders and laughed. "We'll be sure to."

"Have you heard anything else from Winward?" Jonathan asked, bringing up the subject on everyone's mind.

"He called last night. They're finishing up their investigation. I can move back in anytime."

"That means they've explored the well," Marsha said, taking Jonathan's hand.

Tom gave a solemn nod. "Yeah. They found the seven victims still unaccounted for. They brought up the last of the remains yesterday."

Jonathan shook his head. "I still can't believe everything that's happened. But, maybe now, everything can be put to rest."

"I hope so."

A soft knock on the heavy door drew their attention. Detective Winward stood in the doorway.

"Mind if I join you?"

"Not at all," Jonathan said, waving him in. "As a matter of fact, we were just talking about you."

Winward's lips creased with a grin. "I'll bet you were," he said as he turned to Marsha. "I wanted to see how you were doing. You look like you're feeling much better."

"I am. The nurses already have me up walking the halls. I'll be out of here in no time."

"That's good. That's real good. I'm glad to hear it."

"How's Brenda Kellerman?" Tom asked.

"She's going through therapy, but she's doing great. She's at home and happy. It's amazing how resilient kids are."

"That's wonderful news."

"I suppose Tom's filled you in on what's been happening?"

Winward's gaze swept the room before resting on Jonathan.

"Yeah. We were just discussing it. It's incredible how things turned out. But what about Robert Manning? Were you able to find out what part he played in all of this?"

"It's obvious he was after the Rage collection, but, as you know, he escaped before Hayes and I could really get to him. Since we had nothing concrete to hold him with anyway—" He shrugged. "We're still looking for him, but I doubt we'll find him. We discovered that Robert Manning wasn't even his real name. It was only one of several aliases."

"How'd you find that out?" Jonathan asked.

"Interpol. Apparently, our thief's been practicing his trade all over the world."

"And you let him get away?" Marsha sniggered, then grimaced with her hand over her abdomen to support her surgical stitches.

Winward gave her a hands-up shrug. "How were we supposed to know? We were busy playing ghosts and goblins with Tom here. And we didn't exactly *let* him get away. He escaped from a secure police cruiser. How does a person do that and not be seen by a half dozen cops milling around?"

"What about the company the van was registered too? What'd you find on it?" Tom asked.

"It's a privately owned company specializing in investigative work, but you won't find an ad in the yellow pages. Apparently, they've earned a reputation on the down low and are very good at finding missing persons and executing extractions. They even have their own lab. It's pretty impressive really. In fact, they came to us. They have a unique tracking device on all of their vehicles. Imagine their surprise when they found it impounded and being held as evidence." Grinning, he put his hands in his leather jacket's pockets and shook his head. "To be honest, I don't think they're involved, but we're still digging. So far, we've only come up with a sole owner: Marcus Hillyerd. Ring any bells?"

Everyone shook their heads.

"So, you have no idea who Manning was working for, if anyone," Tom said.

"Well now, I didn't say that. There was one surprising development to come out of it."

"Which was?"

"Hayes and I went to pay a visit to Mr. Craig Raymond and his son, Michael. When we got there, it was obvious Raymond senior was having a hard time controlling his temper. He was very evasive and abrupt with our questions, so on our way out we talked to a few employees."

"And?" Tom pressed when Winward paused to draw out the suspense.

Winward's dark eyes twinkled. "Raymond junior was nowhere to be found. Apparently, Michael skipped town the night Manning was apprehended. We went by his residence and it had been cleared out. Empty."

"I still don't understand why the Raymond's would want the collection badly enough to try and steal it," Kelly replied.

"Did Tom tell you of the conversation he had with Merideth Chandler regarding Craig Raymond?"

"Yes, he did."

"Emmy was the illegitimate child she referred to. Her mother was Craig Raymond's mistress, as well as Carson's mother. After she committed suicide, Raymond fell into a deep depression. He became unbearable. That's when his wife finally left him."

"How do you know all of this?" Tom asked.

"Raymond admitted it."

Jonathan raised a brow. "And how did you get him to do that?"

"After we found out about Michael, we went back to have a little chat. I told him if he didn't come clean he would be charged as being an accomplice to his son's illegal activities."

"So," Tom said, "he lost a child, a mistress, and a wife all within days of one another."

Jonathan shook his head. "I'm surprised his wife put up with it as long as she did. Can you imagine sticking by a man through years of infidelity and then one day, you wake up to realize he was in deep mourning for the other woman?"

"Did Michael know about Emmy?" Kelly asked.

Winward nodded. "Raymond told me he got drunk one night and told the boy all about it. He even had a picture to show him."

"That explains why Michael was so interested in seeing the Rage collection the day he came to the gallery to pick up the paintings his father had purchased," Tom stated. "Raymond had been adamant about buying the collection. When Michael saw Emmy's portrait, he understood why."

"It would seem your Rage collection made a huge impact on a lot of people, Tom," Jonathan replied.

"On Russ Carson most of all," Kelly said, claiming a corner of Marsha's bed. "When I was with him, before you guys showed up, he was ranting about his mother. About how she'd made him into what he was. That she'd made him love her and then threw him away. I think his breaking point came when she took another lover and got pregnant. He stood in the shadows for years, his anger and resentment growing as the little girl, as Emmy, received all of the love from their mother that he thought should have been his. He hated her and thought if the child no longer existed, his mother would start loving him again. But that didn't happen. He said she knew what he'd done. He said she'd known and it drove her crazy. That's when she sold everything to Theodore Chandler and then burned the money in the fireplace while he watched. Soon after, she committed suicide. She left him destitute until Mr. Chandler took pity on him and helped him get through college."

"So that's how his hatred for the female gender was born," Winward replied.

"Yes," Marsha answered. "And he probably murdered Theodore Chandler because he gave Carson's mother the means to ruin him, then commit suicide, leaving him destitute and alone. Carson blamed Mr. Chandler for causing his impoverishment. Not to mention the humiliation he must've felt for being forced into taking advantage of the charity Mr. Chandler offered afterward. His resentment had years to simmer and when the opportunity presented itself, he took advantage of it."

"He must have been proud of himself when he staged Chandler's suicide and the commissioner bought it," Winward stated. "It gave him a clean slate to start abducting again somewhere else."

"When I went to him about defending Tom against your suspicion, I have to admit, I was surprised he even considered taking the case. Now that I think about it and know what I know, he must've been busting at the seams to meet Tom and to see his collection."

"No doubt," Tom replied.

"I can't imagine what he must've thought when he first saw it, to have his victims staring back at him," Kelly said. She shook her head. "I'll never understand what could drive a person to do such horrible things, especially to children."

Marsha gave a helpless shrug. "For the most part, the brain and the mind within it are still a big mystery, Kelly. For some people, being grossly abused as a child destroys them. Some grow up to become abusers themselves. Others take it a few steps further to create an existence of hatred where all other emotion is void. The only thing they feel is that tangible part of them that relishes lashing out at the weak. On the other hand, others who suffered the same degree of abuse fight to hold on to their sanity. Therefore, they learn to accept themselves and what happened to them and become a stronger person because of it. They're survivors."

"But children shouldn't have to suffer. They shouldn't have to try to survive."

Marsha smiled sadly and shook her head. "No, they shouldn't. But until our society stands up and takes notice, things aren't going to change."

"I don't know about that," Tom said. "Just think about what happened. Those little girls manipulated Kelly and me to get closer to Carson, then they decimated him. They were allowed to have their revenge. But who allowed it? God? Nature? The cosmos? I don't think change is going to wait on society, I think it's happening now."

"What are you saying?" Winward asked.

"Think about it. In the past few weeks, I've seen and done things I would've said were impossible six months ago. We all have. We can no longer turn a blind eye to what's termed the paranormal."

Marsha held up her hand. "I never saw the girls."

"Maybe not," Tom said. "But you sensed them. You've got your own woo-woo going on with your clairvoyance thing."

She opened her mouth and Jonathan shook his head. "Don't try to deny it, darlin'," he said. "Tom's right. You might call it intuition, but it's more than that and you know it."

"Why would you deny it?" Kelly asked. "It's a gift. You should develop and use it."

"In my profession?" Marsha shook her head. "Too many clinical, closed minds."

"Why would those old fuddy-duddies even have to know about it?" Jonathan asked.

Her eyes went to Tom. "I'll never tell," he said.

She looked at Winward. "Tell who what?" he asked.

Marsha's gaze shifted to Kelly and she scowled at the smirk she saw. "And what about you?" she asked.

"I won't tell anyone if that's what you want."

"That's not what I mean and you know it. I'm talking about *your* gift," Marsha said. She watched Kelly and Tom exchange glances. "Ha," she said, pointing a finger at Tom. "You know what I'm talking about."

"I'm glad somebody does," Jonathan said, looking at Winward. "Do you know what she's talking about?"

Winward shrugged, shaking his head. "Not a clue."

"I bet you don't even need that sling, do you?" Marsha asked Tom, ignoring Jonathan and Winward.

Tom opened and closed his mouth, then looked at Kelly. Her half-stricken expression dissolved into one of resolve as her gaze fell on Marsha.

"I understand why you have to keep it secret," Marsha said. "If you didn't, you'd have desperate people lining the streets wanting your help. But it's just us here, people you can trust."

Kelly bit her bottom lip as she held Marsha's gaze, then she sighed, looked at Tom, and nodded. He took off the sling and raised his arm above his head.

"What the hell?" Winward exclaimed. "I saw your wounds, man. You shouldn't be able to do that yet, at least not without screaming." His eyes narrowed on Kelly, then went to Marsha. "Are you saying she healed him?"

"Why not? She's been healing me all week." She chuckled, then grimaced as her hand went to the sutures in her abdomen again. Kelly removed Marsha's hand and replaced it with her own, closing her eyes. Her brow creased in concentration. Marsha relaxed, releasing a sigh. "Thank you."

"What? You mean she's doing it right now?" Jonathan asked, staring at Kelly's hand.

"Yes. The heat feels wonderful," Marsha answered with a serene smile. She looked at Winward and her smile widened. He stood like a statue, staring at Kelly slack-jawed. "I've baffled the doctor's, you know." Winward twitched like he'd been poked, meeting her gaze. "They told me I died from my injuries during the operation, and that my recovery would take weeks. I should be in ICU right now, hooked up to machines. Instead, I'm sitting up in bed, walking the halls, and taking showers." She laughed and her eyes widened as she looked at Kelly. "I barely felt that. Laughing didn't hurt." Marsha rolled her eyes to the ceiling. "Thank God, I can sneeze now."

Everyone chuckled in a half-hysterical way. Kelly withdrew her hand, leaning into Tom as he wrapped his arm around her.

"Are you okay?" he asked.

"Yes. Just a little tired," she said, smiling up at him.

Tom kissed her brow. "I love you."

"When you heal, you have to share your energy, don't you?" Marsha asked.

"Yes, but it's worth it. It won't take me long to recharge."

"How long have you been able to do this?" Winward asked, a look of wonder on his face.

"I think I was seven the first time," Kelly said. "Our cat caught a chipmunk, but didn't kill it. I cried as I held it and wished with all my heart that its injuries would go away." She laughed. "They did. My mom almost fainted when it jumped out of my hands and scampered away."

"I'll bet," Jonathan said, looking at Kelly like she was an exotic bird speaking Swahili.

Kelly grinned, shaking her head. "Not because I had an ability," she said. "That was no surprise. My family history is full of people with different gifts. It's just that healers are rare. They have to be protected, kept secret."

"Some people would argue that you have a responsibility to the masses that are sick or injured," Jonathan said.

"If I took on that responsibility, it would drain me and I would die," she told him.

Silence fell around the room. Winward cleared his throat. "Well, that's not going to happen, is it? If you ever need me, I'll be there."

Kelly stood and walked to Winward. She wrapped her arms around him and kissed his cheek. "Thank you," she whispered. "Same here."

Winward tightened his hold and gave her a squeeze. "Deal," he said.

Marsha raised her hand like she was in class. "I'd like in on that deal."

"Me, too," Jonathan said.

Tom nodded. "Ditto."

Jonathan snickered. "Damn, what a team," he said, slapping his thigh. "So far, we've survived a psychopath, ghosts, and a freak snowstorm." He lifted Marsha's hand to his lips. "We've accepted psychics and healers. What's next? Shape-shifters, maybe? Vampires?" He waggled his eyebrows. "Aliens?"

Winward snorted. "Get real, Fields. Little green men, maybe, but not shape-shifters and vampires."

Tom chuckled. "Yeah, and a month ago, I would've sworn there were no such things as ghosts." They all shared startled, speculative glances. Then their heads started shaking and a chorus of voices said, "Naw."

Turn the page to read a section from
the second installment of The Marcel Experience

*Eyes of Autumn*
by Cynthia H. Wise

# PROLOGUE

*October 1903*

As he carried the lifeless body through the garden, the wind rose to a deafening roar. Trees swayed around him. Menacing clouds, heavy with moisture, roiled. When he reached the rock wall edging the forest, lightening seared the midnight sky, thickening the smell of ozone, and a tremendous clap of thunder shook the ground. He struggled with the latch before pulling on the heavy door, using his body to keep it open against the wind. Once he was through, the door slammed shut with a bang.

Sweat stung his eyes and his arms ached. The body grew heavier with each step. The storm masked the babble of running water, but he found the bridge easily. After crossing, he veered from the path, pushing his way through thick, grasping underbrush, and moved deeper into obscurity.

Shifting, phantom-like shadows seemed to reach out from every direction. The moaning wind caused the trees to creak, giving a voice to the shadows that made his skin crawl. Breathing hard, he stopped and dropped the body to the forest floor. A flash of lightening lit the darkness and he caught a glimpse of the discolored, swollen gash on her forehead. Blood matted her auburn hair.

He turned away and retraced his steps. By the time he returned carrying a traveling case, lantern, and shovel the storm had begun to rage. Rain fell in sheets, lashing like razors, as he dropped the case beside the body and began to dig.

———— ⚙ ————

Nathan Hillyerd stood head and shoulders above the maid. Tan breeches hugged his long, muscular legs. The high, stiff collar of his white shirt and the skillfully knotted silk cravat stood out against his dark brown waistcoat. Silver was beginning to streak his sandy blond hair, giving a hint to his forty-five years.

"Where is she?" he demanded.

The timid maid wrung her hands. "I don't know, sir. I swear it," she said, her Scottish accent thickening with fear. "I went up to dress milady like I do every mornin', but her rooms were empty."

"Well, find her," he ordered. "She knows I don't like to be kept waiting."

Ignoring the maid as she bobbed a curtsy and hurried away, he moved to the head of the table and sat. His amber eyes narrowed on the door at the sound of booted footsteps.

"Brian," he sneered as the man stepped through the door. "I thought you were gone." "Good morning to you too, brother," the younger man said, catching the furtive glance the maid cast over her shoulder as she left the room. "I see you're scaring the help again."

He moved like a feline predator. His broad shoulders and lean, muscular body proclaimed strength and agility. Brown leather riding chaps accentuated his masculinity and roguish, dark good looks.

"Why are you still here?" Nathan growled, ignoring the remark and the plate of food that was placed in front of him by the serving maid. "I told you to leave last night." The maid made a wide-eyed, hasty retreat.

"In case you didn't notice, Nathan, there was a storm last night.

It would have been insane to ride into the heart of it. I'll leave after I fill my stomach and pack some provisions."

"Get your provisions and leave now. The storm's over."

"Is it?" Brian held Nathan's gaze with his own amber eyes.

"For you it is," Nathan said. He focused on his plate, dismissing his brother.

Brian's grip tightened on the saddlebags in his hand. "Where's Catherine?" he asked. His voice matched the steel in his eyes.

"If you're stalling to say farewell to her, don't bother."

"Why?"

"Why!" Nathan exploded, pushing up from his chair. It crashed to the floor as he advanced toward the other man. "It might serve you well to remember the lady is spoken for! Last night should have taught you that."

"Spoken for. I guess that's one way of putting it."

Nathan's expression turned murderous. "It might also serve you to sheath your edged tongue."

"Why?" Brian asked again. "Does the truth bite? You brought her here from Scotland with no more intention than to make her your exclusive whore. And that's exactly what you did. You'll never make her your wife, babe or no babe."

"And whose babe is it?"

"Now that's the question, isn't it?"

The blow that struck Brian's jaw would have put a weaker man on the floor. Instead, it only spun him around causing him to take a stumbling step to keep his balance. He faced Nathan with menacing hatred, wiping the blood from his split lip.

"Get out," Nathan ground out. "Now."

Defiantly, but without another word, Brian moved toward the kitchen.

"Don't come back, Brian," Nathan said. "Don't try to see Catherine again."

Brian stopped and turned his head. "If it's what she wants, you can't stop us," he said over his shoulder before pushing through the door.

Nathan stood for a moment staring at the door that had closed behind his brother. "I already have," he whispered.

# CHAPTER ONE

*Present Day*

Katie felt a quickening deep within her. She heard whispered secrets as the golden oak shed its leaves, and knew what she felt was excitement mixed with trepidation. Change was coming, yes, but not just to the landscape around her.

She lifted her face to a brilliant blue sky and felt the sun on her skin. As Katie turned her gaze to the rolling pastures, she could see the brittle green-gold they would become. The North Georgia Mountains, part of the Appalachian chain, stood like a fortress in the distance and were nearing their fall peak. Blazing reds and shades of orange, soft yellows and gold would soon be gone. Only the varying greens of pines and spruce would remain to mingle with the browns and grays of the trees that had been stripped.

Katie sketched what she saw on the artist's pad in her lap. A lilting tweet brought her eyes up to a fiery dogwood tree and a brown thrasher perched on a limb. A smile touched Katie's lips as it put on a show of fluffing its feathers. Then it lifted its wings and flew away, like it too sensed the life changes Katie could feel coming.

She took a deep breath, smelling the sweet, clean air, and sighed. Then she stood, folded her blanket, and began the long walk back down the slope and across the pasture to the farmhouse. A flash of gold drew her eyes and Alex let out a gleeful woof as he bounded up to lather Katie's hand with slime.

"Eeeew!"

She wiped her hand on her jeans. The golden retriever seemed to smile as he circled, lashing her legs with a whip-like tail, before beginning a thorough sniff-search to find any new scents she might've picked up.

"Stop that," she said, laughing as she defended her dignity by holding her pack at crotch level. "Some areas are off limits, pal."

Katie crossed the backyard as Uncle Fred emerged from the barn carrying a pail. When he saw them, he let out a chuckle and threw up a work-roughed hand. "You have to be firm with males, Katie-girl," he called. "If you're not, they'll think it's a game and you'll only encourage them."

"That's good advice," she said, climbing the porch steps. "Let's see if it works." Katie looked Alex in the eye and pointed to the floor. "Sit."

Alex sat, letting his tongue loll from the side of his mouth as he panted and Katie scratched behind his ears. "You've got it made, you know that?"

She opened the screen door and stepped into a kitchen that had changed very little since her childhood. Aunt Lou was peeling potatoes and she looked over as the door closed with a soft screech.

"Hey, there," she said. "Did you have a nice day, honey?"

"It was great," Katie replied. "I love it here."

"I understand why you go up there to draw. It's a pretty place. I go there myself whenever I need a moment." Lou turned back to her potatoes with a resigned chuckle. "That is, I used to, until my bones got too old to make the trek."

Katie put her arm around her aunt's shoulders and gave them a squeeze before turning to lift her purse from the back of a kitchen chair.

"Aren't you staying for supper?" Lou asked, watching. "You need a good meal in your stomach, child."

Katie gave her head a regretful shake. "I wish I could, but I have to get up early in the morning. Weekends don't last long enough, do they?"

The thought of returning to the office and having to face Mr. Kregg brought a sense of panic. She squelched it behind a smile. "I'll see you soon, though. Will you tell Uncle Fred good-bye for me?" she asked.

"I will, sweetie," Aunt Lou said, wiping her hands on her apron as she followed Katie to the front door. "You be sure and drive careful. I just don't know how you can drive in all that city traffic. I'd be a bundle of nerves."

Katie laughed. "You get used to it." She kissed Lou's cheek. "Take care of yourself."

Aunt Lou waved goodbye from the porch as Katie got into her mint condition, midnight-blue '69 Mustang. She couldn't wait to get home to soak in a hot bath. She would just take tomorrow as it came.

"What else can I do," she muttered as she turned the key, causing the engine to rumble to life.

———◦◦◦———

Katie lay listening to the drone of her neighbor's mower as he gave his yard its final manicure of the season and was relieved when it stopped. She rose from the sofa to raise the window and inhaled the sweet aroma of cut grass. In the yard across the street, two little boys were lying on their bellies, staring at the ground.

*Probably ants,* she thought, returning to the sofa. Plumping the blue and gold pillow beneath her head, Katie remembered when she used to lie in the backyard, studying the world beneath the grass.

The nightmares had begun by then. Katie slid her eyes closed.

Her cellphone vibrated on the coffee table. She reached over, checked the caller ID, and saw her roommate's name displayed.

"Hey, Angie."

"Hey. I'm at the market. I thought we could have spaghetti tonight with some of that Merlot we have in the wine rack. We still have sauce in the freezer, don't we? What else do we need?"

Katie suddenly felt hungry. "We need angel hair. Since you're shopping, I'll cook.""Deal. I was hoping you'd say that. I won't be long."

Katie disconnected thinking of the inseparable friendship that had been forged while she and Angie shared a box of crayons in fourth grade. Then she remembered the day they'd moved into their little house a mile from the Square in Marietta. The escapade they'd had with the clogged fireplace flue had Katie grinning as she pulled a zip-lock bag of marinara from the freezer and put it in a sink of warm water to thaw.

Back in the den, Katie curled up in the recliner and picked up the flat-screen's remote control. She found a marathon of the Andy Griffith Show and was laughing, watching Andy and Barney talking to Otis through cell bars, when Angie arrived.

"What all did you buy?" Katie asked, seeing a package of Oreo cookies in one of the bags she carried into the kitchen.

Angie began putting the groceries away. "I shouldn't have gone in hungry," she stated and gave Katie a sidelong glance. "So…, tell me about your day."

Katie thought she detected a slight twitch at the corner of Angie's mouth. Even the television conspired against her as a fake audience chose that moment to burst into laughter.

"Oh, lighten up," Angie said, seeing Katie's frown. "He's just a horny, middle-aged man who thinks he has something to prove. Nothing will happen if you don't let it."

"I know," Katie said, leaning against the counter. "I just hate that

I might have to give up my job." She shook her head. "Maybe I'm making this whole thing out to be more than it is."

"Don't start being naïve. You've told me how Mr. Kregg treats you."

Thinking of the way her boss watched her when she pretended not to notice, Katie scowled as she stooped to withdraw two pots and a cookie sheet from a low cupboard. They made a grating sound as they met the electric coils of the stove. She glanced at Angie and saw her friend watching.

"What?"

"What, what?" Angie asked, handing her a package of angel hair pasta.

"You're looking at me like you're trying to read my mind."

"I *am* trying to read your mind," Angie admitted, giving Katie a pointed look before turning and walking out. A moment later, the TV went silent and music from The Eagles followed Angie back into the room. "Something's bothering you. Are you going to tell me what it is or not?"

Katie poured the thawed sauce into a pot to simmer then exhaled a resigned sigh. "Besides the fact that he's getting more aggressive," she said, "I went into his office today and saw him extracting a DVD."

"So?"

"Mr. Carlisle had just left."

"Who's he?"

"A very wealthy client," Katie replied. She put down the bread-knife she was using and looked at Angie. "Why would he want to record their meeting?"

"I don't know. Isn't that illegal?" Angie asked, pulling a bottle of Merlot from the wine rack.

"I think so, especially if the person being recorded doesn't know about it. There *is* such a thing as confidentiality." She preheated the oven and began buttering the sliced bread.

"I don't know what to tell you, Katie, but if he's doing something that could get him in trouble, I'd watch my back, if I were you."

"Yeah, no kidding," Katie said, sprinkling the bread with garlic and parsley. "When Detective Winward and his partner, Detective Hayes, came in today to talk to Mr. Kregg, I thought 'this is it.' But then I remembered they were from homicide. Kevin Ramsey, another client, was found a couple of days ago with his throat slit."

"And they think Mr. Kregg did it?" Angie asked, wide eyed.

Katie chuckled. "No. I don't think so. It's not that unusual to have detectives drop by. Mr. Kregg *is* an attorney, after all, and Mr. Ramsey was his client."

"You said something about him getting more aggressive," Angie said, uncorking the wine. "How? What did he do this time?"

"While I was taking dictation, he passed behind my chair and placed his hands on my shoulders. I could feel him bend over me. I had the distinct feeling he was going to try and nibble my ear or something."

Angie tried for sympathetic, but giggled instead. "What did you do?" she asked.

"I stopped writing, pulled away from him, and gave him a deadpan stare laced with disgust." Katie frowned. "At least, that was the look I was going for. Anyway, at my withdrawal, his expression grew smug and he continued dictating. He ignored me for the rest of the day."

Katie stirred the simmering sauce. The scent of garlic and basil filled the air.

"Are you worried about tomorrow?" Angie asked.

Katie thought about it as she filled a pot with water to boil. "I don't know," she answered. "I'm hoping the look I gave him today will make him think twice about trying anything else."

"Don't count on it."

"I really can't understand why he's being this way," she said, sliding the cookie sheet of garlic bread into the oven.

"What?" Angie exclaimed, handing her a glass. "I can't believe you just said that. Haven't you looked in a mirror lately? You're gorgeous."

Katie shook her head and sipped her wine. "I'm passable. But the thing is, I've never given him any reason to think of me as anything more than a personal assistant."

She released a resolved sigh. "What I need to do is find another job." Her brow furrowed. "But I love this job. I wish he wouldn't be this way. The money's too good."

"Don't let the money stop you. We'll be fine," Angie stated. "Tonight, we're not going to worry. We have plenty of wine so we're going to eat, drink, and get silly."

The corner of Katie's mouth curled as she added angel hair to the boiling water. "Sounds like a plan." She raised her glass, tapped it against Angie's, and took a drink.

As Angie topped off their glasses she said, "I talked to dad today. He asked me to ride up to the cabin and check on the place. I bet it's really pretty up there right now."

Katie thought of the cabin the Perkins' had on Lake Blue Ridge in the North Georgia Mountains and remembered the first vacation she had taken with the Perkins family. She and Angie had been miserable with a case of poison ivy, but it was also when her nightmares had become more vivid.

"Do you remember the time – ?" Angie began.

"We got poison ivy at the cabin," Katie finished and smiled. "That was awful. My skin was on fire, but your mom wouldn't let us scratch."

"We were crusty with calamine lotion." Angie chuckled. "I still think she did it to make it look worse than it was so we wouldn't wander so far away again." Angie paused before saying, "Mom always was over-protective."

Katie knew from experience what it was like to lose a mother. It would be a long time before the hurting eased for her friend. "Hey," she announced, tilting the steaming pasta pot over the colander in the sink, "dinner is served. Grab a couple of plates."

Angie's smile looked forced. "Great! I'm starved."

As Katie spooned sauce over the pasta, she asked, "Are you going to go?"

"I don't know." Angie shrugged. "I really don't want to go by myself."

"It would only be for the weekend, wouldn't it?"

"That's a long way to go for just a weekend," Angie said, carrying her plate to the table. "And if I stayed longer, I'd want someone to go with me." She shook her head. "It doesn't matter. I don't have the time to go, anyway."

"Don't you have at least two weeks of vacation coming to you?"

"Yeah well, I still wouldn't have anyone to go with me."

Katie sat across from Angie and began twirling a bite of food between her fork and spoon. "Is that the only reason, Angie?" she asked softly.

"What do you mean? Of course, it is." Angie forked a bite of pasta and chewed, avoiding Katie's gaze. Then she swallowed and took a drink of wine.

"Okay. So that's not the only reason," she said. "I just don't know if I want to go. I haven't been there since she died."

Angie was like her mother in many ways. She had the same straight, silky blond hair. Her generous mouth always had a ready smile, while her soft brown eyes hinted at her warm and giving nature. But where her mother had been small boned and petite, Angie's regal grace was enhanced by the slender height she had inherited from her father.

"Maybe that's the reason you should go," Katie said, keeping her voice soft. "At least think about it. Okay?"

Angie met Katie's gaze, then nodded. "Okay. I'll think about it."

They ate in silence until a whimsical smile curved Katie's lips. "You know what we need?" she asked.

"Uh-oh," Angie said, her fork halting in midair. "I know that look."

"We need a couple of Lancelots to come along and sweep us off our feet."

"Oh, is that all?" Angie smirked. "Katie, the last Lancelot bought it with Arthur and Merlin. Besides, didn't Arthur catch him boinking Guinevere?"

Katie stopped and stared. "Oh yeah," she said, "I didn't think of that." She gave her head a dismissive shake. "That's beside the point. Don't be such a cynic. We can dream, can't we?"

Angie's expression softened as she topped off their wine and raised her glass. "To our dashing Lancelots – may they carry us away on their galloping steeds before we know we've been snatched."

Katie grinned as their glasses clinked. "Amen to that!"

After dinner, they settled down with a romantic comedy re-run, taking turns refilling each other's glass. When Angie began to giggle, Katie's intoxicated smile widened. "What?"

"I was just thinking about Doris, a woman at work. She's getting married Saturday. Ever since he popped the question, she's been bubbling around the office like a love-struck twit. From the way she talked, I had this picture in my head of a dashing, debonair man with a centerfold physique, so when she said he was picking her up today I stuck around to meet him."

"And?"

"I met him alright," Angie stated, emitting another giggle. "When I saw her parading him through the office, I laughed out loud. I couldn't help it. I had to hide in the lounge until I could compose myself."

"Why?" Katie's grin widened. "What was wrong with him?"

Angie hooted with laughter. "The guy was a genuine nerd. His pants were belted just below his ribs and he had all these pens lined up in one of those plastic pocket protectors. He even wore thick, black frames that kept sliding down his nose.

"I couldn't believe it," she continued over Katie's laughter. "He reminded me of George McFly in *Back To The Future*. I'd set my expectations so high it was like someone burst my bubble with a shotgun."

Katie's lips still quivered. "Looks aren't everything, you know. He might have a secret weapon under that high belt that drives Doris wild."

Angie threw back her head and laughed. "I hadn't thought of that. Considering Doris and her dirty mind, you're probably right."

"It sounds like you had a good day."

"Yeah, I did."

"I'm glad," Katie stated, her words beginning to slur. "Tomorrow's my turn. I deserve an enjoyable Tuesday."

"Well, if Mister Horny Toad gets any bolder, just let him have it in the family jewels and walk out. I can handle the bills until you get back on your feet."

"Ouch! You're vicious. I don't really think that'll be necessary, though."

"You never know."

Katie smiled and shook her head. "I'll keep your suggestion in mind." They clinked glasses again and drank.

CPSIA information can be obtained at www.ICGtesting.com
Printed in the USA
LVOW11s1737301113

363347LV00001B/1/P